Inath-Wakenti is no sanctuary for the united Qualinesti and Silvanesti elves who followed Gilthas Pathfinder out of Khur. Forced to abide there or face their enemies, the elves find themselves choosing between dying of starvation and dying in combat. Some choose combat, and Porthios takes his army to Qualinesti to fight for the liberation of that benighted land. Kerian and Gilthas do what they can to hold their remaining people together and discover the secret to freeing the valley from its mysterious will-o'-the-wisps and its ghosts, but even their efforts are not enough.

Faeterus's plans are nearly complete, as he makes his way to the Stair of Distant Vision, there to take the power granted by the Father Who Made Not His Children before he abandoned the valley to its sterile fate. No one is left to oppose the evil sorceror, save one frightened archivist, all too aware of Faeterus's power - and willingness to kill those who try to stop him.

Help for the elves finally arrives from an unexpected source, dragged forcibly to the valley by the Lioness, but there is no guarantee of victory even then. No one knows if there is a reward for their patience or merely a faster death, and there are no battle lines to draw, for there is no enemy to fight. The will-o'-the-wisps cannot be killed, the ghosts cannot be banished, Inath-Wakenti cannot be made to bloom.

Hope does not flourish in the valley, not even as the Weya-Lu leave off their attacks and Sa'ida brings them hope. All is staked on the vision of the Speaker of the Sun and Stars, the elf who united the tribes and brought them on their journey to this place, Gilthas Pathfinder - and he is dying.

ALSO BY PAUL B. THOMPSON & TONYA C. COOK

THE ERGOTH TRILOGY

VOLUME ONE
A WARRIOR'S JOURNEY

VOLUME TWO
THE WIZARD'S FATE

VOLUME THREE
A HERO'S JUSTICE

THE BARBARIANS

VOLUME ONE
CHILDREN OF THE PLAINS

VOLUME TWO
BROTHER OF THE DRAGON

VOLUME THREE
SISTER OF THE SWORD

DESTINY

ELVEN EXILES
VOLUME THREE

PAUL B. THOMPSON &
TONYA C. COOK

DESTINY

©2007 Wizards of the Coast, Inc.

Published by Wizards of the Coast, Inc. DRAGONLANCE, WIZARDS OF THE COAST, and their respective logos are trademarks of Wizards of the Coast, Inc., in the U.S.A. and other countries.

Printed in the U.S.A.

Cover art by Matt Stawicki
First Printing: October 2007

9 8 7 6 5 4 3 2 1

ISBN: 978-0-7869-4273-2
620-95939740-001-EN

U.S., CANADA,
ASIA, PACIFIC, & LATIN AMERICA
Wizards of the Coast, Inc.
P.O. Box 707
Renton, WA 98057-0707
+1-800-324-6496

EUROPEAN HEADQUARTERS
Hasbro UK Ltd
Caswell Way
Newport, Gwent NP9 0YH
GREAT BRITAIN
Save this address for your records.

Visit our web site at www.wizards.com

DEDICATION

Amid the groves, under the shadowy hills,
The generations are prepared; the pangs,
The internal pangs, are ready; the dread strife
Of poor humanity's afflicted will
Struggling in vain with ruthless destiny.
                    —*William Wordsworth, "The Excursion"*

prologue

Shadows were thick in the windowless corridor deep inside the Khuri yl Nor. Open oil lamps were set on corbels at intervals along the wall, but their flames scarcely penetrated the gloom. Here in the Nor-Khan, the central citadel of the khan's palace, the corridors were not as confusing as those farther out. Even long-time courtiers had been known to wander for hours in the outer palace, seeking a particular chamber.

Sahim Zacca-Khur, Khan of All the Khurs, was not troubled by the maze of passageways or the lack of light. He had traveled the path from his private quarters to the throne room so many times, he could do it in utter darkness. He entered a small, private side chamber and paused, taking time to gather his thoughts and smooth his elaborately curled beard. Although he was past middle age, his black hair and beard showed no gray at all.

Lastly, he adjusted the crown on his head. The crown seemed heavier lately. True, he wore a mail coif beneath it to foil assassins, but the crown itself—a ten-inch-tall hat of stiff red leather, its lower edge decorated by strings of gold beads—felt weightier these days. The departure of the *laddad* ought to have lightened his burdens, but it had not. Even with the exiled elves now deep in the desert, Sahim's troubles were no fewer.

1

PAUL B. THOMPSON & TONYA C. COOK

The *laddad* had fled their devastated homelands of Silvanesti and Qualinesti to fetch up against the walls of Khuri-Khan like debris driven by a sandstorm. For five years, Sahim had allowed them to remain in exchange for the treasure they contributed to his coffers. With them gone, he was back to squeezing coppers from the *soukats,* and the merchants of Khuri-Khan were notoriously tight-fisted. Of course, Sahim knew how to squeeze.

He opened the door, and the guards within the throne room raised gilded swords in salute. Sahim waited for his eyes to grow accustomed to the light. Braziers and brass candelabra were thick around the room's perimeter, and all were lit. Considering the two guests awaiting him, he felt it desirable to banish as many shadows as possible. The usual menagerie of courtiers and councilors was long in bed. Only his bodyguards and the two visitors greeted Sahim. The visitors had arranged themselves as far apart as the space of the hall permitted.

Sa'ida, high priestess of Elir-Sana, stood near the throne. Her white robe and long white hair gave her an ethereal quality at odds with her matronly build and the unhappy expression on her face. The most senior cleric of the Khurish god of healing, she seldom left the confines of the holy temple, where men were strictly forbidden. Spending any time with a reprobate and heretic such as Condortal could hardly please her.

Lord Condortal, emissary to Khur for the Knights of Neraka, had come no farther into the room than absolutely necessary and stood close by the grand doors of the main entrance. Dedicated to increasing its power, and embracing sorcery and all manner of dark mysticism to obtain that end, Condortal's Order had been working hard to extend its influence over Khur. Sahim always had walked a fine line with the Nerakan Knights, refusing a greater presence in his cities yet allowing a measure of freedom in the open deserts that surrounded them.

The dome of Condortal's hairless head glistened with sweat.

DESTINY

Sahim knew it was not merely the heat of Khur's climate that troubled him. The khan's recently-enacted protocol required Condortal to leave his personal retainers outside, and the knight felt naked without them.

An anxious visitor was an incautious visitor, so Sahim had kept them waiting, stewing in each other's company in the overheated hall. Sahim himself had worn his lightest robe, of fine red silk. Embroidered in white and gold, two rampant dragons, the symbol of his own tribe, faced each other across its chest.

He did not bother to acknowledge the salutes of his soldiers or the bows of his visitors but crossed the floor with a deliberate tread, enjoying the immensely satisfying sight of the throne that awaited him. It was his people's greatest treasure, hidden from the dragon overlord Malys during her occupation of Khur. The tall, heavy chair was covered in sheets of hammered gold. Its fan-shaped backrest was set with two star sapphires, each twice the size of Sahim's fist and known as the Eyes of Kargath, for the Khurish god of war. Raised panels on the gilding depicted glorious events from the reigns of Sahim's predecessors.

Once he was seated and his robe arranged to his satisfaction, Sahim acknowledged the holy lady first.

"Great Khan," she said immediately, "the followers of Torghan are again harassing my priestesses in the city. Today alone, three were accosted in the Grand Souks."

"Assaulted?"

Sa'ida firmed her lips. "No, sire. Manhandled, but not molested. The goods they carried were struck from their hands and trampled underfoot."

"Deplorable. Wouldn't you agree, Lord Condortal?"

"Deplorable," repeated the distant Nerakan, "but hardly my affair, mighty Khan."

"No?" Sa'ida turned toward him abruptly, the tiny brass bells braided in her hair clashing to underscore her anger. "It is said the Sons of Torghan take money from Neraka."

3

"A vicious rumor, started by our enemies, the elves." Condortal bowed to the outraged priestess, but there was no deference in his voice. As usual, he spoke much too loudly, and Sahim was glad he stood so far away. "Mighty Khan, is this why I was summoned? Crime in the city is not the concern of my Order. I will take my leave—"

"I have not excused you."

Condortal, half turned toward the doors, halted, and turned back. The khan's mask of royal composure had not altered, but his voice was imperious.

Shifting tone, Sahim assured Sa'ida her concerns had been noted. The City Guard was on watch for Torghanist activity. "These provocations are aimed at me, not your temple, holy lady, and I will deal with them. Several Torghanist leaders have been taken."

He did not have to add *and quickly executed;* that was understood by all. The followers of Torghan the Avenger, the Khurish aspect of the god Sargonnas, reviled Sahim as a tyrant and a nonbeliever more interested in accepting foreign treasure than in keeping Khur pure of outside taint. Once mainly confined to the nomads of the desert—renowned for their distrust of all foreigners, by which they sometimes meant city-dwelling Khurs too—veneration of Torghan was spreading in the cities. The god's small shrine in Khuri-Khan was seeing a steady increase in activity. That this might be due to Nerakan influence was a worrisome notion—not surprising to Sahim, but certainly worrisome. A cynic, he believed Nerakan money a far greater spur to Torghanist boldness than religious fervor.

"You both were called here to receive news," he went on. "The *laddad* have reached the Valley of the Blue Sands. They prevailed against the nomads that dogged their journey from Khuri-Khan, and entered the valley ten days past."

The news likely came as no surprise to Condortal. His Order had spies and informers everywhere. The priestess's face displayed a series of emotions—surprise, relief, and curiosity. She asked what the event meant.

"It means the *laddad* are beyond the borders of my realm."

That surprised Condortal. "Surely, great Khan, this valley is Khurish land."

"It is no man's land. If the *laddad* remain there, they are no matter for Khur."

Silence reigned as Sahim refreshed himself from the brass goblet placed into his hand by a waiting servant. His visitors pondered the news he had imparted. Although both had heard the same words, the interpretations each placed upon them were very different.

Sa'ida understood the khan to be asking her, most subtly, to assist the *laddad* in their struggle for survival. He had no special fondness for them, but neither had he sought their destruction in the years they had dwelt in his realm. His relationship with their leader, Gilthas, might best be described as profitable. And there was profit in allowing the *laddad* to live in the Valley of the Blue Sands. The Knights of Neraka had long plotted the elves' destruction and had once invaded and occupied both elf homelands. A *laddad* state in the valley would act as a distraction, keeping the Order's attention focused away from Sahim's capital. Having the *laddad* outside the boundaries of Khur also would help placate Torghanist fears of foreign influence. The Torghanists hated the *laddad* even more than they despised Sahim-Khan.

For his part, Lord Condortal interpreted the khan's words to mean he counted himself lucky to be rid of the elf pestilence and would no longer intervene on their behalf. While the elves had lived in the Khurish capital, Sahim was bound to honor his promise to protect them—a promise purchased by elf treasure. With the flow of treasure cut off, the elves' welcome in Sahim's realm had run out. They were naked, without a defender in the world. The Order's efforts against them no longer would be hampered by a need for circumspection, the need not to offend the khan's pride.

The knight asked leave to depart. Sahim lifted one hand in an idle wave. "Yes, go. Tell your masters what has come to pass."

Before he departed, Condortal asked, "Great Khan, may I inquire after Prince Shobbat? I have not seen him in some weeks. I pray His Highness is well."

It required all of Sahim's skill to keep his face calm and unconcerned. "The crown prince is very well. He is away. Hunting."

Sa'ida knew this for a lie. Weeks earlier Shobbat had come to the Temple of Elir-Sana seeking her help, but the affliction that had fallen upon him was not one Sa'ida could cure. She had no idea whether the khan was aware of his son's condition. Perhaps Shobbat had fled to keep him from learning of it. Being the well-informed despot he was, Sahim probably knew all, but she felt it best to keep her own knowledge of the matter to herself. After bestowing Elir-Sana's blessing upon the khan, she left the sweltering throne room.

Freed of his audience, Sahim leaned back, feeling the coolness of the golden panels against his back. What a pair! Sa'ida was half again his own age, as patient and intent as an adder. She could speak to the gods as easily as she addressed Sahim and had the power to heal nearly any calamity fate could inflict on a living body. Yet she only watched and waited, complaining about Torghanists she could vanquish in a single night. Who could fathom such a mind?

On the other hand, Condortal was like a weasel, a weak predator who struck from ambush and was not averse to carrion. His predecessor, Hengriff, had been a bold and dangerous man. Sahim had understood Hengriff. He could deal with men like him, but Condortal hadn't even an assassin's scruples. He dreamed of a Khur torn apart, fighting over the *laddad*, so his Order could step in and pick up the pieces. With rebellion smoldering in Qualinesti and the *laddad* fled to the Valley of the Blue Sands, what would Condortal's masters do?

DESTINY

Sahim lived in a dangerous time and place. He played friends and foes against each other and emerged enriched and unscathed. No one was better than he at balancing on the knife-edge of disaster, at turning situations and people to his own advantage. It was a risky game he enjoyed to the fullest.

Except . . .

Where in Kargath's name was Shobbat? And what had become of that damned sorcerer Faeterus and the bounty hunter Sahim had sent to drag him back?

1

Wind cool and damp tore at the griffon rider's face. Reins wrapped tightly around her left fist, Kerianseray bowed low over the neck of her steed, urging him on to greater effort. The will-o'-the-wisps were closing in, and their number had increased. She counted at least a dozen now. And Eagle Eye's sides heaved with exertion as the lights darted and wove, spiraled up and corkscrewed down, all the while gaining on her. She hoped the others in her patrol were safe.

Safe. The notion was ironic. How safe could any of them be so long as they remained in this blighted valley?

Inath-Wakenti, the ancient elf chronicles called it, the Vale of Silence, and silent it surely was. It lay on the northern edge of the Khurish desert, and not so much as a fly or flea called it home. Kerian had led the first reconnaissance party inside. They discovered the valley contained many secrets and nearly as many curses. Its plant life comprised mainly stunted pines and inedible scrub. Huge standing stones littered the valley floor, rising up white and bare of decoration from the oddly tinted blue-green soil. The elves suspected the stones were the ruins of some long-forgotten city but could discern no logic to their arrangement, so the stones' true purpose remained a mystery. Stranger still, Inath-Wakenti was utterly devoid of animal life large or small, and by night it was infested with floating balls of light, will-o'-the-wisps, whose touch caused elves to vanish without a trace.

Eagle Eye veered upward suddenly, and Kerian leaned forward, gripping his sides more tightly with her knees. She made no other move, nor any sound. There was no need. Eagle Eye was a Royal griffon and more intelligent than many a two-legged creature Kerian had known. He seemed to understand the danger posed by the balls of light and knew they were in a race for their lives. Flying flat out wasn't working; the will-o'-the-wisps continued to close. So Eagle Eye strained every sinew in a steep climb. The ground fell away with stomach-churning suddenness, and Kerian, attuned to the griffon's every shift of weight and tensing of muscle, suddenly realized what he intended. She gave the leather belt around her waist a quick jerk to tighten it, and the horizon inverted.

Wings stretched wide, Eagle Eye soared over the top of the loop. Upside down, Kerian spared a look at her pursuers. Her heart sank. No longer a dozen, at least three times that number of glowing orbs chased her across the sky. They fanned out in a wide cone from her original position. Already, the half dozen in the lead were rising after her. They were pale, as if the effort of the chase was finally telling on them, leaching their color. Those farther back still pulsed in vibrant shades of green, blue, crimson, purple, and gold.

Eagle Eye rolled left, bringing them upright again. They had gained some breathing room but were flying in the wrong direction, deeper into the valley instead of south to the elves' camp near its entrance.

As always, dusk had come early to Inath-Wakenti, the high, encircling mountains blotting out the sun's light. In the course of the chase, the bright sky had darkened, but no stars had yet appeared. The will-o'-the-wisps stood out in brilliant relief against the indigo backdrop. Far below, Kerian could see more points of light glimmering among the twisted pines and featureless standing stones. A hundred?

Five hundred? A great many, in any case.

She urged Eagle Eye higher still. Insects could rise only to a certain height. Bats and small birds had a limit above which they could not fly. Perhaps the will-o'-the-wisps were likewise constrained.

She and six other griffon riders had left camp two hours before sunset to patrol the inner valley. In all their previous flights they'd not been troubled by will-o'-the-wisps. The eerie lights appeared at dusk, but none ever rose higher than tree-top level. Tonight was different. The orbs suddenly appeared in midair all around the griffon patrol. Kerian had ordered the patrol to scatter. The sheer number of lights chasing her was a sort of grim triumph; perhaps none had gone after the others. Perhaps they and their griffons had made it back to camp unmolested.

Eagle Eye was panting deep in his chest as he climbed. Foamy sweat collected on his lion's body, staining the white plumage of his neck and Kerian's leather breeches. Her legs were achingly cold. But the desperate gamble was paying off. The lights had risen to maybe forty feet and swooped in flat circles, never rising any higher. By twos and threes, her erstwhile pursuers winked out like dying embers. Already the number of lights had fallen by half. They were giving up the chase.

Kerian was too exhausted to rejoice. She steered Eagle Eye in a wide turn for camp.

From that height she could see the silvery line of Lioness Creek, named in honor of Kerian herself. Beyond it burned the campfires of her people's temporary home. The survivors of Qualinesti and Silvanesti were crammed into the narrow strip of land between the valley's mouth and the creek, thousands packed into an area that represented the only safety from the nomads outside and the mysterious forces in the valley.

Eagle Eye had fallen into an easy lope. Once every four or five beats, he held his wings out and glided. He was very tired.

DESTINY

So was his rider. Kerian couldn't remember the last good sleep she'd had. The challenges of life in the valley were partly to blame, but she was a fighter and accustomed to physical privation. Much harder to face were the unresolved difficulties of her relationship with her husband.

Gilthas of the House of Solostaran was Speaker of the Sun and Stars, king of the exiled elf nation. Just before the departure from Khuri-Khan, he had dismissed Kerian as head of his army. Their breach over whether to bring their people to Inath-Wakenti had seemed irreparable, calling up all the old enmity between royal Qualinesti and forest-dwelling Kagonesti. But with the deed done, with their people in the valley, those differences had been overshadowed by the day-to-day needs of the nation and by one other inescapable fact.

Gilthas was dying.

* * * * *

Against a background of purple sky, clouds drifted by, sending rain coursing down to darken the granite mountain slopes. It was a common enough sight in Inath-Wakenti. Rain fell on the distant heights but seldom in the valley proper. As the light faded and the first stars appeared overhead, the clouds were submerged in the mountains' dark bulk. The smell of rain lingered.

Gilthas stood atop a crude watchtower of logs and stared northwest, watching the far-off shower. The elves had constructed thirteen watchtowers, ten along Lioness Creek and three at the valley entrance. All were kept occupied day and night. But Gilthas wasn't watching for enemies. His wife was on patrol, flying on her griffon over the silent valley. Gilthas could not be easy until she was with him again. The elf standing watch in the tower had positioned herself as far from the Speaker as possible in the close confines, motivated less by awe of her sovereign than by sympathy. His worry for his intrepid wife was obvious.

The view into the valley was unchanging: spindly trees and

pale stone monoliths scattered in the distance like dice dropped by a giant. No fireflies lit the night; no frogs or crickets broke the silence.

When the elves had first reached Inath-Wakenti, they'd been overjoyed. Their constant tormenters, the Khurish nomads, would not enter the taboo confines of the place they called *Alya-Alash*, "Breath of the Gods." The elves collapsed onto the sandy blue soil and rejoiced in their deliverance.

Disenchantment with their sanctuary wasn't long in coming. The valley that sheltered them from desert heat and nomad attacks provided very little else—absolutely no animal life and precious little edible flora. Warriors and civilians alike clamored for permission to search the inner valley for food, but the Speaker forbade anyone to cross Lioness Creek, reminding them of the deadly will-o'-the-wisps encountered by Kerian's original expedition.

Hungry and desperate, some broke the Speaker's stricture, convinced they could return with provisions to allay his wrath. Most did not come back. Those who did only confirmed the Lioness's warnings. Floating lights emerged at night to drift between the standing stones. The orbs' movements seemed aimless, until an elf drew too near, then escape routes were cut off and elves vanished as soon as the orbs touched them. The few who escaped did so by various methods. One stood still as a statue all night long as glowing balls hovered, seemingly confused, around him. Another pair survived by distracting the will-o'-the-wisps with thrown rocks. The orbs followed the stones arcing into the darkness, and the elves were able to elude them.

Gilthas ordered an end to the unauthorized excursions. Now, the only explorations sanctioned by the Speaker were carried out by air, on griffonback. The griffon patrols watched for any disturbances inside the valley, even as cavalry patrols watched the valley's entrance for any sign the nomad tribes were regrouping. When the elves had entered the valley, the majority of the Khurs had turned their horses away and dispersed. But a small band remained, carrying out a plan devised by their leader, Adala Fahim. They were erecting a stone wall across the mouth of the pass to trap the elves within. It was a futile, crazy project, and only the most fanatical of Adala's followers still worked on it.

Gilthas's vigil was interrupted by a voice, hailing him from the ground. "The patrol has returned, Great Speaker! There was trouble."

The messenger was a Qualinesti known to Gilthas. A former silversmith, he was meticulous and careful by trade and not one to spread false alarms. Gilthas climbed down at once.

Although he took pains to hide it, the climb was not an easy one for him. His hands trembled as they grasped the crudely shaped rungs of the ladder, and pain like hot needles stabbed through his ribs. He had taken a blow to the back from a nomad tribesman just before the elves entered the valley. His people put his continuing weakness down to that cowardly attack and he allowed the mistaken impression to stand. Only a handful of elves knew the truth. Consumption, true to its harsh human name, was eating him from the inside out. The sickness had only worsened in the damp, chill air of Inath-Wakenti. By the standards of his long-lived race, Gilthas was still young, but appeared decades older, cheeks sunken and eyes deeply shadowed. He slept little, ate less, and worked as steadily as his failing health would allow.

When Gilthas reached the bonfire in the center of camp, he knew immediately what the trouble was. Only five griffon riders stood by the blazing fire. Two were missing.

"Where is Lady Kerianseray?" he asked immediately.

"I'm here," she answered, arriving at a jog. She stripped off her gauntlets and took the cup of water offered by a nearby elf. She drank it quickly, but before she could finish, the other riders were clamoring for permission to seek their missing comrade.

From the darkness another voice asked, "What has happened?"

Gilthas turned. The newcomer was Porthios. Covered as always by a shapeless, ragged robe and cloth mask, he halted at the edge of the firelight. Porthios was brother to Lauralanthalasa, Gilthas's mother, who had perished in the fall of Qualinost. Each was very nearly the only family the other had left, yet there had never been much love between uncle and nephew. Proud Porthios had not approved of Lauralanthalasa's choice of husband and felt Gilthas carried the taint of his half-human father, Tanis. Formerly Speaker of the Sun, Porthios had been horribly burned by dragonfire during a battle. The fire that had nearly killed him seemed to have hardened his emotions further, scarring him inside as well as out. Gilthas doubted Porthios cared for anyone, save perhaps Alhana, his wife.

Firelight glinted in Porthios's eyes as he scanned the group. "Who didn't return?" he asked. He knew the griffon riders well. They had flown from Qualinesti with him and Kerian only weeks before.

"Hytanthas," was Kerian's grim answer.

Hytanthas Ambrodel was one of her loyal followers. She and the young warrior had fought together in Qualinesti against bandit invaders. More recently, he had served in her army in Khur. When a vast nomad army threatened to attack the elves, believing Kerian had led a massacre of one of their settlements, Kerian had ridden into their midst, hoping to appease their wrath by her sacrifice. Instead, she'd been plucked from the desert seemingly by a divine hand and deposited on the other side of the continent, in occupied Qualinesti. Hytanthas Ambrodel had undertaken a daring mission to find her. He had succeeded, very nearly at the cost of his own life.

Porthios put his back to the bonfire and stared into the haunted land across the creek. "How was he lost?"

"The lights," Kerian replied.

"They've never taken a flier before," said Porthios. "This is a dangerous development."

DESTINY

"We must take steps."

Kerian stiffened. Porthios was among the handful of elves who knew the true state of Gilthas's health, and she knew he was implying the Speaker could not handle the problem himself. She started to make a harsh reply, but Gilthas quelled her with a glance and she bit back angry words, wondering how her husband could be so blind to Porthios's maneuvering.

Gilthas was not blind. He, too, had bristled at Porthios's comment. But unlike his volatile wife, the Speaker of the Sun and Stars was accustomed to keeping his reactions private. He was quite aware of Porthios's insolence. It was always present, like a thorn constantly pricking him, yet never obvious enough that Gilthas could confront him about it.

Gilthas ordered the griffon riders to stand down. Watch would be kept for Hytanthas, but they couldn't risk losing more riders in a futile search. The will-o'-the-wisps had never yet given back a victim.

"Food and water are waiting for you in my tent," Gilthas told his wife.

She nodded but excused herself to tend her griffon first. If Porthios's tone tended toward insolence, Kerian's held no emotion at all. Gilthas knew she would defend him against anything. But what she thought of him and still felt for him, he had been unable to divine.

Porthios followed him as he traversed the crowded camp on his way to his tent. Elves of all stations greeted their Speaker with warmth. Porthios trailed behind, as unheralded as a shadow. No one spoke to Porthios lightly.

Qualinesti and Silvanesti alike had an ingrained horror of disfigurement, making Porthios's return to prominence all the more discomforting. Bathed by dragonfire, Porthios should have died. Instead, he emerged from the forest of the land he'd once ruled to launch a rebellion against the occupying forces of the bandit lord Samuval. Anonymous behind his mask, Porthios freed a Qualinesti town with only a handful of followers and sparked revolts all over the country. Elves as disparate as the displaced Kerianseray, Alhana Starbreeze and her Silvanesti guards, and a loyal cadre of Kagonesti had rallied to his cause.

When Hytanthas Ambrodel arrived bearing news of the elves' imminent destruction in Khur, Porthios left the revolt in the hands of a Kagonesti lieutenant. Then he, Alhana, and Kerian led a small band of newly-made griffon riders to Khur and saved the exiled elf nation from annihilation. In the final confrontation with the nomad leader Adala Fahim, Porthios had revealed his identity and the ruin of his face to the world. Word spread through the elf nation and Porthios's name was secret no longer. He retained his concealing attire to hide his deformities, but Gilthas believed the odd clothing served another purpose. Mask, gloves, bandagelike wrappings, and tattered hooded robe all lent the former Speaker of the Sun an air of mystery and authority he cannily exploited. It was considered ill luck to be long in Porthios's company or even to meet his eyes, but everyone in Inath-Wakenti was grateful for his miraculous arrival at the head of the griffon riders.

Gilthas lived and held court in a great sprawling tent. A forest of pine poles supported much-patched tarps, with only a few low screens as internal partitions. When Gilthas ducked under the low entrance, he could see the entire covered space. Everywhere there were soldiers—veterans of the ride across Khur still dressed in desert attire and sporting an assortment of Qualinesti and Silvanesti armor—as well as civilians of every age and background who carried out the myriad day-to-day tasks required by the Speaker. Through an opening on one side of the tent, Gilthas could see a blazing forge, where broken swords and dented armor were being restored to lethal service. On the opposite side of the pavilion sat a group of scribes, copying orders and other documents for the Speaker.

Gilthas headed for a camp chair near the scribes. Softened by pillows, the simple chair served as his throne. A few yards away was his sleeping pallet, a mound of blankets and rugs. He answered questions and dictated orders until Kerian arrived; then he called for the food and drink that had been held for his wife. When the meal was assembled and the servers departed, Porthios drew near. Kerian stepped in his way and stared him down, nose to nose, until he backed off. Others might be fearful of meeting his eyes but not the Lioness.

As Kerian ate her small meal, she studied her husband. Torchlight was not Gilthas's friend. His cheekbones stood out like hatchets. The flesh between his throat and collarbone was so sunken, cold sweat collected in the hollow. His skin was pale and parchment-thin. The slightest knock would bruise him for days. All his inner strength seemed to be concentrated in his eyes. They were clear and calm, burning in the meager flesh of his face like twin torches.

She finished, and Gilthas lifted a hand. A scribe seated himself nearby, stylus poised. Gilthas bade his wife tell what she knew about the loss of Hytanthas.

"You look terrible," she said instead. "You should be resting."

"I am resting. And I've been feeling better today. The healers have been feeding me beef tea."

She snorted. "Where in this lifeless valley would they find beef?"

"I thought it best not to inquire." It probably came from boiling leather belts and shoes.

She made her report, outlining the stories of the other riders and telling of her own escape from the great mass of lights. The other riders had been pursued by only a few lights, and none of the elves had seen Hytanthas or his griffon, Kanan, after Kerian ordered them to scatter.

Despite her calm recitation of facts, Gilthas knew she was deeply angry. Any death among her warriors was painful to her, but Hytanthas was special, one in whom she'd seen great potential. Gilthas understood the loss of a valued friend. His long-time bodyguard and comrade, Planchet, had died in the desert fighting nomads. Planchet's absence was a wound that had not healed. Each morning when he awoke, Gilthas expected the trusted valet to be there, protecting his back, chiding him for not eating enough, and offering sage, pithy comments on Gilthas's dealings not only with councilors and common folk but with his hot-tempered wife as well.

A tide of longing rose in Gilthas. The need to hold his wife close was nearly overwhelming. But, mindful of his healer's stricture against too-intimate contact with others, he had to content himself with reaching for her hand and saying, "I am sorry. Young Ambrodel was worthy of his name."

She knelt by him, holding his hand carefully. It was little more than bones covered by skin, hot and dry as the sands of Khur.

The moment was all too brief. Her voice was grim as she said, "If the lights can catch griffons, we have no hope of penetrating the inner valley."

"You must be confident, my heart." He shifted position, vainly seeking a more comfortable pose for his emaciated frame, and she let go his hand. "The best minds of our race are in this camp. We shall yet find the answers to the mysteries of this place."

Time was she would have called him a fool and a dreamer. Now she only watched him walk alone to his pallet (with the eyes of those in the tent on them, he would brook no support from her), made an excuse to leave, and bade him good night. Alhana and Porthios awaited her outside the great tent.

"Is the Speaker lucid?" Porthios asked.

Kerian snapped, "He retains both his mind and his grace, unlike you!"

"Captain Ambrodel's griffon has returned," Alhana put in quickly to halt the argument that simmered beneath every exchange between them.

"Injured?"

"There's not a mark on him," Porthios said. "Alhana has treated him for exhaustion."

Alhana's special skill with the griffons had been of inestimable value in the elves' efforts to tame the wild creatures. The note of pride in Porthios's voice amused Kerian. Only with his beautiful Silvanesti wife did the arrogant Porthios come close to being personable.

Lowering her voice, Alhana said, "We have a greater problem. The food supply is dwindling faster than we thought. At the current rate of consumption, it will be gone in a month."

Kerian was aghast. According to the survey taken when they'd entered Inath-Wakenti, there should be at least twice that much remaining. What had happened to the food?

"Theft. Hoarding," Porthios said flatly, but Alhana disagreed. There was no evidence anyone had stolen the food, and hoarding was hard to imagine given the close confines of the camp. Too, the missing food was all meat: stocks of smoked goat and mutton, as well as dozens of live chickens.

Kerian wondered whether the disappearances could be connected to the valley's antipathy to animal life. If so, the ramifications were frightening. They'd thought themselves safe here on the south side of the creek. If that were no longer true . . .

Porthios's hoarse voice interrupted her dark thoughts. "The provisions that remain will go further once we depart for Qualinesti. It's past time for the army to be gone."

Since arriving, he had been agitating to lead the army back to Qualinesti to rejoin the battle against Samuval. Many elves, including Alhana, thought it a good plan. As long as they were safe from the nomads, Kerian agreed. At first reluctant to surrender command of the army to Porthios, she had changed her mind when she realized his departure might help prevent an open break between the interventionists, led by Porthios, and the valley colonizers, led by Gilthas. The only stumbling block was Gilthas himself. He adamantly refused to divide the nation in the face of the perils, known and unknown, that lay beyond Lioness Creek.

Kerian wondered whether that was his only concern or whether he also worried about placing an army at Porthios's disposal. That had concerned her as well, but she still believed the advantages outweighed the risks. With thousands of trained warriors as its core, a great army of rebels could be raised to drive out the bandits once and for all. The liberation of their homeland had never been so close. Gilthas must be made to see that.

Alhana touched Kerian's hand. "We cannot continue as we are."

Porthios was less tactful. "Waste no more time, Lioness. You and I know war is the only way to free our homeland."

For an instant, Kerian wondered whether Porthios might have stolen the food himself to force this very crisis. There was little he wouldn't do if he thought it would advance a cause he believed just. In any case, it really didn't matter. The army must go to Qualinesti to liberate their homeland—and to get Porthios away from Gilthas.

Evading both Alhana's compassion and Porthios's penetrating stare, she said, "I will put it to the Speaker."

2

Wind swept through the elves' camp, snatching at desert *gebs* and courtly robes, both much patched. The usual ebb and flow of the morning's work had come to a stop as elves young and old gathered at the only open ground wide enough to hold them, the pass into Inath-Wakenti. They congregated by family or clan, by former trade or station in life, and sat in orderly rows facing an enormous flat-topped granite boulder. Warriors on horseback were drawn up on either side of the slab. Those who had lost their mounts stood on the hillside behind. Still higher up were the griffon riders and their mounts, far enough away so the griffon scent would not alarm the horses.

The leaders of the exiled elves stood on the granite slab: generals Hamaramis and Taranath, Kerian, Alhana, and Samar, commander of Alhana's royal guard. Porthios stood apart from the rest, at one end of the improvised dais, idly tapping his leg with a stick.

An hour before noon, the last elves filed into place. The crowd quieted. As the silence lengthened, Alhana looked inquiringly at Kerian. The Lioness's lips firmed with distaste. She would have ceded the task of addressing the crowd to Alhana, but the former queen was adamant. Kerianseray, as wife of the Speaker, had precedence over

21

everyone else present. Kerian had acquiesced; if she refused, she had no doubt Porthios would leap at the chance to assert himself.

True to her word, she had spoken to Gilthas, urging him to allow the army to go to Qualinesti. The discussion had not gone well. Her husband stubbornly held fast to his idea that the nation was too vulnerable to be left without defenders. She reminded him she'd encountered nothing in the valley that could be defeated by massed troops and a small portion of the army would remain with them anyway. Such well-reasoned arguments did not sway him, so she spoke of the advantage of having Porthios far away, where he no longer could stir up dissent among their people. Gilthas dismissed this notion with an impatient wave of one hand, and that was when the Lioness's temper began to fray.

"He wants to be leader in your place, Gil! Are you blind to his intentions?"

They'd kept their voices low out of deference to the crowded conditions in the Speaker's tent, but her words had fallen into an unlucky lull in the conversations. A few heads turned their way. A glare from the Lioness sent everyone back about his or her business.

"Keep your voice down."

Kerian was ashamed at having spoken so intemperately, but her husband's hoarse command rekindled her anger, and the apology she'd intended to make went unsaid. Their conversation ended only moments later. Gilthas was seized by a fit of coughing so intense that his chief healer, Truthanar, rushed to him from across the tent. The elderly Silvanesti pushed Kerian aside in his haste to minister to his patient. She made no demur, only watched helplessly as Truthanar worked to get an elixir between Gilthas's blue lips. An age seemed to pass before the attack finally ended and Gilthas lay unconscious, but breathing more easily.

Despite his continuing weakness, Kerian had not wanted to delay the gathering any longer. As Alhana said, they simply could not go on as they had been.

DESTINY

Kerian looked out over the multitude of Silvanesti, Qualinesti, and Kagonesti assembled before her and felt a lump form in her throat. From every corner of the old realms they had come, driven out of the lands in which their race had dwelt for millennia. Many had perished during the long journey. Some had been born.

Clearing her throat, she began to speak.

"People of our ancient race! Many twists of fate and fortune have brought us to this place. Thousands have fought and died so we might live. As we honor those who sacrificed for us, we come together now to consider our future. Because so much depends on the choice we make, we speak before you all in a new Sinthal-Elish."

That was the conclave that had established the first elf realm, Silvanesti, and had made Silvanos Goldeneye the first Speaker of the Stars.

Someone in the crowd called, "Where is the Speaker? Where is the Pathfinder?"

Others took up the call. The cries angered Kerian. A furious retort hovered on her lips, but a touch on her wrist drew her attention. Alhana whispered, "They are afraid, niece, not angry. Reassure them."

As usual her advice was sound, but Kerian's ire was not easily dismissed. She had no wish to parade her husband's condition, not before the nation that loved him and certainly not before Porthios's knowing gaze.

She raised her hands and the cries ceased. "The Speaker knows of this meeting," she said. Grudging every word, she added, "He is . . . unwell today. His healers have advised him to keep to his bed." Truthanar would prefer the Speaker remain in bed permanently, but Kerian wasn't about to reveal that.

Confused questions traveled round the crowd. Their Speaker was ill? How ill? He must be very sick indeed to miss so momentous a gathering. Seeing the Lioness's very evident worry only exacerbated their concern and frightened exclamations erupted.

"Perhaps a litter should be sent for him," Alhana murmured to Kerian as the noise level increased.

"Cease your chattering!"

Porthios's command sliced through the crowd's babble. He walked up the slight incline to the higher end of the granite slab. Most of the elves quieted; the rest were shushed by their neighbors. If they were to hear his hoarse voice, all must be silent. Although they were willing to listen, a great many averted their eyes from Porthios's damaged form.

"We are here," he stated, "to decide matters far more important than the life of one elf."

Kerian took an angry step toward him, but Alhana held her back, hissing, "No! The people must not see us argue."

"Then they'd better close their eyes," Kerian growled but remained where she was, for the moment.

Porthios continued. "The only question we face is this: Shall we remain here and die of starvation or be carried off by the phantoms beyond the creek, or shall we take back what is rightfully ours?"

A large number of warriors thrust their swords and spears skyward, shouting lusty approval. The mob of civilians before Porthios did not echo their fervor.

"Did we endure the desert crossing only to straggle back again?" asked General Taranath, a highly regarded Qualinesti veteran and the Lioness's second-in-command.

"Not straggle—strike!" Porthios rasped, straining his scarred throat to speak more loudly. "A burning brand has been thrown into the tinderbox of Qualinesti. With the army we have here, we can fan that blaze into a conflagration that will consume the invaders and give us back our country!"

"You speak of the army. What of the people? Are they to cross desert, mountains, and sea with nothing more than the rags on their backs? They would not survive such a march."

Taranath's statement was no more than simple truth. While some still hailed Porthios's call to liberate Qualinesti, it was clear Taranath's position had the greater support. Most of those gathered on the alien soil of Inath-Wakenti were not firebrands or warriors. They had fled their homelands to escape genocide, endured years of exile in a hostile land, fought off nomad warriors with rocks and bare hands at times, and followed their Speaker across the desert cauldron to reach the valley he had promised would be a new home. Now Porthios stood there telling them their sacrifices had been for naught, that they must turn around and go back into the desert, with diminished supplies of food and water, easy prey for nomad attacks and the murderous heat. Any who managed to survive the long journey to Qualinesti would face Samuval's bandit horde, perhaps even the dreaded Knights of Neraka, or the army of minotaurs said to be spreading across the continent.

"What choice do they have? Should they stay here and starve?" Samar demanded of Taranath.

Hamaramis, commander of the Speaker's private guard, shook his head. "None need starve. The valley may be devoid of life, but there's game in the high hills. With griffon riders to spot for us, we can send hunting parties after game."

Samar snorted. "For how long?"

"Until crops can be planted and harvested."

"How do you know anything will grow in this dismal spot?"

And so it went. Porthios, Samar, and Alhana wanted to go. Taranath and most of the crowd believed remaining was the only choice. Hamaramis, unflaggingly loyal to his Speaker, was uncertain. While the argument raged, Kerian turned and stared toward the valley mouth and the torrid wasteland beyond. She hated the desert and everything about it. Her brief time in the green forests of home, drenched in blood though that time had been, had only heightened her loathing for all things Khurish. Taranath, finally noticing her silence, asked for her opinion of Porthios's plan.

"No one wants to go home more than I," she said, her gaze roaming slowly over the crowd. "I have been back to

Qualinesti. I have seen what the bandits are doing. Slavery, squalor, senseless death—that's what our country lives with every day.

"Here, we are safe from nomads and bandits, but . . ." Her voice trailed off, and she shook her head. "This is not a place to live. It's a place to die." She gestured toward the monoliths beyond the creek. "Our headstones are already in place."

Porthios sensed the subtle shift in the crowd's emotions. They were wavering, ready to be swayed. He spoke quickly, grasping the advantage.

"Come back with us, Lioness. The army of Qualinesti is yours to command. With you at its head, the army will liberate our rightful lands in no time!"

A cheer erupted from the warriors, and they began to chant, "Liberation! Liberation!"

Hamaramis shouted them into silence. The old general was shocked that the Speaker's wife would side with Porthios and the Silvanesti. He did not realize how difficult it was for her to say what she had said. Her unflinching sense of honesty would not allow her to lie to their people, even if speaking the truth made it appear she was siding with Porthios.

A new disturbance erupted far from the granite platform. Elves in the back of the crowd got to their feet. Like a wave, the motion spread from the rear of the crowd to the front. All eyes turned toward the disturbance.

"The Speaker! The Speaker is coming!"

Gilthas approached, leaning on a short wooden staff. Healer Truthanar followed at his heels, watching with grave concern. The crowd parted for the Speaker, every elf bowing as he passed. Twenty paces from the granite slab, he halted.

"A grand assembly," he said, smiling. "I seem to have misplaced my invitation. How can there be a Sinthal-Elish without the Speaker of the Sun and Stars?"

Kerian leaped down from the stone slab. The eight-foot drop bent her knees and scattered the elves nearest her. She hurried to Gilthas's side. He took her hand, forestalling the attempt to slip a supporting arm around his waist. As though leading a royal procession, the two of them walked to the base of the granite slab. Porthios descended. Gilthas greeted him genially.

"I understand you want to borrow my army. Why?"

"To free our homeland from the filth that occupies it!"

"A worthy goal. But what of the rest of our people?"

"Any who wish to join us are welcome."

Gilthas released Kerian's hand and gestured to the assemblage around them. "No one doubts our people's courage, but they are unarmed and untrained," Gilthas said. "And they would encounter enemies every step of the way, and once home, an army of foes united in their hatred of us."

Porthios reminded them of Bianost, the Qualinesti town he had wrested from Samuval's grip. Inspired by the example of Porthios's tiny band of rebels, the townsfolk had risen up and overthrown their bandit overlords.

"Their valor shall be recorded in the annals of our people," Gilthas agreed. "But they were there, in the town, under the enemy's heel. No one asked them to march hundreds of miles, turn around, march back, and then fight. What you suggest is madness."

"Do you offer a better choice, Great Speaker? This valley is dead. If our people stay here, they'll die and accomplish nothing!"

Gilthas shook slightly, and Kerian realized he was striving to suppress a cough. Raising his voice as much as he was able, he addressed the gathering.

"My people, we have been driven from our ancestral lands and persecuted by barbarians of every stripe. This valley is our destiny. Where we now stand is the only place on this continent that is ours for the taking. No one else wants it. I don't deny its disadvantages. It harbors secrets so dark, our wisest sages have not yet fathomed them, but I believe they will. As I see it, in this sheltered spot, we will heal our many wounds and grow strong. As surely as day follows night, so the fortunes of races change. Today our nation is at low ebb. Tomorrow we will be better, and in a thousand tomorrows, we will have regained what we have lost. But only if we have a haven from which to start!"

A roar went up from the assembly. Alhana applauded the Speaker's vision, but Porthios made a scornful, dismissive gesture.

When the tumult died, Samar asked, "What about those who wish to go, Speaker? Will you keep them here?"

"I will bind no one to my will. But even if every soul departs, I shall remain in Inath-Wakenti."

The assembly fell into loud debate once more. Atop the slab, Samar and Taranath exchanged words. Hamaramis climbed down to stand by his Speaker. Porthios, like Kerian, watched Gilthas. Alhana listened to the crowd for a time, gauging emotions, studying expressions; then she hopped off the rear of the slab. A minute later, she came and spoke privately to Gilthas, then remounted the slab.

When Samar realized she was trying to address the throng, he put a ram's horn to his lips and blew. The high, ululating note echoed down the pass. The crowd grew still.

"Elves of Krynn," Alhana said, "whether we go or stay, nothing will be served if we wreck our unity. Our nations fell because they were divided. We must not be divided again. But there is a way to let all choose."

She held up her hands. In each was a stone. One was a smooth pebble of common white quartz; the other, a rough piece of blue-gray granite. "Let every elf find a stone. Blue granite for those who wish to stay in Inath-Wakenti, white quartz for those who join our crusade in Qualinesti. No blame will attach to either choice. Each chooses his or her own fate, and that choice is final."

Gilthas praised her idea, but Kerian saw no reason for waiting. Why not have the assembly divide into two groups immediately?

DESTINY

"Such a decision should not be made in haste, in the heat of excitement," Alhana explained. "The search for a stone will give each elf time to reflect."

Gilthas decreed the voting would take place the day after tomorrow, at daybreak. All would return to this spot and make his or her decision. Those voting to depart would do so immediately.

The Sinthal-Elish was at an end. Truthanar handed a cup to the Speaker. It contained more of the white medicine.

"I thought you were resting," Kerian said. "What were you thinking of, coming here like this?"

"I was thinking of the future."

"Don't you get tired of talking like that?" she muttered.

"Like what?"

"Like a prophet . . . or a player in some low drama."

He smiled. "Being Speaker requires a sense of drama."

Their walk back to camp was accomplished amid a happy mob of the Speaker's loyal and confident subjects. They knew firsthand their king had spared himself none of the hardships of their exile. When the danger from the nomads was greatest, Gilthas Pathfinder led his people onward with no thought of his own safety. Although he wore the mantle of legendary rulers such as Silvanos and Kith-Kanan, Gilthas had proven himself their equal in valor and majesty.

Their faith was so heartbreakingly profound, Kerian couldn't bear it. "Do you have any plan for those who remain, Gil? What are you going to do?"

He squeezed her hand. "The day after tomorrow, I will cross Lioness Creek and lead our nation into Inath-Wakenti."

Hamaramis, walking next to them, exclaimed, "Great Speaker, is that wise?"

"Yes. We've lingered on the doorstep long enough. It's time to take possession of our new home."

"If it doesn't take possession of us," Kerian said darkly.

* * * * *

Wind blew out of Alya-Alash like a great exhalation. Breath of the Gods indeed! The gusty wind rattled the threadbare tents pitched in the center of the pass. Fifteen cone-shaped shelters woven from dark wool were arranged in a semicircle. They were the last remnants of the once-mighty force that had dogged the elves' every step from Khuri-Khan. The nomads had fought with great courage and ferocity, but the *laddad* outlasted them. Griffons had soared down from the sky, one of them ridden by a hideous demon. When he ordered the nomads to depart, most of them did. It was easy to justify the retreat. So many had died battling the *laddad,* some of the tribes would require years to recover.

Adala Fahim dipped her hands in a dented copper basin. The tepid water stung her scratched fingers as she washed away a thick layer of grime. Known as the Weyadan, the "Mother of the Weya-Lu" tribe, she later had come to be called Maita for the divine, inescapable fate that guided her in the war against the *laddad.* Little of the divine remained; there was only endless, back-breaking labor. The day the *laddad* entered Alya-Alash, Adala had begun the wall across the pass. Some of her former followers returned to help. A few were warriors, but most were older folk who still believed in her godly mission. From sunrise to sundown, they dragged stones from the surrounding slopes. Lacking mortar or tools, they piled the stones in a long cairn, its base wider than its top. Thus far, the wall was head high and about a hundred yards long. The pass was a mile wide. A great deal of work remained.

Adala toiled without complaint, her faith undiminished. The very falling away of the tribes' support convinced her she was in the right. Everyone knew the path to truth was narrow and hard, while the road to error was easy. Her only regret was the betrayal of her cousin Wapah. He had turned his back on her, his people, and his homeland by helping the foreign killers escape justice. His actions were unforgivable.

DESTINY

A few days after he'd led the *laddad* into the valley, Wapah had returned. He rode straight out of the pass, in broad daylight, with his head uncovered for all to see. Outraged warriors wanted to slay him as a traitor, but Adala showed them he was not worth even that. She turned her back on him. The rest followed her example, and Wapah passed through the camp and out into the high desert with no eye upon him. His image diminished to a silhouette, then softened in the heat, wavered, and vanished. Since then, no one else had entered or left the forbidden valley.

Finished with her ablutions, Adala shook her hands carefully over the bowl, allowing every drop to run back inside. Water was plentiful here, but the habits of a lifetime in the desert were unbreakable. She looked up as the thud of hoofbeats announced the arrival of a rider. It was Tamid, a Weya-Lu from the Cloudbender clan.

"Maita! Our hunting party was attacked!"

She stood quickly. *"Laddad?"*

"No. A beast!"

Unlike the deep desert, the foothills abounded in game. Tamid and a party of three hunters had flushed a stag and a wild sow in a rocky ravine east of camp. On their way back with the dressed carcasses, the hunters were set upon. Two men were unhorsed, and the creature had carried off the game. Few animals were bold enough to attack armed and mounted men. Fewer still were strong enough to carry off two carcasses at the same time.

Adala asked if the creature was a desert panther. The long-legged cat, large as a donkey, was nearly extinct in the deep desert but might still prowl in the shadow of the mountains. Tamid vowed the beast was no panther, although it walked on four feet. None in his party had ever seen its like before. He had left the others to trail the beast while he came back to report to Adala.

Such a creature was too dangerous to be allowed to remain so near their camp. Adala sent Tamid to round up more men. The creature must be killed.

When Tamid returned with eleven mounted men, he was

surprised to see Adala herself mounted on Little Thorn, her tireless gray donkey. She was going with them, and as usual she was unarmed. The men did not waste time protesting. She was the Maita, and she would do what she would do.

Tamid led them southeast along the edge of the lower range of hills. The ground was stony. Cacti and bone-colored spear bushes were thick on the ground, forcing the horses to pick their way carefully. Adala's sharp nose detected the strong scent of *soter*. She noted a small stand of the evergreen shrub and marked the spot for a later return. From *soter* she could make a natural wound cleanser, and her store was sorely depleted after the recent battles.

When the nomads reached the spot where Tamid had parted company with his fellows, they halted. One man raised a short, curled ram's horn to his lips and sounded a long note.

In less than a minute, an answering bleat came from ahead and above. The slope was steep. Adala's donkey was more sure-footed than the horses and outpaced them, but soon all of them were struggling upward, leaning forward to keep their balance. Loose stones rolled down the hill behind them. The distant horn blew again, twice, sounding more urgent.

A mile passed before they spied two riders waving swords over their heads. The slender blades, bare of crossguards, caught the setting sun and flashed like beacons. Adala tapped Little Thorn's rump with her stick. The stalwart donkey increased its pace, leaving the horses behind.

"Where is it?" she called.

One of the riders pointed with his sword to the sun-washed crest at his back. "Beyond the ridge yonder, Maita."

At the end of another steep climb, the group came to a plateau perhaps a hundred yards long and forty yards wide. The last member of Tamid's hunting party awaited them at the far end. He was mounted, his bow at full draw. His target was hidden by intervening rocks, but its presence was obvious. The archer's horse, trained to stand quietly in the face of nearly any danger, stamped and shied, shaking its blunt head.

DESTINY

"Keep back, Maita!" called the archer, never shifting his gaze. "It can leap far!"

She acknowledged his warning but tapped Little Thorn urging him forward. The donkey snorted and balked. Stolid even in the presence of griffons, Little Thorn did not like whatever was ahead. Adala chided him as though he were a naughty child and tapped his flank with her stick. He shuffled forward, obedient but unhappy.

Adala knew every beast that roamed the desert, but she'd never seen anything like the animal perched on a low pinnacle at the extreme end of the ledge. It was fully six feet long and covered with dark reddish-brown fur. The upright ears of a cat were oddly mixed with the muzzle, brow, and liquid-brown eyes of a canine. Its forelegs were half again as long as its stubby rear legs. Adala's approach set it to snarling, revealing long, yellow teeth.

"Kill it," Adala commanded.

The archer loosed. The arrow was tipped with a hunting point, shaped like two miniature swords crossed. It flew straight and true at the creature's chest. The beast held its place until the arrow was an arm's length away then snatched the shaft from midair. Shocked by its uncanny speed, the nomads only then saw that its front paws were articulated like fingers.

The men uttered oaths. Adala did not. "Spears!" she ordered. "Spit that monster!"

Riders crowded forward. Half a dozen iron spear points bored in. The creature dropped the arrow and lowered its chin to the stone.

"Do . . . not . . . " it rasped.

The attackers halted in shock.

"Did you speak?" Adala demanded.

Black tongue lolling, the beast nodded, a bizarrely human gesture. "Do . . . not . . . kill . . . me," it said, brown eyes never leaving Adala's face.

The Mother of the Weya-Lu was not known for indecision. Summoning the strength of her *maita,* she ordered the men to fall back. Tamid protested, but she cut him off.

"Withdraw, I say. Those on High will not allow me to be hurt."

Grumbling all the while, the men turned their horses and moved to the far end of the ledge. There they halted. Despite her urging, they would go no farther. Several kept bows in hand, arrows nocked, just in case.

"You have faith," the beast said. It spoke slowly, each word seeming to require great effort.

"Who are you?"

The creature slunk off the pinnacle. Crawling on its belly, it halted five feet from Adala. Little Thorn trembled violently but did not bolt. Adala heard bowstrings creak to full draw behind her, but she kept her attention fixed on the creature. She repeated her question.

The creature answered, and Adala's mouth fell open. "How did this come about?" she demanded.

The beast stared at her for a long moment then rubbed its head on the ground. Its frustration was pathetic. Clearly its speaking abilities were not up to answering her question. Once more she made a swift decision.

"You will come with us. If you behave as the person you claim to be, all will be well. But if I find out you're lying, I'll have you skinned alive."

The nomads at the other end of the ledge stared in amazement as she approached, passed, and descended the steep hill with the weird monster tamely loping at Little Thorn's heels. Despite all they'd been through with her, Adala Fahim still had the power to amaze. Her *maita* was indeed more powerful than any wicked spell. They trailed her back to camp under a sky aflame with sunset. High clouds covered the western third of the sky, and they blazed ruby and gold, strange to nomad eyes accustomed to the pristinely clear vault over the deep desert.

None of them could know the whirlwind of questions that raged behind the serene face Adala allowed the world to see.

DESTINY

The new wonder had set her mind spinning. Why had Those on High delivered into her hands a monster claiming to be Shobbat, Crown Prince of Khur?

3

Far into the night, Gilthas listened to scribes reading from ancient chronicles of the elf kingdoms. He couldn't yet make out the whole story of Inath-Wakenti. Like a mosaic viewed from too close, those fragments of truth he had wouldn't resolve into a pattern. Every time a pattern seemed to be emerging, it fell apart when examined too rigorously.

He lay on his pallet, back propped against a rolled rug, listening to the *Leaves of the Sacred Grove of E'li*. Although Silvanesti, not Qualinesti, was the first of the elf nations, the clerics of E'li in Qualinost had in their archive some of the oldest records of the elf race. They had been carried out of Silvanost at the end of the Kinslayer War, when Kith-Kanan led his followers westward to found Qualinesti. Kith-Kanan's brother, Speaker of the Stars Sithas, was furious when he learned the ancient scrolls had left his realm. Wars had been started over less, but Kith-Kanan, newly anointed Speaker of the Sun, sent back the documents to appease Sithas's anger. As Kith-Kanan had hoped, his twin never noticed the returned scrolls were copies. Kith-Kanan had kept the originals in a special archive. The yellowed parchment scrolls were a thousand miles from either country, being read to the first king of the combined elf nations. The Speaker of the Sun and Stars had abandoned much on the march to Inath-

Wakenti, but not the ancient annals of his race.

Gilthas had charged one scribe with the sole duty of keeping a list of the Speaker's ideas on the subject. Eventually, Gilthas was sure, answers would appear.

"Varanas," he said to that scribe, "read back my list of questions."

The elf held the scroll up to the wavering lamplight. " 'First: Inath-Wakenti has a connection to the gods. Is it where some of them first set foot in the world? Is it where they dwelt? Second: The *Chronicles of Silvanos* say the five dragonstones were buried in the Pit of Nemith-Otham in the northern mountains. Is Inath-Wakenti the location of this pit, and might residual magic remain, though the stones themselves are gone?' "

The dragonstones, containing the essences of the five original evil dragons, had been buried after the First Dragon War. Dwarves dug them up, inadvertently releasing the dragons and starting the Second Dragon War. The scribe Varanas swallowed hard. The notion that even the dregs of such evil might lie beneath their feet was extremely unsettling.

Gilthas prompted him to continue.

" 'Third: Neither the first nor second proposition explains the valley's hostility to animal life or the identities of its ghosts. Fourth: Are the will-o'-the-wisps the valley's defenders or its last inhabitants, and is there a way to nullify or eliminate them?' "

Gilthas lifted a hand, and Varanas paused, allowing him to ponder what he had heard.

None of the old histories mentioned the strange will-o'-the-wisps. But other annals recounting past ages of elf greatness did contain references to spirits set to guard enemies of the state, enemies too well connected to kill. Speaker Silvanos would exile them to distant points in his realm, and they would be watched over by ever-vigilant sentinels created and maintained by magic.

Two of the most famous exiles in Silvanos's time were Balif and the wizard Vedvedsica. A dark scandal had rocked the latter days of the Speaker's reign. Vedvedsica, a retainer of Lord Balif, the commander of the Speaker's armies, had been tied to unnatural and horrifying doings and was sent away to a northern outpost—perhaps Inath-Wakenti? After Sithel succeeded to the throne, Lord Balif left Silvanesti under a cloud and Vedvedsica returned. His presence was kept secret, but Sithel consulted him on matters of the gravest import, such as when the queen gave birth to twin sons.

Many questions remained unanswered. Gilthas had no one among his followers with the skill and power of a sorcerer such as Vedvedsica. After the fall of Qualinost, the Knights of Neraka had made a special point of eliminating priests and sages of the highest rank. Assassins from the Black Hall had roamed occupied Qualinesti, killing elves who had magical knowledge and ability. The only sages remaining in Gilthas's service were lesser clerics, natural healers (such as Truthanar), and a handful of learned scholars. And the very best of those, the royal archivist Favaronas, had vanished with the rest of Kerian's original expedition to the valley.

A different cause denied Gilthas any sages from Silvanesti. The occupying minotaurs suppressed them but took no special pains to root them out. Long before the bull-men landed on the sacred shores, Silvanesti priests and magicians had been driven underground by the Chaos War. As far as was known, they remained underground, hidden in the green fastness of the woodlands.

As the silence lengthened, Varanas looked up, expecting to be told to continue, but the Speaker had fallen asleep. Signaling to the other scribes, Varanas rose quietly. As he withdrew, he saw Lady Kerianseray standing at the edge of the light cast by the lamp. He bowed and left her alone with her husband.

Kerian drew the blanket up to Gilthas's chin. The blanket was actually her own warrior's mantle, the crimson cloth softer than the horse blanket that had formerly been his night wrap.

DESTINY

How far they had fallen when the king of two realms must use horse tack to keep out the night's chill.

She gave the scattered scrolls only a cursory glance. Gilthas continued to seek answers in moldering documents, convinced he eventually could fathom the valley's mysteries. Yet they knew no more now than they did about the far side of the world.

Truthanar had advised her not to sleep by her husband. Elves were resistant to consumption, but repeated close exposure would be tempting fate, and once the sickness took root, it was fiendishly hard to cure. In Qualinost, with excellent care and the finest medicines, Gilthas would have had a decent chance at recovery. Here he had virtually none. She brushed a strand of lank hair from his forehead and left him.

She slept on a bedroll on the west side of the pass. She hiked up to the spot, so weary she fully expected to be asleep as soon as she lay down. Before she could do more than unbuckle her sword belt, however, a black silhouette appeared atop the hill a few yards away. No tents were pitched there. There was no reason for anyone to be wandering about. She called out a challenge.

A low voice answered. Porthios.

"Don't you ever sleep?" she grumbled.

"I'll be brief. Are you coming with us to Qualinesti?"

"I thought the answer to that would be obvious." She turned away.

"He will be dead before we reach the New Sea, you know."

Whipping back around, she snapped, "You go too far, Scarecrow." That was the derisive nickname given him by his human captives in Qualinesti. At times Kerian found the coarse human word particularly apt.

He trod carefully over the loose stones until he was close enough for her to see his masked face.

"You're a fighter, Kerianseray. We march to free our homeland.

39

Isn't that what you want more than anything?"

"Yes!" Then: "No. Not more than anything."

"You cannot stand by and watch us march away. If you miss this fight, you will always regret it." His voice was inexorable. "Anyone who doesn't fight for the freedom of Qualinesti cannot claim it after the victory's won."

Appeals to her fighting pride had failed, so he was threatening her? Join me, or never come back to Qualinesti? How dared he! Her hand closed around the hilt of her sword.

"Get away from me, Porthios. Get away before I finish what the dragon's breath started!"

He came closer still. All that kept her from making good on her threat was his unarmed state. He was as bad as Gilthas. What was wrong with them? Did they think the world was so in awe of their royal blood that they didn't need to bear arms? Damn all high-born idealists anyway!

Voices put an end to their confrontation. One was shouting for the Lioness. She shouted back. A pair of guards, spear-armed civilian volunteers, hurried up. One sported a dented bronze buckler, and the other wore a once-elegant (but now badly corroded) Silvanesti helmet. Both elves were out of breath not from exertion, but from excitement. There was a disturbance in the food cache, they reported. An intruder could be heard moving about inside, but he returned no answer to their challenges. Warriors of the regular army had been sent for and were surrounding the cache.

On went the sword belt again. Kerian was certain the strap had worn a permanent groove in her hip.

A single griffon and rider wheeled above the cache, trying to spot the intruder. The low stone wall protecting the food supply was surrounded by two dozen warriors. The officer, one of Alhana's Silvanesti guards, gave Kerian a whispered report. Movement had been heard from within, but no one had yet entered to investigate.

Kerian drew her sword. Any place else, the intruder would

probably have been nothing more mysterious than a wild dog. Khur was full of them, permanently lean creatures who usually hunted by night. A pack could surround and kill a good horse or drag away an imprudently sleeping elf. But they'd seen no signs of any such animals in Inath-Wakenti, and with their food supplies so low, they could ill afford any loss.

Two guards pulled aside the entry barrier and Kerian ducked in. Crates, barrels, and wicker bundles of provisions were stacked in head-high piles arranged in neat, concentric circles. An all-too-familiar rustle of old cloth told her Porthios had slipped in behind her. She ordered him out.

He pulled a chalk pebble from a pocket and drew a thick white smudge on his masked forehead. "If you see anything without this mark, kill it," he said and melted away.

For a moment, she could only stare after him. Minutes ago, he'd seen her ready to draw steel on him. Now he was going up against an unknown intruder, unarmed, and with only Kerian to protect him should it come to a fight. Whatever else she thought of him, she must credit him with courage.

A metallic clatter sent her jogging around the outer ring of provisions until she came to an opening. A pale shape flashed across the gap. It was slight but stood erect on two legs—not a wild dog. Kerian called a challenge and gave chase. It darted away sharply right and disappeared into the next ring of provisions. She sprinted after—

—and crashed into a solid wall of crates.

Where in the name of Chaos had the thing gone? She began to climb. From atop the crates she spotted the gray-clad intruder in the path below her. It stood facing Porthios.

She shouted for Porthios to grab him, but he didn't move. She jumped down and started to put her sword to the intruder's back but realized the gray figure was translucent. She swept her blade back and forth, but it was like slashing at smoke. The figure had no substance at all.

She moved around to face it. Its eyes were dark holes and its mouth a narrow line. The shape was vaguely elflike, upright, with two arms and an indistinct head.

"Who are you?" she demanded. The gray figure immediately vanished, as though the sound of her voice had chased it away.

Porthios still had not spoken or moved. He seemed rooted in place, staring at the spot where the ghost had been.

"What's the matter? Did it hurt you?" she asked sharply.

When he didn't reply, she grabbed his arm. He flinched hard and jerked free.

"It called me . . . 'Father,' " he whispered.

For an instant she was taken aback, but common sense quickly reasserted itself.

"These ghosts have been here for thousands of years, Porthios. It might as easily have called me 'Father.' There's no logical reason to think it was your son."

"Yet I felt as though I knew him."

His expression was hidden by the mask, but the gloved hands knotted together at his waist were an eloquent sign of his agitation. Silvanoshei, son of Porthios and Alhana, had died at the end of the War of Souls, killed by his lover, Mina. That she had been an agent of the evil goddess Takhisis was well known; less clear, at least to Kerian, was just how deep Silvanoshei's betrayal of his people had gone. Whatever his sins, Silvanoshei had paid for them with his life. Kerian could only imagine the pain Alhana and Porthios had faced, losing their only child.

Porthios had stepped into the space where the apparition had stood. By his very silence and immobility, he seemed oddly vulnerable.

"Nothing more than a trick of the night, I'm certain," Kerian said.

He gave no reply, so she turned to go.

"Say nothing of this to Alhana," he said. "Her wounds are too deep."

For once she was happy to do just as he said. Soldiers called for her from elsewhere in the enclosure, and she left Porthios to go to them.

DESTINY

The warriors showed her discarded cheesecloth bags. The bags once had held haunches of meat. Kerian ordered the soldiers to scour the cache. "Look for footprints, handprints on the containers, anything unusual," she advised. She did not mention the apparition that she and Porthios had seen. Specters did not steal meat.

While the soldiers searched, she examined the bags more carefully. They weren't torn and the neck of each bag was still tied, the wax seal on the knot unbroken.

The soldiers found no traces of any intruder. Carefully folding the empty cheesecloth bags, Kerian tucked them into her sword belt. Her sun-browned face wore a grim expression.

There seemed no doubt their losses of food were due to the valley's weird influence. Mere theft or hoarding couldn't explain the sealed, empty bags. She must tell Gilthas. His plan to cross Lioness Creek and take possession of the valley would have to wait.

* * * * *

The eastern half of the valley stayed light a little longer than the west because of the shadows cast by the western mountains. As the sun slipped below the peaks, two elves walked through waist-high marlberry and olive bushes toward the eastern side. The elder was a Qualinesti, his body haggard and thin from long privation. Favaronas, formerly the archivist of the Speaker's library in Qualinost, was unaccustomed to such strenuous exercise.

"Less haste, if you please," he gasped.

His companion, a Kagonesti years younger, halted only briefly. He sported hunter's togs and hair closely cropped after the fashion of some humans.

Robien the Tireless was a bounty hunter hired by Sahim-Khan to capture Faeterus, a mage formerly employed by Sahim. After years of service to the khan, Faeterus suddenly abandoned Khuri-Khan and had caused Sahim no small amount of trouble before leaving, Sahim-Khan was not a forgiving man. Robien's charge was to find the rogue sorcerer and return him to Khuri-Khan to face his former master's wrath. He said, "I want to find open ground before nightfall. I don't want those lights popping out of the brush so close we can't avoid them."

He was right. Favaronas had been in Robien's company only a short time but had come to realize Robien usually was right. Exhausted, perpetually fearful, Favaronas did not find it an endearing trait.

Favaronas had encountered the hunter after a chance meeting with Faeterus back at Lioness Creek. Desperate for aid and ignorant of Faeterus's identity, the archivist had agreed to work with him in trying to fathom the valley's secrets. Once Robien revealed what he knew of the magician's past crimes in Khuri-Khan, Favaronas found himself caught between the two, wishing to confide all in Robien, but cowed by Faeterus's threats. The hapless scholar did what he could to aid Robien's quest, never at all certain the Kagonesti was capable of capturing the sorcerer before Faeterus destroyed them both.

Robien pushed on, breaking trail for Favaronas. It was heavy going. Marlberry branches were slick but clinging. They constantly wound around Favaronas's ankles and threatened to trip him. Olive bushes, not to be confused with the noble olive tree, had spiky leaves that seemed determined to poke out his eyes. Favaronas's hands and face were streaked with tiny cuts. He could hardly credit Robien's assurance that their prey had passed this way. Faeterus was a mysterious sorcerer, but hardly a vigorous person. Far older than Favaronas and burdened by the heavy robes he wore, how could he have traversed such a terrible thicket?

Robien pointed to faint marks on the highest branches. "He walked up here."

Favaronas squinted at the marks, barely visible to him even once he knew where to look. The sorcerer had walked on *top* of the brush? Swallowing hard, Favaronas the inveterately curious decided that knowing a thing was sometimes far more unsettling than not knowing it.

Their shadows stretched farther and farther in front of them as they traveled. Based on the archivist's theory that Faeterus was seeking a high spot from which to oversee the entire valley, Robien had deduced that a peak called Mount Rakaris was his goal. The trail did seem to be leading directly there. Favaronas believed the valley's monoliths weren't the remains of a long-deserted city, but formed some sort of map or sigil. Viewed as a whole, from a high vantage, their meaning would become plain to Faeterus, allowing him to tap into the hidden power of Inath-Wakenti. What form that power might take, Favaronas did not know, but he was certain Faeterus must not be allowed access to it.

Not until the last sliver of sun was slipping behind the mountains did Robien at last take pity on the struggling Favaronas and consent to make camp. At the archivist's urging, they diverted to a clearing dominated by a trio of standing stones.

The stones were sixteen feet high but looked even taller perched on a low mound of the valley's usual blue-green soil. Favaronas staggered out of the hateful brush and dropped on his hands and knees. Robien went to the stones. He touched the nearest one lightly, staring up at its squared-off top. His enchanted spectacles could detect any trace of living beings, and they showed him that no one had touched the stone in a very long time.

The eastern mountains were still far away, two, perhaps three days even at Robien's pace. Numerous ledges and plateaus were visible on the steep granite slopes. Any one of them might serve for viewing the valley, but Favaronas believed the monolith builders had created one specific place where the grand plan of the scattered stones would be plainly visible. He was certain Faeterus was seeking that spot and that spot alone. The sorcerer's trail would lead them to it.

Tracking wary prey and avoiding the ghostly lights that haunted the valley required stealth, so Robien allowed no campfire. Favaronas resigned himself to another meal of dried fruit and venison jerky, and another night spent shivering beneath his meager blanket. He shrugged the heavy sack from his shoulder. It fell over and the three stone cylinders inside rolled out onto the ground.

Robien looked up from his own small pack. "The way is difficult enough for you, scholar. Why are you carrying rocks?"

Favaronas hastily shoved the cylinders back into the sack. He muttered something about "interesting mineral formations," and Robien seemed content to leave it at that.

The strange cylinders weren't rocks at all, but scrolls. Magically petrified, they unspooled only when exposed to filtered sunlight. Favaronas had discovered them in a tunnel while a member of Lady Kerianseray's original expedition to the valley. By the time he puzzled out some of the text they contained, the expedition was leaving the valley. He had slipped away from the others and returned to the valley alone. He was still working to decipher the ancient books. The writing inside them was a severely abbreviated form of Old Elvish in which each word was reduced to a single syllable, such as *om.hed.thon.dac,* a phrase he recently had worked out to mean "the father who made not his children." This epithet was used frequently in the texts and referred to the leader of those who had built the standing stones. Whether these builders had been colonists or prisoners, Favaronas was unsure.

He'd unlocked only a small portion of the scrolls' meaning, but the implications of even that much were terrifying. His surreptitious return to Inath-Wakenti had been fueled by the desire to harness a great power and help his beleaguered people. Now all he wanted was to bury the knowledge as deeply as possible. No one must learn what he knew. He hadn't told even Robien of his connection to the Speaker's household and his acquaintance with Lady Kerianseray. Simpler if the bounty hunter thought him no more than an unimportant, wayward scholar. Fortunately, Robien was concerned only with capturing Faeterus. He showed little interest in anything that did not directly affect his search.

Robien settled down with his back against a monolith and braced his short, recurved bow. It was his nightly ritual. He never lay down to sleep without the bow, complete with nocked arrow, on his lap. Favaronas had heard it said that the best Kagonesti hunters could hear a leaf bend under a grasshopper's foot. Close association with Robien taught him that was no fanciful tale. Robien could detect impossibly faint sounds and smells, and his eyesight, even without his enchanted glasses, was far more acute than that of any other elf Favaronas had known.

Favaronas lay down a few feet away, in the center of the triangle formed by the three stones. The scholar found the valley's enormous silence very wearing on his nerves. The lack of night sounds made it difficult for him to fall asleep. To fill the void, he made conversation, asking Robien how long he'd been tracking Faeterus.

"Twenty-two days and twenty-three nights," the hunter replied evenly. "The first three nights I spent in a cistern beneath Khuri-Khan." Leaning back against the monolith, his eyes closed, Robien frowned. "Vile place."

"When you find him, how will you hold him?"

He gave a small shrug. "By pinning his wings."

With that, Robien was asleep. Favaronas envied his ability to fall asleep between one breath and the next. Although Favaronas lay quietly and tried to think calming thoughts, rest eluded him. His head was filled with a cacophony of questions and fears. An hour went by, and still he was wide awake. Perhaps a drink of water would help.

The tepid liquid tasted like the skin in which Robien carried it, and Favaronas wished it were wine. On his second swallow, it was—a potent red. Astonished, he choked, dribbling wine down his chest.

"That's your favorite vintage, isn't it. Black grapes of Goodlund, two years old?"

Favaronas's pulse raced. He knew that voice!

From the deep shadow of the westernmost monolith, Faeterus emerged. The sorcerer's habitual raiment—a heavy brown robe—made him appear huge and hulking. He glided forward, feet invisible beneath the trailing robe but seeming not to touch the ground.

Favaronas darted a glance at Robien, certain the wily Kagonesti must know his quarry was at hand.

"The khan's hireling cannot help you."

Faeterus held out a bony hand, and a flame ignited in his palm. Its light revealed Robien to be in no shape to help anyone, not even himself. His eyes were closed, as though he still slept, and the bluish soil was rising up around him, bubbling like thick mud. The growing mound of dirt already reached his waist, immobilizing his legs. Its bottom edge, where the oozing earth met the ground, had hardened to a lapislike stone, and the effect was creeping upward. Soon Robien would be entombed alive.

"When the grains reach his lips and nostrils, they will fill him like a living hourglass," Faeterus explained. "When the sun rises, the heat of the day will fuse the soil into hardest glass. His agony will be intense . . . and lingering." The sorcerer's cowled head turned back to Favaronas. Favaronas had never seen his face; it was always shadowed by the robe's deep hood. "But his fate is easy compared to what I have reserved for you."

Favaronas prostrated himself, begging for mercy, insisting he'd had no choice but to join with Robien. His flailing hand touched the sack of scrolls. Thinking fast, he shoved it forward, spilling the cylinders onto the ground. "Look, master! See what I have found!"

Faeterus uttered a surprised oath. Knobby fingers reached toward a scroll, hovering inches above its surface. "You kept these from me." That was patently true, but Favaronas denied it anyway. The sorcerer asked if he knew what the scrolls were.

"Yes, master! They're chronicles written by those who raised the standing stones," gabbled Favaronas.

Prompted, he went on to relate how he had learned to open the scrolls, and that he could, with difficulty, read some of the text within. A great force grasped the neck of his robe and hoisted him into the air. The sorcerer still had the flame in one hand. The other hand he held aloft, fingers clenched.

"I accept your tribute," he said. "You will survive this night, wretched fool, if you read to me the Annals of the Lost."

The invisible hand dropped Favaronas onto his feet. Pale and trembling, he restored the cylinders to the sack and clutched the bundle to his chest.

As he followed the sorcerer, he glanced back once. The receding glow of Faeterus's light showed Robien encased up to his chest. Like living creatures, grains of sand were racing up to pile themselves one upon the other around his shoulders. Favaronas turned away and trudged on. He was as helpless as the bounty hunter, both of them at the mercy of a pitiless master.

4

T he Speaker's day began with a trip to the creek. Gilthas
sat on a rock between two small willow trees and drank
water from a bowl. Cold, fresh water was one of the valley's
advantages—according to his wife, perhaps its only advantage. The early-morning sun painted the crests of the western
mountains in golden light, but the valley itself was still in
shadow. Morning mist hovered in the low places. Despite
layers of clothing, Gilthas shivered. He just couldn't seem to
get warm anymore.

When the water was gone, he started to rise, to refill the bowl,
but before he could do more than shift his weight, the vessel was
taken from his hand. Kerian dipped the bowl into the creek and
returned it to him.

"Are you warm enough?"

He nodded and used the water to wash his hands and face.
"They're voting now," he added. "I wonder if I shall be alone
by sundown."

"Don't be ridiculous. You're the Speaker of the Sun and
Stars. Your people won't abandon you."

Eagle Eye landed on the other side of the creek. Unlike
the wild Golden griffons they'd captured in the Kharolis
Mountains, he was of the Royal breed, larger and with
white neck plumage. In Kerian's biased view, he was also far

smarter than any of the wild creatures they'd found.

He gave an inquiring trill and flapped his wings. Kerian nodded, lifting an arm. Eagle Eye launched himself skyward and went off to hunt his breakfast.

"Are you sure you can't read that beast's mind?"

The querulous tone in Gilthas's voice brought a faint smile. "I leave that to Alhana," she replied, drinking a handful of water. "But griffons are uncomplicated creatures."

Unlike elves. The words seemed to hang unspoken between them. Kerian trailed her fingers in the creek. Gilthas used to joke about being jealous of the attention she paid to Eagle Eye, but she had begun to see it as more than mere humor. For a long time, all husband and wife had shared was hard work and confrontation, and lately, because of Gilthas's illness, careful neutrality.

Against her better judgment, Kerian had obeyed his order to lead a company to survey Inath-Wakenti's fitness as a new home for their people. The passage of her expedition through the desert had precipitated violence from the Khurish nomads, and its brief time in the valley had led to wholesale disappearances and a battle with a rare and vicious sand beast. In the end, far more questions had been raised than answered. For Kerian one fact had been made plain: the valley was no fit home for the elf nation.

Then had come her decision to depart the valley alone on Eagle Eye, after she received a vision of danger stalking Gilthas. He had survived, but their marriage nearly did not. He dismissed her as commander of his army for abandoning her warriors in Inath-Wakenti. Only eight were ever seen again. Gilthas's archivist, Favaronas, was lost, as was Glanthon, brother of Planchet, the Speaker's late bodyguard and close friend. According to the survivors, the company became lost in the desert, so Glanthon divided it into bands of ten and sent each in a different direction. Eight stumbled into the Khurish town of Kalin Ak-Phan; none of the others was ever seen again.

"What of you? What choice will you make today?" Gilthas asked.

"There is nothing to choose."

"But you want to go."

She didn't answer, only shifted position on the rock and dipped her bare feet in the creek. That put her back to him. She wanted a bit of privacy, time to collect herself. The question of going or staying was one she had preferred not to address until absolutely necessary. The decision wasn't a matter of head versus heart; that was a battle Kerianseray fought frequently. It was heart versus heart.

For much of her adult life, she had battled for the freedom of Qualinesti. She'd plotted and planned, fought and maneuvered to return home with an army behind her. Only the most extreme events had forced her to leave. Her desire to free their homeland had been the cause of a long-standing disagreement with Gilthas. She wanted to take the army back to Qualinesti. He wouldn't allow it, saying that while the elves lived in exile in Khuri-Khan, the army could not be spared.

After many complex developments, it was going to happen. The army would march to Qualinesti, and the Lioness would not be with them. She must stay behind, in a place she loathed, carrying out a mission she felt in her heart to be utterly pointless. Yet no amount of railing against fate could change the single most important fact: she would not leave Gilthas while he was riddled with consumption and marooned in the lifeless cemetery of Inath-Wakenti. Strong as her ties to her warriors were, the tie to Gilthas was far more powerful.

"Go if you want."

His attempt at a careless tone infuriated her, but still she didn't reply, only looked beyond the wide, slow-flowing creek into the valley. The mist was evaporating, thinning to reveal stunted trees and the standing stones beyond them. Her keen ears detected no sounds at all. Even the noises made by the great mass of elves some distance behind them were swallowed up in the deathly stillness of Inath-Wakenti.

"Keri-li." Gilthas used the most intimate form of her name. "I won't allow my sickness to keep you here. Go to Qualinesti. Win it back for us."

It was the final straw, his selfless offer of the one thing that could tempt her from his side. Shame washed over her, and pain clamped itself around her heart and would not be dislodged. For all their differences—and they were legion—she loved him still, and he might very well be dying.

As was usually the case with the Lioness, strong emotions manifested as anger and action. She came swiftly to her feet and stalked to him. With shocking ease, she hauled his wasted frame upright, her hands knotted in the front of his Khurish *geb*. His eyes widened in surprise.

"Hear me, Great Speaker! I am not going anywhere! Do you understand? You are cursed with me forever! We will cross this creek, battle ghosts and dancing lights and anything else that gets in our way, then plant every seed we've hoarded since leaving home. We will make this damned valley bloom, and *then*—" She kissed him with fervor. "Then I will go to Qualinesti and return it to its rightful king!"

He smiled into her flushed, angry face. "What a curse," he whispered.

* * * * *

He was running through tall grass. Exhilaration sang in his veins. Unlike most of his forest-dwelling kind, Porthios loved the savannah. The broad vistas, clear for miles in every direction, made it his favorite country in which to hunt. He could push his swift legs to their limits without impediment. The swish and sway of the grass was music for the chase. The air was cool, with the bite of early autumn, but the sun was pleasantly warm on his bare face. His legs moved smoothly, so fleet and nimble, his toes left barely any impression on the ground. His chest expanded easily with each deep breath. He was whole, unburned, and gloriously alive. The sheer joy of it brought laughter bubbling from his lips.

Hunting the usual sorts of game required stealth and cleverness. The prey he chased now was different. Strength was needed, strength of mind and of determination. The future of his entire race was at stake. To preserve that future, Porthios would do anything. The chase pushed every sense to its limit, but his will was strong, his resolve unshakable. Eventually the usurper would be caught.

He fell. The abruptness of it caught him by surprise, and he hit the ground hard. High grass had concealed a ditch, but that was no excuse. He was never caught off guard. He was never so clumsy. He moved to stand up again, but roots clutched at his booted feet. Each time he pulled a foot free, the grass whipped around his ankle again. In seconds he could no longer break free, no matter how hard he tried or how nimbly he twisted, and he lost his balance. He fell onto his back. Grass closed over him, blotting out the sky.

What had been a thrilling chase had become a nightmare. More grass gripped his arms and legs, encircled his throat, and rose up to cover his face, burying him in a sea of green. The shoots snaked into his ears, pushed between his lips, and invaded his nostrils. He could not breathe!

Get up!

The command sounded clearly in his mind. The tendrils were remorseless. Although he clenched his eyelids tightly, the tendrils worked their way beneath his eyelids, crawling into his skull. The agony was awful. He wanted to scream but couldn't draw breath for even that.

Are you a coward? Free yourself!

Slowly, Porthios closed his fingers around clumps of grass. Mustering every ounce of strength he possessed, he heaved his hands free of the clinging grass. Then his fingers went to work on the greenery encasing his face. The smothering darkness eased. He could see light, he could breathe!

Don't stop now. Stand up.

DESTINY

Enraged by the anonymous patronizing voice, Porthios redoubled his efforts, twisting first his head then his torso from side to side. The strangling growth crumbled and fell away. He looked around to see who dared speak to him in such a fashion.

He was still on the savannah. The flat grassland stretched away in all directions beneath a sky decorated with puffy white clouds, and there was not a soul in sight.

His legs were still encased. Marshalling his formidable resolve, he tore his right leg free then concentrated on the left. He must return to the chase. He could not allow his prey to escape.

"No."

Porthios's head snapped around. The grassland was no longer empty. A human was approaching. Although he was still a dozen yards away, the man's voice carried easily. He was old, clean shaven, with unkempt white hair cut short. His homespun robe was of a clerical cut, and he gripped a blackthorn staff. Porthios recognized him immediately.

"Is this your doing?" he demanded, gesturing at his trapped leg.

The old priest shrugged. "I can't visit you openly, so I borrowed a dream."

A dream? Porthios put a hand to his face. The skin was smooth, untouched by fire, and damp with sweat. He'd never experienced a dream so real.

The human was looking at him expectantly. Testy but curious too, Porthios asked what he wanted.

The priest sighed. "You keep asking me that."

"And you always answer in riddles!"

The human turned and walked away. The arrogant dismissal was just the spur Porthios needed. He tore his leg free of the last of the confining grass and stormed after the human.

"Don't walk away from me!" he commanded, reaching for the priest's arm. As soon as he touched it, the ground heaved beneath his feet. The sun-drenched savannah shimmered and fell away.

They were in Inath-Wakenti. The sun was high in the sky, but the air still held the clammy chill characteristic of the cursed valley. The two of them were alone, with only a scattering of the purposeless white monoliths for company.

"I risked much by coming to you," the priest said. A shower of meteors streaked across the sky, leaving trails of silent fire. Frowning at the display, he added, "This must be the last time."

"Why did you come? Why interrupt a simple dream so harshly?"

"Simple?" was all the human said.

Even as he continued to glare at the old man, Porthios suddenly remembered who he'd been hunting: Gilthas. To save the elf race from his folly, Porthios would kill Gilthas. He would kill Lauralanthalasa's son. It was not a simple dream at all.

"You stopped me. Why?" he asked.

The human's eyes were sad. "Sometimes even dreams are forbidden."

With breath-stealing suddenness, the dream world shifted again. Smooth skin shriveled, muscles knotted and drew in upon themselves, scars sliced across chest, arms, and legs. The remembered joy of Porthios's run through the grassland vanished, swallowed up by the truth of never-ending torment. He stood naked and twisted beneath the open sky. The unaccustomed feel of air against his bare flesh made his head swim. He howled his agony to the staring sun.

With that cry still echoing around them, the old man lifted his staff in both hands and rapped its butt end against the ground. Night fell at once and brought with it Porthios's familiar rags. They seemed to emerge from the ground beneath his feet, rising up to wrap themselves carefully around him, cloaking his shame from the world.

In the distance, thunder rolled. "This is a dangerous place.

It affects me. I cannot stay," the priest murmured, raking his staff through the turquoise turf. Thunder rolled again, closer and louder.

Speaking quickly, he said, "Leave the Pathfinder to his own fate, lost one. Yours rests in the dark and bloody land of Kith-Kanan's realm."

Like water drying on a hot stone, he faded from view, becoming translucent then disappearing altogether. Where he'd stood, a slender ash sapling pushed through the ground.

Porthios woke. He lay on his lonely bedroll outside the exiles' camp. Dawn was breaking. It was the day the people would decide: blue stone or white, stay or go.

Let Gilthas keep his cursed valley. Porthios had spoken with a god. Cryptic words and elliptical answers, true, but he had the guidance of the divine. Elves with the right spirit would follow him. Together, they would begin a new chapter in the history of the First Race.

The god was right about many things. A dark and bloody land, he had called it. When Porthios reached Qualinesti, he intended to make the god's description perfectly apt.

* * * * *

The elf race, divided for so long into two nations and briefly united, was divided again. Stones had been gathered and choices made. Along the west bank of Lioness Creek stood the elves who had chosen to stay. Arrayed opposite them were those who meant to go. All but a few hundred of the Speaker's warriors intended to depart. They were soldiers, and fighting was what they knew. Fathoming the puzzles of a mysterious valley was beyond them. Building houses and tilling the earth was not for them. Each felt he would be more useful in Porthios's battle to free Qualinesti. If death was to be their fate, they preferred to meet it in the land of their ancestors, fighting the enemies of their race. The decision was not an easy one, and theirs was not a happy leave-taking. Bidding good-bye to family or comrades was difficult but expected in a warrior's life. Disappointing their Speaker was not.

Alhana, Samar, and the griffon riders mustered in the area between the two groups. Two griffons were staying behind: Eagle Eye and Hytanthas's Kanan as there was not enough time to bond the latter with another rider.

At least one person was pleased by Kerian's decision to remain. In her absence, command of the Army of Liberation fell to Samar. The proud Silvanesti warrior had never savored working with the hard-headed Lioness. Samar also was pleased that all the civilians had chosen to remain in the valley. Some had wavered, but eventually all realized another desert crossing would be the death of them.

By midafternoon, all preparations were complete and the groups were gathered near the creek.

"We will stay in communication," Alhana promised. "Once we're back in Qualinesti, we'll send regular reports by griffon rider."

"And we'll send news of our progress the same way," said Gilthas.

Porthios was not part of the group around the Speaker. He stood aloof a few dozen yards away, shaded by the low branches of a pine tree. He disliked appearing in full daylight, but Kerian doubted that was the only reason behind his rudeness. Since he was leaving, she made allowances. Skirting the group of griffon riders and their mounts, she crossed the open ground between the two groups of elves and called out to him.

"Scarecrow!"

"Don't call me that."

"You'd better get used to it. The bandits will call you nothing better."

His shadowed eyes narrowed. "Who will you insult once I am gone?"

"Gilthas," she shot back. Halting a few yards away, she asked, "Which route do you take?"

DESTINY

He planned to depart through the pass after dark, he said, then head overland to the New Sea. There, the Army of Liberation would either hire ships or march along the shore until it reached Qualinesti.

Samar's mount, Ironhead, trumpeted impatiently, and Kerian glanced at the big Golden griffon. When she turned back, Porthios had left the shade of the pine branches and was standing only a few feet from her. "I expect you will join us, when the time comes."

When Gilthas was dead, he meant, and she was furious not because he was wrong, but because he'd so easily divined her reason for asking his route. He walked away without another word, and Kerian was left trying to decide whether the odd expression in his eyes might have been pity.

Alhana approached, holding out a hand to her young successor. With characteristic grace, she made her good-byes, but even as they embraced, Kerian was trying to fathom why kind, cultured, civilized Alhana tolerated Porthios for an instant.

"You did not know him before," Alhana said. "He was a different person."

Kerian realized she'd muttered her thoughts aloud. Shaking her head, she asked, "So the fire took his morals and manners too?"

"His looks are the very least thing he lost. He does intend good."

Kerian doubted that but knew argument was pointless. Fortunately, Gilthas arrived and Alhana turned her attention to taking a fond leave of the Speaker. Then it was time for the army to depart.

In close column of sixes the mounted warriors fell in behind Porthios, who traveled on foot for the time being. He would hold the army at the mouth of the pass until dusk then push through the few nomads known to be there. He could have waited till nightfall to leave the exiles' camp, but he worried about losing warriors if he delayed. The bond between the

Speaker and his faithful fighters must not be allowed to sway any wavering minds.

Next to leave were Alhana's griffon riders. All but the former queen were mounted and ready to take wing. Chisa, Alhana's female Golden, stood quietly as Alhana embraced Gilthas one last time and clasped hands with Hamaramis and Taranath. When she embraced Kerian, the Lioness offered her a final blunt warning.

"Watch out for him." Kerian didn't bother to lower her voice, and all within earshot knew who she meant. "We're all pawns in the game he's playing, even you."

Alhana smiled. "I know him, niece." Violet eyes flickered toward Gilthas, standing a short distance away, and Alhana whispered, "You watch out for *him*."

Kerian's hands tightened convulsively on Alhana's arms. Alhana kissed her on both cheeks and stepped quickly away. With practiced ease, she climbed into Chisa's saddle, wrapped the reins around her left hand, and gave the word. Chisa bounded forward. On the third leap, the griffon was airborne, wings beating hard. Samar and the other riders followed their lady into the sky.

The flight of griffons was quickly lost from sight among the low peaks. No rising dust marked the departing column of horses. The damp soil of Inath-Wakenti did not fly up like desert sand. In a surprisingly short time, the elves remaining behind were watching an empty pass and vacant sky.

The Speaker's cough broke the stillness. All eyes went to him, then away, giving him a sort of privacy as he fought the spasm. Truthanar offered a draft. Gilthas sipped it and ignored the healer's worried questions. The past had just ridden away. There was no reason to delay any longer.

Pointing to the center of the valley, Gilthas raised his voice, saying, "My people, our future lies that way."

The Speaker did not have to make the journey on foot. A band of eight elf women came forward bearing a high-backed chair cunningly crafted from mats woven of local grass. They had made the palanquin for the Speaker, to spare him having to walk. Gilthas was deeply touched. So was Kerian, although she covered it with gruffness. The chair was unfolded, and a stout pole run through woven straps on either side. Two male and two female elves stood by the poles, waiting to hoist the Speaker onto their shoulders. Gilthas would have protested—the Speaker of the Sun and Stars ought not be borne on his people's backs like some cruel despot—but one look at Kerian silenced him. If he were honest with himself, he knew he had no choice. He simply wasn't up to making so long a journey on foot.

However, he intended to make one small portion of it under his own power. Taking Kerian's hand, he stepped into Lioness Creek. The stream was slow flowing and not above knee deep there, so the crossing was simple enough. On gaining the far side, Gilthas halted then realized he was holding his breath. Such a simple thing, the fording of a creek, but fraught with great import. From here on, they would be subject to the strange forces at work in the valley. Yet Gilthas was aware of a great exhilaration flooding through him. The last part of their journey had finally begun.

The bearers brought the palanquin across, and Gilthas seated himself in it. The bearers lifted the poles. A flush of embarrassment gave Gilthas's face more color than it had had in a long time.

"Forward, my people," he said. "To the land of our dreams!"

5

Adala slapped the lump of cold dough against her palm. The patty was half the size it should be for a proper loaf, and the coarse flour they'd had to accept in trade felt gritty under her fingers, but it was all they had. The black iron pan was ready, so she laid the dough in the scant smear of cooking oil. The dough sizzled.

The beast lay next to her. Saliva trickled out its open black lips. Adala pinched off another ball of dough and worked it into a patty. The beast's tongue came out.

"You are hungry?" she asked.

"Yes!"

"Supper will be ready soon." The meal would be a poor one, but what she had she would share. Adala would not let a guest starve, no matter how strange the guest might be.

Work on the wall had ceased for the day. Exhausted men and women trudged back to their tents to eat a similarly paltry meal and fall immediately to sleep. Four had watch duty atop the wall. Adala had kept twenty on watch at first, but as the days passed and the *laddad* did not emerge, the size of the night watch shrank. Too many exhausted sentinels had fallen asleep on the cairn and hurt themselves tumbling off.

The beast had been with them two days. At night it hunted, appeasing its hunger with the odd ground rat or rabbit, and returning before dawn. By day, it kept to Adala's tent, only the greenish reflection of its eyes visible to anyone passing. Few passed. Word of the beast's supposed identity had spread. Nomads believed curses were catching, like a disease, and that anyone who strayed too close to the afflicted prince could fall victim to the same misfortune. Adala's followers begged her to kill it or send it packing. No good could come of having such an unnatural thing close at hand, they said. But she did not heed them.

With her unshakable *maita,* Adala did not fear the monster. Its submission to her proved Those on High had sent it to her for a purpose. Normally, she would not have hesitated to destroy such an abomination, but it told her of its intention to enter Alya-Alash and she stayed her hand. Let the beast kill *laddad* if it wished, then let it be killed by them in turn.

The bread was done. Adala removed it from the pan. She poured in a bit of water. Gouts of steam hissed upward. Pieces of dried mutton went into the bubbling liquid. A hairy paw came into view, reaching for the small pile of flatbread. Adala rapped it smartly with her brass ladle. The paw retreated.

"You may eat when all is ready," she said. "Not before."

She dropped a handful of rice into the simmering broth then covered the pan with an inverted wooden bowl to hold in the steam. Despite the cookfire, Adala shivered. The sun had set, and an unhealthy chill was creeping into camp. Clammy cold oozed out of the valley every night. It seeped into the bones and set the body to aching as though every particle of warmth was being leached away. Only a good, hot fire kept the gravelike chill at bay. If the cold was bad there, at the mouth of the valley, she could only imagine how much worse it must be within. Perhaps that was the death Those on High had chosen for the *laddad,* freezing them into corpses while they slept.

When the rice was done, Adala removed the covering bowl and spooned a modest portion of mutton and rice into it. Two loaves completed the meal, and she passed it to her peculiar guest. Shobbat inhaled deeply over the steaming bowl and licked his chops.

"When will you enter the valley?" Adala asked, partaking of her own meager meal.

"Soon. Wait for sign."

He'd said the same each evening when she'd posed the question. This time she did not accept it.

"Tomorrow."

Shobbat's tongue ceased lapping up food. He regarded the somber woman with a twitch of his brow.

"Why . . . tom-ow-row?" His beastly mouth was ill suited to forming certain sounds.

"Those on High teach us to be hospitable for three risings of the sun. After that, a guest becomes a pest. You will go tomorrow."

"I Shobbat!"

"So you have said, but prince or monster, you have worn out your welcome. Go of your own will or be driven out. It is your choice."

He snarled, baring wicked fangs. She pulled a burning branch from the fire and thrust it at him. He shrank back. Lips writhing to cover his long teeth again, he capitulated.

"Tom-ow-row."

Since the beast began sleeping in her tent, Adala had taken to sleeping outside. She unrolled her bedroll in front of the tent and settled herself for the night. Although she trusted her *maita* to protect her from the craven creature, she also kept a dagger hidden underneath her round, brocade pillow. As always, the day's work had exhausted her so thoroughly, she was asleep seconds after closing her eyes.

* * * * *

Atop the unfinished wall, the four nomad sentinels drew scarves close around their necks and huddled together. With no fire to keep the cold at bay, their duty was misery. An enterprising Weya-Lu provided the next best thing to fire. A flask of palm wine was passed from hand to hand. One of the watchmen left to answer nature's call. He'd gone only a few steps when his feet suddenly flew out from under him and he fell into the shadows on the valley side of the wall. His comrades laughed and called out rude comments about his inability to hold his drink. One nomad, more sympathetic than the rest, went to help him. He stumbled down the rock pile, calling his comrade's name. The calls abruptly ceased.

The last two Khurs waited, but the missing men did not reappear. They called for their missing comrades.

before they'd done more than exchange a befuddled look, the darkness came alive. Phantoms swarmed noiselessly up the cairn, overwhelmed the two sentinels, and carried them away to be dispatched just as silently. Then the raiders subsided back into the darkness.

With the force available to him, Porthios could have ridden straight through the nomads. The majority of those remaining were old people, but stealth suited Porthios better than brute force. It spared his army any unnecessary losses and concealed their departure from the wider world. Otherwise, every informer and loose-lipped traveler between Khur and Qualinesti would spread the news that a force of armed elves was on the move. It would not require a military genius to deduce the goal of such a force. Samuval and the Nerakans would be forewarned.

Alhana, leading her griffon by the bridle, joined Porthios as he waited at the head of the concealed cavalry. He explained his plan.

"We'll circle around the end of the wall. We must be utterly silent. No one is to fight unless attacked. The griffons will be muzzled."

"There's no need. I've explained to them—"

"Muzzled, Alhana. All of them." He drew his cloak close and walked away.

A snort from Chisa drew a conciliatory pat. "I know," Alhana murmured, resting her forehead against the griffon's feathered neck. "It will be for only a short time, I promise."

Alhana had suggested the griffon riders take to the air well in advance of the nomad camp and fly high enough to hide the animals' scent from the Khurs' ponies. Porthios said no. His best archers were among the griffon riders, and they might be needed should the nomads try to fight. Alhana did not dispute with him as the Lioness might have. She simply waited, and Porthios found himself offering a compromise. The griffon riders would fly over the camp, but only after the army, leading its horses, was safely by.

Elves and horses crept along in a narrow column. The nomad camp was located not behind the wall, but a short distance from its unfinished end. The rocky terrain meant the elves had to pass much nearer the human camp than Porthios would have wished. All went well for a time; then a Khurish pony neighed suddenly. Perhaps it scented the foreign horses, or perhaps it was unsettled by the strange, dank atmosphere near the pass. Porthios, waiting at the rear of the warriors, gestured toward the griffon riders. One put down the animal with a single arrow.

Shobbat opened his eyes. He did not go out to hunt until the night was well advanced, but something had disturbed his rest. He nosed the tent flap open. The camp slept. He sniffed deeply several times. The odors of wood smoke and charred meat interfered, but he caught the scent of blood, newly spilled, coming from the wall. Never taking his eyes from its dark bulk, he skirted the sleeping Adala and stalked toward the cairn. The smell of blood grew stronger the closer he came. His ears swiveled forward and back. Sounds came to him, sounds out of place in the sleeping nomad camp: the creak of harness leather, the deep breathing of horses on the move, and twice, the muffled clink of metal on metal.

In one bound he gained the top of the wall. There was movement to the northwest. A line of dark figures was coming through the gap. Although they were wrapped in cloaks and scarves, Shobbat's beast-sharpened eyes detected the telltale glints of metal armor. The elves were on the move. He threw back his head and howled.

Adala awoke at once. She looked to the wall, expecting to see four sentinels. Instead, she saw the beast silhouetted in the pale starlight. He was galloping to and fro and howling as though he had gone completely mad. She pushed herself to her feet and ran to her banked campfire. She dropped a few handfuls of kindling onto the faintly glowing embers. The twigs blazed up.

A line of men leaped into view. They were on foot, leading horses. No, not men: *laddad!*

"To horse! To horse!" Adala cried. "The *laddad* are here!"

She ran through the camp, rousing everyone and rekindling campfires where she could. Worn out by the day's work, most of her people hadn't bothered to bank their fires; nothing remained but dead ash. Befuddled by sleep, her people were in disarray. They stumbled through the poorly lit camp to their horses but were forced to halt as arrows rained down from the night sky to land in front of them. They were cut off from their animals.

Alhana saw fires blooming in the semicircle of tents and knew surprise was lost. There was worse to come. Samar hurried back with an appalling report. Porthios had ordered the cavalry to attack. He intended to extinguish Adala's followers once and for all. Alhana and the griffon riders were aghast, but Samar had seen no hesitation in the cavalry. Elves who'd fought their way to Inath-Wakenti through hordes of merciless Khurs had no compunction about obeying their leader's ruthless order.

The griffon riders took flight. Alhana led them straight to the fore of the galloping warriors, hoping to prevent a massacre. The griffons landed amid the swirling melee. Taking advantage of their intervention, many nomads fled, abandoning everything but the clothes they wore, making a dash for the open desert.

Porthios strode through his thwarted cavalry, his ragged robe whipping around his legs.

"What are you doing?" he demanded.

"What are *you* doing?" Alhana replied, face pale as alabaster. "The archers had cut them off from their horses. You could have ridden away and left them behind. Why attack?"

"Dead humans cannot speak."

Furious, Alhana jerked the reins and Chisa reared, scattering the nearby horses. Porthios did not flinch. "If you have no stomach for this war, you may rejoin the Puppet King," he said bluntly.

She devoted a few seconds to calming her fractious griffon, using the time to get herself under control as well, then proclaimed, "I am going with you, Porthios, as your wife and your conscience. Do not try to evade me in either role!"

So caught up were the elves in the confrontation between husband and wife, none noticed Shobbat creeping along the wall. When the Golden griffons had swooped overhead, Shobbat flattened himself on the rocks and froze in place lest he be torn apart by their powerful talons. Then he was on the move again, resolved to strike. His target was not the *laddad* woman mounted on one of the terrible griffons, but the masked elf in front of her. His voice rang with cold command, as did the voice of Shobbat's father, the khan. The masked one apparently was the leader of the *laddad,* and Shobbat intended to kill him. Moving with patient care, Shobbat crept closer and closer then gathered his rear legs. He sprang.

A hardwood shaft hit him in midflight, sending him crashing among frantic horses and hostile warriors. The arrow had come from the hard-faced elf mounted on the largest griffon.

Even an argument between Alhana and Porthios could not long interrupt Samar's vigilance for his lady's safety. He took aim to finish off the beast, but it scrambled away. Yowling horribly in pain, it zigzagged between the horses' legs and was quickly lost in darkness.

DESTINY

The shock of the creature's attack put an end to the argument. Porthios ordered the site cleansed of any evidence of the elves' passage. Arrows were retrieved, tracks cleared away. What remained of the camp was put to the torch.

Warriors on the edge of the group noticed her first: a lone woman clad in a black *geb*. She walked slowly toward them. A donkey followed close behind her, although its reins hung free, dragging in the dirt. The elves watched her warily but allowed her to pass unhindered. She moved like a sleepwalker, eyes staring straight ahead, shuffling feet stumbling occasionally on loose stones. When she drew near, Alhana recognized her.

"Go back, Weyadan," Alhana warned. "The fight is over."

Her warning went unheeded. Adala kept coming. She veered toward Porthios. Drawing to a halt, the nomad woman said, "Faceless One, you were cursed by Those on High. Adala Fahim curses you too. By your bloody deeds, all shall know you for the insatiable monster you truly are!"

Porthios turned away from her in silent disgust.

"The lightning will take you," Adala added and stared up at the night sky, waiting. Nothing happened. The night was cold and quiet but for the crackle of the fire consuming what remained of the camp. Those of Adala's people who had survived the fight had fled into the desert. The Weyadan was alone.

The warriors, with Porthios at their head, turned their horses and rode away. The griffon riders lingered, awaiting their mistress. Alhana dropped a skin of water and a bundle of food for Adala. The nomad woman did not even look at them. Her unblinking gaze was focused on the departing Porthios, as if she could compel his destruction by her will alone. There was nothing more to be done for her. Alhana signaled the riders to fly.

The dust and ash churned up by griffon wings slowly settled. Adala sought her tent. Little Thorn clopped along patiently behind her.

Her tent had fallen but was unburned. Kicking at it, she wondered what Those on High intended for her now. How could she complete the wall by herself? A weaker person might have yielded to despair. Adala decided there was a greater plan at work, a plan so vast and complex she couldn't see it yet. But she would.

Her fallen tent rippled, though no breath of breeze stirred. Little Thorn brayed.

The beast exploded from the collapsed tent, teeth bared and paws extended. He hit Adala and knocked her flat, rolling her over and over on the ground. His head thrust forward, and he sank his fangs into her throat. To ward off the valley's cold, she wore several layers of cloth around her neck, and those stopped his teeth from piercing her skin. His four legs securely pinned her limbs.

"You," he rumbled. "Sign is you. Now you die!"

She twisted her face away from his foul breath and groped with one hand, seeking the dagger hidden in her bedroll. Her questing fingers found cold metal. Heedless of the pain, she grasped the bare blade and pulled the weapon closer so she could take hold of the hilt. She plunged the dagger into the beast's neck.

Shobbat grunted in pain, but his suffocating grip on her throat did not ease. Instead, he rose up on his haunches, lifting Adala off the ground. With a single sideways snap of his wolfish head, he silenced her breathless gasps.

Immediately he released her. It felt as though the dagger had gone completely through his throat; he could hardly breathe. He managed to hook the thick fingers of one front paw around the slender cross guard and drag the blade out. Next, his blunt fingers gripped the *laddad* arrow. It had hit at an oblique angle and hadn't gone deep but had scored a long bloody trail in his furry flesh.

The Weya-Lu woman hadn't moved. She didn't breathe. Her neck was twisted so that her open eyes gazed unblinkingly at the stony soil.

DESTINY

Shobbat had killed. As prince, he had ordered the deaths of others, but never had he killed anyone personally. Killing was an ugly business, but the ignorant desert fanatic was too unpredictable and too proud to be a loyal underling. Better for him if she be dead. Such were the choices of fortune.

An owl hooted nearby, and Shobbat flinched. His injuries were painful but not grievous. Already the arrow wound was clotting, and the bleeding from the knife thrust had slowed to a trickle. His beast form was strong, but more than ever he was determined to find the wayward sorcerer Faeterus and force him to lift his curse. Shobbat was Crown Prince of Khur. With the nomads defeated and their fanatical Weyadan dead, Khur would be ready for a new leader, a prince who (at least outwardly) revered the old gods and decried his father's corruption.

He loped away through the destroyed camp. The fires had died. The pass was once more cloaked in darkness. Shobbat circled the end of the unfinished wall and trotted north, into Inath-Wakenti. The owl did not speak again. But a cloud of bats whirled overhead, squeaking like a palace full of rusty door hinges.

* * * * *

The elves were camped atop a knoll surrounded on three sides by titans of stone. At Gilthas's command, bonfires had been kindled along the open fourth side and in the gaps between the monoliths. The fires would be kept burning all night. Guards on top of the stones reported will-o'-the-wisps darting in the darkness, but none came near the encampment. The light or heat of the bonfires seemed to keep them at bay, for the moment.

The first day's trek had proceeded without incident. Since no other goal had presented itself, Gilthas had decided they would make for the center of the valley. The lifelessness of Inath-Wakenti was disrupted by the tramping of feet, by elf voices, by the bleat and snort of the few domestic animals they retained, and by the occasional calls of Eagle Eye and Kanan circling overhead. Royal griffons and Goldens were rivals in nature, competitors for territory and food, and Kerian hadn't been sure how the two would get on. Alhana had suggested that Kanan, being young, would submit to the elder beast, and pining for his rider, would be glad of Eagle Eye's company. She had been proven right.

Soon they came to a wall of massive white blocks. Kerian said it ran for more than a mile in each direction, northwest and southeast. Blocks up to twenty feet long and eight feet high lay end to end, but there were plenty of breaks between the blocks. Hamaramis commented on its unsuitability as a defense and Kerian shrugged.

"I don't think it was meant to defend," she said. "None of the ruins make sense. They don't connect. They don't seem to be parts of buildings, just enormous blocks of stone dropped at random."

Gilthas let himself be carried to the wall, then ordered the bearers to rest while he left the palanquin to study one of the blocks more closely. The stones were noticeably colder than the surrounding air, neatly dressed, with precise corners and smooth surfaces worn by the passage of a great deal of time. He identified the stone as snowy quartz. Nothing marred the white surface. Normally a boulder exposed to such a climate would be studded with lichens and moss and have a vine or two wedged in its fissures. All the blocks in sight were so clean, they might have been recently scrubbed. And as enormous as each was, rising above the turquoise turf, Gilthas knew from Kerian that quite a bit of each was buried in the ground.

As his palanquin was carried through the gap in the wall, Gilthas glimpsed someone at the far end of the block he had touched. He had a fleeting impression of dark eyes, a shock of brown hair, and tanned skin, but when he turned to see better, the figure was gone. Taranath and Kerian investigated, but found no one. The general was inclined to think the Speaker had been mistaken, but Kerian disagreed.

DESTINY

"The ghosts in this valley are real, Taran, make no mistake. It troubles me they're showing themselves in broad daylight. Sunlight used to keep them away."

They were witness to even stranger things as the night wore on. Slender, luminescent forms drifted out of the trees, passing on either side of the knoll on which the elves had camped. To those on the ground, they resembled nothing more than luminous fog, but the watchers on the monoliths saw them as upright, walking shapes. Like the will-o'-the-wisps, the glowing ghosts did not try to enter the fire-girded camp. After midnight the lights and phantoms went away, but the bonfires were kept burning. Wood ran low three hours before sunrise. As the flames died back a bit, the elves saw the most ominous manifestations yet.

Figures appeared outside the camp, in the deep shadows beyond the firelight. In shape they were both like and unlike elves. They were shorter than an adult elf but stockier than children. Their faces were brown, like those of nomads, and their unblinking eyes reflected the bonfires in red and orange. The strangers did not move or speak. At one point Taranath and Kerian counted fifty of them. Their silent vigil cast a pall over the camp, smothering all conversation. Warriors and civilians alike nervously watched the empty faces watching them.

Gilthas's calm voice and confident presence eased the tense silence. He moved through the camp, speaking to elves of every station, calling each by name. When he reached the place where Kerian, Taranath, and Hamaramis were keeping an eye on the phantoms, he greeted them loudly.

"Has everyone decided not to sleep this night?" he said. "If so, this is the dullest party I've ever seen."

"We have grim guests, Great Speaker," Taranath said wryly.

Leaning on his staff, Gilthas looked beyond his wife's shoulder at the far-off, vacant faces. "What sad creatures." The others regarded him in surprise. "Don't you feel their terrible loneliness?"

Kagonesti warrior and Qualinesti generals traded skeptical looks. Over Kerian's protests, Gilthas had himself boosted atop a head-high monolith. From there he found the impression of sadness to be even stronger. Although the strangers said nothing, made no moves, something about them conveyed to the Speaker a desperate sense of abandonment. Their loneliness was so palpable, he was moved to address them, despite the warnings of his generals.

"Hello! We don't mean to intrude, but we've come to live in your valley! We wish to live in peace! Spread the word! The elves have returned to Inath-Wakenti!"

As he climbed down, his legs betrayed him and he stumbled. Kerian steadied him.

"Do you honestly think those things understand you or care what you say?" she muttered.

"Who can know? Maybe no one's ever tried to speak to them."

Whatever else he accomplished, his actions broke the spell of fear on his own people. Seeing their Speaker face the ghosts on their behalf made them less afraid. Conversation resumed, hushed and tentative at first, then more and more normal. Elves gave up their worried watching, drifted away from the fire-lit ring of standing stones, and returned to their simple beds at last to rest.

Outside the camp something quite singular occurred. The phantoms went away. Their staring eyes closed, the red and orange reflections winking out two by two. The dark silhouettes remained a moment then, without fanfare or fury, submerged into the surrounding shadows. The elves were alone once more.

"How do you do it?" Kerian whispered to Gilthas.

He sighed and shook his head. "If I knew, I'd do it more often."

6

Dawn brought good news. No elves had vanished during the night. Gilthas accepted that news with quiet satisfaction. Perhaps the valley was learning to accept them, he said. Kerian's view was less rosy.

"Whatever lurks here is not stupid, Gil. It learns from its mistakes. We puzzled it last night, probably because there were so many of us. It will adapt, and people will disappear again. That's what happened to us the first time we came here."

He frowned. "It? Who or what is 'it'? The ghosts? I always heard spirits were moved by an unresolved need for revenge or justice. Are the ghosts here of a different order?"

"How should I know? I'm no mage. But whatever it is, it will learn."

They'd been climbing slowly all morning and were crossing a forested plain. Unlike the majestic trees of their homeland, these were spindly evergreens, pines and cedars mostly, and widely spaced. Gilthas traveled in his palanquin, and Kerian walked at his side. A few hundred yards ahead rode a squadron of cavalry led by Taranath. The mounted elves combed through the sparse woodland, keeping an eye out for trouble. All they found were more megaliths, each as inexplicable as the last. These here on the plain had a somewhat different character than the ones left behind in the lowlands near Lioness Creek. The lowland monoliths were square-cut, cyclopean blocks. The upland stones had rounded contours. Vertical stones tapered to blunt points, looking for all the world like enormous teeth growing out of the ground. Riders found cylinders, and even perfect spheres twenty feet in diameter. One feature they shared with the lowland monoliths was their seemingly random arrangement. It was as if they'd fallen from the sky with no more plan than raindrops.

A warbling cry caused Gilthas to look up. The two griffons, Eagle Eye and Kanan, wheeled overhead. Eagle Eye was a mature adult and the younger griffon's attempts to match his flying prowess afforded Gilthas a welcome distraction from the lifeless terrain. When Eagle Eye executed a particularly deft turn and roll, placing himself above and behind Kanan, the latter flared his wings and screeched. In flight against the cloudless blue sky, the creatures were a beautiful sight and offered a measure of reassurance. If danger lurked nearby, the griffons would spot it before the elves did.

Pulling his attention earthward once more, Gilthas said to Kerian, "You're no wizard, that's true. So look at Inath-Wakenti with your warrior's eye and tell me what you see."

"I see a valley where no one lives. No cities, no crops, no herds. It's completely empty, yet defended against all comers. Who is defending it?"

"The ghosts of its long-ago inhabitants."

"I don't think so." She eyed a towering, hourglass-shaped block of white quartz ahead. "There are at least two stories here. First are the ghosts, the tunnels, and the giant stones. They're connected to each other somehow."

Her expedition had found the tunnels after accidentally upending a monolith. Beneath it was an entrance to the underground passageways. And the ghosts seemed to enter and leave the tunnels at will.

"But I believe the will-o'-the-wisps are different," she added.

DESTINY

When similar lights had claimed Kerian on the battlefield outside Khuri-Khan, she thought she was destined for oblivion, like the warriors who'd vanished during her initial trip to the valley. Instead, she found herself dumped into the loathsome Nalis Aren, the Lake of Death, in Qualinesti. Her adventures with Porthios, Alhana, and the griffons followed. Why the lights had transported her away from Khur remained a mystery but she'd decided they were different from the lights here. Inath-Wakenti's will-o'-the-wisps flew meandering, irregular courses, drifting and dawdling until their target was lulled into a false sense of safety. The lights that had kidnapped her were larger, faster, seemingly more direct of purpose. Their source, she felt, was different from whatever drove the valley lights.

"They are attracted to living creatures," she reasoned. "Over the centuries, they've eliminated every living animal from this valley, right down to the flies and fleas."

"What does that suggest?"

"They're guarding the valley—not only to keep people out, but to keep the residents in."

Gilthas nodded slowly. "The inhabitants of the valley were not intended to have contact with outsiders. I imagine they never did. One by one they died, as we all die, and their spirits haunt the land. They don't present a threat like the lights. If we could find a way to persuade the will-o'-the-wisps to leave us alone, we'd be a long way toward making this place home."

"Maybe you can talk to them," Kerian said dryly.

Whatever he intended to say was swallowed up by a furious bout of coughing. So wracked was he by the spasm, Kerian ordered his chair lowered and the healer summoned. Truthanar brought more of his palliative drink, but Gilthas could swallow very little.

"Great Speaker, you must rest!" Truthanar declared. "If you continue on like this, I will not be responsible for the consequences."

Gilthas's answer was some time coming, but at last the coughing subsided and he wheezed, "I'm in a chair already. How more rested must I be?"

Blood oozed from his nose. Kerian, kneeling at his side, carefully wiped it away with her fingers.

"Sire, you must lie in a warm bed and sleep," Truthanar insisted.

"Soon, noble healer. Soon."

Kerian followed Truthanar as he returned to his place in the milling throng. "Tell me plainly," she said in a low voice. "What is his condition?"

The aged Silvanesti was blunt. "He is burning his candle at both ends, lady. Even if he took to a bed right now and kept warm and quiet, his life still would be measured in months."

She had known her husband's health was bad, but hearing the prognosis aloud was still a shock. Returning to the palanquin, she found Gilthas had succumbed to the medicine and was slumped in the chair, sleeping, chin on his chest. The cup had fallen from his slack fingers. Kerian picked it up and handed it to one of the Speaker's aides.

"Follow the scouts," she told the bearers, gesturing at Taranath and the cavalry. The bearers lifted the chair and resumed walking. They were not the same four who had carried the palanquin at the beginning of the journey. Every hour or so, a new quartet replaced those carrying the chair. It had required Kerian's intervention to put such a rotation in place. The bearers were volunteers, and none wanted to give up his or her place. If Kerian hadn't insisted, they would have carried on until exhaustion dropped them in their tracks.

When the palanquin resumed its progress, the crowd of elves behind it picked themselves up too and continued their steady tramp toward the center of the valley. None knew what, if anything, might be there, but it was the Speaker's will they go, and for him, they would walk into the Abyss.

While Gilthas slept, Kerian decided to reconnoiter ahead. She whistled loudly and Eagle Eye, circling above her, landed a few yards away. She swung into the flat saddle and urged the griffon aloft. Kanan followed them but a sharp scream from Eagle Eye sent the younger beast back.

They flew northeast, just above the low trees. The late-morning sun was in their eyes, and their combined shadows chased behind. The cavalry waved as griffon and rider flashed over them. Kerian easily picked out their leader, although he wore nothing to set him apart. Taranath was out in front, as usual.

The mountains ringing Inath-Wakenti were high and very rugged. Shreds of cloud drifted over their peaks, pushed by an east wind. The air was warmer aloft than on the ground. One of Inath-Wakenti's many oddities was the chill of its soil. The elves quickly learned the ground drew off the heat of their bodies, so they slept on padding made of whatever was at hand—blankets, spare clothing, pine boughs. Fires died quickly too, and the embers went cold faster than normal. Cruising five hundred feet over Inath-Wakenti, Kerian was warm for the first time in days.

White monoliths crouched among the low trees or towered impudently above them. There still seemed no rhyme or reason to their placement. Favaronas had told her the stones were not native to the valley, so they must have had been hauled in for a purpose. What weird, useless purpose, she could not imagine.

The farther she flew, the more numerous the monoliths became. At last night's campsite, the sarsens had been ten to twenty yards apart. Now, only a handful of yards separated them. The stunted trees thinned, then ended. Abruptly the ground below Eagle Eye's driving wings was solid white, like a plain of snow. The griffon reared back, hovering, startled by the blinding reflection of sunlight from the enormous field of dressed white stone.

Kerian turned the griffon's head and they flew along the edge of the pavement. It was perfectly circular, at least a mile in diameter, and from this height, featureless. Grass and weeds grew up to its edge, but as with all the other stone structures, nothing encroached on the pristine surface. The assemblage of monoliths stopped thirty yards or so from its edge, leaving clear ground in between. Judging by the position of the mountains and the distance the elves had come, Kerian realized she must be looking at the center point of Inath-Wakenti.

Her circumnavigation of the enormous disk complete, she steered Eagle Eye toward the center. He balked, tossing his head and fighting the reins. She couldn't blame him. A wave of cold air rose from the pavement and hit the soles of her shoes. When she let the griffon have his head, he flapped hard to get back outside the perimeter of the stone pavement. She had him land a few yards from its edge. He lay down facing away from the circular slab, and she proceeded on foot.

The pavement was knee high, its edge cut square, but worn by the elements. Although white like the monoliths, it wasn't made of snowy quartz, but a denser rock. A series of tremendous pie-shaped wedges had been neatly joined to form the mile-wide disk. Gingerly she climbed onto the platform. The flow of cold air she'd felt aloft was discernible at ground level too. Air temperature atop the platform was noticeably colder than the usual chilly feel of the valley.

On closer inspection, the stone wasn't unmarked after all. The surface was covered with carved lines. Weathering had softened them, but their intricate patterns of curlicues and flowing curves was still visible.

Her journey to the center of the platform took a while, and the farther she went, the more isolated she felt. The mass of featureless, flat stone seemed to steal her sense of direction and distance. When she checked her position relative to her sleeping griffon, she realized she'd been walking in a circle. She sought one of the radial joints between the wedge-shaped slabs and used it as a guide to the center.

Sounds of whispering came to her ears, and she stopped immediately. In a silent land infested with ghosts, every noise was significant. Unfortunately, the sounds were too faint for her to understand, so she resumed her trek.

DESTINY

The center of the great disk was marked by nothing more than the simple confluence of all the joints, but as she drew near it, the voices became louder and more distinct. She kept going but slowly, turning her head left and right, alert for she knew not what. When her foot touched the center point, the voices instantly became comprehensible. They were nothing more than mundane conversations—about fresh water, clean clothing, the health of the Speaker.

Kerian was amazed. She wasn't hearing ghosts, but the voices of her own people as they advanced across the wasteland! Whether by magic or the strange effect of the valley's shape, voices from many miles away were reaching her with perfect clarity. By shifting her position slightly, she could bring even individual conversations into focus. But however much she tried, she couldn't locate Gilthas's voice in the welter.

"Gilthas, can you hear me?" She stopped, frustrated.

Instantly the muddle of conversations died. Hard on this silence came ten thousand variations of "who said that?" Not only could Kerian hear them, but they could hear her! The peculiar effect worked both ways.

She demanded quiet. When the amazed chatter died, she identified herself and called for her husband again.

Hamaramis answered, "The Speaker sleeps, lady. Where are you? We can't see you."

She told him, provoking another cacophony of questions. She shouted them to silence again.

"Is it safe for us to proceed there?" Hamaramis asked.

"It seems so. Just continue north-northeast, and you can't miss it."

She seated herself at the center of the disk. As her people advanced, she spoke to Hamaramis and Taranath as easily as if they were standing beside her. When Gilthas awoke, she regaled him with the tale of her discovery. By midafternoon the first riders appeared beyond the distant edge. They came to her on foot; their horses liked the cold, white pavement no more than Eagle Eye had.

"Welcome to the navel of the world," she hailed Taranath. The warriors laughed, but her old comrade in arms frowned.

"Are you well?" he asked.

"As well as ever, Taran." She grimaced. "Actually, my legs have cramped. Give me a hand."

Pulling her upright, he exclaimed, "You're cold as ice!"

She put a hand to her face, but felt nothing untoward. Yet her legs had stiffened and her arms were bloodlessly pale, her fingernails blue. She and the others returned quickly to the pavement's edge. Jumping off the stone to land on the grass, Kerian felt as though she were entering a steam bath, such as the plainsmen enjoyed. After a few hours on the great platform, the cool air of Inath-Wakenti felt positively hot.

Taranath offered her a flask from his belt. She pulled the stopper, recoiling at the sharp odor. The flask contained *fluq*.

The Khurish beverage was distilled from the fermented juice of the corpse cactus, so called because its fleshy, pale blue fronds resembled the limp hands of the dead. The flavor was unbelievably bitter, almost metallic, but the liquid flooded Kerian's veins with heat.

When she'd caught her breath again, she ordered everyone kept off the platform. "It finally occurs to me (thank you, *fluq*) that if you all could hear me talk, then so could anyone else in this blasted valley."

Taranath swallowed *fluq* and nodded. It would be poor tactics to announce their plans and position to all and sundry, but he wondered whether there was anyone in the valley to hear them.

"We're surrounded, remember?" she said. "Despite the Speaker's hopes, the ghosts in this valley are not our friends."

*   *   *   *   *

The only thing worse than pursuing Faeterus across the eerie valley was traveling with him. Favaronas was accustomed to Robien's swift step.

But however persistent the Kagonesti was, he wasn't heartless. He moderated his pace to accommodate the scholar's needs, and he halted a few hours each night for sleep. Faeterus did not. His progress wasn't terribly rapid, burdened as he was by heavy robes and by Favaronas, but he never rested, not even for a moment.

At first Favaronas thought him preternaturally alert and magically attuned somehow to his surroundings but gradually came to realize a more fundamental process was at work. Faeterus was afraid, and Favaronas did not know why. Poor Robien was no longer a threat. The arrival of the Speaker and the elf nation, although imparting a sense of urgency to the mage's as-yet unknown master plan didn't seem the cause of the deep fear Favaronas sensed. He couldn't decide whether he should be glad or worried about whatever it was that terrified Faeterus. Humans had a saying: the enemy of my enemy is my friend. In this case, the enemy of Favaronas's enemy might simply kill them both.

By dragging his feet, falling, and veering off course at every opportunity, Favaronas hampered their progress as much as he dared. He had little hope of rescue or escape, but if Faeterus wanted haste, then Favaronas would do all he could to delay. His tactics finally goaded the increasingly anxious sorcerer into action.

Mount Rakaris was no more than a day's march away when Favaronas took a calculated tumble into a dry ravine. Faeterus stood on the edge, fists on hips, and raged at him.

"Torghan save me! Get up! Get up, or I'll give you frog's legs to stand on!"

In trying to protect his bundle of stone scrolls during the fall, Favaronas had earned himself a bloodied upper lip.

"You go too fast," he complained, putting a plaintive whine into his voice (it wasn't difficult). "Why such haste? The bounty hunter is finished, and the Speaker's warriors are nowhere near."

"I wasted too much time playing cat and mouse with Sahim's hired killer. I intend to be there by first light." It was midafternoon. "Whether you are still alive then is entirely up to you, elf spawn!"

He'd used that epithet once before, and it still made no sense to Favaronas. Of course he was the spawn of elves, as was Faeterus. But perhaps one of the sorcerer's parents had been a human. That would explain a lot. Favaronas had heard half-breeds were anxious, cruel creatures.

Painfully, he climbed back up the steep bank. When his eyes reached ground level, the sorcerer's deteriorating, rag-wrapped sandals were only inches from his face, giving him a clear view of Faeterus's left foot. He gasped.

The foot had only four toes. Each ended in a thick, down-curving yellow nail. No elf had such an appendage. Nor did any human Favaronas ever heard of.

Faeterus jerked his foot back beneath his robe. He extended a bony finger, pointing at Favaronas. Immediately, the archivist felt his lips close together. One hand flew to his face, and he gave an inarticulate cry. His fingers found only smooth skin between nose and chin. His lips weren't simply sealed, they were gone!

"Unless you want to lose your ears as well, be silent. And keep up."

Turning, the sorcerer plunged through a waist-high growth of wild sage. With Robien's death, there was no reason to conceal his tracks or walk atop the greenery.

Scrabbling at the edge of the ravine, the scholar hauled himself out and hurried to catch up. His breath whistled through his nose. His teeth and tongue were still there but sealed away. Horror threatened to overwhelm him, but he told himself that what the sorcerer took away he could restore. He claimed he wanted Favaronas to read to him from the stone scrolls but had not asked for that. His haste to reach the eastern mountains superseded all else.

As if reading his captive's thoughts, Faeterus pointed at him again, and just like that, Favaronas's mouth was restored. The sorcerer commanded him to read as he walked.

Favaronas stretched his jaw wide and licked his lips. "The scrolls will never open in such strong sunlight," he warned.

"You're a scholar. I'm sure you have transcriptions."

DESTINY

Favaronas had indeed begun to make a handwritten copy of the text. He pulled a sheaf of pages from an inner pocket in his bag. The parchment was covered with the miniscule script he had mastered during his years in the Speaker's service.

He began with an explanation. "The cylinders are numbered, but they're not in sequence. The lowest number I have is 594. The text begins in midsentence: 'our most gracious lord, *Om.hed.thon.dac* (the Father Who Made Not His Children), stood upon the, um, mountainside to say farewell. He could not touch the soil of the place without provoking death. "My children," said he, "bear this exile in good grace. Do not make this an island, but a fortress. In time I will return and free you.'"

"He never came back."

Faeterus did not amplify on this bitter comment but did halt long enough to conjure a path ahead of them. The sage had become so dense, their progress had slowed to a snail's pace. When the sorcerer spread his hands, the thick bushes split apart as if cleared by a scythe. They set out again and Favaronas continued.

" 'The Father rose on the wind and departed to the—' " Favaronas frowned. "Southland? Homeland? 'The place on which he stood was named *Ro.bisc.ro.pel.*'"

The abbreviations had eluded Favaronas's attempt at translation. Faeterus calmly provided it. *"Rothye biscara rolofassos pelmany."*

Pelmany meant stair. Favaronas muttered, "Stair of Distant Vision?"

Faeterus swung around to face him. Although the front of the hood was only a few feet away, Favaronas could make out little more than a faint suggestion of the face within its deep shadow. "That is our destination."

"Are you him, the Father Who Made Not His Children?"

"No. He passed out of this world long ago." The hood shifted and Favaronas glimpsed two dark eyes within. "I was the only one to escape. I have come back to claim the heritage of the Lost Ones, my people."

Favaronas shivered. If the sorcerer were telling the truth, then he was unbelievably old. Recalling his own ghostly encounters with the valley's half-animal inhabitants, Favaronas blurted, "Then you're not an elf!"

"Thanks be to the Maker! For fifty centuries I have lived in the shadowy edges of the mighty elf race. I found Father's writings, and learned how to prolong my life until the day of retribution. That day has finally come! Your people's power is broken. I shall complete their destruction. When I stand on the Stair of Distant Vision, the key to unlocking this valley's power will be revealed to me. I will make that power my own and use it to work my will!"

The sheets of parchment fell from Favaronas's hand. He finally understood the danger awaiting them all.

The hooded head turned away from him, but the sorcerer's pointing finger sought him out again. Favaronas's slack mouth closed with a snap, and his lips once more vanished.

"Pick up your notes and follow," Faeterus said. "What you know, you will never tell."

7

There was nothing but dreamless void. He could sense nothing at all beyond himself. Then a voice spoke and nothingness became . . . something. The voice spoke again, and he felt himself slowly sinking in the boundless darkness. By the time he made out the words, he had fallen hard onto a cold, gritty surface.

"—Where are you?"

Hytanthas raised his head from the coldness beneath it. "Commander?"

"Can you hear me?"

Pain thudded inside his skull. The sound of the Lioness's voice seemed to ebb and flow with the pain. Pushing himself up onto his hands, Hytanthas called to her again. The effort of speaking loudly sent paroxysms of agony lancing through his head, and he finally gave up shouting. It was clear that although he could hear the Lioness as if she were only a few feet away, she couldn't hear him. She seemed to be conversing with others, but hers was the only voice he could hear.

The blackness around him was absolute. Elves are gifted with the ability to see even in lightless conditions, yet Hytanthas could see nothing at all. He feared he had been blinded. Fighting back panic, he concentrated on his other senses. His questing hands encountered hard stone arching overhead and stone walls on either side, but open air in front and behind. He was in a tunnel. He recalled the Lioness describing the tunnels her expedition had explored beneath Inath-Wakenti. The return of that memory brought the rest flooding back.

He had been flying night patrol on Kanan. A group of will-o'-the-wisps appeared, trying to surround him. At his command the griffon dove. Down and down they plummeted, Kanan never wavering although it seemed they would smash into the blue soil. They leveled off only yards above it. The lights were left behind, and Hytanthas did a foolish thing. He relaxed, exulting in his triumph over the mysterious lights. A trilithon loomed out of the shadows, two tall, white stones supporting a third laid horizontally atop. With Hytanthas's hands slack on the reins, Kanan chose to dive under the lintel. His rider didn't react in time. Hytanthas's forehead struck the stone, and he fell from the saddle, unconscious. Awakening a short time later, he saw no sign of Kanan, so he shucked his dented iron helmet and leather skullcap and prepared to walk back to camp. The instant he dropped the helmet, a will-o'-the-wisp appeared. It touched him, and next thing he knew he was here.

Was that what happened to all the others who vanished? Were they whisked away and deposited in the maze of tunnels underneath the valley floor?

Time enough later to worry about such things. He didn't know how long he had been here, but his throat was parched and his belly protested its emptiness. He had only the gear attached to his person: a fighting dagger, a light grapnel with thirty feet of thin rope (commonly carried by griffon riders for retrieving messages from the ground), and a bit of hard biscuit rolled inside a bandanna. Sword, water bottle, and flint and steel had been lost with Kanan.

The hard biscuit eased his hunger pangs, and he explored his surroundings more carefully. The wall had a slight curve, which increased the higher he explored. The ceiling curved above him. The opposite wall, some seven feet away, was exactly the same, made of small, cleanly cut blocks fitted together without mortar.

Which way should he go? There seemed little difference. He felt no breeze on his face, so he chose a direction and started off, feeling his way along the wall and shuffling his feet to avoid tripping over unseen hazards. The stone wall was smoothly dressed, but his sensitive fingertips noted tiny imperfections. Like some grades of marble.

Every now and then, he heard the Lioness; she was talking to Hamaramis and Taranath by the sound of it. Hytanthas called out periodically but never earned an answer. He had no idea why he was hearing his commander but was certain he owed his life to the sound. Her voice had brought him back from a place he suspected he might never have escaped otherwise.

In the perfect darkness, his sense of time became confused. He seemed to have been walking for ages. At times his booted feet crunched through loose gravel or sent larger fragments skittering aside. From the lack of strain on his leg muscles, he deduced the tunnel was continuing straight and level, neither climbing nor descending.

When a faint, purplish glimmer appeared far ahead, he feared it was no more than a mirage conjured by his light-starved brain. The glimmer persisted. Relieved beyond words at the return of light, he put aside the puzzle of his inability to see in the blackness and forced himself to hold to his slow but steady pace. He didn't want to risk a fall.

The glimmer was not an exit. It was another will-o'-the-wisp. The fist-sized purple light appeared to be hovering in place. Despite his approach, it never moved. He poked at it with the tip of his dagger. His probing dislodged the globe and it began to fall. Without thinking, he reached out and caught it in midair. The globe was weighty for its size, smooth and hard, and slightly warm. By its amethyst light, he saw that the column on which it had sat was extremely slender, no thicker than his finger, about three feet high, and made of some sort of polished black stone. When he bent low to study its base, he got his first glimpse of the debris on which he'd been walking. The shock caused him to drop the smooth globe.

The tunnel floor was covered with bones. Most were the remains of large animals, but here and there he saw the tiny skeletons of birds and rodents.

When the globe hit the floor, its light had grown brighter, changing from purple to indigo. He picked it up and carefully dropped it again. The impact brightened its light considerably, to a sky-blue shade.

Whatever else its purpose, the light made the going easier. Resuming his trek, he ate the last of his dry bread and pondered the significance of the bones. Could they be the remains of Inath-Wakenti's missing animals?

He'd not traveled far when the light illuminated something more substantial than dry bones. A body lay near the right wall. Its posture told Hytanthas the person was dead, although there was no smell at all, only the dry, dusty odor of the bones. He intended to pass the corpse quickly but pulled up short when he realized the body was that of an elf. Metal armor was easily discernible beneath the sun-bleached *geb*. Hytanthas crouched to see the warrior's face.

The dead elf was known to him—a Qualinesti named Marmanth who had ridden out of Khurinost with the Lioness so long ago to search for Inath-Wakenti. He must have been taken by the will-o'-the-wisps and left in this tunnel, just as Hytanthas himself had been. But Marmanth had died, while Hytanthas lived. Why? Did the will-o'-the-wisps sometimes kill their victims outright, or had Marmanth never awakened from the strange sleep?

Elves dislike touching their dead, but Hytanthas steeled himself and searched the corpse. It showed no signs of violence. The debris around it had been disturbed by nothing but Hytanthas's own footprints. It was as though Marmanth had appeared there from nowhere and never got up again.

DESTINY

Hytanthas stood and resumed walking. Hungry, his throat achingly dry, he knew that if he couldn't find a way out, he'd end up like poor Marmanth, like all the creatures trapped down there: a corpse, slowly drying and turning to dusty bones.

* * * * *

Night came again. The elves camped near the huge circular platform amid the dense gathering of monoliths. A defensive perimeter was created by filling the gaps between standing stones with barricades of brushwood. Kerian and the professional warriors thought it futile to erect barriers to keep out ghosts and flying spirit lights, but the rest of the elves took the effort seriously. Barricades and bonfires had kept the phantoms at bay before. The civilians trusted they would do so again.

The elves tried cutting sod to strengthen the barrier, but the sandy soil fell apart on their spades. Turning the dirt revealed the soil's strange sterility. No worms wiggled in the cuts, no pill bugs turned armored carapaces to the intruding light. For its top three inches, the dirt was blue-green and very sandy. Below that was black loam of the finest sort. Elves who had been farmers in Silvanesti and Qualinesti grew quite excited when they saw that. Kerian crushed a handful of dirt in her fist.

"How will you grow anything without insects to pollinate it?" she asked.

"Some things do grow here," Gilthas countered. Vines and bushes propagated through their roots, and trees could pollinate with the wind. Still, her point was a valid one. A lack of insects would make it difficult to grow fruitful crops.

Before all light had left the valley, strange shapes could be seen flitting among the standing stones beyond the barricade. They were not at all like the somber, staring figures Gilthas had spoken to, but four-legged creatures that bounded between stones. They seemed so solid and real, hunters begged for permission to go outside the wall.

91

"If you do, you'll never be seen again," Kerian warned.

One elf insisted he'd seen a rabbit. With a few questions, Gilthas determined that for the creature to be visible at such a distance, it would have to be at least three feet tall. The animal was only another apparition. The disappointed hunters tightened their belts and departed, turning their backs on the "animals" still cavorting from one shadowed thicket to another. Some of the creatures were four legged; others bounded along on two.

Alone with his wife, Gilthas watched the display.

"Perhaps we should have a look around out there," he murmured.

Exasperated, she reminded him of what she'd just said to the would-be hunters. "They're nothing but the same ghosts we've seen before," she added.

"Can we be certain? Your expedition didn't penetrate this far, did it?"

Kerian shook her head and looked away, toward the capering shadows. Her earlier visit and the subsequent loss of nearly her entire command was still a very sore subject for her. None of the eight elves who survived blamed her for the deaths of the others. She'd believed the Speaker to be in grave danger and had acted to protect him. No warrior would have expected any less. Kerian knew she could not have done other than she had—yet she felt guilty. The memory of those who'd perished in the desert would never leave her.

"Come," Gilthas said, holding out a hand. "Let us take a stroll in the twilight."

She tried to laugh, but there was more exasperation than amusement in the sound. "Do you have a death wish?"

"Do you want to live forever?"

Her breath caught as if a hand had squeezed her heart. The teasing tone sounded so like the Gilthas of old, utterly at odds with the emaciated figure before her, but the irony of his words struck like a knife.

DESTINY

He recognized the direction of her thoughts. The pain on her face was reflected briefly in his eyes, but his hand didn't waver. Kerian took it. Sword at her hip, bow and quiver of arrows slung across her back, she walked at his side with bemused pride. She could only marvel at the indomitable will that burned inside him.

A gate in the barricade had been fashioned under a soaring trilithon. Casks filled the gap between the upright stones. Hamaramis was there with his lieutenants. When the old general heard the Speaker intended to leave camp with only the Lioness as his escort, he protested vigorously.

Gilthas wasted no breath in discussion; he merely waited for the general's exclamations to run down.

"The Speaker will do as he will," Kerian told Hamaramis. "I'll try to bring him back alive."

Those nearby spread the word. While the casks were being rolled away, scores of elves crowded the rough wall, anxious to see their sovereign challenge the valley's ghosts.

As the royal pair passed through the trilithon, a fit of coughing staggered Gilthas. Kerian supported him with one arm. He tried to pull away, protesting she could hardly use bow or sword while holding him up.

Her grip tightened. "Don't worry. If it comes to that, I'll drop you like a hot rock."

With a nearly soundless chuckle, he straightened. They started across the open ground between the camp and the stunted forest. Gilthas glanced back.

"I'm evolving a theory about this place," he said. "I think—"

"Long live Gilthas Pathfinder!" cried a voice from the camp.

"Long live the Speaker of the Sun and Stars!" added another, and for a time the Silent Vale echoed with a chorus of elf voices.

When the tumult died, Kerian asked Gilthas about his theory. He squeezed her arm and shook his head. His eyes, fixed on the camp, were bright with unshed tears. "Not just now," he said, voice roughened by emotion.

He lifted an arm, acknowledging his people's cheers. He and Kerian continued their slow walk.

The thickets ahead were touched by the failing light. When the two elves were halfway to the line of gnarled trees, a creature dashed between a pair of stunted oaks. The Speaker halted, and Kerian unslung her bow.

"Not unless I say so," he said quietly.

A grimace twisted her lips but she nodded.

Something stood by one of the trees. Speaker and consort continued their advance watched by dark eyes. The eyes were close-set and low to the ground.

"Don't be afraid," Gilthas said. "We mean you no harm."

For her part, Kerian meant plenty of harm, but she kept the broadhead pointed at the ground. Abruptly Gilthas crossed in front of her. She made a sound of protest, but he gestured sharply for silence. She edged to her left, seeking a clear line of fire. He gave no sign of noticing her movement. All his attention was focused on the staring eyes and the shadowy shape behind them.

"Can we help you?" he asked, keeping his voice low and calm.

More eyes appeared around the first pair. They were of various sizes and heights. Each pair appeared suddenly and silently—first they weren't there, then they were. Gilthas introduced himself simply, by name only, perhaps not wishing to frighten the evanescent creatures before him with his full title. He told them the elves had come to live peacefully in the valley and asked what the creatures wanted.

While he talked, Kerian realized something odd was happening. Her legs began to feel heavy, as though dragged down by invisible weights. She was having trouble moving. Each step was more difficult than the last. Her fingers holding the arrow went numb. Breathing was becoming a chore. She could think of no reason for it but malign magic, and she tried to warn Gilthas, but he didn't hear her gasped words. More and more figures were materializing in the misty twilight around them. The shadowy silhouettes were becoming more distinct, resolving themselves into elves dressed in white shifts. All were barefoot, with long, tangled hair, and all were a head shorter than she. Their faces were indistinct, blurred like reflections in water disturbed by ripples. She could get no clear impression of their appearance.

"We were driven from our homelands by invaders," Gilthas was saying. "This valley is our last refuge."

You cannot stay. This is no place for such as you.

The whispery voice teased Kerian's ears, and Gilthas's startled reaction showed that he'd heard it too. Coolness played on Kerian's arm. One of the translucent elves had touched her. She wanted to pull away, but her muscles seemed to have turned to wood. None of the creatures was near enough to touch Gilthas, and he droned on and on as though negotiating with Sahim-Khan's unctuous minions. More ghosts touched Kerian, their small hands cold as mountain snow.

Gilthas said, "Perhaps we can help you. Why do you haunt this valley? What makes your souls so restless?"

We are forgotten. We are the lost. But we live. We live!

With that, the ghosts changed abruptly. From pallid specters, they became more corporeal. White shifts and pale skin darkened. The ghosts were feral creatures, covered by fur, no longer resembling elves at all. The chill, feather-light fingers were claws, and they raked over Kerian's arms, drawing blood.

Dragging in as large a breath as she could manage, Kerian expelled it in one great heave: "Trap!"

He turned. Shock bloomed on his face. "Let her go! In the name of the Speaker of the Sun and Stars, let her go!" he cried. Astonishingly, the creatures obeyed. They fell back. Gilthas went to his dazed wife, and this time it was he who offered support.

Speaker? You are Speaker?

"I am!"

Blood of the Goldeneye!

Regaining command of her limbs, Kerian grasped her husband's arm. "They're not elves, they're monsters!" she said wildly. "We have to go back!"

The specters went with them as they fled. The creatures didn't follow, but vanished from one spot and reappeared again a few yards farther on.

Kerian ran faster, her grip on Gilthas's wrist painfully tight. The first stars were winking into view overhead. The will-o'-the-wisps could appear at any time, but they were most obvious just as the stars began to shine. Despite his best efforts, Gilthas was falling behind, and Kerian's attempt to drag him along only threw him off balance.

"Let me go," he insisted. "I can run!"

She released him but told him to run faster.

They were only halfway to the camp when she jerked him to a halt. "Don't move!" she hissed, pointing.

High above, a score of lights bobbed and swooped. Crimson, gold, sapphire, vivid green—they descended swiftly and converged on the two elves.

"What do we do?" Gilthas demanded.

"Stand still."

"What of the ghosts?"

Kerian dared move enough to look over one shoulder. The ghosts had halted. The expression on each twisted, beastly face was dreadful. Grimacing with hate, the ghosts bared long, gray teeth and made tearing gestures with their claws. They advanced no farther and, as the lights descended, shrank from them as thoroughly as the living elves did. The ghosts seemed terrified of the will-o'-the-wisps.

The colored lights darted past, missing Kerian's head by a few feet and flying straight at the retreating spirits. An amber light caught one slow-moving ghost, and both vanished in a silent flash.

"They hunt the spirits as well as living creatures!" Gilthas whispered.

Kerian, consumed by the need to remain still when every muscle screamed to run, clenched her teeth. Three will-o'-the-wisps passed within arm's length. Their slow, meandering flight was deceptive. They could move as swiftly as an arrow when the situation required it.

Two more ghosts were taken by the lights before the rest vanished into the silent forest. More will-o'-the-wisps appeared, drifting in from north and south. As she and Gilthas stood elbow to elbow in the deepening twilight, Kerian could see elves standing on the stones ringing their camp. All watched helplessly as half a hundred dancing lights filled the ground between the camp and the two trapped outside its safety. The Lioness was furious. She wasn't angry at her husband for venturing outside the camp, but at herself for allowing it. He had always led by example; it was his nature. The responsibility for his safety was hers and hers alone. Even if it meant offending the dignity of the Speaker, she should not have permitted him to leave the camp.

"Does it hurt when they take you?" Gilthas asked, interrupting her self-recriminations.

Gruffly, she said it did not.

"Keep close, then," he said. "If we are to be lost, we will be lost together."

Their resolve to remain motionless met an abrupt end when his illness rose up to choke him. He tried to stifle the cough, but the spasm was too strong. As it bent him double, only Kerian's strong arms kept him on his feet. The orbiting will-o'-the-wisps drifted closer.

The spasm passed, and Gilthas straightened, striving to catch his breath.

"Here they come," she said.

"I love you."

She swallowed hard. "And I love you, dreamer."

"That's good. Perhaps you'll forgive me as well."

Before she could ask what he meant, the lights closed in and he reneged on his pledge. Gilthas summoned his strength and shoved his wife away. Two will-o'-the-wisps met at his chest and exploded in a blaze of light.

8

Kerian hurled herself at Gilthas as the corona of light engulfed him, and they both went down. She tried to twist and fall beneath him, to cushion his landing, but she was only partially successful. For a moment she lay unmoving, not breathing, eyes closed. Who knew where the will-o'-the-wisps might have sent them.

Nowhere, it seemed. She and Gilthas had done nothing more than strike the ground. They were still in Inath-Wakenti. The night sky still arched over them. And Gilthas was held fast in her arms.

"So," he grunted, opening his eyes. "Apparently I am not worth taking."

"Be still," she hissed, listening intently. "I don't think that's what happened."

A troop of cavalry galloped up, forestalling further discussion. Leading them was Hamaramis, pale with shock.

"Great Speaker! Lady Kerianseray! Are you all right?"

Kerian helped her husband stand, and they reassured the old general. The spectral monsters were gone. Will-o'-the-wisps were maneuvering in the mist, rising along the tree line a dozen yards away, and the elves did not hang about. Hamaramis offered his horse, but Gilthas climbed up behind him instead. The Speaker was swaying on his feet and even

Hamaramis's well-behaved bay might prove too vigorous for his unsteady hand. Never one to worry about protocol or appearances, Kerian simply vaulted up behind the closest soldier, a young Qualinesti much astonished to find himself sharing a horse with his queen.

Shouts greeted the Speaker and the Lioness on their return. Everyone marveled at the Speaker's miraculous survival. Elves crowded his horse, eager to confirm Gilthas was truly unharmed.

After reassuring his people, Gilthas headed for his tent, ordering a council be convened immediately. Soon enough, Hamaramis, Taranath, and the chosen leaders of the people—members of the Thalas-Enthia, the Qualinesti senate—had joined the Lioness in the Speaker's tent. Gilthas was seated in his camp chair, legs covered by Kerian's crimson mantle. Despite Truthanar's worry for his health, the healer had to be content with serving his king a draft of soothing elixir then retiring into the background.

Gilthas and Kerian related their experiences. Unlike his wife, at no time had Gilthas been paralyzed, but he had felt very strongly the specters' opposition to the elves' presence. The sensation emanating from the ghostly assemblage was hatred, pure unvarnished loathing, he told the council. Gilthas's reassurances had had no effect.

"You did stop their attack on me," Kerian pointed out.

A puzzling development, but true, Gilthas admitted. When he commanded them to release his wife, the angry ghosts surprisingly obeyed, but their hatred had grown stronger. They had retreated only when the will-o'-the-wisps appeared, demonstrating the two presences were at odds.

Much as he regretted causing distress to so many unhappy souls, Gilthas was adamant. "They must give way. They will give way. We are here, and I intend we shall stay."

"Could we lay the ghosts to rest somehow?" asked a Silvanesti, a minor member of House Cleric.

Gilthas was doubtful. No one among the elves had the knowledge and skill. And an ordinary cleric might banish one or two ghosts in his entire career. What could be done against hundreds of malevolent specters?

A pall descended on the group. Nothing was to be heard but the crackle of torches and the scratching of Varanas's quill. The scribe was seated on the Speaker's right, slightly behind the makeshift throne, dutifully taking notes on all that was said. In the shadows behind Varanas, the healer fidgeted, shifting from one foot to the other, obviously impatient for the council to end so his patient could be put to bed.

The discussion resumed, in an unfocused, halfhearted fashion. No one had any useful suggestions to offer. Gilthas listened, chin in hand, a frown of concentration on his face. Kerian wasn't fooled. She knew he was nearing the end of his endurance. Exhaustion had sharpened the lines on his face even as it blurred his gaze. She was about to insist they adjourn for the evening when a thought struck her with blinding suddenness.

"I know someone wise enough to tell us if it is possible to put the ghosts to rest," she exclaimed. "Lady Sa'ida!"

Sa'ida was the high priestess of the Khurish goddess Elir-Sana. During the elves' exile in Khuri-Khan, the priestess had proven herself a valuable ally, albeit a covert one given her desire not to offend her people's sensitivity to all things foreign. She had loaned the Speaker the temple documents that mentioned the valley. Gilthas had them carefully copied and continued to study them alongside the wise works of his own race.

"She might as well be on one of the moons," observed Hamaramis.

No party of elves could hope to make it to the capital city and back. If the desert and the nomads didn't kill them, Sahim-Khan might. Once, the khan had tolerated the elves because of their contribution to his coffers. But they no longer had enough money in their treasury to tempt him, especially given the troubles he faced from those who despised the elves, including the followers of the god Torghan.

"Eagle Eye can take me there," said Kerian.

She could fly to Khuri-Khan and fetch Lady Sa'ida, she explained. It was an intriguing idea. Gilthas disliked the notion of sending her alone, but no one could ride Hytanthas's Kanan. A griffon would accept only his or her bonded rider. The formation of such a bond usually required many months of patient attention. Alhana had been able to break wild Golden griffons to the saddle by means of a special ritual, but there was no one in the valley who knew how to do what she had done.

"Even if you reached the city safely, we can't be certain Sa'ida would agree to help us," Gilthas added.

That was true. Whether Sa'ida's help in their time of exile stemmed from true generosity of spirit or a more pragmatic desire to aid the enemies of her enemies, Kerian couldn't say. Even if the human priestess was sympathetic to their plight, she might refuse to leave her sanctuary and undertake a journey to a haunted valley. It was well known she rarely left the temple's sacred precincts. Kerian was confident she could persuade the woman to come back with her to the valley, but Gilthas put an end to the discussion.

"A proposed mission to Khuri-Khan is not practical. I cannot allow it."

His peremptory tone caused Kerian to stare. He sat, frowning at no one in particular, his face so bloodlessly pale, it might have been carved of pure white Silvanesti marble. Kerian allowed the matter to drop, but while the others took a moment to pass around waterskins, she continued to observe him. He didn't return her gaze, only stared down at the cup of medicine he held.

After sipping from the cup, he continued in a more measured tone. "I believe my experience tonight solves one of the valley's mysteries. We face not a single malign force, but two distinct ones. The apparitions are ghosts of those who once inhabited Inath-Wakenti. Who they were, I don't know, but they are at odds with the will-o'-the-wisps. When the lights appeared, the ghosts fled."

"But we don't know who created the lights or how they are controlled," Taranath put in.

"Guards?" mused Hamaramis. "The will-o'-the-wisps guard the valley from intruders like us, but they also keep the ghosts of the original inhabitants inside."

Gilthas supported his intriguing theory, and the group fell to speculating about why the lights hadn't carried off the Speaker.

"Blood of the Goldeneye."

All eyes turned to Varanas, and Gilthas asked what he meant. The scribe looked up from his writing. Realizing he'd spoken aloud, he flushed to the roots of his pale blond hair and begged forgiveness for having interrupted.

Assured by the Speaker that he'd given no offense, the scribe answered, "That's what the spirits called you, sire, Blood of the Goldeneye. They obeyed you once they knew your identity." Varanas consulted his notes. "But their hatred of you only grew."

"Maybe Silvanos Goldeneye was responsible for them being here," Kerian said. "And maybe those of his line are immune to the guardian lights. I'm no scholar, but there is a certain warrior's logic to it. The ghosts may have been elves once." She hadn't mentioned the spirits' beastly metamorphosis. She would discuss that with Gilthas privately first. "Exile, imprisonment—however it was styled, suppose they were sent to this distant valley, guarded by powerful magic in the form of the floating lights. If Speaker Silvanos, or another of his line, had sentenced these wretches to eternal exile, it would make sense for his blood descendant to be immune to the spell that created the guardians."

Again silence descended. The Lioness's words hinted at a bleak tale rooted in the distant past. What crime could these malefactors have committed to earn such a terrible punishment? What sort of elves had the ghosts been?

Gilthas ended the silence. "An interesting thesis," he said and turned the talk to other issues. A senator reminded him of the dwindling food supply. Meat continued to disappear even though the caches were heavily guarded. Grain, vegetables, and potable liquids were untouched, but animal flesh seemed utterly unwelcome there, even when cooked or preserved. Water supplies were adequate, but no new source had been found since they had left Lioness Creek. A former member of House Gardener claimed water abounded just below the surface. Divining rods wielded by sensitive elves detected plenty, and wells could be dug fairly easily.

With food the greatest priority, the Speaker decreed search parties would be dispatched the next day to comb the surrounding area for anything edible.

"What of the ghosts, sire?" Hamaramis wanted to know.

"If we don't find food soon, we'll all be ghosts," grumbled Kerian.

The most distant searches, Gilthas said, would be carried out by mounted scouts, who might outrun any hostile spirits. All parties would return to camp an hour before sundown to avoid the marauding will-o'-the-wisps.

With that, the council broke up. As the last councilor was departing the Speaker's tent, Truthanar stepped forward and conducted a brief examination of his king.

"Your fever is up. Too much exertion. Too much night air."

"Too much being Gilthas," said Kerian.

Smiling, the Speaker pled guilty to all charges then told Truthanar he could go. Plainly dissatisfied with his liege's frivolous attitude, the healer took himself off to his own bedroll. The Speaker's scribes approached, ready to take their places for the night's reading and dictation, but Kerian dismissed them. Gilthas did not protest.

When the Speaker's tent was empty but for the two of them, his brave posture collapsed. He leaned heavily on his wife's arm for the short walk from camp chair to sleeping pallet.

Soon he was settled, sitting up beneath a pile of blankets and rugs that would have suffocated Kerian, and he asked her to refill his cup of medicine. As he sipped it, grimacing mightily (for it was exceedingly bitter), she broached a subject she knew he would not like.

"I can fetch the holy lady. I can convince her to come."

"I can't spare you."

His comment held more of petulance than truth. She reminded him there was no overt threat that Hamaramis or Taranath couldn't handle just as well in her stead. Her presence would confer no special advantage to the hunt for food. But having Sa'ida on their side might make all the difference in the world.

Elir-Sana was not only the goddess of plenty, she was also the deity of healing, the Khurish aspect of the goddess known to the Qualinesti as Quenesti Pah. Sa'ida was her highest representative in Khur, a favored daughter of long standing. The priestess had saved Khuri-Khan from plague after the death of Malys and ministered to the reprobate Sahim during years of intrigue, power plays, and poison plots. If anyone could heal the dying Speaker of the Sun and Stars, Sa'ida could.

Personal concerns would never carry the most weight with Gilthas, so Kerian said only, "Even if she cannot defeat the army of ghosts and floating lights, her counsel will be invaluable."

"Khur is dangerous. Khuri-Khan doubly so," he said stubbornly.

He'd been shivering during their exchange. Shuddering more violently, he abruptly fell back onto his pallet as if his body simply refused to support him any longer. He tried to sit up again, but his trembling arms weren't strong enough to lift him.

She dropped to her knees by his side. "Gil!"

"I'm so tired." Closing his eyes, he whispered, "And I'm afraid, Keri-li. If you go away, I fear I will not be here when you get back."

He had never before admitted fear, nor the severity of his illness. She felt tears come to her eyes. She took him in her arms with heartbreaking care; one hand guided his head to rest on her shoulder, and the other smoothed the hair from his face.

"You put up such a front," she murmured, her tears falling unchecked. "Why didn't you tell me you were so gravely ill?"

"I can't admit it too often. It's bad for my morale." He chuckled weakly.

"You need to rest—"

He turned his face to the warm hollow of her throat. The inane words of comfort died on her lips.

"I will do what I must for my people—even die, if I must," he said. "But I can't do it without you. I lost Planchet. I can't—"

The agonized confession choked off abruptly. He pushed a little away from her. She watched him gather his strength, drawing it around himself like a threadbare robe.

She regarded his shivering form for a few seconds then asked, "Do you trust me, Gil?" A wordless nod was his answer. "We cannot live in this valley unless its enmity to animal life is overcome. We don't have the resources to overcome it. Lady Sa'ida is our best hope. I can go to Khuri-Khan and return in a day and a half. Give me your permission to go."

"You're always storming off somewhere. The missions are always vital. You don't value your life enough, Keri-li. When you rode out of Khurinost to face the nomads, I thought you were going to die."

That had been her goal at the time, although he didn't know it. She'd overcome that bit of madness.

"Now you want to go away again." He sighed, eyelids drooping. "I'm in no condition to stop you."

She rested a hand on his cheek. "You are my sovereign. You can stop me with a single word."

Light sparkled briefly in his eyes. "If only I could find that word." The eyelids came down, and the spark was gone. "You may go."

DESTINY

Sleep stole him away. Kerian remained beside his pallet a long time. Several times his breathing went so shallow that she thought it had ceased, but her hand on his chest still felt the slow beat of his heart.

"I am your wife," she said, although she knew he couldn't hear. "And I will return."

*   *   *   *   *

Two riders picked their way through the debris of the nomad camp. The man wore brown trews and boots, and his leather jerkin concealed a mail shirt. His sword he wore openly. His dark hair had grown long and was grizzled at the sides. The woman was fifteen years younger. She wore her hair in a single black braid that reached the middle of her back. Her outfit was much like his but black instead of brown. A crossbow of unusual design rested across the pommel of her saddle.

Breetan Everride, Knight of the Lily, and Sergeant Jeralund had traveled a very long way to reach this point. They had come from Qualinesti by foot, by ship, and by horse, pursuing a legend in the making. Their quarry was the stranger who had emerged from the depths of the forest in the former elf kingdom. He had incited a rebellion against the bandit lord Samuval with startling success. Although he was covered from head to toe by a rough robe, gloves, and a mask that bared only his eyes, they had reason to believe him to be an elf of good birth.

When the efforts of that troublemaker came to the attention of the Knights of Neraka, Breetan was sent to collar him. Her command was wiped out but for a handful of men, including the sergeant, who had dubbed the rebel leader "Scarecrow" for his ragged appearance. Breetan's superiors had given her one chance to redeem her failure: find the Scarecrow and kill him before the revolt he had inspired consumed all of Qualinesti.

She thought she had him cornered in the Skywall Peaks south of Qualinesti, but he managed to flee on a griffon before she could put a crossbow bolt through his heart. From one of the elves he'd left behind, Breetan learned the Scarecrow's destination. The answer was puzzling. The griffon riders were making for a spot in far northern Khur near the mountain range that separated the desert kingdom from Neraka.

Puzzled or not, Breetan had maintained the chase. Her burning haste cost them a fine saddle horse apiece just getting to the west shore of the New Sea. A fast ship carried them to the far end of the sea. On land again, skirting the western edge of the Khurish desert, Breetan found nomads who loved Nerakan money more than they hated Nerakan Knights. They told her the exiled elves had left behind their sanctuary at Khuri-Khan, crossed the desert, and taken refuge in a valley known variously as Alya-Alash, Valley of the Blue Sands, and the Silent Vale. Whatever its name, it was located in the northernmost reaches of Khur—the very place the Scarecrow and his griffon riders were reputedly going. So there she and the sergeant were, many days and many miles later.

Nothing usable remained in the wreckage of the camp. What hadn't burned had been scavenged. Dead horses lay where they had fallen. Broken arrows and shattered swords littered the stony ground. A rubble stone wall ran straight as an arrow across the pass, yet it could not have been intended as a defensive work. It was incomplete. The ruined nomad camp lay between one unfinished end and the west side of the pass. No wonder the Khurs had been routed. Well-trained elf cavalry sweeping around the head-high wall would put any barbarians to flight.

Jeralund dismounted and picked through the debris for clues. Breetan rode slowly along the wall. The dead had been removed, but the amount of blood spilled on the stones gave ample evidence of the fight that had raged. Near the end of the wall, she reined up. The desert stretched out ahead, shimmering in the pitiless sun. It was only midmorning, and already she felt as though she'd been hung over a fire to roast. She pulled her wide-brimmed Khurish grass hat lower on her head and pulled away the loosely woven linen strip that protected her eyes from the sun's glare. The sand around her was churned with the prints of horses and human feet, but the trail leading away was obvious. Defeated at the valley mouth, the nomads had fled into the realm they knew, the great wasteland.

Her appraisal was interrupted by an odd sound: the clatter of stone on stone. It came from somewhere to her right. She rode toward the sound, gripping the wrist of the crossbow with her free hand.

In a hollow behind a sandy knoll, she found a lone man. He knelt amid scattered stones, piling rocks onto a new cairn. By its size and length, Breetan knew it for a grave. Alert for ambush, she gave in to her curiosity and urged her horse down the sand drift. She circled around so when she halted, the sun was behind her.

"Greetings," she said. "What happened here?"

He glanced up from under his wide-brimmed hat then resumed stacking stones. "One of many pointless battles," he replied. "This is the grave of the last to fall."

"A kinsman?"

"My clan, my tribe. The Weyadan."

The intricacies of Khurish relations did not interest Breetan. She asked the Khur whether he'd seen any elves.

"Who wants to know, Neraka?"

Apparently her accent was clear enough, even if her garb was that of a western rover.

"I am Breetan Everride, Knight of the Lily. I seek a *laddad* wanted for crimes committed against my Order."

"Your law means nothing here." Two more rocks thunked into place. "This is a land of hard edges, where right and wrong are always clear—even if men and women choose not to see them."

Breetan drew a purse from her belt and tossed it at his feet. The rattle of coins within was unmistakable. "Perhaps steel will encourage a change in your philosophy. The *laddads* are in the valley, yes?"

"Whether one or one hundred, it is only *laddad*."

He went back to work on the grave, and Breetan gave up on amiable persuasion. She leveled her crossbow at his right thigh. "Whether whole or lame, you will answer me, Khur," she said, mocking his elaborate manner of speech.

He pushed himself to his feet and doffed his hat. His eyes were grey. None of the nomads she'd encountered thus far had such odd, pale eyes.

"The *laddad* went into the valley twenty days ago," he said.

Jeralund appeared atop the dune. He gestured for the young knight to join him. Breetan lowered the heavy repeating bow. From all she knew, the Khurs always had been willing friends of Neraka. And they had little love for the elves.

"Work hard, old man," she said. "And keep the purse. You earned it."

She cantered up the long slope and disappeared over the crest.

Wapah shook his head. He'd learned long ago not to bandy words with fools or killers. Still less should one waste wisdom on killers who were also fools. He put his hat back on and resumed piling stones on Adala's grave. When his hand, seeking a stone, touched the purse instead, he picked it up. The velvet bag was heavy. He dropped it into a hollow between two rocks, and covered it with more stones.

After saying the proper prayers, begging Torghan to accept the soul of Adala Fahim, he was done and a great emptiness chilled his soul. He had thought balance would be restored when the *laddad* found their valley. Adala's death, unwelcome though it was, also had redressed the hard edge of justice. The arrival of the *nemosh* (the "over-the-mountain people") threatened to upset the balance again. Trouble would continue unless the *laddad* were very watchful.

Wapah felt no guilt for misleading the *nemosh* woman. Many *laddad* had gone into the valley, just as he had said. Of course, some had come out again, so where her quarry might be, only Those on High could know.

A final glance at the cairn and Wapah turned away. His horse, waiting in a nearby hollow, came when he whistled.

He put the mountains at his back. He wanted to see the ocean. For four nights, he had dreamt about walking on the beach with the ceaseless waves lapping at his feet. Such recurring dreams were sent by Those on High, and the message of that one was clear. He would not return to the desert, but would abide by the ocean till the end of his days. The sea would wash his bones. His soul would dwell evermore among the righteous.

A mile away Jeralund and Breetan rode into the narrow pass, eyeing the peaks rearing up on either side. It was, as Jeralund pointed out, an excellent place for an ambush. He wondered why the elves weren't defending it.

"They don't expect anyone to follow them in here," she said. "Khurish nomads are superstitious savages, and our armies are far away."

Nonetheless, it offended both soldiers' tactical sense to ride openly into territory held by an enemy. Jeralund was a soldier of wide experience. He said they should hug the eastern side of the pass. They'd be in shadow in the morning and could travel during the coolest part of the day. They would watch the line of sunlight advance, and when their position was about to be exposed, they could rest and await sunset before resuming their trek.

Breetan found his reasoning sound. They rode to the eastern side of the pass. When the terrain grew rough, they dismounted and led their horses along a track barely wide enough for a goat. No sooner had they gained the first prominence than a squadron of cavalry came trotting down the pass. The Nerakans pulled their horses behind the cover of a large boulder and watched the patrol go by. Jeralund counted forty mounted elves.

He whispered, "Those aren't foresters or town elves, lady."

Breetan's assumption was proved incorrect. Gilthas, the exiled elf king, had fled with more than civilian refugees. The pass was patrolled.

"It doesn't matter," she said, blithely dismissing the elf cavalry. "If the Scarecrow were in a crystal tower in Silvanost, I'd still get him!"

The sergeant made no reply. A dozen times on their journey, she would have been lost without him to set her straight. Breetan Everride was brave and tenacious, but far too arrogant and inflexible for her own good.

The mounted elves divided into three groups, each riding off in a different direction. When the rumble of hooves faded, the Nerakans moved out again. Jeralund judged they had about three hours before sunlight hit them. By then they would be two thousand feet higher up, and well inside the wall of mountains that guarded Inath-Wakenti.

9

Kerian reckoned the flight to Khuri-Khan would take about ten hours. Departing Inath-Wakenti an hour or two after sunrise would put her in the Khurish capital after dark, which would be advantageous to her stealthy mission. Her leaving was not meant to be a secret, but neither did she announce it. Hamaramis knew and Taranath was told just before she left. The Speaker's many councilors were not informed.

Gilthas would not be seeing her off. He'd passed a restless night, only consenting to swallow a sleeping draft when he realized his anxiety was keeping Kerian awake and hovering nearby. Afterward he slept deeply. The draft was a mild one, but Truthanar said all the Speaker's energy was engaged in fighting the disease inside him. He had none to spare to turn over or even dream.

After assembling her scant baggage for the trip, she conferred with Truthanar. He met her outside the Speaker's tent.

"I will make all possible speed," she said. "You must keep the Speaker with us until I return."

"Of course, lady. The human priestess is a skilled healer, I hear."

His tone carried more than a hint of wounded pride. He

had worked tirelessly to help Gilthas, and Kerian had no wish to shame him. Many were the nights he'd sat awake by his patient, trying to ease Gilthas's suffering. He had few medicines or common comforts at his disposal, and little expertise fighting an ordinarily human disease such as consumption. Yet he had persisted with art and courage, as befit a member of his ancient fraternity.

"Do not feel slighted," she said. "No one could have served the Speaker better. He has asked me to bring the holy lady to counter the curse hanging over Inath-Wakenti, not to replace you as his physician. But if she can—"

"Lady, if she can make the Speaker well again, I shall be the first to bless her efforts." It was a difficult admission for a proud Silvanesti.

"Keep him well, Truthanar. Tie him to his pallet if you must, but keep him well until I return."

Taking leave of him, Kerian went outside the elves' hastily erected barricade to the open ground where Eagle Eye awaited her. She secured her few bags to his saddle. Her baggage comprised an assortment of weapons, a tiny hoard of gold and steel to smooth the way in Khuri-Khan, and a little food for Eagle Eye. Hamaramis had urged her to take rations for herself, but she refused. With food so scarce, she would eat in Khuri-Khan.

The sound of pounding hooves announced the arrival of Taranath and Hamaramis. They dismounted a short distance away, and Taranath jogged up to the waiting Lioness. Old Hamaramis approached more slowly.

"Commander, I . . ." Taranath began. His voice trailed away, and he looked distinctly uncomfortable. The veteran warrior, formerly a commander in the Qualinesti royal guard, had been her second-in-command in Khur for the past five years. They had not always agreed—the Lioness had little use for fawning favor-seekers—but they were comrades, united by service to their Speaker, bound together by the terrors and triumphs of many battlefields.

Kerian held out her hand. Taranath clasped it warmly in both his own.

Hamaramis's farewell was gruff and brief. Then he added, "I've been thinking we should build a temporary citadel—a place where we could take shelter if things go badly. Barricades between the standing stones are hardly adequate."

"What would we build it of?" Taranath wanted to know.

"There's plenty of stone lying about. We can put it to good use."

Kerian mounted. "Good idea. Remember to stay off the circular platform. There's no telling how far that thing throws voices. Till we meet again!"

She tapped Eagle Eye's flanks with her heels. The griffon spread his broad wings and, with two mighty bounds, took off. Before she could turn his head to Khuri-Khan, a high-pitched cry captured Kerian's attention.

Kanan had taken flight from the far side of the camp. The riderless griffon arrowed straight for Eagle Eye.

"No, no!" Kerian shouted. "Go back!"

The young beast paid her no heed but did take notice of Eagle Eye's more forceful comment. The Royal griffon screeched twice. Kanan's answering chirrup sounded quite forlorn. Head drooping, Kanan descended to the camp.

Kerian urged Eagle Eye higher. She spared a last glance over her shoulder. The camp buzzed with activity, but all was still around the Speaker's tent. Truthanar was making certain the Speaker's repose was undisturbed.

Aloft, the air was cold. Kerian had brought a heavy cloak for the journey. She pulled its hood up over her head. Her golden hair, which she'd hacked off during her stay in occupied Qualinesti, had grown out but still didn't cover her neck. She was grateful for the cloak's deep hood.

The southern mountains, lowest of those encircling Inath-Wakenti, were her first goal. The three snow-capped peaks that marked the entrance to the valley were in fact ranged along the sides of the pass, two to the east and one westward, so she wouldn't be required to skirt their broad slopes. Morning sun glared off the western peak and colored the mountainside in golden light.

The stark landscape below, untouched as yet by the sun, unrolled with a monotonous sameness: widely scattered cedars, pines, and rock maples; vines engulfing boulders and filling ravines; flows of light-colored gravel from the slate hillsides. The standing stones appeared gray in the shade cast by the high mountains and looked even more enigmatic than usual with the last ribbons of mist curling around them. Kerian longed to see a deer or wild goat on a lonesome crag. An eagle or vulture sailing on the rising air would have been a revelation.

She saw none of those things, of course. The Silent Vale was as devoid of animal life as ever, but eyes of a different sort were watching her in flight.

Faeterus and Favaronas had reached Mount Rakaris late the night before and begun the long climb to the Stair of Distant Vision. They had covered no more than a third of the distance before a dozen will-o'-the-wisps materialized higher up the mountainside and drifted down toward them. Despite Faeterus's forceful commands, the lights closed in, forcing him to fend them off individually. Favaronas clung as close to the sorcerer as he dared, hoping he would be protected. Faeterus dispatched each light with arcane gestures and shouted words that were unintelligible to the archivist. These efforts reduced each will-o'-the-wisp to a smoky dot, gray-white in the darkness, which finally disintegrated and vanished.

By the time the last fireball was banished, the sorcerer was reeling with exhaustion. He collapsed but retained enough presence of mind to put Favaronas to sleep with a wave of his hand before succumbing. The two passed the night where they dropped.

The griffon's cry as it rose from the camp roused Favaronas and sent a thrill of hope through him. A griffon meant the Speaker and his loyal warriors could not be far away. He hauled himself to his knees, shading his eyes against the bright sky, searching for the source. But Faeterus had awoken as well. A stoppered gourd was slung over his shoulder on a thong. The sorcerer pulled it forward, uncorked it, and thrust its long neck deep into his hood. He drank, swallowing more and more quickly as the liquid revived him. The smell coming from the gourd made Favaronas's stomach clench. He knew that reek. The sorcerer was drinking blood and not very fresh blood either.

Revived, Faeterus stood and looked skyward. He intoned a long sentence. A prickling sensation washed over Favaronas's face. It felt as if every hair on his head were standing on end. The sorcerer pressed his palms together. When he drew them apart again, a bar of white-hot fire stretched between them. Favaronas threw himself face-down on the ground, arms covering his head. A heartbeat later a crack of thunder assaulted his ears, and a blast of heat scorched his back.

Kerian didn't see the lightning bolt coming, but Eagle Eye did. His huge raptor eyes could see in almost a complete circle for miles around him. The flash was far away but bright and strong, rising from the ground on the griffon's left rear quarter. Without waiting for guidance from his rider, he banked steeply away. Taken by surprise, Kerian pitched sideways. She threw her arms around the griffon's neck and protested loudly.

Her complaints died when the sizzling bolt of lightning roared past them. Kerian yelled as the metal gear she wore burned through her clothes. Eagle Eye continued his maneuver, making a complete roll and coming right side up. Although griffon and rider had turned away just in time, Kerian's eyes were dazzled by the blast. When she'd blinked her vision clear again, she saw Eagle Eye's left wingtip was singed, and fur on his left hindquarter was scorched and smoking.

"Well done!" she praised him, patting his feathered neck.

Uncharacteristically, the griffon flinched as she patted him.

Leaning far forward, she waved her hand before his left eye. Eagle Eye didn't blink or give any other sign he'd noticed the motion, and she realized the lightning bolt had blinded him on that side. His right eye was undamaged.

Gently, she directed him into a steep climb. High, icy cloud fingers streaked the new day, but otherwise the sky was clear, unbroken blue. None of the previous griffon patrols had encountered random lightning bolts over Inath-Wakenti. That didn't rule it out as some strange manifestation of the valley's hostile magic, but it was more likely someone down there was hurling thunderbolts.

Eagle Eye climbed cautiously, flying in flat, wide curves quite unlike his usual bold style. Kerian looked past the beating wings, seeking the possible source of the deadly lightning. All she saw were rocky crags spinning past.

When they had doubled their height, she set the griffon's head south again. It was pointless to remain, inviting a second attack. Nothing more happened, but she didn't stop looking over her shoulder until they reached the far side of the mountains. Stalwart Eagle Eye flew steadily on, head tilted to compensate for the loss of sight on his left side. Kerian forced herself to remain calm so her emotions wouldn't agitate the griffon. But inside she was boiling mad. Someone would pay for this treacherous attack.

Had she but known, she was in no danger from a second assault. Favaronas cautiously lifted his face from the dirt and saw Faeterus sprawled nearby. The effort of hurling the single bolt had flattened the sorcerer. The breast of his robe moved, the shallow breathing his only sign of life.

Favaronas himself was unharmed, though his head reeled from proximity to so great a discharge of energy. The ground sloped steeply there. Getting to his feet required caution lest dizziness send him cartwheeling down the mountain. Still, he made all the haste he could. His chance to escape had come.

Whispering voices brought him whirling back toward Faeterus's unconscious form. Four spirits had appeared higher up the slope. Apparitions did not manifest in Faeterus's presence while he was awake (and he never slept). With him laid out cold, that protection was gone.

The specters regarded Favaronas with unblinking eyes. Their faces were unnervingly devoid of expression. At first they floated in midair, their bodies fading away a foot above the ground, but as the apparitions solidified, their lower legs appeared. It was impossible to tell whether they were male or female. All had hollow, emaciated faces framed by long, tangled hair.

Favaronas stared in fear, falling back and sending pebbles skittering down the mountainside.

"Don't hurt me!" he rasped, holding out both hands to ward off the ghosts. "I mean no harm. He forced me to come!"

One of the four spirits took a step forward and spoke—at least, the words seemed to come from it.

He still lives. We cannot claim him yet.

"Is he one of you?" The spirit answered in the affirmative. "Who is he?"

Look on him yourself.

More whispers filled the air. Other spirits, less solid-seeming than the first four, had materialized above and below Favaronas. His escape blocked, the scholar gave in to curiosity and crept toward his immobile captor. The knotted rag that held the hood tight around Faeterus's throat finally yielded to his trembling fingers. He pushed the hood back and beheld the sorcerer's face for the first time.

Faeterus had implied that he was thousands of years old. Favaronas might have disbelieved his claim to such an improbably great age, but the sorcerer's hands were those of a very old elf, with prominent knuckles, so he expected to see a wrinkled, withered visage. Not so—the sorcerer's face was smooth and unlined. His forehead was high, his chin sharp, and his ears rose to the expected points. His white-gold hair was short and curly. He looked like an elf in the very prime of life.

Or did he? When Favaronas looked more closely, certain oddities became apparent. The ears were not quite right; their peaked tips were too long and pointed not up, but back. The nose, though long and narrow as was common among Silvanesti, was dark around the nostrils. What Favaronas had taken for pale skin was in fact a coat of downy hair. No true elf grew such hair on his face. It wasn't even a beard such as humans or half-elves wore. Fine, white hair covered Faeterus's entire face from forehead to chin. To confirm the evidence of his eyes, Favaronas put out a tentative finger and touched the sorcerer's cheek. The hair was soft as velvet.

Stranger still, a shadow under Faeterus's nose proved to be a faint scar, as though his upper lip had been split in two and sewn back together.

Favaronas backed away, still staring. The more he looked, the weirder the face appeared. The sorcerer's tongue, just visible between his parted lips, was dark as sandal leather. His eyebrows seemed to meet over his nose, or was that a trick of the light? Taken as a whole, the face seemed somehow animal-like, as though a beast had tried to transform into an elf and failed.

Only he had the power to leave, and he abandoned us.

"Why do you walk the mortal plane? What do you want?"

To be away from this place. You can help. Go to the place of Distant Vision.

With a sinking heart, Favaronas glanced up the slope beyond the four specters. Distance and the steep angle reduced the Stair of Distant Vision to nothing more than a horizontal band of dark rock. "Why? What's up there?"

The crowd of apparitions vanished, leaving only the first four. They wavered like an image seen through desert heat. Desperate, Favaronas repeated his questions.

Seize the key before the door opens.

The four blinked out of existence.

"Wait! What does that mean?" he cried, the scholar in him already puzzling over the words.

"It means," said a voice behind him, "time is short."

Icy defeat lanced through Favaronas as he turned on leaden feet. Faeterus was himself again, sitting up. The sorcerer put a hand to his head, realized his concealing hood was askew, and cast a venomous glance at his captive.

"Well, elf spawn, what have you learned?" His voice was weak, but hatred dripped from every syllable.

"Nothing, master. The more I hear, the less I know!" the archivist gabbled.

Faeterus held out a hand, silently commanding assistance to stand. As soon as Favaronas drew near, the sorcerer grabbed his arm and jerked him off his feet. Favaronas quickly realized he could not move away. Faeterus's hand, clamped onto Favaronas's bare arm, adhered as though grafted flesh to flesh.

"Now we are one. Until my work is done, you'll not wander off or talk to the dead again."

The archivist stared down at the unnatural bond, nausea rising in his throat. Their skin appeared to have melded together—did the link go deeper? Did the tainted blood of the creature called Faeterus mingle with his own?

He turned away from the hooded head that was much too close and struggled to his feet, awkwardly pulling the sorcerer upright as well. Favaronas took a step, then another, dragging the weakened sorcerer along with him. The ledge seemed as distant as the sun. Faeterus's sustenance might be vile, but at least he'd eaten recently. Favaronas could scarcely remember the last food or water he'd had.

As he climbed, outwardly resigned, he distracted himself from his misery by concentrating on the many questions raised by the encounter with the spirits. What exactly did they want—to put off their half-life and rest or to rejoin the mortal plane? How did having their betrayer here help them? And what was the key he was supposed to seize?

Favaronas was widely read, but he was no sage. All he

knew of magic were the few basic concepts he'd gleaned from ancient manuscripts. The stone scrolls might contain further clues. The conundrum was how to peruse them without alerting Faeterus to his intentions.

His thoughts continued to wander until Faeterus rapped him sharply on the head. "Watch your step!" the sorcerer snapped.

Unthinkingly, Favaronas had taken them to the crumbling lip of a ravine. Two steps more and they would have tumbled a hundred yards onto toothy rocks. For a moment he considered rushing forward and taking those steps.

"Don't assume what kills you will harm me," Faeterus said. "Remember the griffon rider's fate."

Favaronas resumed the climb. So Faeterus thought the griffon rider dead? The scholar knew better. After the mage had fallen unconscious, Favaronas had seen the griffon circle briefly then continue south. No sooner had the thought entered his mind than he drove it away, filling his head with stanzas of a particularly dull Silvanesti epic poem. Joined as they were, the sorcerer might be able to read his thoughts. No sense giving away everything.

* * * * *

Pairs of mounted elves rode through the stunted elms and oaks littering the eastern half of the valley. They were part of the Speaker's widened patrols, desperately seeking sustenance in the barren landscape. So far they'd found nothing. Even the trees were sterile. Oaks bore no acorns; elms did not scatter winged seeds before the breeze. Given the strange climate of Inath-Wakenti, it was impossible to tell how old the trees might be. An eight-foot tree might be a young sapling or a mature plant a thousand years old, forever arrested by the weird influence of Inath-Wakenti.

The morning was still fresh when flankers came riding in to Taranath to announce a strange find. Not food or a water source, but an elf.

DESTINY

"Alive?" Taranath asked.

"It seems so. But you'd better come see. It would be easier than explaining!"

The two riders led him nearly a mile south of his original line of march, to a clearing containing three tall standing stones. Four more mounted warriors were drawn up around one of the monoliths, the elves staring at something on the ground. Taranath started to dismount. The soldiers advised him not to draw too near. After admonishing them not to be so fearful, the general got down and pushed between two horses. He beheld the strangest of many strange sights he'd witnessed of late.

A mound of blue-green sand was humped up by the base of the white monolith. Buried up to his mouth in it was an elf with tanned skin and dark hair cut short. His eyes were closed as if in death, but his nostrils flared ever so slightly. He was breathing.

Even more remarkable, the dirt mound was covered by live bats. Taranath could hardly believe his eyes—living creatures in Inath-Wakenti! The bats reacted not at all to the approach of elves. They were clustered so thickly, their wings completely hid the surface of the mound. The seated elf was encased from toes to lips. The bats covered only the portion illuminated by the rising sun. As he stared, another bat flew squeaking by his head and landed near the bottom edge of the living mass. The newcomer spread its wings and positioned itself just where the line of sunlight was starting to creep downward on the entombed elf's torso.

"Careful, sir," said one of the warriors, breaking the stunned silence. "The sand is alive."

Something skittered over the surface of Taranath's boots, and he looked down. Streams of turquoise-colored dirt were flowing over his feet like water. With an oath, he shook free and stepped back. Fortunately, the creeping sand didn't extend more than a few feet from the trapped elf.

The unknown elf was a Kagonesti, Taranath thought. From

the look of him, he had dwelled among humans. If they didn't free him soon, the sand would bury him completely. The presence of the bats was as inexplicable as the rest, but they must give way if the fellow was to be dug out.

He set the warriors to work. For foraging, they carried gear such as short-handled spades and vials for sampling any water they might find. Two riders got down and tried to drive the bats away by shouting and waving their spades. The bats chittered and squeaked, but stayed put. Only when Taranath probed among them with his saber did they take flight. As soon as they were gone, the sand they'd been shading ceased roiling and hardened with an audible creak. Wherever the sun touched it, the flowing soil went rigid as stone. The imprisoned elf groaned very weakly. The solidifying sand was squeezing the breath out of him.

"Break him out!" Taranath cried. "Hurry!"

The hardened sand was like glass—very hard but ultimately brittle. As they hacked at it with spades, the elves were cut by flying shards, but they kept at it. The flock of bats circled just above their heads, making a terrific din. Soon the elves had the hardened sand cleared away from the Kagonesti's torso. His chest expanded with a great, shuddering breath. Immediately, the bats dispersed. They were gone from sight in seconds.

The warriors turned their attention to the glass encasing his legs. When they had freed his legs, two seized his arms, heaving him upward. The spell that had animated the soil was broken. The blue-green dirt lay quiet beneath their feet. To be safe, they carried the stranger a few yards away. Taranath splashed water on his ashen face.

The Kagonesti came to with a vengeance. Jerking free of the hands supporting him, he rolled away and was on his feet in a heartbeat. Elves are a dexterous and nimble race, but the Kagonesti's quick recovery and terrific reflexes startled them all.

He didn't reach for a weapon, only seated a pair of tinted

spectacles on his nose. Peering at them through the yellow lenses, he said, "You're not ghosts!"

Taranath folded his arms. "No, my friend, but you nearly were."

10

H er dreams were filled with sky.

A strong breeze sang in her ears and played over her bare arms and legs. It was both pleasant and shockingly chilly. She walked along a narrow marble causeway surrounded on all sides by open blue sky. Neither end of the path was visible; the marble simply blended into the sky before and behind. On each side stone monuments reared up, each shaped vaguely like an elf. She amused herself by affixing identities to the amorphous blocks: Alhana, delicately slim, strong as steel; Samar, standing so rigidly at attention his back might snap from the strain; Porthios, lean and angular, turned slightly away from the causeway. The flowing figure with arms spread wide could only be Gilthas. But what of the gnomish shape at his side? As she studied it, the rounded block moved, the egg-shaped head turning. It had her face.

Kerian flinched awake. She was still surrounded by sky, but this was no dream. A chilly wind chapped her face. She was leaning forward against Eagle Eye's neck. Below her dangling fingers the wastes of Khur whirled by, their pale brown color gone gray by starlight. After sunset, she had cinched her saddle straps tight and allowed herself to nap. Eagle Eye snorted and bobbed his head, sensing his rider was finally awake.

Clouds billowed around them, blue-white in the starlight.

Khur did not often play host to clouds, and she immediately wondered if Eagle Eye had veered off course. A check of the stars and the horizons fore and aft confirmed it. Without her watchful hand on the reins, the strong headwind had pushed Eagle Eye slightly eastward, toward the Gulf of Khur, the horn-shaped bay west of the Khurman Sea. Proximity to the sea accounted for the clouds.

Khuri-Khan lay near the west coast of the gulf. She loosened the reins from the saddle horn and turned Eagle Eye southwest. The griffon's wings rose and fell in a smooth rhythm. His eye injury had slowed him only a short while. He had adapted quickly, although he continued to favor the injured side. They should reach Khuri-Khan well before midnight. Kerian was pleased. She had no time for diplomacy or combat. She intended to swoop into the night-cloaked city, locate Sa'ida, and wing away again as quickly as possible.

The coast appeared, lines of breakers foaming white under Eagle Eye's left wing. Kerian followed the coastline until the sprawling, man-made mountain that was Khuri-Khan appeared. Gilthas had admired the city's alien beauty: the squat towers and encircling wall built of native stone, strengthened by a facing of tiles glazed in creamy shades or bold, primary hues. He had a taste for the exotic, even though he lived austerely. For her part, Kerian found the city gaudy, and crude. The fine Temple of Elir-Sana was the only structure she found at all attractive.

Her eye was drawn to the dark scar that marred the land west of the city—all that remained of Khurinost, the tent city that had been the elves' home for five years. Burned and thoroughly looted, the makeshift city was only a field of ashes standing out starkly against the pallid desert sand.

She steered Eagle Eye down into the lowest layer of clouds. By remaining within their shelter for as long as possible, she would be hidden from observers on the ground and from the sentinels on the city wall. When griffon and rider emerged from the cloud, they were well inside the city's outer defenses.

The Khuri yl Nor, the "Palace of the Setting Sun," frowned

down on the city from atop its artificial hill. Markets, known as *souks,* were paved with terra cotta, making them stand out as pink patches against the dark sea of rooftops. All were empty at this hour. The Temple of Elir-Sana glowed like a pearl on a bed of coals. Its dome, thirty-five feet in diameter and made of a single piece of pale blue marble, was truly a marvel. None knew how the long-ago Khurs had managed to polish marble to the thickness of a fingernail then raise the delicate dome into place. Farther down the ceremonial street were the other temples of Khur's gods. The spiky towers of the sanctuary of the fierce desert deity Torghan had been built to resemble upthrust spears. Sacred flames billowed from tower tops at several temples, but there were no people in sight on any of them.

At her command Eagle Eye spread his broad wings and glided in, silent as an owl descending on its prey. The low wall surrounding the Temple of Elir-Sana was decorated by brass chimes. The griffon's rear claws missed the chimes by inches, and he alighted inside the temple enclosure. Kerian dismounted, a little dizzied by the sudden cessation of motion after such a long flight. She bent her knees and stretched her back, glad to be on firm ground again. She led Eagle Eye to a small pool of water in the courtyard and let him drink. When he finished, she fed him from the store of food in one saddlebag. He caught the skinned rabbit she tossed and bolted it down in a single gulp. She threw him another, the last. It was a lot of meat for the hungry elves in Inath-Wakenti to sacrifice, but it wouldn't do for her mission to fail because of Eagle Eye's hunger. Her own pangs she ignored.

Tying the griffon to a stanchion by the pool, Kerian headed for the temple's entrance. As she did so, she heard a scuffling sound and saw movement on one of the buildings outside the wall. Something darted away into the shadows. She stared at the spot a long time. Was it an errant husband, a prowling cat, or a spy? Unable to discern more, Kerian hurried on.

The temple door had no knocker. Instead, a brass chime,

gracefully formed, hung on the doorpost. Kerian struck it once. The sound was lovely but faint. As she started to ring it again, the door swung inward. A young acolyte stood in the opening, a fat candle in one hand.

"Who calls at such an ill-fated hour?" she grumbled.

"I have urgent business with your holy mistress. Let me in please."

"The holy lady sees no one at this hour—"

Firmly but gently, Kerian put a hand on the acolyte's chest and pushed her back through the deep portal.

"I've no time for manners. The lives of thousands are at stake." Not to mention the life of her brave, misguided husband. "I would not intrude otherwise. Rouse your mistress now, or I'll do it myself."

The girl eyed her silently. The Lioness had left her heavy cloak on Eagle Eye's saddle. The acolyte saw a leather-clad, tattooed Kagonesti whose short, burnished gold hair stood out in disarray around a face chapped brick-red by the wind. Despite the weariness that darkened Kerian's brown eyes, the girl also saw the resolve in them.

"Very well." The acolyte departed, her white *geb* swirling around her ankles as she strode swiftly away.

Alone Kerian attempted to contain her impatience. Elir-Sana might be a Khurish deity, but Kerian would not defile her house by stomping to and fro, much as she might itch to do just that. Another short, thick candle provided the only light in the antechamber. The air was as Kerian remembered it—clean and fresh, unlike the incense-heavy atmosphere in most shrines—and she could hear the gentle rise and fall of singing, muffled by the thick stone walls. However late the hour, the Temple of Elir-Sana was not sleeping.

When she rested a hand on her sword hilt, another thought occurred to her: weapons were not allowed here. She unbuckled her sword belt and wrapped the belt around the scabbard. Her desire not to offend ended there. She tucked the sword beneath one arm. She wouldn't surrender her blade.

A quartet of priestesses arrived. Older than the girl who had answered the door, each carried a wooden staff as thick as her wrist. Although they leaned on the staffs like walking sticks, Kerian had no doubt the priestesses had been summoned in case the temple required protection. The four didn't speak, apparently content to stand and stare at her forever. She could barely restrain herself. If Sa'ida didn't come soon, she would search the stone pile room by room.

"It is not lawful to bring weapons within."

Kerian recognized the low, slightly husky voice immediately. Sa'ida, high priestess of Elir-Sana, appeared out of the gloom, trailed by the young doorkeeper. The stern look on the holy lady's face changed to astonishment as she took in the sight of her late-night visitor.

"Lady Kerianseray?" she exclaimed. "Venea said an armed elf had entered. She didn't say it was you!"

"I didn't introduce myself."

Sa'ida dismissed the somber foursome of priestesses. "You surprise me. I never thought to see you again."

"I surprise myself, Holy Mistress." Kerian's gaze flickered toward the acolyte. Taking the hint, Sa'ida sent Venea away.

The last time priestess and Kagonesti warrior had met, the elves still dwelled in the tent settlement by the city wall. Gilthas had sent Kerian to learn what Sa'ida, leader of the esteemed priestesses of Elir-Sana, might know of the purportedly mythical Valley of the Blue Sands. In the temple courtyard, Kerian and her escort, Hytanthas Ambrodel, had been set upon by murderous Khurs. Sa'ida herself had identified the men as followers of the Torghan sect; she recognized the crimson condor tattoo that marked the would-be killers.

When they were alone, Kerian drew a deep breath and said, "I am sorry to intrude, but I come on a vital mission for my people—to ask you to come back with me to the Valley of the Blue Sands."

To forestall the expected argument, she gave the priestess

no time to reply, but immediately launched into an explanation of the valley's haunted nature, how no animals lived there, and that thousands of elves were slowly starving.

"It is a sad tale, but I'm no farmer," Sa'ida said when Kerian finally paused.

"You're a healer, and many are sick. You have the power of holy magic. You can banish the spirits that keep animal life from flourishing." Kerian swallowed, fighting her emotions. "And you can save the Speaker of the Sun and Stars."

She described Gilthas's illness and explained the elf healers could do little more than slow the human malady's inevitable victory. Since the Speaker had most likely contracted the disease in Khurinost, didn't Sa'ida have an obligation to help him overcome it?

The priestess shook her head. "You have my sympathy, lady, and as always, my admiration for your courage, but I cannot leave the sacred confines of the temple for so long. I took an oath to dwell here."

"You need be gone only a few days." Kerian told her that Eagle Eye was waiting in the courtyard. He would take them both there and back in short order.

"Fly!" Sa'ida paled. "Human beings are not meant to fly!"

The Lioness dryly agreed with her. "But in this case you must make an exception. I beg of you."

"I cannot," Sa'ida said, not without regret. "I am sorry."

Kerian persisted, employing all the arguments she had marshaled during the long flight south and repeatedly assuring the priestess that Eagle Eye would bring her back to the temple as soon as possible. But Sa'ida would not be budged. The situation in Khuri-Khan was volatile, she explained. Even if her vows did not preclude it, her absence at such a time might be used as an opening for greater violence. She sympathized with the elves' predicament. She offered to prepare special nostrums for the Speaker, but she would not go with the Lioness to the forbidden valley.

Their exchange was interrupted by a commotion outside. The chime had rung, and the acolyte, Venea, went to open the door. As it swung inward, a gout of flame came with it, setting the girl's gown on fire. She fell screaming to the floor. Hands spread wide, Sa'ida shouted a brief spell and the flames died. The priestess called for aid as loud voices sounded outside.

Kerian rushed to close the door but found the opening blocked by a pile of blazing debris. Beyond it, highlighted by the flames, were several figures. They hurled javelins at her, crying, "*Laddad!* Spawn of evil! Give us the foreigner to kill!"

The four guardian priestesses arrived. Together, they and the Lioness shoved the heavy panel closed and secured it. One of guardians panted, "Holy Mistress, those are men! Men in the sacred compound!"

"Not only men," Sa'ida said grimly. "Followers of Torghan!"

She ordered the temple sealed. Kerian expected the women to race about, shutting doors, but they did not. They remained where they were, each woman lifting her clasped hands to her chin. Their lips moved in silent invocation. Distant slams began to echo through the temple. The structure was windowless with only a handful of entrances. The multiple banging sounds meant more was happening than the mere shutting of physical portals.

When the clamor ended, Sa'ida rounded on Kerian. "You brought them here!" she charged.

"Never! My mission is secret!"

"It is secret no longer. The Sons of Torghan must have been watching the goddess's house."

The high priestess spoke in low tones to her followers. The other women departed. Turning to Kerian, Sa'ida said, "Not since the dragon's day has this place been so violated. You must leave at once!"

"Every time I come to this place, I'm set upon by Torghanist fanatics!" Kerian snapped back. Striving for a calmer tone, she added, "Who do you think they fight for, their god or their paymaster?"

DESTINY

The high priestess was concerned for her temple and its inhabitants, but Kerian's point was well taken. Both of them knew Nerakan coin was behind much of the Khurs' supposed religious outrage.

"My apologies, Lady Kerianseray. You are blameless," Sa'ida said. "You must go before they breach the wards we have erected. If they do not find you here they will not dare further outrages against this temple." Given time, clerics of Torghan could overcome the protective spells. So could certain orders of Nerakan Knights.

"Your beast is in the courtyard." Kerian didn't ask how Sa'ida knew that but had no doubt she was correct. "I will drive them back, and you can reach him. Your destiny lies in the Silent Vale, not here. Good luck to you and your people."

Kerian believed a wise warrior made her own luck. If Sa'ida wouldn't come willingly, Kerian would get her by hook or by crook. Once the holy lady was in Inath-Wakenti, once she saw their suffering, she would understand how great was their need and would forgive her rash act. The Lioness drew her sword as Sa'ida turned toward the entrance. She would have to choose her moment carefully.

Kerian counted to three, and Sa'ida threw open the door. A wall of bright blue light surrounded the temple. In the courtyard beyond that protective barrier skulked a gang of masked Khurs armed with clubs and daggers. As the women emerged, the Khurs set up a shout.

"Don't worry," Sa'ida said. "We can pass through the barrier, but they cannot."

No sooner were the words out of her mouth than Kerian grabbed her wrist and dashed through the shimmering blue wall. They were on the other side before Sa'ida could catch her breath.

A Torghanist attacked with a club. Kerian parried high, swept under his upraised arm, and thrust through his chest. A second man stepped in, aiming a dagger at her belly. A heartbeat later, his severed hand, still gripping the knife, lay on the ground. Shocked by their comrades' quick defeat, the Khurs edged back but continued to pace the women as Kerian made for her griffon.

Sa'ida hissed, "You know you cannot force me! Let me go!"

"I'm sorry. In the valley you will see."

The priestess's wrist seemed to turn to smoke. One moment, she was in the Lioness's grip; in the next, she was free. Before she could flee, a Torghanist ran up behind her, dagger raised high. Kerian lunged, knocking the woman out of the dagger's path. Her sword caught the Khur in the throat, but the need to shove Sa'ida out of the way had thrown off her aim. Rather than a killing stroke, she scored a bloody line across his neck. He drove his own weapon's point toward her shoulder.

Her reflexes saved her life, but the dagger pierced her high on the right arm. Kerian aimed a backhanded stroke at her attacker, and the Khur's head went flying from his shoulders.

More than two dozen Torghanists swarmed into the courtyard. Judging by the torches outside the wall, even more were gathered in the street. Their spies must have summoned every loyal Son of Torghan in the city.

Sa'ida sat on the ground, dazed. Blood trickled from a cut on her forehead. Kerian hauled her to her feet.

"If you want to keep living, come with me!"

The woman was too dazed to answer. Kerian whistled shrilly and was answered by a loud and even more piercing cry. Following the sound, the Lioness spotted Eagle Eye on the far side of the courtyard. The four foolish Torghanists who had tried to subdue him lay torn and bleeding at his feet. Catching sight of Kerian, he reared and rent the air with another shriek. He came galloping to her, awkward on the ground but too fearsome to be stopped.

He bent his forelegs to allow Kerian to heave Sa'ida aboard.

DESTINY

A weak, "No, no," came from the priestess.

The Torghanists were converging on them. Griffon or no griffon, they knew the penalty for allowing their prey to escape. An arrow flickered past Kerian's nose. She wrapped the reins around her fist as a group of men entered the gate in the wall. They weren't Khurs. They wore western clothes. One was tall and gray-bearded. The others carried crossbows. Nerakans!

The bowmen suddenly turned their faces away, and Sa'ida cried, "Your eyes!"

The warning came too late. A tremendous flash filled the courtyard, and an unseen force slammed into Eagle Eye, knocking him onto his side and spilling his passengers to the pavement. A mass of shouting Torghanists rose up like a black wave and engulfed them. Dazed, blind from the flash, Kerian felt her sword snatched away. A rough burlap sack was dragged down over her head, her hands bound in heavy cords. Blows rained down on the sack, and the fight was over.

* * * * *

Hytanthas lay still, cheek pressed to the cold tunnel floor. A dull boom had awakened him, and he wondered whether it was real or yet another hallucination. Wandering in the tunnels, he had found himself prone to all sorts of imaginings. He'd heard approaching footfalls, the clatter of rocks, whispering voices, even the clang of metal on metal. All proved to be unreal.

For a time he'd kept the light globe burning constantly. Each time it went out, he struck it to rekindle its light, but the resulting glow was weaker and weaker. Inevitably he struck it too hard and the outer shell cracked. Whatever volatile spirit had been held inside escaped, the stream of faintly luminescent purple smoke flitting away down the tunnel. When it was gone, the darkness again closed in.

By then Hytanthas hardly cared. Prowling the endless dark was leaching away his sanity and his resolve. Once he had been hungry and thirsty. Those appetites had dulled. He no longer wondered at his strange inability to see in the dark. Time itself was meaningless. He had no idea how long he'd been down here. Perhaps the exit he sought did not exist. Perhaps he was dead and did not realize it yet. Was that how the apparitions in the valley had come to be? Was he just another of those spirits, doomed to roam the blackness for all eternity?

A second boom sent vibrations through the stone beneath his cheek and blasted away his despair. That was no hallucination! That was real!

He hurried down the passage, seeking the source of the sound. Friend or foe, it didn't matter. He could not remain alone in this terrible place.

The sound of a voice came to his ears. It was speaking his own language! He shouted, "Hello! Hello, can you hear me?"

After a long moment of heart-pounding silence, the single voice replied, "Who said that? Where are you?"

He gave his name and rank. Another interval of silence ensued; then a different voice said, "This is the Speaker. What proof can you give that you are Hytanthas Ambrodel?"

The notion that his sovereign might also be lost in the tunnels did not dampen Hytanthas's relief. He was so glad not to be alone, he nearly wept. He named his father and mother, sketched his service in Qualinesti and Khur, and related how he'd been transported to the tunnels by the lights of Inath-Wakenti and had been awakened by the Lioness's voice.

"Where are you, Great Speaker?" he asked.

"A long way away." The reply came only after a long pause.

Hytanthas didn't believe it. The Speaker must be close since they could converse. "I'm coming to you, sire!" he cried.

He began to run. Every two dozen steps he called out to the Speaker again, assuring Gilthas he was on the way. When he tripped on the loose debris covering the tunnel floor, he picked himself up and went on, never slackening his pace. The Speaker called to him, but he ran wildly, and it wasn't until after his third such fall that he heard the Speaker say, "Take care! I am on the surface, not underground, and I fear I may be miles away from you."

It seemed ridiculous. Hytanthas had heard of mountaineers conversing across wide valleys by using echoes, but surely this was different. He heard no echoes, only the strange delay before the Speaker's answers. Still, he heeded the Speaker's words and slackened his pace, trying to look around and choose his path more carefully.

"Where are you, sire?"

"On a wide stone platform in the center of the valley"— some words were lost—"Where are you?"

Rather plaintively, Hytanthas explained he didn't know exactly where he was but thought himself in one of the tunnels under the valley.

Conversing back and forth, they established that each could hear the other better now than when they'd begun. It seemed Hytanthas might be closing the distance between them. The young warrior began counting paces softly. He'd left five thousand behind when Gilthas spoke again, sounding much closer. In fact, Hytanthas could hear his sovereign's teeth chattering.

"The air above this disk is cold indeed," the Speaker confirmed. "Too cold to be natural."

"How fare the people?" asked Hytanthas, slumping down to rest for a moment.

Holding on, said Gilthas. Food was dwindling fast. Porthios, Alhana, and most of the warriors had departed for Qualinesti, and Lady Kerianseray had flown off to bring back Sa'ida to help ward off the ghosts and will-o'-the-wisps. Hytanthas knew the holy lady. She had aided him and Planchet when they were caught inside Khuri-Khan after the khan's curfew. If not for her intervention, they would have been murdered by bloodthirsty Torghanists.

When the Speaker told him he'd been missing for more than a week, the warrior shook his head in amazement. No wonder he felt wrung out.

The Speaker assured him his griffon was fine, although pining for his rider. The elves had found the vast stone platform at the focal point of the valley. Standing on its center, one could hear things from all over Inath-Wakenti. Gilthas had been experimenting with the effect when he heard Hytanthas calling for help. He asked what the warrior had found in the tunnels.

"Nothing but bones." Hytanthas explained how his discovery of the body of one of Lady Kerianseray's warriors, as well as layer upon layer of desiccated animal bones, had led him to conclude that the animal life captured by the will-o'-the-wisps was transferred into the tunnels to die.

"Take courage, Captain," Gilthas said. "We'll get you out."

Hytanthas jogged onward. After a time he reported, "Sire, I have found a body."

The corpse was that of another elf warrior, although blind as he was Hytanthas couldn't identify him. The dead elf was lying faceup with a dagger buried in his throat. Hytanthas's first fearful thought was of murder, then his hand went to the warrior's scabbard. It was empty. The blade in the elf's throat must be his own.

Haltingly, Hytanthas described what he'd found. The Speaker was shocked the warrior would have given up on finding escape.

"Perhaps he was grievously injured before he was transported to the tunnel?" Gilthas suggested.

Hytanthas's examination of the body revealed only the one wound. But unlike his king, the young captain could understand how the elf might succumb. Without the voice of his sovereign to buoy his spirits, Hytanthas himself might have given in to despair.

He found a crust of bread in the dead elf's belt pouch. It fell to powder in his mouth, but he choked it down anyway. Shifting position, he put his hand down on something hard and sharp. The characteristic shape and feel told him it was a piece of knapped flint. Perhaps the lost warrior had been trying to start a fire and the stone had gotten away from him. Disoriented by the darkness, he'd been unable to locate it and had given up, though the flint lay just a few feet away.

Piling up strips of the dead elf's cloak, Hytanthas struck the flint against the hasp of the dagger. Bright orange sparks showered onto the tinder. He nursed them carefully until they flickered to life. His triumph was quickly tempered by grief. As the feeble light illuminated the features of the dead elf, he recognized Ullian, who had been in the Speaker's service for only a short time. Hytanthas was one of the few who knew of the human blood in his heritage, and Ullian had been a staunch comrade.

The Speaker congratulated him on his acquisition of light. Putting aside his sadness, Hytanthas tore Ullian's cloak into strips then wrapped the strips around the end of his sword to form a torch. The tunnels were a maze, but as long as he could see, he might be able to find a way out. There was nothing he could do for his lost comrades. All he could do was try to survive.

Torchlight brought a fresh revelation. Wall paintings around him leaped and danced in the flickering light. He described the frescoes to the Speaker. Beautiful scenes of gardens and parkland covered both walls. The paintings had been rendered with amazing skill, giving them an unusual feeling of depth. The colors were so fresh, they might have been painted just the day before. The only jarring notes were the portraits of lean, angular-looking elves, rendered life size, interspersed with the peaceful sylvan scenes. The elves glowered balefully at the viewer.

The Speaker theorized the paintings had been done by the people who'd once lived in the valley. The very ones whose spirits still haunted it.

With the aid of his makeshift torch, Hytanthas soon found a crossing tunnel, which branched off to the right. When he reached the intersection, he halted, uncertain which way to go. The tunnels looked identical.

"Are there portraits at the intersection?" the Speaker asked. Hytanthas said there were. "Do they face any particular direction?"

Hytanthas dutifully studied the portraits. Those in his original tunnel looked toward the intersection. Those in the crossing tunnel faced *away* from the intersection. The news excited the Speaker.

"You should take the new tunnel! I believe the paintings face something important, like a way out."

With no better alternative, Hytanthas did as the Speaker suggested. After being so long deprived of company, the young captain felt miraculously refreshed and talked almost nonstop as he walked. The Speaker listened silently, now and then prompting him with questions. Hytanthas reported the thinning of the debris on the floor. Fewer and fewer bits of bone crunched beneath his boots. Then he saw something more interesting to report.

"Sire, the tunnel ahead slopes down. And a white mist swirls near the floor."

His voice had taken on a hollow quality, as though he spoke inside a large, empty room. The Speaker asked about the frescoes. They were gone. Where the tunnel began its downward slope, the frescoes ended.

He was seeking the surface, not a passage to take him farther down. Still, the tunnel might level out and begin to climb. He told the Speaker he would scout ahead. If the passage continued to slope downward after a hundred steps, he would go back.

The tunnel walls were plain gray stone, unadorned by paintings of any sort. The white mist filled the passage from side to side. First curling about Hytanthas's ankles, it deepened as he advanced until it reached to his chest. It was cold and clammy, and remarkably cohesive. He swept a hand through it, and the mist rippled like water rather than flying about like fog. The air grew steadily colder. Hytanthas's garments sagged with damp. Water dripped from his hair down his back. Reaching another branching of paths, he halted. The intersection was very wide, at least twenty feet across. A sense of unease filled Hytanthas. He couldn't see anything untoward, but he sensed danger nearby.

Gilthas urged him to go back, but Hytanthas drew his dagger and moved forward slowly. His caution was well founded. The toe of his left boot suddenly found open air rather than solid rock.

There was a great hole in the floor, nearly as wide as the tunnel. He dropped a bone chip into the hole. His keen ears never heard the chip hit bottom.

As he turned to go, the air around him trembled once then again. A loud boom echoed down the passageway.

The Speaker heard it as well and demanded to know what was happening. A wind had begun to blow, Hytanthas told him. The mist was being drawn down the pit. The pull was strong. It tossed Hytanthas's long hair and dried the dampness from his clothes. When all the mist was gone, the wind ceased.

"I see light in the hole!" Hytanthas exclaimed. Deep within was a pale white glow. It showed him the sides of the shaft were polished smooth and free of embellishment.

When a minute passed with no other occurrences, Hytanthas turned and retraced his steps to the crossing tunnel.

He had no idea what might be in the deep hole, but as he walked, a more pressing question came to his mind. The rush of air suggested the tunnels had been unsealed somewhere. The last time that happened, he had heard the Speaker's voice. Who knew what had been admitted into the tunnels?

11

Caressed by the soft light of ten thousand stars, the stone scrolls softened, opening one by one like exotic flowers. Never before had Favaronas laid them all out at once. A trained librarian never opened books he knew he would not have time to read because even the finest vellum inevitably cracked with use. The scrolls were even more delicate than most, despite their rock-solid appearance. He had no way of knowing how many times the stone could soften, open, and harden again. Overuse might destroy them. But Faeterus wasn't concerned with such niceties. He'd ordered all the cylinders placed where starlight would work its magic on them.

The climb to the Stair had proven too much for them to complete in a day. They were still several hundred yards short of their goal when Favaronas collapsed. As the sorcerer's hand was still joined to Favaronas's arm, Faeterus dropped with him. The archivist's exhaustion was no ploy; he couldn't go a step farther without rest. Food and water would have strengthened him, but Faeterus offered none. He did sever their unnatural bond. As Favaronas slid into sleep, he was grateful for that small blessing.

Awakening after nightfall, Favaronas found the sorcerer's manner much changed. Having rid himself of Sahim-Khan's bounty hunter, destroyed (so he thought) an elf griffon rider, and with the Stair of Distant Vision in reach, Faeterus was more relaxed, even expansive. When he asked Favaronas to read from the scrolls, his voice sounded much less arrogant than usual. Favaronas was emboldened to ask, with all deference, why Faeterus didn't read them himself.

"Their meaning is shielded from my eyes by a very old and potent ward."

Storing away that bit of knowledge, Favaronas knelt to study the scrolls. Faeterus had forbidden a fire—no sense attracting potentially unfriendly attention—but had cast an illumination spell around Favaronas to brighten the air enough to permit reading.

As the archivist feared, the randomly collected cylinders belonged to different chronicles. None was a continuation of any of the others. In addition to the one he'd already sampled, the second contained a record of the original inhabitants' attempts to foil the powers that confined them. It bore the cryptic title *Ten Thousand and One*, and interested Faeterus greatly.

The scroll began in midsentence. The inhabitants of the valley had employed many methods to catch and destroy the lights that patrolled the valley. The lights were referred to variously as "night wardens," "watchers," and "vigilants." Many were caught in nets and other traps, but it made no difference. However many will-o'-the-wisps were caught, the next night saw no shortage. Two of the valley's inhabitants, Stabo and Mexas, engaged in a long debate on their captors' nature. Stabo claimed new lights were created every night, so capturing any was pointless. Mexas countered that their number was fixed, although not all appeared at any one time. If enough could be captured, the total would lessen.

When Favaronas showed a tendency to dwell on the scroll's long-winded recitation of the disagreement between Stabo and Mexas, Faeterus commanded, "Spare me these mediocrities," and Favaronas skipped ahead.

Anyone who entered Inath-Wakenti eventually was taken by the lights, according to the scroll; the inhabitants were immune to them unless they tried to leave. Then it was noticed the animals were disappearing. The beasts were not trying to leave, yet their number steadily diminished. Facing starvation, the prisoners (as Favaronas had begun to think of them) tried tunneling out. They dug miles of passages beneath the blue-green soil, but the lights found them there too.

The scroll ended there. Still curious, Favaronas asked, "Is that how they died?"

"Eventually. They could not live off each other's flesh forever."

Favaronas turned away, aghast at the horror Faeterus revealed so casually. The archivist silently bemoaned his foolishness in returning to this place. He had been safely in the company of Glanthon and his warriors, outside the valley's dreadful influence, and he'd thrown that safety away for the hope of power. If he managed to survive, he would confess his crimes to the Speaker and beg forgiveness. Whatever punishment was meted out, Favaronas would embrace it with joy.

The final scroll had the shortest text of the three—a stanza of verse. When Favaronas began a halting translation, the sorcerer surprised him by quoting the lines in full. Hooded head tilted up toward the starry sky, Faeterus recited.

> *The sun's eye grows dark. No moon loves him.*
> *The stars sleep and answer not the night. Until*
> *The father holds the key in his hand,*
> > *standing before the Door*
> *And reads the Holy Key.*
> *From the Stair of Distant Vision,*
> > *under the sun's black eye*
> *The Door is opened. The Light revealed*
> *Burns all, consumes all, kills all*
> *Unwraps the flower, cracks the egg*
> *Pulls the seed from the ground.*
> *If the Holy Key is broken.*

DESTINY

In Elvish, each line had the same number of syllables, which made it doggerel by the standards of Silvanesti poesy. Favaronas commented on its poor quality.

Faeterus chuckled deep in his throat. "Not good poetry perhaps, but excellent prophecy, elf spawn."

With that, he rose and ordered Favaronas to do likewise. The archivist intended to roll the still-softened scrolls carefully for transport, but as soon as his fingers touched one, it disintegrated. Cracking and popping like sheets of softening ice, each scroll fell into shards that crumbled further and further until only a fine white dust remained. The archivist turned a stricken face to his captor, but Faeterus only shrugged.

"I shouldn't have spoken the words aloud. It matters little now. The play is nearly done."

The illumination spell ended, and Faeterus reached toward Favaronas.

Shying from his touch, Favaronas hurried up the mountainside as quickly as he was able.

The pebbly soil crumbled under their feet, hampering their progress. In firmer patches of ground, Favaronas caught sight of Faeterus's unbroken footprints—broad but short, with only three thick toes. Wedge-shaped impressions at the front of each toe print were made by his clawlike nails. When he'd glimpsed the sorcerer's foot during the trek across the valley, it had sported four toes. Now it had only three. The sorcerer seemed to be losing his elf appearance, perhaps reverting to his natural form, a notion that only fueled his captive's terror. There was no saying what sort of creature Faeterus might truly be.

They reached a level place and Faeterus halted. Favaronas immediately collapsed, determined to rest for however long he was allowed. Looking around, he realized this was no narrow ledge, but a large open space. Other features were difficult to discern. His eyes were so tired, he had trouble focusing in the dark. His silent speculations came to an end when Faeterus spoke.

"The Stair of Distant Vision," the sorcerer declared. "Here begins the end of your race."

* * * * *

Breetan and Jeralund had picked up a promising trail. Two people—elves, from the size and shape of their footprints— were heading east into the high mountains. Wondering why two elves would be out, alone and on foot, so far from their camp, Breetan decided to track them. After a day's stalk, she and the sergeant glimpsed their quarry along an open ridge. One was a middle-aged elf so exhausted he staggered like a drunkard. The other was completely covered by the heavy layers of a hooded, ragged robe.

"The Scarecrow!"

Jeralund agreed with Breetan's whispered evaluation. Who else in this lifeless place would need to burden themselves with such a supremely uncomfortable disguise?

Knight and sergeant stalked their prey with utmost care. The range was too great for her special crossbow, so Breetan forced herself to be patient. Her target would not get away. The Scarecrow must have a good reason for being up there, perhaps heading for a secret rendezvous with other elf rebels.

After nightfall, a pale greenish light brightened their quarry's campsite. Breetan, climbing some ten yards from the sergeant, wondered if it was meant to be a signal, but she could discern no answering gleam from the surrounding peaks, so she resumed the climb.

Less than a minute later, she did notice light, a faint, diffuse glow on the rocks around her. She turned to look behind. A swarm of small, glowing globes was sweeping upslope at considerable speed. Since arriving in the valley, she and Jeralund had seen similar lights in the distance. Breetan thought them lamps carried by patrolling elves, but the lights closing on them belied that theory. Each was a floating fireball, colored green, red, blue, or yellow.

They whizzed overhead, emitting a sizzling sound as they passed. Breetan loaded her crossbow with a hardwood quarrel and raised the sight to her eye. The lights were small but so bright that they were easy to see. She loosed. The black-painted quarrel flew true. A golden light dropped to the ground. She went to retrieve her prize.

The light was much dimmer, and Breetan was certain she'd injured it, whatever it was. When she got close, she realized it wasn't actually lying on the ground, but hovering a few inches above it. Even as she noticed that, the dim light suddenly brightened and leaped off the ground straight at her face. Flinging herself backward, she tumbled down the slope, losing her crossbow and finally fetching up against a gnarled juniper tree. The little globe of golden fire, shining brightly, sailed well overhead.

Jeralund had made no headway against the lights either. He'd drawn his sword when they approached and slashed at them as they dodged and dashed around him. The only result was exhaustion. Sweating despite the coolness of the night air, he lowered his blade and stood panting. Surprisingly, the lights stopped as well. He decided they were reacting to his movements. When he fought, they swarmed. When he stood still, they quieted.

Moving slowly and carefully, he sheathed his sword. A single orange light left the swarm above him and plummeted directly at his face. Jeralund's reaction was immediate and unfortunate. He flung up a hand to ward off the light. When he touched the ball of fire, both it and he vanished in a flash of white. A heartbeat later, a dull boom echoed over the mountainside. The remaining lights winked out.

Breetan disentangled herself from the juniper tree. She found her crossbow, undamaged by the fall, but wasn't so fortunate herself. It felt as though she'd broken a rib. Wincing, she looked up in time to see Jeralund engulfed in light. She stumbled to the place where he'd been, but he had vanished.

The echoes of the boom faded away. Unnatural silence reclaimed the night. Casting a final, fruitless look around, Breetan shouldered her crossbow and resumed the chase.

* * * * *

"Pull! Heave away! Smartly now, smartly!"

Hands cupped around his mouth, Hamaramis shouted encouragement as a hundred elves strained on ropes and levers, trying to upend a giant block of stone. Hamaramis had chosen one of the smaller stones within the elves' camp, but smaller did not mean small. The block was twenty feet high, ten wide, and as much as six feet thick. Affixing hooks to its top had been easy. Shifting the massive block was not.

The Speaker had returned from a long sojourn at the center of the mysterious platform and had ordered Hamaramis to bring down a monolith immediately. The general had wanted to topple a block all along, to strengthen the defensive wall When the Speaker explained why he wanted to move the stone, Hamaramis feared the disease attacking the Speaker's body had begun to affect his mind as well.

"While on the platform I spoke with Hytanthas Ambrodel!"

With the care of one humoring a disordered mind, Hamaramis replied, "With his ghost, sire?"

Gilthas made a dismissive gesture. "He lives, General, but is lost in the maze of tunnels under the valley. I mean to break into them and find him."

The Speaker insisted no one else be told of this. Hamaramis understood the need for secrecy. From what Hytanthas had reported, the other missing elves were most likely dead, but if the news of Hytanthas's survival spread, bereaved family members would mob the scene and impede their efforts. The old general's notion of shoring up their defenses would be a good cover.

Hamaramis called for more hands on the ropes. Onlookers crowded in to take hold wherever there was space. The general sent a volunteer up the stone to make certain all ropes were pulling equally. Behind the block, elves wielded levers made of the valley's twisted trees. They piled dirt under the levers to improve their lifting ability.

"Once more then. Heave!"

The ropes went taut. Elves strained and groaned and

sweated. The block leaned forward a few inches, buckling the turf before it, but no amount of pulling could budge it further. Hamaramis finally called a halt. The elves dropped the ropes and nursed their aching limbs. The old general went to consult with his Speaker.

The unnatural cold atop the circular platform had worsened Gilthas's condition, and the palanquin's original design had been modified. Rather than sitting upright, the Speaker reclined fully, with pillows to prop head and shoulders and a number of mantles and cloaks tucked around him for warmth.

"It's no good, sire," Hamaramis declared. "Eight or ten feet of its length must be buried. We'll never move it this way."

Gilthas shook his head in wonder. The original inhabitants, slight in size and few in number, must have employed magic to erect the thousands of ponderous stone blocks. Unfortunately, magic was in short supply among the new occupants of Inath-Wakenti.

Sunset had come and gone. Hamaramis suggested they call a halt for the night. Gilthas agreed. He dismissed the volunteers and gave permission for the levers to be taken for firewood. Closing his eyes, he lay quiet for a long minute.

"Amazing, isn't it?" he finally murmured.

"What, sire?" Hamaramis asked.

"How empty the valley feels without Lady Kerianseray."

Quieter too, the old general thought, but merely agreed with his king.

As the volunteers streamed away, a few youths removed the ropes still atop the stone. Gilthas, watching their nimble ascent of the stone, sighed with envy and tried to sit up. Hamaramis objected, telling the Speaker he was overtaxing himself. Gilthas held up a silencing hand. Only a very few were allowed to chide him, however well-meaning: his wife was one, Planchet had been another.

Gilthas's attention turned to the turf buckled in front of the stone. He leaned over the side of the palanquin, the better to see, and steadied himself by resting a hand on the block.

The monolith shifted.

The elves atop the block protested, thinking Hamaramis was trying to overthrow it.

"It's not us!" he yelled back, assuming they had somehow upset the stone's equilibrium. "Clear off now!"

With a noise like a great waterfall, the stone continued to lean forward even as the elves scrambled down. Alarmed, the bearers took up the palanquin's poles and carried the Speaker out of harm's way. As soon as his hand left the stone, the movement stopped. The monolith remained where it was, canted halfway to the ground.

Hamaramis stared at his king. "I have an idea, Great Speaker," he said and asked Gilthas to approach and touch the stone again.

Understanding dawned on Gilthas's face. "You think I did that?"

"Please, sire."

It was ludicrous. Gilthas was no iron-arm, endowed with preternatural strength. Of late his lungs were so congested, he could walk barely ten paces without gasping for breath. Feeling foolish, Gilthas had the bearers carry him back to the leaning block, and he pressed a palm against the stone. It shifted immediately. Startled, he snatched his hand away and the movement stopped. He looked from his hand to the stone, unable to believe the evidence of his own eyes. Moving the great monolith had required no more effort than opening one of the well-balanced doors in the palace of Qualinost.

"Get everyone clear," he said hoarsely. Hamaramis and the bearers moved back. He put a hand on the stone and gave a modest shove.

The monolith moved as if weightless.

The twenty-foot-tall block fell heavily onto its face. The base, pulling free of the ground, flung dirt skyward. Shouts of joy erupted all around. Still seated in his palanquin, Gilthas was leaning on the fallen slab, his shoulders and head liberally sprinkled with dirt, his face wearing a very bemused expression.

DESTINY

Where the monolith had stood, there was a deep hole. Hamaramis went to the edge and looked in. The pit was dark, deep, and cool. Fingers of mist coiled around the old general's boots. He wondered aloud whether every standing stone concealed a tunnel opening. One of the Speaker's bearers asked a different question: Why had the inhabitants of Inath-Wakenti used such weighty doors?

Hamaramis's first concern was the defense of the camp. If all the stones could be moved easily with the Speaker's help, they could be used to create a stronger perimeter. On the other hand, it wasn't prudent to open so many holes into the tunnels. There could be dangers below as unfriendly as the ghosts and will-o'-the-wisps above.

"Don't worry, General," Gilthas said quite casually. "When we've finished exploring the tunnel, I'll just put the stone back where it was." The bearers and the general stared at him and he laughed.

Hamaramis summoned warriors to guard the opening. Gilthas told the general he wanted the tunnel explored immediately.

"At night, sire?"

"It's always night down there."

His logic was impeccable. Hamaramis quickly put elves to work erecting a frame so the explorers could be lowered into the hole. Workers skilled in woodworking and rope craft were summoned. Additional torches were lit.

While the work was underway, the Speaker sent for a scribe to map the tunnels. The warrior sent to fetch a volunteer returned alone. The scribes were notably lacking in enthusiasm for the quest.

Hamaramis berated the warrior for failing to carry out the Speaker's command. "I'll bring a scribe, sire—at the end of my sword, if necessary," the old general growled.

Gilthas stopped him. He would not force anyone to face danger. He wished he could enter the tunnel himself. He once had been quite skilled with an ink brush. Of course, such adventures were beyond him at the moment.

He had decided to send only warriors down when a young elf emerged from the camp, running full out. Catching sight of them, the newcomer slowed abruptly. Despite ink-stained fingers and the short haircut of a scribe, the newcomer was very young and female. She bowed quickly to the Speaker, to Hamaramis, and even to Truthanar, just arriving with his helpers.

"Great Speaker, I am Vixona Delambro, apprentice scribe. I come in answer to your summons," she panted.

"You're a child!" Hamaramis exclaimed.

"I've taken the scribes' oath." That meant she was at least eighty, though she looked much younger.

Gilthas asked, "Why do you want to go?"

"To serve you, sire." He regarded her steadily, and she blurted, "And to show those old cranks I'm as good as they!"

He understood. His senior scribes were from a generation that hadn't allowed females into their profession. In Qualinesti the prohibition against females had been rescinded long ago, but few women were motivated to buck the formidable oldsters who guarded the scribal tradition so jealously. Scribes' oaths of discretion, probity, and accuracy were not empty mouthings. The penalties for violating any part of the code were severe and the damage to one's honor even more so. In all his life, Gilthas had known fewer than a dozen female scribes.

Something about Vixona touched Gilthas. Perhaps it was her faint resemblance to Kerian—she was blonde, but had the same heart-shaped face as his wife. More likely it was Kerian's stubbornness Vixona brought to his mind.

"You've got fine mettle, young lady. Don't fail me."

"I won't, Great Speaker. I won't!"

Rather sourly, Hamaramis asked her if she could handle a weapon.

"I fought in the desert against the humans."

So had every elf in the valley. "Do you have any proficiency with weapons?"

She was forced to admit she did not, but the general's obvious disapproval could not quench her enthusiasm.

DESTINY

The exploration party would be led by Hamaramis, and he chose three warriors to accompany him. Each would take two torches, one burning and one in reserve. Lamps would have been better in a tunnel, but all the oil had been requisitioned as food. They would be armed with swords only, no bows. The general tried to press a borrowed blade on Vixona, but she demurred, being already burdened with parchment, inkpot, and brushes. He looked to the Speaker for guidance. Gilthas waved the borrowed blade away. Let her take what she wanted, he said.

As he watched the preparations, Gilthas ate the tiny meal Truthanar had brought. The Silvanesti healer had touched his king deeply. Arriving at the worksite with the usual dose of unpleasant-tasting medicine, he also brought a surprise: a small pot of *kefre*.

Gilthas had developed a liking for the Khurish beverage during the exile outside the desert capital. The healer had found the *kefre*, as well as the white clay pot and tiny matching cup in which it was traditionally drunk, among the Speaker's baggage where they had been carefully packed away by Planchet before the desert crossing. Truthanar had hoped the drink would help awaken his king's vanished appetite.

Cradling the cup in his thin hands, Gilthas inhaled deeply. The pungent aroma of *kefre* enveloped him, even as thoughts of his lost friend and absent wife filled his mind.

The frame slowly rose over the pit.

12

When Kerian regained her senses, she was being dragged down a murky lane, her toes bumping over uneven cobblestones. She had wit enough not to struggle, instead using the opportunity to size up her situation.

Two men had her by the arms. Her empty scabbard flopped against her leg, but she felt her concealed knife still in place, hidden in the small of her back. Her upper arm throbbed where the Torghanist dagger had sliced it. A crude bandage had been tied around the wound, and the bleeding had stopped. Her captors smelled of wood smoke, goats, and sour milk, aromas associated more normally with nomads than city-dwelling Khurs.

The tiniest lift of her head gave her a glimpse forward. A pair of Khurs carried the unconscious Sa'ida. Several other men accompanied them. The Khurs' faces were hidden by scarves and broad-brimmed hats pulled low. The progress of the silent procession could be judged by the sound of slamming shutters and doors that preceded them. The locals had learned to make themselves scarce when the Sons of Torghan were abroad.

She first thought they were bound for the Temple of Torghan, but her surroundings told another tale. This was not Temple Walk, where Khuri-Khan's important sanctuaries were found. Temple Walk was a broad paved avenue. This was a shadowed, mean-looking lane fronted by tall mud-brick houses. The buildings suggested Arembeg, the city's southern district, a maze of tight lanes and alleys unrelieved by squares or *souks*. Arembeg was a good place for cutthroats to hide from the khan's soldiers and his legion of informers.

Her captors halted at a nondescript door in a dead-end alley. One Torghanist lifted his cudgel and rapped a sequence of knocks on the door. The narrow portal opened inward a few inches.

"We have them," the Torghanist said, and a voice from within ordered them to enter.

The room was wide. Furniture was scant. Common Khurish chairs were short and three-legged, with a single pole sticking up as backrest. Sa'ida was set onto one, her hands tied behind her back. One of the Torghanists holding Kerian's arms muttered about ill luck befalling those who mistreated a holy woman.

No such worry affected their handling of Kerian. They did not bother with a chair, but dropped her facedown on the dirt floor. When she hit, she contrived to have her left arm fall limply across her lower back.

"What of the beast?" The voice asked. His accent was foreign to Khur, and his voice was loud in the low-ceilinged room.

"It was too fierce. We didn't have the proper weapons. It killed two of my men and tore up four more. We threw a net over it and left it there."

Kerian silently rejoiced. Eagle Eye was alive.

"Are the implements ready?" asked the leader.

Kerian heard the clink of metal, and a grunted remark that the irons would be hot enough soon. She had no doubt who the "implements" were for and what their purpose would be. From beneath slit eyelids, she watched the Torghanists come and go from a brazier heaped with glowing coals.

"You were right to watch the temple, my lord," said one of the Khurs. "How did you know the *laddad* would return there?"

"I didn't. But I marked Sa'ida for a traitor long ago. It doesn't surprise me the elves would remain in contact with her. She was their ally when they were here. Even now she works to undermine your nation and your gods."

The Khurs' replies told Kerian that any squeamishness they'd felt at capturing the priestess was fading rapidly. One man asked what was to be done with the *laddad* woman. "I doubt we'll get anything out of her," the foreigner said coolly. "Perhaps if she sees what the priestess must endure, she'll be more willing to share what she knows."

The Khurs engaged in ugly speculation about Kerian's own fortitude in the face of pain. Their leering laughter steeled her for action. When enough of them were looking away, she'd show them what fortitude really meant.

The foreigner uttered a sharp reproof. "Why is the elf not tied?" he demanded. The Torghanists laughed off his concern. They'd worked her over well. She wouldn't wake up any time soon.

"Idiots. You have no idea who you're dealing with." He ordered the closest man to bind Kerian's hands and ankles.

The fellow's rag-wrapped sandals advanced toward her. He bent to grasp her slack arm. Using his body to shield the motion, she drew her concealed knife and buried it in the man's chest. He gasped and sagged to his knees. Kerian put the blade in her teeth and catapulted to her hands and knees. She shoved the dying man at the next nearest thug. Before he could react, she was on her feet. The knife flashed. A second Torghanist collapsed onto the first, his throat slashed.

The room's dim lighting kept the men from understanding exactly what she'd done. Not realizing she was armed, they thought she was simply making a desperate attempt to overcome far superior numbers. Only their foreign master was disturbed by her sudden revival. Kerian spotted him for the first time. He was seated at one end of a long table on the far side of the room. A lamp on the table before him illuminated his face. Kerian had never seen him before, but he was easily recognizable as a Nerakan. He was past middle age, bald, with bushy brown eyebrows. His thin cloak did nothing to conceal the armor and bejeweled court sword he wore. All of this she took in with one swift glance before he turned down the lamp's wick.

"Didn't you search her for weapons?" he barked.

The Torghanists hefted their cudgels and closed in. Kerian dropped to a crouch. She slashed a third Khur across the chest. He let go his weapon and staggered back, bleeding heavily. Taking up his cudgel, she fended off a hail of blows and attacked again. A Torghanist cried out as her knife opened his gut, and the rest backed off.

She gave them no time to organize but hurled the cudgel at the light. The Nerakan, thinking the blow was meant for him, jerked back. The hard wood struck the brass lamp, knocking it to the floor. Oil poured out and tiny blue flames danced across the spreading spill.

"Kill her!" the Nerakan bawled. "What are you waiting for? Kill her now!"

The Sons of Torghan tried. They were rough and ready fighters accustomed to street brawls, but they were out of their depth against the Lioness. Eight Khurs had entered the room with her. Minutes after the Nerakan ordered her death, only three still stood. Meantime the burning oil pooled around the leg of the table and ignited it. Dull orange flames flickered, giving the scene a wild, distorted look.

A Khur landed a stunning hit across Kerian's shoulders. She whirled, driving him back with knife thrusts but received a nasty whack on the thigh from another quarter. The Khur who struck the blow got a deep cut across the forearm for his temerity.

The room was filling with smoke. The long table was alight, and flames were spreading to a dusty wall hanging. The Nerakan had fled. Coughing heavily, his Torghanist hirelings who could still move were abandoning the fight as well.

Sa'ida still slumped in her chair, unconscious. Kerian cut her bonds and carried her to the door. It was a perfect place for an ambush, but the Nerakan and the Khurs were gone. Kerian paused at the mouth of the narrow alley.

The street was empty and dark and little wider than the alley in which she stood. The fire was not yet visible out here, but smoke was seeping from beneath the eaves. The second-story dwelling above was abandoned. The roof was gone and the shutterless windows showed sky beyond. No one was going to notice the fire until a neighboring structure caught.

The priestess's weight pulled on her injured arm. She shifted the unconscious woman to her other shoulder. Taking a deep breath, she left the deeper shadows of the alley and hurried away from the house. She prayed she wasn't following in the footsteps of the fleeing Torghanists.

Her chosen route was north, opposite the way she'd been brought. Heading uphill past a line of tightly shuttered houses, her luck held. She paused several times to listen for sounds of pursuit, but other than the sound of a dog barking, the quarter was calm.

The narrow alleys of Arembeg gave way at last to a wider street. Kerian's progress was slow, hampered as she was by the unconscious priestess and her own injuries. She had to halt and catch her breath several times. Each time, she tried to rouse Sa'ida, but the human remained senseless. Kerian wished for a fountain with water to revive the priestess, but Khuri-Khan had few public water sources.

After what seemed an endless hike, she came to a small *souk*. Half a dozen *soukats* were just beginning to set up for the day's market. When they realized the elf woman sought water not for herself but for the unconscious priestess of Elir-Sana, a water bottle was promptly produced. Sa'ida commanded the highest respect, and the *soukats* seemed inclined to think Kerian was to blame for her current state. The Lioness didn't bother enlightening them. For all she knew, some of them were followers of Torghan. She poured water into her cupped hand and applied it to Sa'ida's face, all the while urging the priestess to wake.

DESTINY

Sa'ida's eyelids fluttered and opened. She sat bolt upright exclaiming in shock.

"Calm yourself, Holy Mistress. You are safe." Kerian said, glancing up at the *soukats* ringing them. None wore a particularly kind expression. "Much has happened, and we should not remain here."

Sa'ida offered the water to Kerian. The owner of the bottle was displeased, but when Sa'ida thanked him for his generosity, he did not demand its return. Kerian's throat was dry as the desert. She drank deeply.

When Sa'ida had recovered sufficiently, she blessed the *soukats* in the name of Elir-Sana, and the two women left the little square. From various landmarks, Sa'ida judged them to be more than two miles from the Temple of Elir-Sana.

Kerian began to relate the events that had occurred while Sa'ida was unconscious. She hadn't gotten far in the tale when a clangor of bronze gongs sounded. A column of smoke was rising from the Arembeg district behind them. Its base was painted red by flames. The gongs were summoning able-bodied Khurs to fight the blaze. Kerian urged the priestess to a quicker pace and finished telling of their capture and escape. Sa'ida confirmed what Kerian suspected: there was no Torghanist temple in Arembeg.

The smoke was no longer a single column, but a wide curtain. The fire was spreading. Sa'ida pitied the poor folk who would lose their homes. Kerian was not so forgiving. Those were the same folk who had bolted their doors and done nothing when Torghanists dragged two prisoners, one of them a holy priestess, down their street.

"Our attackers may worship the desert god, but they take their pay from Neraka," Kerian said. She described the bald man she'd seen in the empty house.

"Lord Condortal!" Sa'ida exclaimed.

She identified him as the official emissary of his Order in Khur, holding the rank of ambassador.

Kerian was not surprised. Wherever the Dark Knights

went, subversion and violence followed. She described the pan of branding irons Condortal was preparing for them.

"How dare he!" The priestess's usually calm countenance was flushed with outrage. "When Sahim-Khan learns of this blasphemy, he'll have the foreigner's head!"

"Calm yourself. It's all part of the game. I've had brushes with his kind before."

"Such insults cannot be borne!" Sa'ida insisted.

"Really? Is that the doctrine of your divine healer, or the creed of Torghan?"

Sa'ida halted in mid-diatribe, ashamed. Her steps faltered and she put a hand on the wall of a house to steady herself. She was not a young woman. Her long hair was tangled. Many of the ribbons and tiny bells woven through it had been lost. Her white gown was torn and dirty. When they were thrown from Eagle Eye, she sustained a hard knock, and a sizable bruise darkened her forehead over her left eye.

Recovering her equanimity, she apologized for her outburst and they resumed walking. More calmly, Sa'ida thanked Kerian for saving her.

Kerian asked, "By the way, what was it that knocked us off Eagle Eye and put you out for so long?"

"A powerful spell."

"Condortal didn't look like a spellcaster," Kerian mused. "Do the worshipers of Torghan have magic like that?"

Sa'ida exclaimed, "They do not! There must have been a Nerakan sorcerer at our temple!"

The possibility upset her deeply. She grew more and more agitated at the idea of a foreigner practicing illicit magic in her city. Kerian comforted her with the thought that the Nerakan and his hirelings hadn't been after Sa'ida. They could have struck at the Temple of Elir-Sana any time. They attacked only after seeing Kerian's arrival. Condortal's hirelings probably had orders to seize any elves who showed up in Khuri-Khan.

"It was simply their misfortune that the elf who showed up was you," murmured Sa'ida.

DESTINY

When they reached the Temple of Elir-Sana, Sa'ida was astonished to see the khan's armored horsemen drawn up in the avenue. They surrounded the blue-domed temple like a wall of glittering steel. Kerian was all for slipping away unseen, but Sa'ida had had enough skulking. Dirty, exhausted, and injured, the priestess stormed into the square. Fearing more treachery, the elf woman followed reluctantly in her wake.

"Marak Mali, is that you? What's going on here?" Sa'ida demanded.

The commander of the troop, a handsome young man with an elegant mustache, looked past the line of horsemen. Shock bloomed on his face.

"Holy Lady, you are well! Bless the goddess!"

Reassured Sa'ida was indeed whole, he explained that he and his men had been sent by the khan to guard the temple from further attacks. The activities of the night had not gone unnoticed. Unlike the cowed folk of Arembeg, those living near the temple had not turned a blind eye. They ran to alert the city garrison. Sahim-Khan ordered a company of his elite horsemen to protect the ancient shrine and crush the Torghanists if they dared show their faces.

"The old rogue did well!"

Captain Mali chose to ignore the priestess's disrespectful remark. His gaze fell upon Kerian, standing nearby, and he asked the holy lady who she was.

Kerian would have given her name, but Sa'ida replied quickly, "A courier from the khan of the *laddad*. She came to see me."

Mali nodded. He'd known a *laddad* was about after seeing the griffon tethered in the temple courtyard. As loyal men of Khur, he and his soldiers had not desecrated the temple enclosure with their presence.

"It is irregular to entertain foreign emissaries without the Khan's approval, holy one," he commented cautiously.

"I wasn't expecting her, was I?" the priestess replied tartly.

"And before I could do more than greet her, the house of the goddess was invaded by mad Torghanists! They dragged us into the Arembeg district, but we managed to escape."

He glanced southward at the smoke blackening the predawn sky. "So I see, beloved of the goddess."

Sa'ida thanked him for his efforts and began to move away. "I must prepare myself," she explained. "I trust you'll be here all day?"

"We remain till the Great Khan recalls us." Brows lifting, he asked, "Prepare yourself for what, holy one?"

"I have decided to go on a journey."

The Lioness was elated, but allowed nothing to show on her face. It would not do for a mere courier to shout triumphantly. Instead, she emulated the priestess's dignified exit, following Sa'ida between lines of horsemen to the gate. The priestess carefully closed the gate behind them.

Sa'ida had taken only a few steps when the temple doors opened. Priestesses and acolytes streamed out, many of the latter in tears. They surrounded Sa'ida, loudly proclaiming their relief, praising the goddess for her safe return, and lamenting her bruised and battered state. With some effort, Sa'ida restored order. One acolyte was sent to bring ointments and clean bandages for the Lioness's injured arm. The others were dismissed to their duties.

Once the youngsters were within the temple and out of earshot, Sa'ida addressed the priestesses. "Thanks to the goddess's mercy—and the wits of Sosirah here—I am restored to you. I am going with Sosirah to minister to the khan of the *laddad*. Prepare my baggage for a journey of ten days, and include the instruments for a great healing."

Bewildered but obedient, the priestesses departed. Kerian and Sa'ida followed them inside while Sa'ida dressed her injured arm. Kerian asked her about her change of heart.

"There is an old saying: 'The enemy of my enemy is my friend.' The Dark Order and its Torghanist minions have grown too bold. Sahim-Khan will strike back at them, but it is time I do something myself."

"And helping us may divert the Nerakans from Khur."

"True, but"—Sa'ida's brown eyes regarded her steadily—"your Speaker has a great soul. There aren't enough like him in the world. He should be saved."

Perhaps it was the fatigue of the long journey or the sudden release of tension after the brawl with the Torghanist fanatics, but Kerian's relief was so strong she felt tears pricking her eyes. She threw her arms around the woman's neck and hugged her hard.

"Ah, lady, remember who we are," the priestess said but patted Kerian's shoulder kindly.

Stepping back, Kerian cleared her throat and assumed her sternest demeanor. "What did you call me out there—Sosirah?"

A smile graced the priestess's lips. "It means 'Lioness' in our language."

Dawn came, the perpetually cloudless sky above Khuri-Khan brightening from cobalt to azure with a swiftness that still surprised Kerian. While Sa'ida met with the elder priestess who would mind temple affairs in her absence, Kerian went to see to Eagle Eye. He was sleeping in a far corner of the court-yard, still weighted down by a heavy fishing net. Sensing her approach, he awoke. She spoke soothingly to keep him from struggling against the net and injuring himself. As soon as he was free, he stretched his limbs, filled his great chest with air, and gave vent to a full-throated screech. Many of the soldiers on guard outside the wall found themselves unceremoniously tossed to the ground as their horses bucked and reared. Kerian smothered a laugh.

Aside from superficial scrapes and his still-blind left eye, Eagle Eye seemed in fine shape. She led him to the same small pool from which he'd drunk on their arrival. While he quenched his thirst, four acolytes came out of the temple. They carried baskets and a brass tray.

"Food for you and the beast," said the eldest girl. "Ointment for the creature's eye."

Kerian made to take the baskets of Eagle Eye's provender, but the acolytes bypassed her. Unafraid, the girls set the baskets directly before the griffon. He watched them with fierce head held high then snapped up the pieces of meat, bolting each in a series of prodigious gulps.

Kerian ate more decorously, though not by much. She was devouring her third peach (Khuri-Khan was famous for its golden peaches) when one of the acolytes approached the griffon on his blind side. She held a jar of unguent. Kerian warned her not to get too close. The acolyte opened the jar of unguent and began to sing.

The Khurish tune was a simple one, a children's song about an injured little girl having a wound dressed. To Kerian's astonishment, Eagle Eye allowed the girl to anoint his injury. He even lowered his feathered head so she could better reach his eye.

"I've never seen him allow a human so close before," Kerian said.

"All creatures know pain," the girl replied. "And all creatures understand kindness."

By the time the sun cleared the intervening buildings and set the temple's blue dome ablaze, Sa'ida was ready. The entire college of Elir-Sana turned out to see her off. Kerian had worried she would try to take too much heavy baggage, but those fears proved unfounded. The holy mistress carried only two modest-sized cloth bags.

Kerian fixed the pillion pad to the rear of the saddle and buckled a spare strap to the harness. After securing the woman's bags, she cupped her hands as a toehold for the priestess.

"I'm not so infirm," Sa'ida said, frowning.

"Humor me, Holy Mistress. I'd rather you not sustain a broken leg even before we go."

The priestess obliged, putting her foot in Kerian's hands and letting the elf woman hoist her up. Eagle Eye turned his supple neck to regard the new passenger. Her face paled a bit at his close, steady regard, but she did not recoil, only bade him a polite good morning and thanked him for carrying her upon his back. Blinking, he turned to look at Kerian, and she was hard-pressed not to spoil Sa'ida's dignified greeting by laughing.

Once Sa'ida was buckled securely in place, Kerian swung herself into the saddle and took hold of the reins. She addressed the throng of anxious women.

"I swear to you all, I will guard Holy Mistress Sa'ida with my life and return her to you safely."

"Peace and good health!" Sa'ida said, and the women called their farewells.

Because of the added weight, Eagle Eye required an extra step to get them airborne. Sa'ida held Kerian tightly around the waist as they climbed skyward, but when the griffon leveled off, she relaxed.

"How long to the Valley of the Blue Sands?" she shouted into the wind.

"We should reach it a few hours before midnight," Kerian shouted back.

Wary of another magical attack, Kerian did not have Eagle Eye circle for height as usual. She put him into a steepish climb, due north out of Khuri-Khan. Sa'ida was looking down, staring at the receding ground. Concerned, Kerian asked if she was all right. The priestess lifted a beaming face.

"This is wonderful!"

From the air the city appeared strangely flat, Sa'ida thought, like an image drawn by a skilled mapmaker. To the south, smoke still stained the Arembeg quarter, but she could see no flames. The fire must have been brought under control. She was still concerned for those injured or displaced by the fire, but the fault for that misery lay squarely with Lord Condortal. Her attention was drawn to the palace, glittering like topaz atop its hill. She wondered whether Sahim-Khan had slept well the previous night.

When he received the letter she'd dispatched to him that morning, she was sure his rest would be troubled for some time to come.

*   *   *   *   *

The frame was in place. A windlass turned by eight elves was set up on firmer ground a short distance away from the pit. The windlass controlled the rope that would lower the explorers into the hole and would raise them up again. A bronze hook dangled at the end of the rope. Hamaramis would descend first. He was adjusting the rope harness around himself. A company of dismounted warriors stood nearby in case of trouble.

Vixona was seated on the edge of the toppled monolith, keeping out of the way until she was summoned. Her attention strayed toward the far-off trees. The usual crowd of silent spirits had gathered to stare at the intruders in their domain.

"I must be getting used to ghosts. They don't seem so frightening today," she commented.

"Then walk out there and greet them," Hamaramis said, fastening the bronze hook onto his harness.

Vixona sniffed. Like the scribes, the general seemed to resent her. The scribes she could understand. They disliked revealing the secrets of their male-dominated craft to a female. General Hamaramis's resentment she could not fathom. She wasn't usurping any of his rights or privileges, only exercising her own hard-won skills.

"Are you ready?" asked Gilthas. Hamaramis nodded and walked to the hole, the heavy rope dragging behind.

The windlass creaked around. Hamaramis went up, his feet dangling over the black opening. He took a firmer grip on his torch and nodded.

"Lower away!"

Vixona had left her perch. One arm wrapped around the frame for support, she leaned over to watch the general's descent. The rope was marked in ten-yard increments with dabs of white paint. He descended three marks, thirty yards, then the rope went slack.

"He's at the bottom!" she called.

Hamaramis jerked on the rope to signal he was out of the harness. It was hauled up, and each of the three warriors made the descent. Vixona was the last to go.

"Good luck," the Speaker said, smiling.

Shyly, she thanked him. It seemed odd to her that it was he who offered kindness. The Speaker was the patron of all scribes, but he didn't seem to resent her a bit. Perhaps, having the Lioness as a wife, he was accustomed to competent females.

Since she needed her hands free for writing and drawing, she carried no torch. The blind drop through inky darkness was not pleasant. The creaking noises the rope made as it twisted her slowly around only added to the eerie feeling. She looked down between her feet. Moving lights meant the warriors already were exploring the tunnel with their torches. She hoped someone would be waiting for her when she reached bottom.

Her feet touched a hard surface, but before she had time to stiffen her knees, she lay sprawled on her back. Quickly she got out of the harness and tugged on the rope with both hands to let those above know she'd arrived.

A flaming brand approached. It lit the face of General Hamaramis. "Are you all right?"

She stood, wincing from her hard landing. "Fine, thank you."

He pulled the harness aside and left it on the floor still attached to the hook. She studied her surroundings.

They were in a circular chamber with a single tunnel leading away. Vixona noted that the tunnel bore due west.

"How do you know its direction?" Hamaramis asked.

She explained that the hoist frame had been raised with its four supporting poles aligned with the cardinal directions. The distance marks had been daubed on the rope's south side. During her descent, the rope had made six complete twists. From the position of the paint marks now, the tunnel must lead due west.

"You noticed all that?"

She blinked, surprised by his surprise. "It's my calling to notice," she said simply.

A shout from within the tunnel had Hamaramis drawing his sword and running for the mouth of the passage. "Stay behind me," he warned. Vixona assured him she had no desire to be first.

They caught up with the three warriors thirty-five yards along. Vixona estimated the distance aloud, in part to distract herself from her pounding heart.

The warriors stood at a crossing tunnel (which ran northeast-southwest, according to Vixona). They had seen a single figure dart across the opening as they approached. Wanting to give chase, they'd thought better of it and had raised an alarm.

"Well done," said Hamaramis. "Chasing an unknown is too risky. It could be a phantom."

During this exchange Vixona had been scribbling rapidly. She pulled Hamaramis's torch closer to her page so she could see what she was writing. The flame wavered and crackled. There was a draft, and it came not from the shaft where they'd entered, but from the crossing tunnel.

"What do you make of the pictures?" she asked breathlessly.

Before he could embarrass himself by saying "what pictures?" Hamaramis saw them. The walls were covered with murals painted in delicate hues. The wall before them depicted a host of elf warriors on griffons and horses.

"It's Balif," Vixona said. The warriors, intent on searching the darkness for signs of trouble, didn't heed her, but Hamaramis prompted her to continue. "This painting shows Balif leading the armies of Silvanos Goldeneye on the Field of Hyberya."

She didn't ask whether he knew the details of the story, but simply launched on an explanation. Some clans in the western provinces of Silvanesti had refused to acknowledge Silvanos as their overlord. Small companies of warriors were sent to enforce the Speaker's will, but one by one they were ambushed and destroyed. Speaker Silvanos sent Lord Balif with the royal army to subdue the rebels. Balif swept the troublemakers away. In a forest clearing called Hyberya, the recalcitrant western elves pledged fealty to the Speaker of the Stars. The battle was one of Balif's greatest triumphs.

Obviously later generations had forgotten it. Hamaramis was frankly astonished. "You mean elf fought elf?"

She nodded. "Hundreds died. As a result, the western forest was divided into military districts, each with its own garrison. The society of Brown Hoods, believed by the Speaker to have been behind the rebellion, was ruthlessly suppressed."

"Brown Hoods?"

"A league of rural clerics and wild magicians. The most famous Brown Hood was Vedvedsica."

By now, all the warriors were listening. They regarded the young scribe with new respect.

"How do you know all this?" Hamaramis asked.

"I'm a scribe. I read."

The draft grew stronger, forcing the warriors to shield their torches with their bodies. Hamaramis considered their next move. The southwest leg of the crossing tunnel would take them beneath the woodland and away from their camp. Northeast led directly to the circular stone platform. Hamaramis thought it likely that if the tunnel system had a hub, it would be found under the huge platform, the valley's dominant feature.

They headed northeast, with the breeze at their backs, walking in single file. Hamaramis led, followed by two warriors, then Vixona, and finally the last warrior. Vixona kept count of her paces, measuring the length of the tunnel as they traveled. They'd gone about a mile when the wind abruptly grew stronger. One warrior, caught with too light a grip on his torch, found it snatched from his hand. The burning brand bounced ahead of them for quite a distance, sending out sparks with each impact. It finally came to rest against the wall. By its light they saw a figure struggling on the floor.

"Help!" The plea was in the Common tongue, flavored by a human accent. "Help me, please!"

The man was clinging to the edge of a wide pit. Only his head and arms were visible. The elves ran to him, and two warriors dragged him to safety.

He was a human of middle years, dark haired, and dressed in brown leather. When the warriors saw his scabbard and knife, they drew their own weapons.

"Who are you?" Hamaramis demanded.

"My name is Jeralund. I'm a hunter—"

"How did you get here? There are no humans in Inath-Wakenti."

"I chased a stag through a narrow ravine in the mountains and emerged in the valley. It wasn't on my map. Last night, before I could get out, some sort of floating fireball touched me. Next thing I know, I'm in these caves."

One of the warriors relieved Jeralund of his weapons. Hamaramis eyed the human's sword with suspicion. It was a war blade. "Are you a soldier?"

"I have been." So had most of the able-bodied folk on the continent.

A further search produced a pouch of coins, new ones. Steel coins usually turned brown after a month or two in circulation. His were still bright and free of rust. They were also Nerakan.

"I'm afraid you must consider yourself our prisoner, at least for now," Hamaramis said. The man protested, but Hamaramis cut him off. "It's for the Speaker to decide what's to become of you."

Vixona, who had moved away from the interrogation for a peek into the pit, called for the general to take a look. The pit was extraordinarily deep. She doubted there was enough rope in the valley to plumb its depths. But that wasn't what interested her.

"Take the torches away and look down," she said. A warrior took their lit torches and moved a short distance away. In the ensuing darkness, a faint, bluish aura could be seen far, far down in the pit.

DESTINY

"And listen," Vixona said.

From the deep shaft came a slow, regular thud. It sounded very much like the rhythm of a beating heart.

13

Showers of rain trailed across Inath-Wakenti like filmy curtains. From the elves' camp in the center of the valley, the entire panorama of clouds and clear sky, sunlight and rain, was laid out like a magnificent mural. Gray clouds advanced rapidly across the heavens, bursts of rain alternating with shafts of sunlight that reached down with golden fingers to caress the ancient white monoliths.

Gilthas stared at the beautiful vista and saw none of it. He was sitting alone in his palanquin at the edge of the great stone disk, recruiting his strength. The explorers he'd sent into the tunnel were overdue. Repeated shouts into the pit had evinced no response. There was no shortage of volunteers ready to go down after the explorers, but Gilthas forbade it. He wouldn't risk more lives.

Even more bitter was Kerian's absence. She had a habit of overcoming long odds, but a trip alone to Khuri-Khan to spirit away the Khurs' most holy priestess might be more than even the Lioness could handle. He intended to use the platform's power to call to his wife and the missing explorers, as he had spoken with Hytanthas before. None of them knew the scope of the valley's strange influence. If Gilthas could shift a gigantic monolith with one hand, perhaps he could send his words beyond the valley's confines to wherever his wife might be. It was the only thing he could think to do for her.

The shaft of sunlight that briefly illuminated the platform was swallowed up by a new squall. The golden light seemed to race across the white granite, trailing rain in its wake. The palanquin had a canvas shade to keep off sun and rain. Gilthas found the sound of the rain pattering on the canvas surprisingly soothing.

He had need of such small comforts. Other problems had worsened. Food supplies continued to dwindle. He authorized more foraging parties, but they returned with frustratingly little sustenance. A few bushels of herbs, some dandelion greens, and a smattering of wild mushrooms would not sustain a nation. For the first time, he questioned his decision to bring his people to Inath-Wakenti. He wondered whether he had made a disastrous choice. Perilous as their existence in Khurinost had been, there they faced enemies they could see and fight. In the valley the foe was a situation, exacerbated by an army of silent phantoms. The elves had paid a high price to get here. Many had died during the march across the desert, and those who survived heat and nomad attacks found death still stalking them, death by starvation.

Could he have chosen another path? Kerian had never wavered in championing her dream of retaking their homelands. Yet Gilthas knew without any doubt that that was beyond their power, at least for the moment. Her secondary plan, to seize Khuri-Khan and hold it as a citadel, was completely outlandish and would have resulted in slaughter and suffering on a terrifying scale. Their one and only advantage—the sanctuary they'd purchased from the khan—would have been lost. Every hand would have turned against them.

The rain fell harder. He shouldn't delay any longer. He stood too quickly. His legs nearly betrayed him, but he bore down hard on his staff and did not fall. Droplets of rain fell on his face. He ignored them and approached the platform. The granite was more finely grained and purely white than any he'd seen before.

Fifteen inches showed above ground. More lay buried. Gilthas should've been able to leap onto the slab in one easy bound. Instead, he struggled as though scaling a mountain.

When he finally succeeded, he was gasping. The rain soaked his hair, streamed over his eyes, and ran off his chin. Rather than a hindrance, the rain was pleasant, almost warm, which was odd since it came from the lofty mountains. Its effect was unexpected. It acted like a tonic, giving his thoughts new clarity, his body new strength of purpose. He pushed forward, making for the center of the huge circular monument.

The tip of his staff slipped on the wet granite, and he went sprawling. He skinned the knuckles of his left hand and got a nasty knock on the jaw. Undeterred, he got himself back onto his feet. Rain rinsed the blood away.

When he reached the exact center of the platform, an odd thing happened. The rain continued to pour down on him and splash onto the stone, but it made no noise. It was weird to observe the fall of rain yet hear no sound of it at all. Curious, he clapped his hands together. They made no sound either. He drove the butt of his staff into the granite. Nothing.

The unnatural silence allowed other sounds to come forth. These grew louder as he concentrated. They were the voices of his people in camp. By facing slightly left or right he could make the voices louder or softer. He shifted an inch here, an inch there, until the voices were gone, then drew a breath and spoke the name closest to his heart.

"Kerian."

His ravaged lungs permitted no loud cry. He spoke in a normal tone. In the noiseless void, his voice rang like a high, clear bell. "Kerian, this is Gil. I pray you can hear me. I'm waiting for you. Don't give up!"

Water dripped from his face as he lowered his head to gather his composure. When he could trust his voice again, he called to the lost explorers. "Hamaramis, this is the Speaker. Come back if you can. We need you. Everyone is needed. Come back."

DESTINY

A beam of sunlight swept across the stone disk. It passed over him like a seashore beacon.

"Come home, everyone. I need you. I need you all."

With that his store of strength was done. His knees buckled, and he collapsed onto the rain-washed stone.

* * * * *

Hunched low over Eagle Eye's neck, Kerian shook her head. "Do you hear that?"

"Hear what?" Sa'ida asked.

"That buzzing sound."

Sa'ida did not. She suggested Kerian's ears were congested from flying. Her own had popped painfully several times as Eagle Eye climbed higher in the sky.

"It sounds like music or a voice."

"None could reach us up here, could they?"

That was true enough, ordinarily. But Kerian recalled how far her voice had carried when she stood on the huge stone platform in the center of Inath-Wakenti. She described the great disk to Sa'ida and explained how it brought voices to her ears from a great distance and likewise projected her own voice over several miles. Perhaps what she'd heard was another such distant call.

If so, Sa'ida reasoned, then why hadn't she heard it too?

They had no answers, and Kerian felt a growing sense of urgency. Beneath them the untamed desert flowed by. The view was unutterably dull to the Lioness and her impatience rendered the endless vista even more unbearable.

For her part Sa'ida never tired of the view. The blank sands were broken now and then by a narrow circle of green grown up around a well or spring. Nomads in sand-colored *gebs* looked skyward when the shadow of the griffon flashed across them. Even at this height, elf and human felt their cold hostility. The nomad children were not so unfriendly. They raced madly below the passing griffon, obviously thrilled to behold such a rare sight. Pointing, jumping up and down, the children waved at the soaring flyers.

Once they plunged into a bank of clouds, a very unusual occurrence over the desert. Warm mist flowed around them. A dark shape loomed out of the murk on their right. Kerian immediately turned Eagle Eye away, banking sharply left.

"What—?" Sa'ida swallowed her question as the dark shape grew more distinct. Long and gray, it resembled a ship's slender hull, bare of masts or sails. Glass portholes dotted its curved side. Lights gleamed within. White steam billowed from a pipe at its stern. The steam was feeding the cloud, thickening it. Mist closed in behind the machine, and as silently as it had appeared, the strange device was gone.

Astonishment kept them silent for a time. Kerian shook her head, saying, "Must be the work of gnomes. I've heard they build strange things."

Sa'ida had heard the stories too, but the device seemed so elegant and purposeful, she could hardly credit it as a creation of that erratic race.

They burst abruptly into sunshine. Kerian exclaimed in surprise. During their passage through the cloud, they had inexplicably climbed several thousand feet. The air temperature had fallen greatly. Their garments, dampened by the heavy mist, chilled them to the bone.

"Look!" Kerian pointed ahead. The blue-gray slopes of the Khalkist Mountains filled the view from horizon to horizon, most prominent among them, the three snow-capped peaks that marked the entrance to the valley. Sa'ida was amazed. She'd never been more than twenty miles from Khuri-Khan in her life. She asked Kerian about the white stain atop the three peaks.

"Is it truly snow?" Kerian nodded. After a pause, Sa'ida asked, "What is snow?"

The Lioness cast about for a reply. She'd never tried to define snow for someone to whom it was utterly alien.

"It's like rain, only much colder. When the air is cold enough, rain hardens and becomes snow."

DESTINY

The priestess was as delighted as a child by this discovery. Although a wise and long-lived woman, her education had been devoted entirely to healing and the doctrines of her goddess. She pulled her heavy cloak closer around herself and enjoyed the adventure, marveling even at how very cold her nose was.

Despite Sa'ida's pleasure in the trip, she was shivering, and Kerian thought better of continuing at this height. It would be easier if they entered Inath-Wakenti at a lower level. To their left, northwest, a square notch in the rugged range beckoned. Green with trees, its slopes were several thousand feet lower than the mountaintops directly ahead. Eagle Eye shifted course and they descended. The temperature warmed.

"Better?" Kerian asked over one shoulder, and the priestess patted her shoulder in reply.

The warmth was welcome but could not dispel Kerian's worries. Eagle Eye had performed heroically, making such a long flight with very little rest between the journey out and the return, but she wished he could fly faster. She couldn't escape the feeling that the strange noise she'd heard was somehow a call for help.

*   *   *   *   *

Trying to find the promised rescue party was no simple task for Hytanthas. Fit as any warrior, he set a rapid pace and tried to maintain it, but hunger and thirst weighed his limbs. Once his torch was exhausted, blindness only added to the strain. Still, his sovereign had promised rescue, and Hytanthas would do his utmost to seek the elves searching for him.

Trailing the fingertips of his right hand along the tunnel wall, he negotiated the featureless dark. One factor worked to his advantage. The tunnel floor was clear of debris. Beneath his feet was only hard, clean stone. He'd come across no more bodies for quite a long time. He was thankful for that mercy. The dead could tell him nothing. They only reminded him of the fate that awaited him should he not find help or an exit from the subterranean maze.

The air shivered as if from a light breeze and a voice said, "Kerian."

Hytanthas halted.

"Kerian, this is Gil. I pray you can hear me. I'm waiting for you. Don't give up!"

The voice belonged to the Speaker. Was Lady Kerianseray in the tunnels?

Hytanthas marshaled his scattered thoughts. The Speaker had told him the Lioness was away on a mission, flying to Khuri-Khan to bring back the priestess Sa'ida.

The Speaker continued, calling to Hamaramis to return. The general of the Speaker's own household guard was away too?

Hytanthas shouted, "Sire, I'm coming!" He strained to hear the reply.

"Come home, everyone. I need you. I need you all."

With that, the peculiar resonance was gone from the air. The Speaker's pleas were at an end. Hytanthas drove a fist into his palm. His sovereign needed him, and he was blundering around in the dark. He fell to berating himself out loud, but broke off abruptly when he detected more voices. Hytanthas held his breath and listened.

He could hear quite clearly the voices and footfalls of five or six people. One tread was heavier than the rest, and the voice associated with it was lower, rougher—a human. How had a human gotten down here?

Hytanthas called to the unknown party, giving his name and identifying himself as a friend. Drained by hunger and the long sojourn in impenetrable darkness, he nevertheless steeled himself for a final push. He continued to call out as he jogged down the passage. After perhaps half a mile, he could hear the voices more clearly and he identified a female and a male as well as a human male. The number of footfalls told him there were several more elves who weren't speaking.

He drew breath to shout, but his warrior training abruptly reasserted itself. What if these people weren't his comrades? Ridiculous, he told himself. What other elves would be in the tunnels beneath Inath-Wakenti? But why was there a human with them?

Stricken with doubt, he fell back against the side of the tunnel. To his surprise, he discovered the wall was fluted by shallow scalloped niches. The niche at his back was just deep enough to conceal him. He flattened himself into the cover and waited, prey to all sorts of fears and uncertainties.

* * * * *

"I don't see how you can be sure we're heading southwest," said Hamaramis testily. "I lost my sense of direction long ago!"

Vixona replied, "It's simple. We made two right-angle turns, then the tunnel made a quarter-radius bend. Therefore we're traveling about 270 degrees from our original heading or, measured another way, ninety degrees—"

"I'm sorry you asked," muttered Jeralund.

"So am I."

Only Jeralund carried a burning torch. The rest had extinguished their brands to preserve them for later use. Jeralund's flame passed just under the nose of a figure standing in a niche in the wall. What he had taken for a sculpture suddenly recoiled from the wafting flame, and Jeralund gave a shout of surprise. Vixona's higher cry echoed his. The figure was no statue; he was alive!

"Put away your swords!" he shouted. "I'm one of you!"

Hamaramis froze, unable to believe what he was seeing. "Hytanthas!"

General and captain fell on each other, embracing like long-lost brothers. Hytanthas recognized the other three warriors. Vixona introduced herself. With her writing down every word, Hytanthas quickly outlined his adventures thus far.

"You've been down here more than a week and haven't spied another living soul?" Hamaramis asked.

"Not one." Hytanthas shrugged helplessly. "Only the dead."

"It must have been terrible for you," Vixona said.

Torchlight played over her upturned face. It had indeed

been terrible, but as he stared down into the warm brown eyes that regarded him so sympathetically, Hytanthas found himself smiling.

Hamaramis related how his party had found Jeralund. The young captain gave the human a considering look, but when Hamaramis mentioned they'd heard the Speaker summoning them, all other considerations were pushed aside.

"So it was real! I heard him too!" Hytanthas exclaimed. "We must get to him!"

They were all agreed on that point. The problem was, even with Vixona's map, Hamaramis's party hadn't been able to retrace their journey. The tunnels seemed to alter after they passed through. Intersections vanished, wall paintings noted by Vixona were no longer present.

"Strange," Hytanthas remarked. "That hasn't happened to me. I'm just lost."

He asked to see the map. With ink-smudged fingers, Vixona indicated her party's path on the small page.

"We tried backtracking from the deep pit where we found Jeralund, but the passages had changed," she said, brow furrowed. She obviously regarded it as unfair for the tunnels to belie her carefully drawn map.

Hytanthas gazed down the tunnel behind Hamaramis. "Let's go back the way you came," he suggested.

The general protested. Hadn't the boy been listening? The tunnel was no longer as Vixona had drawn it.

"Nevertheless," the warrior said and set off.

Hamaramis was put off by his blithe manner, but Vixona said, "We should follow him, sir. He's been here much longer than we. He might notice something we missed."

Taking the torch from Jeralund, Hamaramis and Vixona followed Hytanthas. The warriors surrounded Jeralund and brought up the rear.

Keeping his voice low, Hytanthas explained to Hamaramis how he'd been prey to hallucinations during his first few days. Those had faded, and he felt able to distinguish between false and real images. He was anxious to see if his hard-won acuity would allow him to see through the illusions that had stymied the rescue party's attempts to find a way out.

Far down the route, Vixona's map showed a crossing tunnel. Hytanthas found it precisely where she had indicated it would be. He complimented her accuracy. The young scribe blushed. Hamaramis was perplexed. His party had backtracked, seeking that very crossing, and it hadn't been here.

They continued on. Hamaramis congratulated Hytanthas on surviving his encounter with the will-o'-the-wisps. The general still found it strange Hytanthas was alive when all the other vanished elves he'd come across were dead. Hytanthas hadn't mentioned his discovery of the warrior Ullian, whom he suspected of having taken his own life. He didn't know why Ullian had awakened down here, and until he could report to the Speaker, he wouldn't engage in speculation. He had no doubt at all why he himself had awakened.

"The Lioness called me back from death," he said simply.

Vixona looked up from her note-taking.

"I heard the commander's voice. I was falling into oblivion, most certainly never to return, but I heard her voice and it drew me back."

Hamaramis offered no comment. They passed a large radial crack in the tunnel wall, positioned exactly as Vixona had noted. Next would come a southeast-northwest crossing passage, she reported. Hytanthas walked faster.

Jeralund, plodding along near the rear of the group, considered trying to escape, but wandering alone and unarmed in the tunnels seemed a far worse fate than remaining with the elves. The conversation also had given him food for thought. Why had he awakened when so many others had not? He had heard no voice calling him back. He simply awoke as from a sound sleep. Perhaps the magic of the floating lights affected him differently because he was human.

Vixona gave a cry of triumph. The intersection was exactly where she had drawn it.

Hamaramis could hardly credit their success. His party had been able to find none of the landmarks on the map once they passed them by.

"Are you a wizard?"

Vixona's question earned a smile. "No, just a hard-working fellow trying to earn his pay," Hytanthas said. "Maybe the lack of light helped me overcome the visions."

They skirted the pit where Jeralund had been discovered. It was silent and dark. The throbbing sound and faint glow were gone. Hytanthas pointed to the footprints left in the dust earlier by Hamaramis's party. It was a sign they were getting near the surface, he thought. Deep in the tunnels, where he'd first awakened, the floor was covered by a thick layer of bones. That thinned until there was only hard stone that didn't show footprints. Here the floor was covered by dust that filtered down from above.

Hytanthas jogged through the last intersection and started up the southeast passage. The others followed until he stopped suddenly, causing Hamaramis and Vixona to blunder into his back. His arms were outstretched to prevent them passing.

"Listen!" he hissed.

A metallic ringing came to their ears. There were three distinct rings, a pause, then three more.

"That's our signal!" Hamaramis exclaimed, rushing by the immobile Hytanthas. "The Speaker is calling us back!"

The warriors, bringing Jeralund with them, crowded in behind their commander. Hytanthas trudged tiredly up the rising tunnel after them. Only Vixona remained with him.

"Don't worry," she reassured him. "General Hamaramis is right. It's our signal."

Hytanthas nodded. He didn't doubt it, but another realization had stolen away the joy of his escape from the tunnels. The other vanished elves hadn't been as fortunate as he. He was bringing the end of hope for a great many families.

Vixona took his arm. "We came to rescue you, but you saved us. The Speaker will honor you for your deed."

DESTINY

Hytanthas looked down at her hand. Although ink-stained, it was well formed, the hand of a strong elf woman. He took a deep breath and increased their pace.

On the surface by the overturned monolith, rain fell in fits and starts. The sun had vanished behind the western mountains, and the last light of dusk was fading from the cloudless sky. Torches had been lit. A large plate of hammered bronze hung in the pit. A mallet rested against it. By hauling the plate up and letting it drop sharply, the elves made the hammer strike. Taranath was there, back from his long patrol. He ordered the gong rung again. The rope gang drew up the heavy plate and let go twice. Before they could do so a third time, something in the pit took hold of the rope.

Hopeful but cautious, Taranath ordered archers forward. The rope twitched and twisted. A voice from the pit shouted, "We're here!"

"Hamaramis?" Taranath exclaimed.

"Yes indeed! And we've brought company!"

Taranath sent elves scurrying to ready the windlass. Others brought shielded torches closer to the hole. A harness was affixed to a second rope and lowered down the shaft. Vixona came up first, dusty, heavy-eyed with exhaustion, but beaming. The next person to appear was Hytanthas. As soon as the captain was free of the rope harness, Taranath clapped him on the back with such enthusiasm, he nearly went sprawling.

The three elf warriors were brought up, and the harness was lowered again, for the old general, Taranath assumed. When the person who appeared was not Hamaramis but a human, consternation bloomed on Taranath's face. The human made no hostile moves, but the three warriors from the rescue party surrounded him quickly and made certain his hands were securely bound.

At last Hamaramis appeared. Before he had even shed the harness, he asked about the Speaker. Taranath was extremely grave.

"I'm afraid the Speaker's condition has worsened," he said quietly. He explained that Gilthas's bearers had found him barely conscious in the center of the circular platform. The Speaker was back in his tent again, quite feverish.

"And Lady Kerianseray?" Hytanthas asked.

No good news greeted this question. The Lioness had not returned from her solo mission to Khuri-Khan.

"She went alone?" exclaimed Hytanthas. "How could the Speaker allow that?"

The two generals exchanged glances, then Hamaramis addressed Hytanthas, his habitual frown softening. "Lad, you'll not serve our brave Speaker nor his valiant lady by standing out in the rain." He gave Hytanthas a push to get him moving.

Hytanthas let himself be herded along. "I would greatly appreciate food and a bath, sir."

The old general assured him that half his request could be provided.

14

Sa'ida was sleeping slumped against Kerian's back. Abruptly she flinched awake and slid sideways. Feeling herself falling, she grabbed wildly for Kerian. The sudden movement caused the elf woman to overbalance. Out of habit Kerian threw herself forward to hug Eagle Eye's feathered neck.

"Peace, holy one! You are safe." The restraining straps buckled around the priestess's waist held her snugly in the griffon's saddle.

"Forgive me!" Sa'ida rasped. The constant wind had dried her throat. "I thought I was falling."

Kerian sympathized. Passing a leather-wrapped water bottle to the priestess she related the experience of her first overnight flight. She'd not secured the saddle rig properly and had tossed so hard in her sleep that she and the saddle ended up hanging underneath the flying griffon. When she opened her eyes, she found herself upside down in a thick cloudbank.

"I thought I had gone over into the next life!" she said. When a mountain peak rushed out of the fog, she nearly was knocked into eternity.

The priestess handed the bottle back. The white scarf covering her head had been knocked askew. She straightened the scarf, tightening the knot that secured it at the nape of her neck, but tendrils of hair still streamed across her eyes. As she worked to tuck them away, she found herself regarding the Lioness's shorn head with envy.

They were still miles away from the elves' camp, descending in gentle stages through cool night air. The range ringing Inath-Wakenti bulked large before them. Sa'ida peered over Kerian's shoulder at the rugged pinnacles. She had never seen mountains before.

Suddenly she trembled down the length of her frame and inhaled sharply.

"Shall I land?" Kerian asked, thinking the priestess was in need of a respite from the unaccustomed constant motion.

Sa'ida shuddered harder. "This place is saturated with power!" she gasped.

"What sort of power?"

"Not godly magic." That was Sa'ida's stock in trade. "Something wilder, very old, and very dark! It's horrible! What a troubled place!"

Kerian made silent note of that. Trust Gilthas to pin his hopes on a sanctuary awash in ancient dark sorcery. She'd make certain Sa'ida shared her impressions with him. Perhaps the priestess's opinion of the peril would carry more weight than hers had so far.

Sa'ida was muttering. Leaning close to Kerian's ear, she said more loudly, "One power balances the other, but both are deteriorating. A war has raged here for untold centuries. Both sides are fading, but their power is still potent." She scanned the shadowy horizons as if she could see the magical forces mustered like armies on a battlefield.

"The lines are blurred. I cannot tell one from the other." She bent forward, resting her forehead against Kerian's back. "Just *sensing* them makes my soul ache."

Sympathizing with her pain, Kerian nevertheless kept Eagle Eye flying straight on to the center of the valley and the camp. However, when the distance to the mountains declined to a few hundred yards, the priestess's trembling and complaints gave way to something stronger. She gripped Kerian's cloak in both fists and jerked hard.

"Turn away! Turn away *now*. I cannot bear it!"

Immediately Kerian steered Eagle Eye into a wide right turn. Sa'ida was hunched against her, fingers gripping Kerian's waist so hard the elf woman was certain they would leave bruises. The priestess's breath came in short, sharp gasps as if she could barely drag the air into her lungs. Her breathing didn't ease until they'd put a mile of clear air between them and the entrance to the valley.

"There is an ancient ward on this place. It is very strong," she said. She didn't know who had cast the confining spell, but was certain her goddess, the Divine Healer, had had nothing to do with it.

Kerian set Eagle Eye to flying in a large, slow circle while she pondered how to get the priestess into the valley. Despite the nomads' superstitious insistence that it was taboo, nothing had interfered with the elves' various comings and goings by horse, on foot, or on griffons. Sa'ida asked whether their sages had experienced any difficulties. Kerian was forced to admit that none among the exiles had Sa'ida's level of expertise and sensitivity.

Frustration rose like bile in Kerian's throat. She could tell by the stars that midnight had come and gone. Her goal was in sight, and every minute's delay propelled Gilthas that much closer to death. Truthanar had done his best but there was little more he could try against the strange human disease. Kerian had snatched Sa'ida from the clutches of Nerakan agents and Torghanist fanatics, overcome the woman's own resistance, and brought them across the length of the Khurish desert. And they couldn't enter the valley!

Sa'ida pondered the situation as well. She suggested they land. The magical barrier was strong, evoking distress and panic, but it was a ward of very long standing. Perhaps its coverage was thinning or there were gaps in it. It might be less dangerous nearer the ground, for example. The priestess could cite precedents—

She broke off in midsentence, yelping in surprise. Kerian had directed Eagle Eye to descend. He put his head down and they sank rapidly. A hundred feet up, he flared out, flapping strongly until they were almost hovering, while Kerian quickly studied the terrain. To the left, she spied a rocky spit of level ground between the peaks and guided Eagle Eye to it.

On the ground wind whistled, setting their cloaks to flapping. Around them were nothing but stone crags, broken boulders, and drifts of pale gravel. They'd landed at a high elevation, above the tree line, and stood exposed to a constant column of cold wind. Far below, beneath the cloudless night sky, the desert lay like a pale tan sea. It stretched from horizon to horizon, west, south, and east. Wide dunes, broken here and there by the dark lines of dry wadis, rolled south toward Khuri-Khan.

"We can't stay here," Sa'ida muttered, giving up her vain attempts to hold her cloak closed against the strong wind. Kerian agreed.

The priestess sought the boundary of the archaic ward. Arms outstretched, palms held outward, she walked slowly forward. Her attention was so concentrated on her work, she lost track of her footing and slid awkwardly on the loose gravel. Kerian leaped forward, grabbing the back of her cloak. It was undignified, but it saved Sa'ida from a nasty tumble. As her racing heartbeat slowed, the priestess gave her a look of gratitude. More cautiously, she resumed the search.

Kerian knew exactly when Sa'ida found the boundary because she stiffened abruptly. She remained frozen in place for half a minute then turned back to Kerian with tears running down her face.

"Bring me the embroidered bag," she said, still weeping.

In one of the priestess's cloth bags, Kerian found a small pouch made of white muslin. She knew better than to open it, but as she hefted it, she felt within several small, hard objects, a few softer pieces, and a light substance that crackled beneath her fingers The bag itself and its shoulder strap were covered

DESTINY

with fine stitching in several shades of blue shot through here
and there with silver. The Lioness was no needleworker, but
even to her untutored gaze, the workmanship was astonishing,
the individual stitches so small and fine it was hard to discern
one from another. There was something odd about the design
itself, though. It seemed to mutate and alter while she looked
at it. The intricate pattern of flowers and silver leaves wavered
like a mirage in the desert, the stitches crawling across the
muslin and rearranging themselves. They formed words but
in no language the Lioness had ever known or seen. Once more
the pattern shifted, the silver threads flashing brightly though
only starlight fell upon them.

"Sosirah!"

The priestess's stern voice jerked Kerian out of her daze.
She gave the bag to Sa'ida, then went to stand by Eagle Eye's
head. The griffon bent down to nuzzle her, trilling a worried
note. She laid a reassuring hand on his neck.

Sa'ida clutched the bag to her chest with her right hand
while holding her left hand high. Over the noise of the
steady wind, Kerian heard her chanting. It sounded more
like a recited list of words than a song or poem. Nothing
happened for a time; then the wind ceased blowing.

Twenty yards away, dust still streamed around a wind-
sculpted boulder. Above, clouds were driving over the peaks;
below, the twisted trees were bent by the punishing air.
Where the two women and the griffon stood, all was calm.
Eagle Eye tossed his head and trumpeted loudly, sensing the
unnaturalness of it.

Kerian led him across the stony ground, coming up behind
the murmuring priestess. Was it a trick of the early-morning
light or was there a faint luminescence around Sa'ida's head?
When Kerian looked directly at her, the glow vanished, but if
she cast a glance to one side or the other, the priestess's head
was indeed enveloped in the palest of firefly haloes.

The murmuring ceased, but Sa'ida did not move. Her eyes
were squeezed shut.

Kerian had to call to her several times before the priestess replied. When she did, it was to ask about the wind. "The wind has died around us," Kerian answered. Couldn't the priestess feel that for herself?

"Very well. We can proceed."

Sa'ida kept her eyes closed and held the bag hard against her chest with one hand. Effectively blind, she held out a hand to Kerian. The Lioness brought her to Eagle Eye's side and boosted her onto the pillion. Cinching her into place, Kerian moved with unusual caution. It felt as though they were inside a delicate bubble, and if she moved too quickly or abruptly, the bubble would shatter, allowing the wind to bluster through once more.

Leaning close to Eagle Eye's head, she whispered, "All right, old monster. Gently we go."

Rather than driving them into the air with bounding leaps, Eagle Eye simply ran straight down the length of the spit and directly over the edge of the cliff. With powerful, deliberate wing beats, he arrested their plummet and sent them arrowing forward.

Kerian had to admit it was as smooth a takeoff as she'd ever felt. Of course her heart was in her throat and she was very glad Sa'ida's eyes were still closed.

"Not too high," the priestess whispered.

Kerian kept them just high enough so Eagle Eye's wing-tips didn't touch the ground on the downstroke. They edged upslope to the gray ridgeback. Normally topping a peak would expose them to strong drafts, but in their current protected state, Eagle Eye sailed over as softly as a dandelion seed. Not only had Sa'ida calmed the natural wind, her spell affected the breeze of their passage as well. The feathers lay flat on the griffon's neck, and no breath of air stirred Kerian's hair.

As Eagle Eye descended the far side of the ridge, Sa'ida slowly opened her clenched fingers, easing her grip on the spell bag. Her eyes opened. At once wind teased their ears and tugged at their clothes, the natural breeze of flight. Eagle Eye, relieved to be out of the unnatural calm, shook his head and chuffed a loud exhale.

Sa'ida sagged against Kerian, drained. The elf woman eased Eagle Eye into a climb. When they left the pass behind and entered the valley proper, they were flying a thousand feet above the ground. Kerian asked Sa'ida how she had defeated the ward.

"The ancient spellcasters made a mistake," the priestess said, leaning close to Kerian's ear so she didn't have to shout. "They tied their barrier to the wind. As long as it blew, the ward remained in place. I had to make a hole in the wind, that's all."

If she'd had any doubts before, Kerian knew at that moment she'd brought the right person to Inath-Wakenti. Compassion and cleverness were rare among the wise folk the Lioness had known and even more rare among humans. Gilthas would be in good hands.

False dawn came. Sunrise was still an hour away and would be hidden behind the high eastern ridge for longer than that, but the sky began to blush with new light. More of the terrain was visible to Sa'ida. The meandering line of Lioness Creek flashed beneath them, and Kerian pointed out what few other features there were, dwelling especially on the scattered masses of snowy quartz: individual monoliths, long walls with pointless gaps, the incomprehensible groupings of gargantuan stone. Did the holy lady know their significance?

Sa'ida did not. Flying a thousand feet above them, no rhyme or reason to their arrangement was apparent. She suggested they might be the foundations of still larger structures of wood, which had decayed after so long. In the coastal districts of Khur, it was common to build on stone pilings.

Kerian shook her head. The monoliths were too large and erratically spaced to have been the foundation of any building. Sometimes hundreds of feet separated them. No wooden beam could span such a gap.

"It's like the gods were playing dice," the Lioness said.

They cast the huge white blocks into the valley then left them where they lay.

"Maybe they were."

Kerian glanced back, but Sa'ida's lined, brown face betrayed no humor.

Several small, bright lights appeared on the ground ahead of them. Kerian tensed. Sa'ida wondered if they were the will-o'-the-wisps she'd mentioned. A few worried seconds later, the priestess felt her relax.

"They're our campfires. Hold tight, Holy Mistress! We may arrive in time to discuss breakfast!"

This bit of irony was lost on Sa'ida, but she would understand soon enough. Food was so scarce in the valley many elves "discussed" meals rather than ate them.

Sa'ida held on as Eagle Eye lowered his head and dived toward the distant fires.

* * * * *

Robien the Tireless was once more on the trail but proceeding with greater caution. He'd had little respect for magic prior to Faeterus's attack. Now, he knew to be more careful. The obvious trail left by the sorcerer also made him wary. Faeterus might be careless because he thought Robien dead, or he might be leading the hunter into fresh traps. Robien knew just how subtle such traps could be.

After his rescue by the elf warriors, he returned with them to their camp but slipped away unnoticed almost immediately. A party of explorers had found its way out of the tunnels, and the excitement over their return provided a perfect diversion. Although grateful to General Taranath and his warriors for their rescue, Robien was determined to get back on Faeterus's trail. He intended not only to complete the commission he'd accepted from the khan, but to free Favaronas in the bargain. The scholar's capture weighed on his conscience. He allowed himself a few hours' sleep then resumed the chase.

He donned his yellow spectacles and surveyed the terrain

ahead. Two sets of footprints were plainly visible, glowing faintly green even where the trail crossed rocks. The tracks ascended the slope in short, stuttering strides. They were two days old, but Robien would not rush. The day was young yet. It would be better to overtake the sorcerer at day's end. Faeterus would be tired from the long climb, and the setting sun would be behind Robien and in his quarry's eyes.

When he pocketed his spectacles again, he was taken aback to find himself surrounded by elves. At first he thought them the Speaker's people, but then he saw they had no legs—long, tangled hair and tattered clothing, and no lower limbs at all.

Ghosts.

He did not fear the dead. He'd been many places and seen many things, and all the ghosts he'd heard of seemed to him sad creatures, deserving more pity than fear. He made straight for those who stood in his path. The spirits raised no hand against him, but when he drew abreast of them, his arms and legs began to tingle. The sensation was not pleasant. Taking heed of the obvious warning, he drew back a few steps.

"Stand aside," he commanded.

The ghosts reacted not at all, only stood silent and immobile. He started forward again. The effect was stronger and sent him stumbling backward, hissing in pain.

The line of spirits extended as far as he could see to left and right. He could not go around them. His sword passed through the ghosts without hindrance. He sheathed it again, frustrated.

"I must get through," he said, and charged.

The shock hurled him to the ground and left him badly dazed, although only for a moment. When his head cleared, he no longer lay on the ground. He was being carried. The spectral figures were far more substantial than when he'd first seen them. Four had lifted him, and the others streamed ahead and behind. Their progress was silent as the sunlight.

Half-formed legs passed through the grass without shifting it at all. The ghosts were insubstantial as smoke, yet their grips on him were solid enough.

The bizarre procession passed between standing stones, their white surfaces washed golden by the morning sun. Robien craned his head up to see forward. Thus far, he'd felt only bemusement. A hunter of long experience, he sensed no menace in the creatures—a great and aching sadness but no menace. When he saw where they were taking him, bemusement vanished and he tried to fight.

A white stone monolith hovered above the ground. Twenty feet in length, it floated as though anchored in the air. Beneath it, a hole gaped. A crowd of ghosts stood around the hole, their empty eyes fixed on his approach. His limbs had gone numb and he had no strength. Attempts to shout met with the same lack of success.

Without a single word spoken, the ghosts dropped him into the hole. He fell eight or nine feet then hit bottom hard. His head swam but he had no trouble seeing the monolith descend, sealing him into the cold, black ground.

* * * * *

For all its evocative name, the Stair of Distant Vision was a great disappointment to Favaronas. The view was fine but hardly the revelation he had expected.

The Stair itself was a sizable tableland cut into the side of Mount Rakaris, semicircular in shape, a hundred yards wide at its outer edge and sixty yards deep at its apex. The pavers covering its surface were set in alternating courses of dark blue slate and creamy feldspar. Ten-foot obelisks rose up on its left and right edges. Those also alternated between dark basalt and alabaster. Additional obelisks dotted its surface, and Favaronas saw no obvious pattern to their arrangement.

From that vantage point, Inath-Wakenti resembled a long, wide bowl, bound on all sides by steep mountains. The regularity of its boundaries suggested the work of unnatural forces. The edge between the valley floor and the mountains was perfectly defined. Here and there, time and erosion had softened the line, but for the most part, the boundary looked as if it had been drawn by a god's hand. The monoliths poked up among the trees and brush, their shape and stark whiteness reminding the archivist of tombstones.

A huge circular feature in the center of the valley puzzled Favaronas. He mistook it for a lake, but Faeterus said it was a huge disk made of wedges of white granite. The sorcerer called it the *Tympanum*, meaning "drum". What its purpose was, he would not say.

Exhaustion claimed Faeterus and Favaronas immediately after their arrival. Unfortunately Faeterus didn't rest long. He kicked Favaronas awake only an hour or so after sunrise then set him to collecting various items with no explanation of their purpose. As Favaronas gathered loose stones and long tree branches, he watched his captor.

Seemingly from nowhere (for he carried no baggage), Faeterus produced a surveyor's transit and a slender tripod. He set it up, carefully aligning it with the far-off Tympanum. Then he moved from spot to spot, making notes on a piece of parchment with a small charcoal stick. He continued for so long that Favaronas, having gathered the required amount of stones and branches, settled himself out of the way and slept.

Thankfully, Faeterus had no immediate need of him, and he was able to rest for several hours before the sorcerer woke him again. When Faeterus did rouse him, the sorcerer sounded almost genial.

"Stand up," he said. "Behold a wonder no other living soul has seen in four thousand years!"

Obediently, Favaronas got to his feet. The sun was low over the western peaks, the brilliant disk suspended between a thick layer of clouds above and the gray mountains below. Its light gave the valley a deep golden sheen. Shielding his eyes against the glare of the low sun, Favaronas could see the Tympanum in the valley's heart glowing with reflected sunlight. A pretty sight to be sure, but surely not what the sorcerer had worked so hard to witness. Yet Faeterus stood transfixed. Perhaps only mages could see whatever it was that—

Favaronas gasped.

As the sun descended further, the monoliths throughout Inath-Wakenti began to shine vividly red. The thousands of stone blocks blazed like a mosaic of fire. The sun sank further, and the reflected glory became so intense that Favaronas was forced to put a hand over his eyes and view the scene through gaps in his fingers. His squinted eyes teared up, bringing on the final revelation.

When the individual points of crimson light blurred together, they formed an image. Not a picture, not writing, but some sort of gigantic hieroglyphic symbol. He could not see it very well. Looking at the array of shining monoliths was like trying to stare directly at the noonday sun. But he had an impression of a complex interweaving of wavy lines and single points. Oddly enough, it reminded him of Silvanesti musical notation but far removed from that ancient art.

The effect lasted only a few seconds. The sun continued its downward journey, and the blazing hieroglyph faded, leaving only a forest of faintly glowing stones. The line of twilight encroached on the valley floor, slowly submerging the monoliths in shadow.

"Amazing," Favaronas breathed. "Does this occur every year on this date?"

The sorcerer flicked a contemptuous look at him. "Barring clouds, it occurs at every sunset, but it is visible only from this exact point in the valley."

That seemed unlikely to Favaronas, knowing what he did about the movement of celestial bodies during the course of a year, but Faeterus's next words explained the discrepancy: magic was at work.

"The glory of the sign," the sorcerer said, "is not a natural occurrence, and no mortal mind can retain its detail. I must make an impression of it when it appears. It is the key to my quest."

The apparition's words echoed in Favaronas's memory: *Seize the key before the door opens.*

Faeterus gave him new instructions. He wanted a small fire kindled at a particular spot on the Stair. Favaronas scurried away to gather tinder. He made several trips, dumping fistfuls of dry leaves and twigs by a waist-high block of dark blue basalt. The block had a shallow depression in its top. While Favaronas fetched and carried, Faeterus produced tiny flasks and small suede bags from inside his ponderous robes. These he arranged atop the stone block, then added a large, shiny coin and a small trinket on a chain. Favaronas managed to pass close enough to identify the coin as a Khurish *begon*, a silver piece whose name meant "loaf of bread." The trinket and chain carried the black patina of tarnish, and the archivist deduced it must be silver too. It resembled a four-footed animal, perhaps a cat.

When Favaronas had the fire burning, Faeterus ordered him to find water. Favaronas's stomach chose that moment to offer a loud grumble. He couldn't remember the last time he'd eaten.

"Care to share my fare, elf spawn?"

Favaronas looked away from the mocking voice and blank hood and went to search for water.

They'd passed no springs on their ascent. He'd have to go higher. With much puffing, he climbed the steep slope behind the Stair. The sun was down, and the growing dark made his quest all the more difficult. He poked among thorny shrubs and peered under rock ledges. All he found were patches of leathery lichen.

Pausing to rest, he looked down on the Stair. The notion of escape was alluring, but he couldn't muster the nerve. Faeterus was in no better physical shape than he and likely couldn't catch him if it came to a foot race. But the sorcerer might hurl a thunderbolt at him or blind him or lame him. Favaronas shuddered at the possibilities his imagination conjured. If a warrior had stood in his place, that worthy might have found an opportunity to escape or to kill his captor. Favaronas was no warrior.

It wasn't only fear that held him back. Weak and beaten as he was, he still clung to a faint hope that he could foil Faeterus's evil machinations. Perhaps he might yet be able to serve his people.

A force tugged on the hem of his robe, pulling him off balance and forcing him to scrabble wildly to avoid a fall. The invisible hand of Faeterus beckoned. Favaronas hurried back down the mountainside and reported his failure to find water.

"A pity. I'll have to use the drinking supply."

Favaronas's throat was terribly dry, but he maintained a prudent silence.

The sorcerer was grinding powders in the hollow atop the basalt block. The tarnished silver necklace and the *begon* sat in a shallow pan. Into the pan, he poured liquid from a pottery flask. The silver items hissed and bubbled, sending an ugly stench into the evening air. Some sort of vitriol. Favaronas edged upwind from it.

The contents of their only water bottle went into the pot. Faeterus sprinkled in the powders he'd mixed then added the hissing, stinking contents of the shallow pan. The vitriol had completely dissolved the silver coin and necklace.

A light breeze had come up, and the fire wavered. A sharp command from Faeterus sent Favaronas hurrying to add more wood.

Faeterus next produced a parchment, one very long, continuous sheet. "Set the pot by the fire," he said. "Stoke the flames to medium intensity. And mind what you do! Spill that pot, and you'll die right now!"

Favaronas placed the pot carefully next to the fire. The corrosive mixture continued to swirl as if stirred by an unseen hand. Its noxious fumes set Favaronas to coughing. Faeterus pointed a finger at him, and the archivist was horrified to feel his lips seal themselves shut again. He inhaled and exhaled rapidly through his nose and retreated to the far side of the platform, but Faeterus wasn't done with him. The finger pointed again, and Favaronas's legs fused at the ankles. As with his mouth, there was no outward trace of a seam. His ankles were welded together as though he'd been born that way. Caught completely by surprise, he lost his balance and fell.

The scroll proved long enough to stretch from one side of the Stair to the other. Unrolling it, Faeterus made use of the stones and tree branches Favaronas had collected. At intervals along the parchment's length, he erected the spindly branches, supporting each with a pile of stones. He lifted the parchment, turned it on its edge, and wove it in and out of the natural forks in the branches. With a scrap of cloth from his robe and a short branch, he fashioned a makeshift swab and dipped it into the liquid simmering by the fire. He painted the liquid onto the upright sheet of parchment, covering only the side facing the valley. Then he settled himself by the dying fire.

"Now we shall see what we shall see."

A wave of his hand brought Favaronas's eyelids down and sealed them. That was a new horror. Blind, mouthless, hobbled, Favaronas screamed against his own flesh until he could scream no more.

15

The sun bathed the city in gentle, golden warmth. Trees spread their shading canopies over broad streets and slender paths. Towers and other buildings rose above the trees, not competing with them, but coexisting in close harmony. Warm stone set off green leaves that exactly matched the green copper sheathing on the tower roofs. Four especially tall towers rose from the city's outer corners. Arching crystalline bridges, delicate as lace, connected the four towers and enclosed the city like a glittering crown.

From the lofty vantage point of the palace's highest terrace, Qualinost seemed unreal in its serenity and impossible beauty. Gilthas stood alone on the terrace, looking out on the city he ruled. He was filled with such peace, he felt his heart would burst from the sheer joy of it. He would be content to remain here forever, drinking in that view. He'd read once that when the emperors of old Ergoth passed away, their bodies were converted by magic into stone statues. Perhaps when his life drew to a close, he could become a statue, and be placed here, forever overlooking the city and its people.

Smiling, he chided himself for such morbid thoughts. A Speaker's duty was to the living. However much he wished to linger, matters of state would not wait. He delayed only a moment longer, drinking in the blue of the sky and the infinite varieties of green in the trees, breathing deeply of the scents of jasmine and orange blossom carried by the breeze. Finally, like a reluctant swain, he turned away, his fingers reaching out for one last touch of the smooth wood of the balcony's railing.

The palace was alive with activity. Servants moved swiftly through side corridors bearing food and drink, hampers of linen, or pots of living flowers. In the main passages, soldiers of the royal guard kept watch as all manner of people strolled the elegant halls. The Speaker's daily audience would commence soon, and favor-seekers already were jockeying for position.

From the seaside provinces came mariners wearing wide canvas pants and carrying rolled-up maps. They wanted royal backing for trading voyages to distant lands. A pair of emissaries from Thorbardin and a trio from Ergoth stood in private conclave. The two dwarves were unrelated to each other yet alike as mirror images: each with a thick, brown beard, bulbous nose, and green eyes. The Ergothians retained an air of imperial hauteur even though their empire had long since fragmented into insignificance. Solamnic Knights, broad shouldered and perpetually serious, conversed in measured tones with lavishly dressed merchants from Palanthas.

Gilthas nodded and smiled to everyone but received little recognition in return. He was accustomed to that. To the world, he was a fool and a dreamer, dismissed as the Puppet King, his strings controlled by Prefect Palthainon. Ostensibly the Speaker's advisor, Palthainon had been installed by the Knights of Neraka as the true power in Qualinesti. The ease with which everyone accepted Gilthas in the weakling's role had worried him at first. He knew the unspoken reason most believed him to be a dupe: he was not a pure-blooded elf. His father, valiant Tanis, had been half human. Although Gilthas's pedigree was otherwise impeccable, many assumed his seemingly pliant nature sprang from the human taint.

He put aside this worry. The Puppet King was a masquerade, a necessary one if he were to save his people. Someday the world would know the truth. Someday they would see his true self. A very different Gilthas would lead the elves of Qualinesti to peace, freedom, and plenty.

The reactions of strangers no longer bothered him. However, when several important senators passed him by without speaking, he was perturbed. When his long-time bodyguard and valet Planchet strolled by without so much as a nod, perturbation grew into anger. He turned and hailed Planchet, but his staunch friend did not even turn around.

"He cannot hear you."

Someone was standing in the shadow of one of the columns that supported the high ceiling. He stepped into the light, showing himself to be an elf of above-average height. He had dark blond hair and the elegantly tall ears common among the oldest families of Silvanesti. Gilthas was taken aback. No one from Silvanost had come to his court in a very long time. More unusual still, the visitor was dressed in a curiously old-fashioned style, like a warrior from one of Silvanesti's epic poems. He wore a banded cuirass, separated pauldrons on each shoulder, and a mail kilt rather than divided trews. Short suede gloves covered his hands. His eyes were an arresting shade of blue. Gilthas had never seen such brilliant eyes in an elf, even a Silvanesti.

"Who are you?"

The stranger bowed, bending deeply from the waist. "Greetings, Great Speaker. My name is Balif, Lord of Thalas-bec and First Warrior of House Protector."

"You bear an ancient name, my lord. I thought it had fallen out of favor long ago among the Silvanesti."

Lord Balif smiled. "It did indeed."

Gilthas gestured at the throng behind him. "What goes on here? Why am I being ignored?"

"They aren't ignoring you. They cannot see or hear you."

Gilthas demanded the reason for this. Had a spell been used to render him invisible? He wanted it stopped immeadiately and the proper order restored. Balif shrugged.

DESTINY

"I cannot change what has been. I have come to guide you. I sought the privilege, and it was granted."

"Guide me where? Speak plainly, sir!"

Sadness shadowed those remarkable eyes. "I am Balif, right arm of Speaker Silvanos. Do you understand? I am he who enlarged the realm, carried the standard of Silvanos to the great mountains of the north, fought—"

Gilthas's laughter interrupted him. "It will take more than antique armor and a quaint accent to convince me of such nonsense. What's the matter, couldn't Kith-Kanan come?" Gilthas joked.

"No, he could not," was the utterly serious reply. "You shall meet him, if you wish. He is an elf among elves."

It was too much. Gilthas dismissed the mad fellow with a wave and walked away. "Play your games with someone else. I have a kingdom to tend."

"No, you don't."

Gilthas's smile faltered and he looked back. "What did you say?"

"This kingdom no longer exists. As we speak, you lie dying on a pallet in the Vale of Silence."

Despite the outrageous words, Gilthas did not laugh. The calm certainty in the stranger's voice gave him pause. But the palace was solid around him, the faint breeze of a courtier's passage ruffled his hair, and he clung to the reality he saw.

"If you're Balif, why do you look so fair? The champion of Silvanos was afflicted with a terrible curse and died in exile."

"My mortal life ended long ago. My appearance is as I choose it to be, just as yours is. You appear now in vigorous good health, but in truth, you're little more than skin and bones, and you can scarcely draw a breath, your lungs are so devastated."

Denying all of it, Gilthas made to turn away again, but Balif took his arm. With gentle yet inexorable pressure, Gilthas's hand was lifted to his own throat. The pulse beating there was indeed very slow, very labored.

"Your life is ebbing. When it is done, you may accompany me to the next world."

"And if I refuse?"

"Then you will wander the land forever, another of the restless spirits in the Vale of Silence."

Gilthas remembered the terrible loneliness he had sensed from the ghosts in the valley. That memory brought with it all the others. His beloved city, the palace, all these people—they were not products of magic, but illusions of his own making. His city had been wiped from the face of Krynn. Alone and gravely ill, his mind had sought a last few moments of peace before succumbing to death.

"This is not how I expected to die," he whispered.

"It rarely is. Come."

Gilthas avoided Balif's outstretched hand but followed the Silvanesti into the throne room. Empty of people, the room was nothing more than an echo in his mind, a faint replica of something lost forever. Balif craned his neck back, taking in the hall's mighty dimensions and the gold and polished crystal columns that soared up to a vaulted ceiling painted to mimic the summer sky.

"Beautiful," he said, like anyone new to the grandeur of Qualinost.

"It was." Tears dampened Gilthas's cheeks. "May I ask something?"

"You may ask. I may not answer."

"Why is your fate such a mystery? You were among the greatest elves of the age. Why were you cast into such obscurity?"

The handsome Silvanesti regarded him with such a fixed stare Gilthas wondered if he had given offense.

"You're embarking on a journey into the unknown, and that is the question burning inside you?" Balif said.

Gilthas shrugged, embarrassed. "I've always wondered."

Balif told the story of his rise, his fall, and his life after that fall. Much of it fit the rumors and speculations to which the Speaker of the Sun and Stars was privy, but the cause and final outcome of Balif's exile shocked him to his core. He looked away, at the floor, the columns, anywhere but at the shade of the ancient hero.

"I pity you," he said.

"Once you pass out of the mortal sphere, life's concerns are mere vanities and completely unimportant. As it was with me, so it will be with you. Come, little time remains."

The throne of Qualinesti stood on its dais, bathed in golden light. Its gilded back, carved in the shape of the sun, reflected the light with painful intensity. Balif held out a hand to the empty chair.

"That is your portal, Speaker of the Sun and Stars. You have but to take it, and all your cares shall end."

All his cares would end. It was a notion both comforting and terrifying. Gilthas didn't want to die, didn't want to leave Kerianseray. And there was so much left undone. A brave, suffering people looked to him for leadership. But he was so sick. Illusion or not, the feeling of drawing an unencumbered breath was intoxicating. He felt young and healthy, just as he should. All he need do was sit his throne and the struggle would be over.

The sound of voices drew him closer to the dais. The voices were coming from the glowing throne, speaking all at once, but not in unison. The sound was like the rolling of ocean waves, lifting and lowering him in a rhythmic, soothing motion. Soon he would be part of that sound, his own voice added to the chorus of the dead.

Pathfinder.

He stopped. That voice had not come from the throne. He glanced uncertainly at Balif. The Silvanesti was looking back toward the far end of the illusory hall. Nothing at all was visible there. The image of the audience hall simply faded into blackness.

Gilthas Pathfinder, come back!

The voice was not familiar, but it pulled powerfully at him.

His foot, lifted to step onto the throne dais, lowered back onto the floor.

"Come," urged the shade of Balif. "Join us."

He wanted to, to become one with great elves of the past like Kith-Kanan, Balif, Silvanos, Silveran, and with those who loomed large in his own heart—his father, and his mother who had died with Qualinost to save them all. The joyous reunion required him to take single step onto the dais and to sit down on his throne.

Gilthas Pathfinder, in the name of the goddess, I command you! Return!

With a knowing smile, Balif said, "Go with the gods, Great Speaker. You shall not see me again."

The Silvanesti's body paled to a translucent silhouette, then vanished. All around Gilthas the remembered beauty of Qualinost likewise dissolved, becoming a confusing welter of gray and brown before gradually resolving into the patchwork roof of his tent in Inath-Wakenti. Above him floated the face of a human woman. Tendrils of white hair curled around a face creased by concern.

The woman's lips moved, but he couldn't make out the words. Drawing a shuddering breath, he croaked, "What?"

The woman moved abruptly out of his line of sight, and her place was taken by someone Gilthas did know. Kerian, looking windblown and sunburned, knelt by his bed and took his face in her hands.

"Who told you you could die?" she said, voice breaking. Tears glistened in her eyes, and Gilthas was concerned. The Lioness never wept in public.

"Don't cry, my love," he rasped. "I met Balif. He told me his true tale."

She called him a fool and he smiled, pleased he had cheered her.

The intimate moment was broken by the human woman's return. She laid damp cloths on his brow. Kerian introduced her as Sa'ida, high priestess of the Temple of Elir-Sana.

DESTINY

"She saved your life," Kerian added.

He felt strangely ambivalent about being rescued. The eternal glory of Qualinost had been within his grasp. Now he had only the sterile despair of the Silent Vale.

No, not only that. He took Kerian's hand. His own was cold, but hers was warm as sunshine.

"Did you hear me call you?" he asked. "I used the stone platform."

"Of course. I came as fast as I could," she said, smiling.

His eyes closed, and Kerian looked to Sa'ida. The priestess was gripping the pendant she wore around her neck. Normally the gold-and-sapphire amulet was kept hidden within her robe, but she held it tightly in her right hand. The Eye of Elir-Sana, the symbol of the goddess of healing.

"He will rest. His soul had almost departed, but he is back." Sa'ida regarded the Speaker's wasted frame. Elves were a naturally slender, willowy race compared to humans, but the Speaker of the Sun and Stars appeared no more than a skeleton beneath the heavy blankets. In sleep he looked far worse than many corpses she had seen. She shook her head. "Consumption is dreadful among my people. It is an abomination in yours."

Kerian looked away. Sa'ida's reaction had caused her to see Gilthas through new eyes. Merciful E'li, they had only just arrived in time!

The Speaker's tent was filled with people. Kerian nodded to Truthanar, and he returned the gesture with a look of dawning relief. Turning, he herded the rest back to a more respectful distance. The air of terrified suspense was replaced by one of cautious optimism.

Kerian touched her husband's face. It was bathed in sweat but noticeably cooler than it had been when she'd arrived. Sa'ida gently but firmly pulled her away from her sleeping husband. They emerged from the close confines of the tent into cool morning air.

"Is he healed?" Kerian asked.

The high priestess rubbed her hands together, flexing her

fingers stiffly as if they pained her. "That was no healing, lady. The Speaker was on the edge of a chasm; I guided him back home, that's all."

She explained the course of treatment the Speaker would require. Healing him would be a long and complicated process. Consumption was a deep-seated malady. It had to be destroyed root and branch, or it would recur.

"Have you told him?" Sa'ida asked.

Kerian, still digesting what the priestess had just said, was lost. "Told who? What?"

"Of the child you carry."

Shock rocked the Lioness back on her heels, and Sa'ida immediately realized she had not known her own state. The priestess apologized for having delivered the news so bluntly.

"How can you know?" Kerian asked hoarsely.

Sa'ida shrugged. "I am the high priestess of Elir-Sana."

Kerian walked on trembling legs to a nearby log and sat down. A child! Her head moved in a denial, but she knew Sa'ida wouldn't mislead her about so important a fact.

The priestess's hand rested on her shoulder. "Don't look so frightened," she said kindly. "It's the most natural thing in the world."

Natural for some, but for the Lioness? The foundations of her world were shifting under her feet, and Kerian wondered how she would cope.

"Motherhood," she said, and the word sounded as strange to her as anything she'd encountered in Inath-Wakenti.

* * * * *

Outside the ring of standing stones and bonfires, unfriendly eyes surveyed the camp. Black tongue lolling, the beast who was Prince Shobbat crouched by a small tree. His belly ached with hunger. Before he'd come into the valley, he'd hunted rabbits and squirrels. In the valley there was nothing. He was sure the *laddad* would have food. Sneaking in would not be easy. *Laddad* senses were far keener than a human's, but so were his, and he was much stealthier than when he'd been human.

He did not debate the question long. His empty belly overruled any qualms. Rising from his crouch, he trotted through the widely spaced trees. It was very early in the morning, and the high mountains shadowed the valley, but he kept to the low places so as not to risk showing a silhouette to elf eyes. Unfortunately, he could find no easy access. The ramparts surrounding the *laddad* camp were uniformly patrolled.

At a barricade spanning the gap between two lofty monoliths, the pair of elves on watch leaned casually on their spears. Their attention was half-hearted at best. Since the Speaker's encounter with the will-o'-the-wisps several nights back, the ghosts of Inath-Wakenti had not reappeared. Eerie silence still cloaked the valley, but the absence of specters went a long way toward lulling elf fears. For the civilian volunteers, guard duty became routine. The hardest part of the job was staying awake.

One sentinel stood straighter and pushed his helmet back from his forehead.

"Did you see that?" he asked.

His comrade had seen nothing but his own drooping eyelids. "What?" he mumbled.

The first sentinel pointed at a gully about thirty yards away. "It went in there," he said. "It looked like a dog. A big one!"

An argument ensued. Both elves knew there were no dogs in Inath-Wakenti, but the first insisted he had not been mistaken. Whatever it was, he had seen something. The discussion grew heated, but he remained adamant. He went to find the captain of the night watch and report the sighting.

The beast noted the departure of the sentinel. Only one elf remained, and the barrier at that spot was only chest-high, made of loose stones. He couldn't hope for better odds than that. Belly low to the turf, he crept forward. Soon he was close enough to hear the crackle of bonfires and to smell wood burning. He could smell *laddad* too. Unlike the pungency of unwashed humans, *laddad* scent was redolent of dry grass, like a haymow.

Gathering his long legs beneath him, Shobbat sprang.

He hit the *laddad* sentinel in the back, and the two of them went down in a heap. Shobbat's jaws locked onto the *laddad*'s throat. How easy it would be to tear the elf apart. Part of him wanted to taste the hot blood flowing, but enough of his humanity remained to resist that savagery. He held on until the *laddad* succumbed to lack of air and lost consciousness.

Pressing on, Shobbat kept to the shadows, avoiding bonfires and the packs of alert *laddad* patrolling the camp. His keen nose detected the aroma of smoked meat. He tracked the tantalizing odor. Once he almost blundered into the path of several mounted warriors. The riders didn't notice him, but their horses did. The front pair reared and lashed out with their shod hooves. Shobbat withdrew quickly into the deep shadows between two large tents. The riders calmed their mounts and moved on.

Shobbat's nose led him at last to a round tent with a conical roof. It was guarded by a pair of spear-armed *laddad* who walked around it in opposite directions. Getting past them was simple. He waited until they met and moved on; then he sprinted for the tent. He put his nose under the fabric and shoved himself beneath.

Within, the tent was dark and full of savory smells. Five goat haunches hung above him. Shobbat tore one down and devoured it immediately. When he reared up to drag down a second, he saw there were only three remaining, not four. Instantly wary, he dropped to his belly. Although he watched and listened to the limits of his beastly senses, he detected no one inside the tent. Perhaps he had miscounted the number originally. The flesh was hard and dry, almost wooden, but to Shobbat's starved stomach, it was ambrosia from the gods. He pulled down a second haunch to eat. He intended to take the last two with him. As he ate, he glanced up.

Only one haunch remained.

That stopped him cold. He might have miscounted by one, but not two. The meat was disappearing even as he stood directly beneath it. Without taking his eyes from the last hanging haunch, he backed away until he came up against the tent wall. The air around the haunch shimmered. Tiny sparks of light darted this way and that. They focused on the goat leg, surrounding it in a faint halo of purple light. The light faded. When it was gone, so was the meat.

The same phenomenon began to swirl around the half-eaten haunch on the ground. Unwilling to let his dinner vanish, Shobbat hurled himself onto the meat. Snatching it up in his jaws, he shook it vigorously. The sparkling aura dissipated, leaving his meal behind. Unfortunately, his noisy movements caught the attention of the guards. They ran in, one of them bearing a torch. Seeing him standing in the middle of the tent, a half-chewed goat haunch in his mouth, they shouted for help. Shobbat galloped between them, knocking them aside.

Outside he immediately ran into a quartet of warriors. Had they been mounted, he would have died beneath their horses' hooves. As they were on foot, he was able to dart between them and escape.

A hue and cry arose behind him. Belatedly, an arrow hissed by his head. Shobbat laid back his ears and ran for all he was worth. The rumble of horses on his left drove him the opposite direction, into a welter of tents. He threaded his way among them, leaving chaos in his wake and earning swipes from tools in the hands of terrified *laddad*. One bold youth tried to bar his way with a loaded crossbow. Shobbat, goat haunch still firmly clamped in his jaws, leaped over the youngster's head, leaving her staring after him in impotent surprise.

He rounded a corner and veered into a broader avenue, choosing it because it was not lit by a bonfire. He quickly discovered his mistake. Several *laddad* were standing outside a very large, patched tent. Shobbat had blundered into their midst before realizing they were there. It was astonishing enough to find himself facing General Hamaramis, commander of the *laddad* khan's army, and

Kerianseray, the khan's warrior-wife, but the identity of the other female in the group was even more amazing: Sa'ida, high priestess of Elir-Sana.

When he'd first become a beast, Shobbat had gone to the Temple of Elir-Sana seeking help to return to his true state. Instead, the high priestess had driven him away. Hunger forgotten, Shobbat dropped the goat haunch, bared his yellow fangs, and snarled at Sa'ida.

Kerianseray and the other warriors drew their swords. Shouts and the sound of running feet told Shobbat the mob that had chased him from the provisions tent was arriving as well.

"Hold!" The voice of Sa'ida carried over the tumult, silencing it. "This is no ordinary beast. He is as foreign here as we are." She named Shobbat, to universal astonishment.

Fury shook Shobbat. He should kill the worthless woman for having refused him aid, but the forest of naked blades before him and the angry crowd behind argued for a different tack.

"Don't . . . kill . . . me," he rasped, lowering his head.

Various exclamations of shock came from the *laddad*, and Sa'ida said, "He bears the curse of a powerful sorcerer."

"Fay'trus!" Shobbat hissed, head bobbing up and down vigorously. "Kill Fay'trus!"

The *laddad* in front of him muttered among themselves and two departed, but Kerianseray advanced on him, sword still out, and his attention focused on her. "You're our enemy," she told him. "You've caused untold suffering with your plots!"

She edged to one side and he shifted to keep her in view. "My country . . . my crown!"

"Now!" she cried.

The two elves who'd left the group had worked their way around to flank him. They came charging at him from each side. The mob was still behind him. He had no place to go but forward.

He launched himself not at Kerianseray, but at the traitorous priestess. For siding with foreigners against her own prince he'd have her eyes for amulets.

DESTINY

Sa'ida stood calmly, awaiting his attack. At the last moment, she raised her hands and mouthed a single word. Shobbat froze in midleap as if stuck in amber. She flung her hands apart, and he up shot into the sky like a missile from a catapult.

He tumbled nose over tail through the air. When he finally landed in a dry ravine, loose sand softened the blow somewhat, but the impact still drove the breath from his lungs. He lay gasping for several long minutes, grateful to have survived such a fall.

The *laddad* camp was a distant glow on the southern horizon. The meddlesome Sa'ida had thrown him several miles deeper into the valley. She'd kept the *laddad* from hacking him to bits but lost him his goat haunch and his way. On a day soon to come, Shobbat would mete out a fitting punishment.

The morning wind brought a new scent to his nose. Faint and fetid, the odor was one he had tasted before, when he was still a man. It belonged to Faeterus. The sorcerer had passed this way.

With a last angry glare at the rising smudge of bonfire smoke marking the elves' camp, Shobbat trotted off among the monoliths.

16

I n the chill, small hours before dawn, three elves came to the Speaker's tent, chosen by Gilthas for a critical mission.

Under Sa'ida's ministrations, his condition had improved. Although he continued to be marble pale and weak, his fever had broken. Able to take in a little nourishment, he was stronger and had left his bed for the first time in days. The three he'd summoned—Kerian, Taranath, and Hytanthas—found him seated in the camp chair that served as his throne.

One other had wished very much to be included in the group. Meeting with the Speaker privately the evening before, Vixona the scribe had argued for the usefulness of her mapmaking skills. Gilthas appreciated her enthusiasm and listened to her passionately delivered argument quite seriously, but her true motivation was not hard for him to deduce. She'd hardly left Hytanthas's side since their return from the tunnels, bringing him food and drink, tending his minor hurts. The young captain, occupied with his duties and the care of his griffon, paid her little attention, but Vixona's attachment to him was obvious to Gilthas. Nevertheless, the mission did not require a cartographer.

Gilthas's voice was still quite hoarse. Kerian, Hytanthas, and Taranath strained to hear every word over the bustle in other parts of the large tent.

DESTINY

"We know the sorcerer Faeterus is in Inath-Wakenti. He must be found and nullified."

It wasn't like the Speaker to mince words. Kerian, certain Faeterus had hurled the lightning bolt that had blinded Eagle Eye, said bluntly, "You mean kill him."

"I mean he must be nullified. If he can be rendered harmless in any other way, that is sufficient." Gilthas coughed to clear his throat. "Do what you must to protect our people."

Each of them understood his instruction in his or her own way. Kerian privately resolved to have the sorcerer's head. Hytanthas, who had fought Faeterus's monsters in Khuri-Khan, assumed the Speaker wanted him brought in to face royal justice. Taranath, with no personal experience of Faeterus, would follow the Lioness's lead. He did ask what was to be done with the human Hamaramis had found in the tunnels.

Kerian had recognized Jeralund as one of the Nerakan soldiers captured by Porthios and taken to Bianost as part of a ruse to free the city from bandits. Comforted by her identification, Jeralund dropped his pose as a "simple hunter" but refused to say why he was in the valley. He had helped free Kerian from the bandits in Bianost who planned to execute her, but his silence about his purpose in Inath-Wakenti was worrisome.

She advised keeping him under guard. "He's a straight fellow, for a human, but we don't know his purpose and can't risk having him escape."

Gilthas concurred. "It's likely he's a spy or a scout for an enemy, no matter how you look at it. There's probably a thousand like him combing every nook and cranny between Kortal and Sanction looking for us."

Taranath and Hytanthas bade farewell to their Speaker, picked up their gear, and departed. Kerian lingered to say her own good-bye in private.

"I thought the holy lady would have you cured by now," she said, frowning as he fought back another cough.

"The infection is entrenched. But don't worry, my heart. I

215

shall be here when you return." He touched two fingertips to her still-flat belly. "Both of you."

She placed her hand over his. "Does it please you?"

"It's the best news we've had since coming to Inath-Wakenti. Does it please you?"

He knew how profoundly stunned she'd been by the priestess's revelation, how hard it was for her to imagine having a child. Her expression reflected her continuing uncertainty, and he sought to reassure her.

"Don't be afraid."

"I'm not afraid!" she insisted. "Well, not much."

She bent and kissed his forehead. As soon as she moved away from him, Truthanar hurried across the tent, ready to offer his arm if support was required. With the brief audience at an end, Gilthas was confined to bed for a few hours of rest.

Kerian caught up to the others as they headed out of camp. They were traveling on foot. Neither Kerian nor Hytanthas wanted to risk making their griffons targets for another thunderbolt, and every horse was needed by the cavalry. Tracking the elusive Faeterus would be more practical on foot anyway. Stealth was more important than speed. Their best hope of overcoming the sorcerer was to take him by surprise.

The trio headed toward the dawn sky. The Lioness had a general idea of where they should start looking, based on the origin of the lightning hurled at her, and she set a steady pace, one they could maintain all day. They put some distance between themselves and the sprawling camp, the exercise chasing away the morning chill. They shed their light cloaks.

As she tucked her cloak into her small pack, Kerian gave Hytanthas a considering look. "You have an admirer," she said. He answered with a blank look. "The scribe. Vixona."

"She's not my type," he said brusquely.

She snorted. "What is your type?"

Rather than responding with a jest, the young captain took a deep breath and blurted, "You saved my life in the tunnels, Commander."

The seeming non sequitur confused her. She hadn't been present when he'd told the Speaker the full story of his adventures in the tunnels. She knew only the bare outline. Hytanthas explained the sound of her voice had brought him back from certain death, waking him when so many others had never opened their eyes again.

She shrugged. "The Speaker has said my battlefield voice can cut down small trees. But no one's ever likened me to a holy chorus."

He insisted he hadn't imagined it, that he would be lying dead in that tunnel if not for hearing her voice. She started to make another joke, but something in his expression stopped her. It wasn't simple obstinacy she saw there. When his eyes slid away from her questioning look and a blush reddened his face, the quick-witted Lioness knew all she needed.

"Vixona is an intelligent girl. Don't squander that. Be grateful for the gifts of chance."

"Spoken like a general," Hytanthas said sourly.

"Spoken as one who has more love than she ever deserved."

Taranath, who'd been ranging ahead, doubled back and joined them. Hytanthas's face was still flushed, and Taranath asked if something was wrong.

"It seems I have an admirer."

With that cryptic declaration, Hytanthas shifted the conversation to his griffon's well-being. Kerian watched him surreptitiously while he and Taranath talked, finally nodding to herself. It wasn't the first time she'd had to deal with an infatuated junior officer, and she knew that in time Hytanthas would be fine.

The disk of the sun was lifting above the mountains ahead. The Lioness quickened their pace toward the shadowed peaks.

* * * * *

Favaronas once more was kicked awake. He'd been deep in a heavy, dreamless slumber, but arose without protest. It amazed how quickly one became accustomed to such battering, how pathetically grateful one could be to have the use of legs, eyes, and mouth.

"Get up the mountainside," Faeterus told him. "Don't come down until I say you can."

Faeterus had created a fence of parchment, chest high and mounted on tree branches, that arced behind the central pedestal at the far end of the ledge. He had painted the parchment with the clear liquid he'd made from silver compounded with other ingredients. Favaronas's assistance was not required. Faeterus had to do the work himself, and every inch of the scroll must be saturated. Now Favaronas must leave the dying fire and remove himself from the Stair. The slightest stray shadow might ruin the sorcerer's efforts.

The spot to which Favaronas was banished was a narrow spire of rock a few yards above the Stair. It was still in deep shadow. He shivered, hugging his arms close. The western mountains were gilded by sunlight. Above, the sky changed from indigo to dark rose to pale blue, and was streaked with high, dry clouds. Faeterus stood atop the pedestal, arms raised high. The sleeves of his robe slid back, revealing narrow wrists and forearms tufted with red-brown hair. Favaronas looked away. Like all full-blooded elves, he had no body hair and found the sight repellant. Faeterus recited a brief conjuration then crossed his arms over his chest and bowed toward the valley.

The sun peered over the mountain behind them. When half its disk was showing, golden light struck the array of monoliths. They glowed steadily as the sun cleared the peak. Faeterus was shouting, flinging ancient Silvanesti words skyward in rapid succession. Favaronas had to avert his eyes from the brilliance of the monoliths, so he stared at the parchment. He couldn't make out any changes to the long tail of paper, but Faeterus continued his exhortation until the monuments lost their fire completely. Then he climbed down off the pedestal and gestured curtly for Favaronas to descend as well.

Drawing near the parchment, Favaronas could see black streaks had formed on its pristine surface. They resembled scorch marks, and he could feel a faint heat coming off the scroll. Even as he stared, the diffuse marks focused and became more distinct.

"Don't touch it!" Faeterus barked, and Favaronas, who'd had no intention of touching the scroll, quickly backed away.

The sorcerer moved sideways along the length of the parchment, studying the darkening marks. He held his ragged robe close to his body to keep the fabric from touching the scroll. Although his face was buried in the robe's deep hood, his gasps and exclamations as he beheld the metamorphosing parchment made his satisfaction plain.

"What does it mean?" asked Favaronas, keeping his voice low and deferential.

"I can't say yet. The result requires study."

"But what is it for, master?"

"You call yourself a scholar! You know nothing, like the rest of your kind!" Faeterus made a sweeping gesture, still careful not to touch the parchment. "This is the secret of Inath-Wakenti, the testament of the Lost Ones. When I have deciphered it, I shall acquire the ultimate power of this place!"

"Power left by the dragonstones?"

Hardly had the words left his lips than he wished them unsaid. Faeterus advanced on him with unexpected alacrity. A wave of one hand knocked the archivist flat on his back.

"What do you know of such things?" Faeterus hissed.

"Only the legends any elf knows of the Pit, master," gabbled Favaronas. "The Pit of Nemith-Otham."

The hood regarded him for several heart-pounding seconds then turned away. "You know nothing. And you have no need to think. Only to do as I say."

Faeterus turned away and began rolling up the long scroll. Marveling that he still possessed his limbs and senses, Favaronas sat up. He wanted desperately to beg the sorcerer to release him. The stone scrolls were dust. Favaronas wouldn't be needed to read them. Faeterus had what he wanted, his key to the valley's secrets. What possible use could Favaronas be to him? What possible threat could one exhausted, starved librarian pose? None and none. Perhaps if he asked in just the right manner, with enough groveling deference, perhaps Faeterus would let him go.

"I'll not be letting you go," Faeterus said, and laughed at Favaronas's expression. "Discerning your thoughts hardly requires a seer. They are written on your face. I have one final use for you, elf spawn. Every good conjuration requires a test subject. You shall be the first to feel the effects of my new power, the first to be destroyed. Then I will know I have succeeded."

Fresh horror coursed through Favaronas. Up until that moment he'd told himself Faeterus would release him when his usefulness had ended. That comforting fiction could no longer be maintained. He was marked for destruction. There was nothing left to lose.

Favaronas turned and ran.

Faeterus watched, all emotion lost beneath the smothering layers of his robe. He waited until Favaronas was within a few yards of the edge of the Stair then lifted his hand. Favaronas's legs jerked together, his ankles fused, and down he went, rolling over and over. When he fetched up against a low outcropping of stone, he discovered his mouth was sealed.

Gravel crunching underfoot warned him of Faeterus's approach. Even from twenty yards, the sorcerer's voice carried with astonishing clarity.

"Don't be so impatient to meet your destiny, elf spawn. You cannot change your fate."

Tears coursed from Favaronas's eyes. Faeterus had left him his sight, and he watched in abject terror as his tormentor slowly closed the distance between them.

DESTINY

"It would be easy to let you die on your belly here. But your death can serve a higher purpose. I wish I could exchange you for the Speaker of the Sun and Stars, but he's unlikely to put himself in my hands. You are the only elf spawn I have, so you will have to do."

A careless wave of one hand freed Favaronas's legs, and he was commanded to stand. "Clear away the stones and branches that held the scroll. Prepare a fire. I will not rest until I have penetrated the meaning of the key."

And so it went. Faeterus sat with the scroll on his lap. He unrolled a portion, studied it, then advanced it to peruse a new section. They had no water, and Faeterus didn't partake of his disgusting victuals. He simply sat and studied the scroll. Favaronas collected wood for a large campfire. Deliberately he kindled it near the front edge of the ledge so the flames and smoke would be more easily visible in the valley, and he loaded the fire with green wood and rotten windfall branches to thicken the smoke. If Faeterus recognized his prisoner's stratagem, he did nothing about it.

Usually Faeterus avoided direct sunlight, keeping to the shadows like some hulking insect, but not today. He remained where he was, hunched over the parchment as the sun rose higher, bathing the Stair in heat. Often Favaronas could hear him mumbling and muttering, and occasionally he would burst out with sudden vigor, shouting unintelligible phrases, then lapse back into more subdued gibbering. Favaronas could make no sense of any of it. The words sounded like Elvish but larded with unintelligible phrases and garbled by a truly barbarous accent. Favaronas couldn't tell whether Faeterus was reading the foul-sounding stuff from the scroll or simply talking to himself. Frankly, he no longer cared. His lust for knowledge and his resolve to stop Faeterus had died beneath the sorcerer's effortless cruelty. All he wanted was to escape and warn his people. Perhaps the Speaker could send his warriors to overcome the sorcerer. Maybe it was already too late. For all Favaronas knew, Faeterus could be reciting his final conjuration at that moment.

As he struggled to yank dead wood from a narrow rock crevice, he tried to remember the verse Faeterus had recited from the ancient scroll. He had an excellent memory, trained by decades of practice. He ceased trying to free the piece of dead wood and closed his eyes, allowing the words to echo again in his memory.

> *The sun's eye grows dark. No moon loves him.*
> *The stars sleep and answer not the night. Until*
> *The father holds the key in his hand,*
> > *standing before the Door*
> *And reads the Holy Key.*

Did the first line mean the release of the valley's power had to take place after sunset?

> *From the Stair of Distant Vision*
> > *under the sun's black eye*
> *The Door is opened. The Light revealed*

"Sun's black eye" sounded like an eclipse, but there were no eclipses expected for many months.

> *Burns all, consumes all, kills all*

Favaronas shuddered. That certainly sounded like a goal Faeterus would embrace.

> *Unwraps the flower, cracks the egg*
> *Pulls the seed from the ground.*
> *If the Holy Key is broken.*

More obscurity. If the Holy Key was "broken" (whatever that meant), would life be restored or forever blotted out?

Although Favaronas didn't know it, his theories about the valley were running along the same lines as his Speaker's: that it was the location of the Pit of Nemith-Otham, where five dragon-stones containing the essence of five evil dragons had been buried. The stones had been dug up later, but Favaronas thought it logical that their power could infect the area where they had lain.

The walk back to the bonfire was a long one. Every strike of his heel jarred like a blow. Faeterus had stopped mumbling. He sat silent, chin on his chest. Favaronas's footsteps slowed, grew more stealthy. If Faeterus were asleep, he might have a chance to get away. He circled wide of the unmoving sorcerer and wondered how to dispose quietly of the wood cradled in his arms.

"Put it on the fire."

He jerked in surprise, dropping several pieces of wood. He snatched them up and deposited the entire bundle next to the fire.

"Fall down," Faeterus said, quite matter-of-fact, and all feeling left Favaronas's legs. He dropped flat on his back. His legs weren't fused together, but they were paralyzed. Unable to sit up, he rolled over onto his stomach and began dragging himself across the rock ledge. Faeterus chuckled.

"Save your strength. Before the sun sets again, you will see the greatest release of power since the Cataclysm. You wouldn't want to miss that. As a royal archivist of Qualinesti, surely you want to witness firsthand the final obliteration of the elf race?"

The paralysis in Favaronas's legs was creeping upward. His belly went numb. With a last, desperate heave, he rolled himself onto his back so he might see the brilliant sky before all went dark.

* * * * *

"Do you see smoke?"

Kerian and Taranath were taking a short rest, leaning against a low monolith. Hytanthas's question brought them to their feet. He was returning from filling their water bottles at a nearby spring. All three shaded their eyes and looked high up on the mountainside.

"That's our target," Kerian declared.

Taranath was skeptical. "How can you know? Anyone could've made that fire."

"Faeterus thinks he's killed the khan's bounty hunter," she said. Taranath had told her of his patrol's rescue of Robien, from Faeterus's magical trap. "He's finally begun whatever it was he came here to do, so he doesn't care whether the Speaker's warriors find him either."

Her logic was good but not impeccable. The Nerakan soldier they'd found in the tunnels might have comrades, Hytanthas suggested, and the fire might be their doing. The Lioness's certainty was unshaken. The Nerakan was a professional warrior; if he had comrades, they wouldn't be so careless with a campfire.

That convinced Hytanthas. He was eager to press on as quickly as possible, but Kerian urged caution.

"You just said he might have begun what he came here to do!" Hytanthas protested. "We have to stop him!"

"We will but not by exhausting ourselves. A steady pace maintained through the night will get us to the source of the smoke by midday tomorrow."

Hungry and strained as they were, an all-night march was not a pleasant prospect, but Taranath and Hytanthas did not object. What had to be done would be done.

Kerian shouldered her bedroll. "I'll take the lead." She strode off among the gaunt trees and standing stones.

The smoke was a beacon rising in clear view of the entire valley. Skulking through the underbrush, Prince Shobbat had come to the same conclusion as Kerian: only Faeterus would be arrogant enough to declare his presence with a bonfire. Since the priestess's magical hand had thrown him several miles providentially in the right direction, the prince had a lead on the *laddad* expedition. He knew they were not far behind him, having first smelled then heard them. He also detected the teeming *laddad* camp, farther back, and tasted the pines and cedars, vines and wild sage all around him. It was quite dizzying, having the senses of a beast.

DESTINY

He broke into a trot, anxious to reach Faeterus first. If Kerianseray caught the sorcerer, Shobbat would never be able to extract the necessary counterspell to undo his transformation. He would spend the rest of his miserable life as a beast. That was not the destiny promised him by the Oracle of the Tree.

He pondered how to convince Faeterus to release him from the spell. The sorcerer was accustomed to life in Khuri-Khan. His sojourn in the lifeless vale would likely make him all the more eager to have his position restored. Shobbat could offer him a place at court, an estate of his own, any amount of money—as soon as Shobbat had taken his rightful place as khan. If that didn't sway him, Shobbat would dismember him, piece by piece, until he agreed.

His lips curled in a snarl. Maybe he should start with dismemberment and to the Abyss with trying to buy the sorcerer's aid. Why waste treasure and privilege on an untrustworthy mage? Pain and terror were far better inducements. He would leave just enough of Faeterus alive to remove the curse then rend him to bits.

Another pair of eyes beheld the smoke rising from the side of Mount Rakaris. They were rimmed with tears. Breetan Everride had worked her way up the eastern slope, just south of the broad ledge where the smoke originated. After scaling the heights above the ledge, she carefully made her away across the higher range toward a boat-shaped rock prominence above the Stair. Fatigue, the persistent pain of her broken rib, and the constant presence of the valley ghosts at her heels had clouded her mind and hampered her pace, until finally she made a crucial misstep. She set her foot on a slab of fractured shale and swung her full weight onto it without first testing its stability. The narrow slab shifted abruptly, sending her plunging, feet first, a hundred yards down the mountainside.

Her fall ended only when her left boot wedged in a gap between an oak stump and a sharp-edged boulder. Her body hurtled past until its momentum was arrested with a jerk that snapped her ankle. The pain was horrendous. A sharp scream was torn from her throat, and she shoved her fist in her mouth. Certain she had given herself away, she waited for the inevitable cries of discovery and the hail of elven arrows that would pierce her battered body.

None came. Wracked with agony, her face torn and bleeding, she carefully freed her shattered ankle and lay back, gasping for air and staring at the sky. Through tears, she saw a thick column of smoke rising from the cut in the mountainside below. There was almost no wind. The smoke rose straight as an arrow. Good conditions for her crossbow, if she could still manage it. Her ankle throbbed mercilessly. It was swelling inside her boot. She'd never be able to walk on it, but if she wanted to complete her mission, she had to move. The nearest place that afforded a clear shot at the ledge below was the boat-shaped prominence to which she'd been heading. It was still three hundred feet upslope.

Breetan pushed herself over onto her belly. If she couldn't walk, then she would crawl.

Twenty feet up the rocky slope, her injured foot snagged on a tree root, and she passed out from the pain. Reviving minutes later in the cool air, she drew a shaky breath, dug her fingers into the stony ground, and resumed her agonizing crawl. Lord Burnond Everride would have expended his last breath carrying out his mission. His daughter could do no less.

17

The preparations were lengthy and obscure. After bringing the Speaker back from the brink of death, Sa'ida sequestered herself in a tent on the edge of camp. There she remained for two days, seeing no one, speaking to no one, and ignoring the food and water left outside the tent. They had no victuals to waste, so morning and evening the untouched food and water was taken away and distributed elsewhere.

At dusk on the second day, the priestess finally broke her silence, asking for water. The warrior on guard outside her tent brought her a cup and brought the old general as well.

The tent flap parted a few inches. From within the dark interior, Sa'ida said, "I shall need more water than that. Much more."

She conveyed her requirements to Hamaramis. His brows lifted, but he agreed without argument. The human priestess had brought the Speaker of the Sun and Stars back from death and promised to free him of the terrible illness. If water she needed, then water she would have.

A motley collection of buckets, jugs, and pots was filled from a nearby spring and gathered outside the priestess's tent. Several hours after dark had fallen, Sa'ida asked Hamaramis to summon the Speaker. She still had not come out of the shelter.

The Speaker arrived in his palanquin. He had slept much of the day. Between the priestess's ministrations and Gilthas's own strength of will, he arrived sitting up in the woven chair rather than lying propped by pillows. Most of his remaining army and a great many ordinary elves were already there, waiting silently. Sa'ida stood just outside her tent, her back to the crowd, her head bowed. The bearers arrived, but they did not lower the palanquin to the chill ground. Hamaramis announced the Speaker's presence.

"You have brought me to the deepest graveyard in the world, Great Speaker," Sa'ida murmured.

"It's our home. Or will be. Can you help us?"

She turned to face him. Those closest in the crowd gasped at the alteration in her appearance. A robust human woman of fifty years with a typically dark Khurish complexion, Sa'ida seemed to have shrunk. Her face was sallow, and her lips were blue as with cold. In her white robe, she seemed a pallid ghost herself. She looked nearly as ill as Gilthas.

"In my service to the goddess, I have communed with many spirits: peaceful and restless, howling mad and serenely content. I have never encountered any like those who dwell in this valley. They have been crowded into this place as salted fish are packed into barrels in the *souks*. Row upon row of dead souls, very old and very angry."

She swayed unsteadily. Gilthas called for a chair. Hamaramis supported her until the stool arrived. Sa'ida sank onto it gratefully. Despite his anxiety to hear what she had to say, Gilthas was concerned for her welfare. But she turned aside his offers of food and drink.

"There are at least four layers of captive spirits here."

"Four?" Gilthas was surprised. "We thought two—the beast-people and the will-o'-the-wisps."

She shook her head. "Deep in the primeval warp and weft of this land are imprisoned the souls of an ancient colony of your race." Grimacing in pain, she pressed a hand to her forehead. "Deeper still are voices so old and so awesome I dared not try to speak to them." She regarded Gilthas with burning eyes. "This is no place to live, Great Speaker."

Murmurs arose from those nearest in the crowd. The mutterings spread as the priestess's words were passed back to those farther away.

"We have no choice," Gilthas told her, raising his voice. The crowd fell silent again. "All other realms have refused us. We must endure here or die."

Sa'ida lifted both hands to knead her forehead. "Then in spite of my misgivings, I shall try to help you."

Gilthas's sigh of relief was nearly soundless. He smiled.

"Protect us from the floating lights, holy lady. Those they touch are transported deep into tunnels beneath the valley never to wake."

"That can be done."

"Our next urgent need is food. Animals must be allowed to live here, and edible plants allowed to thrive."

"Ah, that requires doing battle with a great power. There is a mighty spell on this place. Life is severely constrained."

"By whom?" Hamaramis asked.

She managed a weary smile. "Spells are not signed like poems. The magic here is so ancient, all telltale marks of its origin have worn off. I can tell you it was the work of *laddad* wizards, a great many of them, acting in concert."

Exclamations came from the crowd. Their survival was being hampered by magic cast by their own race? The irony was very bitter.

Gilthas asked Sa'ida to bend her efforts first to controlling the will-o'-the-wisps. The elves could work on making the valley bloom if they were free of the fear of being snatched away.

He expected her to give him a list of items necessary to fulfill his demand or perhaps to say that she must rest and gather her strength before embarking on the task, but she did neither. She set to work immediately.

Rising, she removed her necklace and held the chain so the Eye of Elir-Sana dangled free at its end. She went to the first of the water-filled vessels, murmured an incantation, then dipped the amulet into the water.

"Pour the consecrated water on the ground all around the camp, being careful to form a continuous line with no gaps. It will create a barrier the guardian lights cannot cross." She moved to the next jug, adding, "Save some of it for your soldiers. When they are stalked, they should fling a few drops at the lights. Any light struck by a single droplet will vanish forever."

The civilians raised a cheer, which the warriors took up. Gilthas praised Sa'ida for her efforts.

"Don't thank me yet, Great Speaker. Without the lights to act as guardians, the spirits of the Lost Ones may be emboldened to act as they have not before." He asked what she meant. "I don't know," she replied, sounding tired and cross. "Just be wary. Any good healer will tell you, sometimes the cure can be worse than the disease."

If her warning provoked any qualms among the elves, they weren't apparent. As soon as a vessel was treated, eager hands snatched it away. Hamaramis laid claim to a few dozen small pots that his riders could carry while patrolling outside camp. The crowd dispersed, leaving the wrung-out priestess alone with the Speaker of the Sun and Stars. Gilthas pressed her once again to eat, saying they would gladly give her the very best they had.

Knowing how short was their supply of food, she assured him she would be well content with whatever was the usual fare.

"In that case, you shall dine like royalty," he said, his shadowed eyes twinkling briefly.

She gave him a sagacious nod. She understood this king well enough to know he would not feast while his subjects starved. The bearers carried his palanquin away. Sa'ida followed. Several of the Speaker's attendants accompanied her, kindly matching her slow pace.

By the time the party reached the Speaker's tent, the repast was laid: rose hip tea, roasted peas, goat cheese, and *kamenty*.

DESTINY

This last was a Khurish staple of olives and nut meats pressed into a loaf. Comprising two elven items and two Khurish foods, the menu was diplomatic if austere. The small table was lit by two candles, the delicate lines of the silver and gold candlesticks only emphasizing their humble surroundings.

Once the tea was poured, Gilthas dismissed his attendants. "Your coming has been a blessing, not least to me, holy lady," he said, sipping his tea. "What convinced you to leave your sacred temple?"

Sa'ida related her adventure with Kerian and the Torghanists. He'd heard the tale from Kerian but listened with interest to the priestess's impressions. He expressed regret that the fanatics had chosen to attack the high priestess because of the presence of his consort. Sa'ida assured him she did not blame the Lioness.

"The Nerakans were behind it," she said. "When I realized that, I knew the best way to strike back at them was to ensure the survival of their most persistent enemy."

Gilthas ate a bit of *kamenty*, chewing with great deliberation. "I am no one's enemy, merely everyone's target."

"You dissemble, Great Speaker."

"Not at all. I would happily have lived my entire life in my own country and never fought a battle, but the world would not allow it."

Sa'ida sipped her tea. It was strong stuff. The rose hips had been grown in Qualinost, dried until they were small and hard as pebbles, then packed in sawdust. The priestess found the scent ineffably sad, the essence of flowers nourished in the soil of a vanished city.

"This valley is a trap," she said very quietly.

"I do not believe it." Despite the warm glow of candlelight, the Speaker's face was pale and hard as a marble bust. "Destiny brought us here. We overcame horrendous odds and survived, for what? To perish in this hidden waste? No. I believe we will make it bloom, as we did our own cities."

Changing tack, Sa'ida said, "I know some things about the sorcerer Faeterus which might interest you." She refilled both their cups. "He has been in Khur only since the overthrow of Silvanesti."

"I thought his service to Kur of longer duration."

"He came to Khuri-Khan by way of Port Balifor on a ship full of *laddad* refugees. Within a fortnight, all the refugees were dead, save Faeterus."

"What happened to them?"

"One of the many misconceptions, half-truths, and lies Faeterus encouraged," she said, nodding. "It was said they died of a plague. The Great Khan summoned my healers to tend them, lest they infect the entire city." Her dark eyes lifted from their study of her tea and bored into his own. "The plague victims were delirious, but they were not sick, sire. They were enchanted."

Her meaning was plain. Faeterus had caused the deaths of a shipload of Silvanesti merely to conceal the reason behind his departure from the elf homeland.

"He wormed his way into the khan's confidence by performing various unsavory tasks. Sahim-Khan rewarded him with treasure and the freedom to work his sorcery, so long as it did not threaten the throne or the security of Khur."

"I'll wager Sahim came to regret his tolerance. Who exactly is Faeterus?"

The high priestess had tried to find out. His presence had caused a disruption in the city's spiritual harmony, the worst since the great dragon. She had no success. "Seeking him out on the spiritual plane was like gazing into an open hole on a dark night. It was not only a cloak of secrecy, there was a genuine *void* around him I could not fathom. All I could discover was that he is very old, he came to Khur from Silvanesti, and he has no loyalty to anyone but himself."

She pushed her teacup aside. The meal had restored some healthy color to her face. "I believe he was a prisoner in Silvanesti. His ship arrived from Kurinost, on the north coast, the location of a large prison. Many of the refugees on the ship were convicts. In the confusion caused by the minotaur conquest, I believe a contingent of prisoners escaped from the Speaker's prison, seized a boat, and made it far as Khur."

"With a viper in their midst."

"Exactly."

Gilthas knew the fortress at Kurinost. It was a large keep, erected on a solid granite pinnacle four hundred feet high. On three sides were sheer cliffs down to the sea. The fortress was connected to the mainland by a single causeway easily controlled by a standing patrol of griffon riders. There was virtually no petty crime in Silvanesti and those banished were not ordinary criminals, but dissidents, subversives, and it appeared, one rogue sorcerer. They were held without trial, often for decades.

"I pray to my goddess your hunting party finds him," she said. "There is power here no mortal should possess. If Faeterus achieves it, we may all be lost—humans, *laddad,* everyone."

With that, the repast was done. Both of them were too exhausted to maintain polite conversation. Sa'ida asked permission to retire, and Gilthas granted it.

The remains of the dinner were cleared away. Every scrap and crumb was carefully conserved for another meal.

Varanas arrived, he and his fellow scribes ready to take the Speaker's dictation, but Gilthas waved them away, declaring himself too weary. When Hamaramis came to report that the enchanted water had been distributed around the camp, he found the Speaker in bed, but the news he brought was welcome. Although many will-o'-the-wisps drifted outside the invisible barrier, none had penetrated.

"And our friends, the ghosts?" Gilthas asked.

"They are there, Great Speaker, as always. They watch but they do not advance."

"Good." The word came out on an exhale as the Speaker's eyelids closed.

Hamaramis departed with a noticeably lighter step. Dining with the human cleric, the Speaker had eaten his first meal of any size in two weeks.

* * * * *

Twenty mounted elves galloped through the night. They were patrolling several miles south of camp, keeping watch for threats as well as any possible provender. As midnight approached, they spotted glimmers of light in a particularly thick stand of monoliths. A host of will-o'-the-wisps emerged in a long line, flying with unusual swiftness toward the warriors.

The elves were carrying two small pots of water blessed by Sa'ida. The warriors formed a circle, facing outward. The two riders carrying the water pots positioned themselves on opposite sides of the circle. One was the commander of the patrol. He balanced the rough clay vessel on the pommel of his saddle. The lights swept in, and he held his warriors steady, counting the will-o'-the-wisps as they came: twenty. Exactly twenty lights and twenty elves. No two globes were the same color. Many were in some shade of white or gold, but greens, blues, and reds were sprinkled through the pack.

The lights formed a ring around the warriors. Horses and riders shifted nervously as the silent sentinels flashed by.

"Stand ready," the commander said.

He dipped a makeshift brush in the water. His first attempt missed, but on the second try, he doused a brilliant green orb as it passed his horse's nose. The effect was instantaneous. The ball of light emitted a shower of sparks. Its color changed to dark red, like a campfire ember about to go out. Falling slowly, the will-o'-the-wisp hit the ground, rolled a short way, and vanished.

The patrol cheered. At the commander's back, his second-in-command showered their tormentors with Sa'ida's special libation. A golden globe fell out of formation, sputtering and sparking, and disappeared.

Three more were dispatched, and their loss seemed to confuse the rest. They darted higher in the air and collided with each other in sudden flares of colored light. Commander and second stood in their stirrups and flourished their brushes at the wayward lights. Four more died, and the others gave up. They darted away like minnows fleeing a pebble dropped in their pool, retreating behind a line of standing stones where they remained, pulsating rapidly.

The elves were elated. For the first time, they had defeated the will-o'-the-wisps. Many of them had known elves who served in the Lioness's first expedition and who died silent, lonely deaths in the tunnels because of the bobbing lights. They were finally getting their own back.

Their commander wasn't satisfied with leaving the lights cowering behind monoliths. He wanted to destroy them. He and his second each had half a pot of water remaining, and he intended to continue the fight. Ordering the rest of the patrol to remain at a safe distance, the two rode slowly toward the monoliths. Strange business, two veteran fighters stalking their enemy with nothing more lethal than a few cups of water and a pair of straw brushes. But there was no arguing with the efficacy of the human priestess's preparation.

The elves veered apart, one passing on each side of a slender standing stone. The will-o'-the-wisps were clustered together, flying in tight circles. They were as far from the elves as they could get within the cluster of stones—only six feet away, the easiest of targets. The commander smiled grimly. What was the kender phrase? "Pickings easy as a one-eyed shopkeeper."

He stood in his stirrups and flung drops at the mass of lights. Five or six immediately flashed out of existence. The rest reacted strangely. Instead of a last, blind charge at their tormentors, they swarmed even more tightly together and dived at the ground. With a loud crash like the fall of heavy stones, the lights bored into the soil. An aura shone briefly from the hole they'd made, then all was dark once more.

Commander and second exchanged an astonished look. They rode forward and the second dismounted to inspect the hole. Four feet wide, it bored straight down through the layers of blue-green soil. The sides were hot to the touch and smooth, but cool, stale air wafted from the hole. Evidently the lights had breached one of the many tunnels.

The warrior lying on the ground by the hole called a whimsical greeting. "Anybody there?"

"Yes! Keep calling! I am coming!"

The elf recoiled sharply and jumped to his feet. His commander set him to shouting into the hole then summoned the rest of the patrol. They all crowded into the grove of white stones, weapons bared. The unknown person in the tunnel drew near the opening and shouted his relief at being found. The commander demanded his identity.

"My name is Robien. I'm a Kagonesti bounty hunter. I met your General Taranath some days ago. He can vouch for me."

They hauled him out, and he offered heartfelt thanks. The tale he told was a strange one—picked up bodily by the valley's ghosts and tossed, weapons and all, down below. Just before he heard the warrior calling, the fleeing orbs had flown straight down the tunnel at him.

"I thought I was doomed! But they passed right through me, harmless as sunlight," Robien finished.

The commander described his patrol's defeat of the guardian lights and the lights' desperate method of escape.

Robien accepted a skin of water from the riders but not their offer of a ride. His deadly encounters hadn't dissuaded him from his original mission, the capture of the sorcerer Faeterus. He settled a pair of yellow-tinted spectacles on his nose.

"Give my regards to General Taranath," he said and jogged away.

The warriors sat staring at each other for several seconds. If not for the hole in the ground, the entire affair would have seemed a collective illusion. One of the warriors, a soldier from western Qualinesti, had heard of Robien the Tireless. Kagonesti by birth, the bounty hunter had lived nearly his whole life among humans, which accounted for his foreign accent and odd appearance. It was said that in all his career, he had never failed to get his quarry. Some he did not return alive, but none ever escaped.

The commander turned his horse's head back toward camp. Despite the encounter with the bounty hunter, the real story of the night was the success of Sa'ida's blessed water. General Hamaramis must be told how well it had worked. The riders followed their leader out of the grove of monoliths.

The water was meeting with similar success in camp. Even after the liquid soaked into the ground, the barrier persisted. Will-o'-the-wisps approached the camp, came to the line drawn in the soil, and halted. They meandered up and down, left and right, but none could advance an inch farther. Everyone was delighted and the children acted upon their jubilation. Standing safely inside the line, they flung stones and dirt clods at the will-o'-the-wisps. The lights were not easy targets, dodging nimbly away from the projectiles, but when a lucky child did connect, the will-o'-the-wisp staggered in flight.

Hamaramis was drawn by the children's loud cheers. To their disappointment, he ordered an end to their merriment. None knew how long the spell would work, he said sternly, and there was no sense antagonizing the lights. He could not be everywhere, however, and the teasing and harassment of the will-o'-the-wisps continued all around the camp.

As the night progressed, more and more lights arrived. By midnight, hundreds drifted around the camp beyond the invisible barrier. Word spread, and elves were roused from sleep to witness the spectacle. The lights represented every color of the rainbow, from deepest purple to pale green to fiery red. White was the commonest hue, and those tended to be the largest will-o'-the-wisps. The lights ebbed and flowed along the barrier like schools of bright fish. Sometimes a pair would put on a burst of blinding speed and chase each other skyward in an ever-tightening spiral. At the apex of the spiral, the pair would collide, and only one would survive. The other disappeared.

The noise in camp roused Sa'ida. Blinking against the torchlight, she emerged from her tent. The festive atmosphere did not please her. After donning her cloak, she stopped the first warrior she saw and demanded to be taken to Hamaramis. The old general was on the east side of camp, halting yet another group of children from throwing pebbles at the lights.

"This must stop!" Sa'ida said, hurrying up to him. "It's very dangerous!"

He gave her a look of deep frustration. "We've been trying to stop it. The children—"

"Never mind the children! The lights are massing for a reason. They're trying to overcome the ward placed around camp!"

"What can we do?"

Sa'ida brushed the tangled hair from her face. "Is there any of the blessed water left?"

Three clay pots set aside for late-night patrols were brought to her. She asked that more water be drawn for her to bless. Hamaramis sent out the order then accompanied the priestess and two dozen warriors to the monolith the Speaker had overturned.

Most of those responding to Hamaramis's call fanned out to search the camp for extra water, but three elves, thinking to save time, took up buckets and rushed toward the spring. Unfortunately it lay outside the warded area. The celebratory air in camp had caused them to forget the very real danger posed by the will-o'-the-wisps at night. Standing atop the toppled monolith, Sa'ida saw their peril and shouted a warning, but the three had already stepped outside the barrier and they were swarmed by dozens of lights. All three disappeared instantly, without time even to cry out. Shocked, the noisy crowd fell silent.

"No one goes across the line!" Hamaramis roared. It was not an order he had to repeat.

Sa'ida had sent for straw brooms. These arrived, and the two dozen warriors were ready. Veteran soldiers, bronzed by the brutal sun of Khur and bearing the scars of combat, they felt faintly ridiculous facing a foe armed only with brooms. Sa'ida made it plain their task was serious. The overturned monolith was near the edge of camp and, thus, near the protective barrier. Each warrior dipped a broom in the water and swung it in a wide arc, flinging droplets at the will-o'-the-wisps massed only yards away.

The first salvo claimed a dozen lights. They vanished in a flare of sparks. The others ceased moving, hanging utterly still in midair. Many emitted a faint buzzing sound.

Sa'ida called for the warriors to resume their efforts, and the motionless lights were easy targets. They succumbed in great numbers. More water arrived. The buckets and ewers were handed up to Sa'ida to be consecrated to Elir-Sana. While she worked, the noise from the will-o'-the-wisps intensified. All were buzzing and the sound grew so loud, it distracted the priestess. She had to begin her incantation all over again.

The soldiers continued flinging water at the lights. The largest, brightest lights ceased buzzing. First one, then a handful, then dozens soared into the night sky, blazing brightly. When they'd ascended several hundred feet, the remaining lights joined them, and the entire assemblage shot upward until it disappeared among the stars.

A profoundly stunned silence blanketed the elf camp. Then a single voice shouted, "Long live Sa'ida! Long live the high priestess!" Thousands took up the cry.

Robe soaked (one of the water pots had spilled) and looking more harassed than heroic, Sa'ida was as amazed as anyone by the departure of the lights.

"Are they *all* gone?" Hamaramis demanded.

She nodded. By her special sense of such things, the priestess knew that not a single will-o'-the-wisp remained in Inath-Wakenti.

A group of elves raised a clamor at the foot of the overturned monolith. They were kin of the three who had disappeared while trying to reach the spring, and they wanted the tunnels searched immediately for their lost loved ones. The frame still stood above the hole at the base of the monolith, and despite a guard's efforts to pull him back, the brother of one of the newly vanished elves clung to the frame and shouted frantically down into the hole.

Hamaramis was trying to address the elves' demands when the sentinels guarding the camp's perimeter raised a warning.

The ghosts were coming.

Sa'ida had seated herself on the other end of the monolith. She jumped up with creditable agility and hurried to Hamaramis's end of the slab. Looking west, she could see ranks of pale, translucent specters appearing from the cover of trees and other monoliths. The spirits were no more numerous than usual, but they moved with slow determination directly toward the camp.

"I feared this," Sa'ida murmured. She held her hands down to the warriors standing by the monolith. Two soldiers helped her descend. "General, without the guardians, the spirits are free to roam at will. They're drawn to the living. They'll move among us, bring panic, melancholy, even madness, if we allow it."

Hamaramis paled. "Allow it? What can we do? More water—?"

"The dead are beyond the goddess's blessings."

"Then what?" he demanded.

The beloved of Elir-Sana responded to his frightened anger briefly and with formidable calm. When she'd finished explaining what must be done, the old general dispatched warriors to ride through camp and spread the word. Everyone was to retire inside their tents, close the flaps, and admit no one. The dead couldn't enter a home closed to them unless they were invited. That was the prevailing theory, anyway. Sa'ida couldn't be certain it would hold true for flimsy tents and the spirits inhabiting the "Refuge of the Damned," as Inath-Wakenti was known in the texts of her goddess.

"How long?" the general asked.

DESTINY

"Until sunrise. I pray the new light of day will banish the spirits, at least until night falls again."

Hamaramis insisted she must pass the night with the Speaker's household. Her lone tent was too exposed. She accepted the invitation and urged haste. Leading elements of the ghostly horde were halfway to the camp.

The sides of the Speaker's tent had been drawn down. Only the main door flap remained open, and the last members of Gilthas's household were hurrying inside. Hamaramis delayed to watch as elves hurried into shelter. Warriors led their horses into corrals. Parents scooped up straggling children. In moments the camp's many paths were deserted.

The old general held back the heavy tapestry that served as the door flap to the Speaker's tent and gestured for Sa'ida to precede him.

"What exactly will they do?" he asked.

"What ghosts always do. Haunt us."

18

The eastern half of the valley had fewer monoliths, and thick foliage filled the void. It wasn't lush, healthy verdure, but a mass of thorny creeper, trumpet vine, and barberry bushes. The ground covers were a tangle guaranteed to trip the unwary. The bushes were head high, with branches thick as an elf's wrist and covered by half-inch spines. Kerian and her comrades were forced to cut their way through. Arms and faces were soon covered by scratches.

Sometime after midnight Kerian halted to catch her breath. Her thoughts turned to her husband. His malady made sleep heavy but unsettled, tormenting him with fever, drenching sweats, and nightmares. As she looked back over her shoulder toward the distant camp, even more than usual she wished him pleasant dreams.

One by one her companions ceased their labors and followed her example, gazing across the starlit landscape in the direction of those they'd left behind. During their eastward trek, the land had risen slowly and they had a clear line of sight to the camp, below them. The bonfires were faint at this distance.

As the three elves watched, a great column of light suddenly blazed upward from the camp. The column resolved into a multitude of will-o'-the-wisps, streaking into the night sky, corkscrewing, crashing into each other, and washing the monoliths in frantic rainbow glory. High in the sky, the lights abruptly winked out, leaving the valley cloaked in darkness once more.

The three elves regarded each other in silent consternation.

"What was that?" Hytanthas demanded.

"The lights must have attacked the camp."

Taranath regarded Kerian in horror. Fearing the worst, he whispered, "The Speaker?"

She reassured them both. The bond between husband and wife was so strong, she knew without a doubt that Gilthas still lived. But something extraordinary had occurred, and she was equally certain he was at the center of it.

No other displays disturbed the night, so Kerian turned her face eastward again.

"It's all right," she said. "Whatever it was, it's all right."

The mountains rose gray and massive before them. The thick growth had seriously impeded their progress. Turning their anxiety into strength, they cleared the bushes with renewed vigor. The vines and barberry gave way to wild sage, and each stroke of their swords filled the air with its heavy odor. The smell was not a pleasant one. Trust the cursed valley, Kerian thought bitterly, to warp a savory herbal aroma into a nauseating stench.

The heavy foliage ended abruptly, and all three elves stumbled gratefully into the open, breathing deeply of fresher air. The ground ahead was dotted with stunted pines and plain gray boulders rather than the usual snow-white monoliths. High, thin clouds had begun to cover the stars above Mount Rakaris.

They paused to clean their blades. Kerian had just slipped hers into its scabbard when she spotted someone sitting on a nearby boulder, watching them. She'd had no warning of his presence. When she glanced up at the clouding sky, he hadn't been there. When she looked down again, he was. Unnerved, she barked a loud challenge. Hytanthas had his sword halfway out of its sheath, but Taranath put a hand on its hilt, halting him.

"Robien," Taranath called. "Kerian, this is the bounty hunter we freed from Faeterus's trap."

Robien slid off the boulder and approached. Starlight glinted off his spectacles. He bowed to the Lioness with a sweep of one hand. "Lady Kerianseray," he said with formal precision.

"Kerian will do. Taran's told me how he found you." Giving him an appraising look, she added, "You have a powerful friend."

He made an offhand comment about the khan, and she let it go. He was alive because a flock of bats had shaded the creeping sand, delaying its deadly effect until Taranath's patrol could dig him out. If Robien didn't realize who had sent those bats to lifeless Inath-Wakenti, it wasn't her place to enlighten him. She asked why he was here.

"We're pursuing the same target. It has occurred to me we should join forces."

The Lioness regarded him in silence for a time. He was accomplished, and his abilities would be useful in their quest to stop Faeterus. But she didn't trust his motives. He'd slipped away from Taranath's elves almost as soon as they'd returned to camp. He hadn't wanted their help then, why did he want it now? In her usual blunt fashion, she put that very question to him. He met bluntness with bluntness.

"What do you intend for the sorcerer?" he asked.

Her eyes narrowed. "I intend to have his head before he can cause more grief."

"My contract is to bring him back to Khuri-Khan alive." She started to argue, but he held up a hand. "Contracts can be amended."

Sahim-Khan would pay more for a live victim to punish. But two brushes with death in the space of a few days had shaken Robien's considerable confidence. He told them of the attack by the spirits, that he might have wandered forever in the tunnels if not for his enchanted spectacles. Not only could they detect any trace of living beings, but they allowed him to see in utter darkness. As it was, he'd been trapped underground for two days, and in that time he'd done some hard thinking. He'd concluded that he could find Faeterus, or he could survive Inath-Wakenti. Doing both might be more than one elf, no matter how skilled, could manage on his own.

"I agree the mage is too dangerous to take alive," he finished. "All I ask is sufficient evidence to prove to Sahim-Khan that Faeterus is indeed dead."

"Two ears and a tail for you, it is," replied Kerian with unconscious irony.

The two elves, both Kagonesti yet so very different, clasped hands, and the Lioness found her small force greatly enlarged.

Now that they were clear of the heavy undergrowth, she wanted to make a quick reconnaissance. In hacking their way through the tangle, they'd lost the trail. Robien offered to find it again because he was the freshest of the group. The other three rested, sharing a water bottle. They hadn't long to wait. The bounty hunter returned and announced he'd found a trail.

"Faeterus?" Kerian asked.

He shook his head. "No, an elf he captured and forced to aid him. I'd know the prints of Favaronas's ragged sandals anywhere."

Kerian choked on a mouthful of water. "Favaronas? He's here and alive?"

"He was two days ago, when the prints were made." Robien was surprised that the Lioness knew Favaronas. He'd thought Favaronas an itinerant scholar.

"He's the Speaker's archivist! The question is how do you know him?"

They had met weeks before, Robien said, by the creek near the entrance to the valley. Scholar and bounty hunter traveled together for a time, and when Faeterus left Robien to die in the grip of the strangling sand, he'd kidnapped Favaronas. From the signs Robien had deduced that Favaronas was doing all he could to delay the sorcerer's progress to Mount Rakaris, even though he must think Robien dead and there was little hope of aid.

Kerian brought the discussion to an abrupt end, telling Robien to take the lead. Once they reached the trail left by Favaronas, she quickened their pace. Hytanthas struck up a conversation to talk with Robien, eager to compare their experiences in the tunnels. The two of them led, with Taranath and Kerian close behind. The Lioness mentioned the part Favaronas had played in her first expedition to Inath-Wakenti. She'd thought him lost with the rest of her unlucky band after its departure from the valley. Robien's news amazed her. Tough, battle-hardened veterans perished, but the inexperienced, comfort-loving librarian survived.

Fate was strange.

* * * * *

Huddled inside their makeshift shelters, the elves listened in terrified silence to the slow, muffled footfalls outside. Lamps were extinguished lest their light attract attention. Some elves, braver or more curious than their fellows, peered out through small tears in the fabric and beheld a prodigious sight. Illumined by only starlight, the dead walked among them.

The ghosts were gaunt, clad in plain shifts or kilts. Faces were greenish pale, with dark holes where eyes should be. They walked with measured tread, heads turning slowly right and left, as though seeking something. Standing outside the tent flaps closed firmly against them, some sobbed and groaned, wringing their hands. Others shook fists at the night sky, or scratched at the tents with spectral hands. A few crawled along the ground, clawing at the dirt to drag themselves forward. Although the elves heard the thud of numerous footfalls and the scrabbling of those who crawled, none of the spirits left any prints in the dust.

Now and then one shrieked loudly, like a victim receiving

a deathblow. The blood-chilling screams sent them hurrying away from spy holes and back to the center of their shelters, where they clung to each other for comfort. The nation that had borne the wrath of the nomads of Khur was paralyzed by an army of ghosts.

Round and round the apparitions tramped. As the priestess had hoped, they could not enter a closed tent, but neither would they give up trying. The assemblage of living souls drew them as a feast draws starving folk.

Accidents occurred. Several tents collapsed when the frightened occupants knocked down the support poles. By the time the tents were up again, the ghosts were inside. They reached out with gray hands, their icy touch straight from the grave. Some elves fled their fallen shelters only to face more spirits outside. Others, frozen into immobility by terror, simply sat in horror as the ghosts clustered more and more thickly around them, crying, wailing, holding out pleading hands.

Up close the specters displayed strange features. Despite having the upswept ears characteristic of full-blooded elves, some had thick tufts of hair on faces and arms. Others had only three or four fingers on each hand or bizarrely shaped ears—not even round like a human's, but triangular and set atop their heads, like the ears of a dog or cat. Long, pointed teeth framed lolling black tongues. Elves who challenged the invaders with sticks, stones, and tools quickly regretted their courage. Ghosts who met defiance seemed to grow stronger and become more solid, and they returned violence with violence. Elves attempting to defend home and family mobbed, buried beneath raving, laughing apparitions. No elf could bear such torment. The fortunate ones lost consciousness. The rest went mad.

In the Speaker's tent, everyone gathered close around their king. The fire in the central hearth burned brightly. Gilthas ordered it built higher, that they should not be cowering in darkness. A terrible scream split the air. No ghostly wail, that sound had been wrung from a living throat, and it brought

Hamaramis and the other warriors to their feet, hands going to sword hilts or reaching for bows.

"This is not a threat weapons can defeat," Gilthas said. Although outwardly composed, he, too, found the anguish of his people nearly impossible to endure. His own physical suffering he'd born with silent fortitude. His nation's pain cut at his very heart.

One young warrior strode to the heavy tapestry covering the opening. Sa'ida warned him not to open the flap. The elf whirled to face her, hand gripping his sword hilt so tightly the knuckles showed white.

"What do they want?" he cried.

"What we all want. To live."

"But they're dead!"

The priestess nodded. "They do not know that. Or they do know but are fighting against that truth."

Obeying the Speaker's quiet request, the young elf returned to the fire. The others gathered around as Sa'ida told what she knew of ghosts. They are, she said, souls trapped on the mortal plane by magic, by the power of a curse, or by their own unspent desires. So numerous a legion of specters in Inath-Wakenti hinted at a great conflict in ages past. Those exiled here had been imprisoned by magical controls so strong that even their souls were not allowed to leave. Like Gilthas before her, the priestess sensed loneliness from them. Being more attuned to such things than he, she went further, explaining that over the centuries, the spirits' loneliness had hardened into a terrible rage, a thirst to be revenged for their suffering. She shivered and rubbed her arms as if chilled.

"Perhaps they'll depart now that their masters, the will-o'-the-wisps, have gone?" Gilthas suggested.

A scream caused all of them to flinch. Something heavy hit the canvas wall of the tent and caromed off. Sniffling sounds followed then slowly faded away.

Varanas dropped his broken stylus, which he'd snapped in two at the sound of the scream. "I cannot bear this!" he said.

"Will it go on all night, lady?"

"The dead have motives the living can scarcely comprehend," Sa'ida answered. She repeated her hope that sunrise would disperse the ghosts.

"Here's to the dawn," said Hamaramis, downing a swallow of potent *fluq*. The Speaker and Sa'ida echoed the sentiment, lifting their small cups of *kefre* in salute.

A reddish glow brightened one side of the great tent, and the smell of burning canvas filled the air. Warriors, attendants, and scribes were on their feet in an instant. They couldn't let the camp burn down around them!

Gilthas rose, leaning heavily on his staff. "Lady?" he said, offering an arm.

A high priestess could not lose face before the *laddad*. Exiled and humbled they might be, but theirs was a civilization stretching back millennia. The Speaker, a young adult by the standards of his race, likely had seen more summers than the most aged Khur alive. His eyes, shadowed by travail, regarded her with steady confidence.

With great dignity, Sa'ida took his thin arm.

He smiled. "There. Whatever befalls me, I shall have a healer close at hand."

The fire was subsiding. By the time the slow-moving Gilthas passed through the door, it was almost out. A neighboring tent, belonging to the high-born Silvanesti clan of Kindrobel, had been reduced to ashes. On each side of the destroyed tent, the lane was full of pallid apparitions. Slowly, their attention shifted to Gilthas, standing in the open doorway of his tent.

He stepped outside. Embers drifted down. Sa'ida brushed stinging coals away from his face. He drew a deep breath.

"Specters of Inath-Wakenti, listen to me! You have no business with us. Begone! Leave us in peace!"

The ghosts started shuffling forward, converging on him.

"I don't think they're listening," Sa'ida murmured.

"They hear me very well." He raised his voice. "The force

that held you captive is gone. Can't you sense it? You can go to your long-denied rest!"

A dry, sighing sound filled the air, as though hundreds of voices all whispered at once.

"I can't understand you," Gilthas told them patiently.

Despite his calm demeanor, Sa'ida, holding his arm, felt his pulse racing. The Pathfinder was good at dissembling, but he was frightened. So was she. She had never been among so many spirits before. The longing, the desperate greed for life emanating from the bleak assembly took her breath away. Waves of cold broke over her like showers of ice. Her magical training caused her to feel it more strongly than the elves but also equipped her to deal with it. Still, she knew a fierce, primal urge to flee.

"You're hurting my arm," Gilthas whispered. Embarrassed, she eased her grip.

Behind them, Hamaramis begged the Speaker to return inside. The advancing spirits were only yards away.

"I'll not be shut in by them. Either they must go or we must." A flash of his old strength, the strength of his illustrious ancestors, straightened Gilthas's back and he shouted, "And we aren't going!" He turned and thrust a finger at the nearest ghosts. "You are dead! Your time in this world is long over. Go now! Return to the realm of peace and eternal rest!"

To the surprise of all, including Gilthas himself, the advancing apparitions faltered. Their whispering subsided. Gilthas turned to the spirits on his left and repeated his command. The creeping advance halted.

Sa'ida no longer watched the ghosts; her attention was on her patient. Such power she felt from his starved, diseased frame! It burned in him like a beacon, unquenched despite his many ills.

"I am the Speaker of the Sun and Stars. I know great wrongs were done to you. You were imprisoned here by my ancestor long ago. I don't know what crimes you committed, and I do not care. I absolve you of any guilt. You have walked the mortal world too long. It's time for you to go."

From the assembled spirits flowed a wave of melancholy so strong Sa'ida felt tears prick her eyes. They did not weep or wail, but their grief was manifest to the sensitive priestess.

"Your chains are broken. The door has been opened. Nothing holds you here but ancient pain and rage. Let them go. Cease your struggles. The inexorable tide of time will bear you away. You have only to cast away your hate, and go."

The night darkened as the last embers of the burned tent winked out. Even so, it was clear to the high priestess and the elves crowded in the door of the Speaker's tent that the ranks of ghosts were thinning. Several spirits had vanished completely. Others were so attenuated as to be barely visible.

Gilthas sighed deeply. The arm Sa'ida held trembled. "I am tired," he declared, still addressing the spirits. "But I cannot rest until I know my people are safe. What you had is gone, but no one can hurt you now, and you must not hurt in return. Farewell to you all. Gilthas, son of Tanis and Lauralanthalasa, bids you good-bye. Rest well."

They went. One by one, the doleful spirits faded away until only darkness remained. When every single one was gone, Gilthas gave up his own struggle. Hamaramis arrived in time to help Sa'ida catch him when his knees buckled. Two warriors lifted him.

"Wait," he commanded, voice hoarse from his oration. "General, inspect the camp for damage and casualties."

Hamaramis watched him carried back inside the tent. The old general tried to comprehend what he had just witnessed. He had seen many things in his long life—terrible things such as the destruction of Qualinost and wondrous things such as the Speaker leading his people down a desert mountain and away from murderous nomads in the dead of night. The Speaker's stand outside Inath-Wakenti against raging nomads had left Hamaramis amazed and awed. But it paled in comparison with the night's events. He led a company of warriors through the camp. They found not one ghost remaining, and still he could not grasp what his sovereign had accomplished. With only the power of his words, the Speaker had exorcised hundreds of malign spirits from the land they had haunted for centuries.

None of them could know with certainty whether the spirits would return, but in his heart Hamaramis believed Gilthas Pathfinder had banished the ghosts forever.

*　*　*　*　*

Favaronas also witnessed the departure of the will-o'-the-wisps. Lying on his side, still paralyzed from the chest down, he was trying to find release from constant terror in sleep when a flash brought his eyes open. The great fountain of light swirling up and away from the elves' camp reminded him of gnomish fireworks he'd seen once in Zaradene. He stared in amazement until Faeterus strode before him, blocking his line of sight.

"There is another here. The Watchers have been dispersed," the sorcerer said.

Favaronas felt hope flicker in his heart. The Speaker had magical assistance! Perhaps all was not lost. If the new mage was powerful enough to send away the lights in the valley, he might be potent enough to forestall Faeterus.

The sorcerer had been staring out toward the now-dark valley. He chuckled, an unpleasant sound, and said, "When I am done, that spectacle will seem like a child's game."

Although Favaronas watched the sky, nothing further happened. Trying to hold on to the ember of hope, he allowed exhaustion to claim him.

Hope did not last long. When he awoke again, the sky was pale gray with the coming dawn, and disappointment chilled him more surely than the cold rock beneath him. Whoever had banished the lights, he hadn't come to defeat Faeterus. The sorcerer was still there, Favaronas was still paralyzed, and this was very probably the last day of his life. If Faeterus had his way, it would be the last day his entire race would ever see.

Flinging his hands skyward, Faeterus exclaimed in the same abbreviated ancient tongue used on the stone scrolls.

DESTINY

Favaronas struggled to decipher the abbreviations and archaic declensions and translate the words into modern Elvish. But understanding the words did not mean he could fathom their intended purpose.

"Awaken land, awaken sky, awaken sun! Ancient shadows long buried, awake! Come forth and blind the sun!" the sorcerer cried then called for the shadows and "forgotten eyes" to do his bidding.

The sky had brightened to shell pink. Thus far the sorcerer's commands seemed unavailing. His booming oratory went on a long time, until the sun cleared the peaks behind them. When light touched the outer edge of the Stair, Faeterus turned to face the new sun. As always, he was swathed in many layers of moldering cloth and Favaronas wondered how he could bear it. The hood must be stifling.

His exhortations in the old tongue gave way to a chant. Only eight words repeated over and over, but Favaronas could not decipher them. The words were not Elvish of any era, nor the abbreviations of the stone scrolls. They sounded coarser than any elf tongue. In the oldest chronicles there were references to *Kevim,* the language of the gods, and Favaronas wondered if that was what he was hearing.

The chant was remorseless. Faeterus's voice marched up the vocal register then down. He punctuated his invocation with eight loud claps then returned to the rising and falling chant. It went on so long, Favaronas thought he would scream. The words hammered at him, bored into his skull. He was sure he would never forget them, just as he was certain he could never pronounce them. He wrapped his arms around his head, trying to shut out the sound and spare his battered ears. It didn't help. The words continued to beat down on him like a hail of stones.

A tremor shook the ground, then another. Faeterus lifted his arms during the chant then dropped them in the brief interval of silence. With his heavy robe flapping, he resembled some impossibly awkward bird trying to take to the air. At one point in the chant, he stamped his right foot, causing the mountain to vibrate like a hammer-struck gong. The blows of his heel sent loose stones tumbling down the mountainside.

Favaronas lifted his gaze. He gasped.

Above the center of the valley, a dark mass had appeared. It hovered high over the Tympanum. To be visible from that distance, it had to be gigantic. With each succeeding eight-word chant, the mass grew. Soon it darkened a sizable portion of the valley beneath it. In growing horror, Favaronas realized the sorcerer's purpose. The verse in the stone scroll spoke of "the sun's black eye." With no natural eclipse available, Faeterus would blot out the sun with a dark cloud of his own creation.

There and then he resolved not to wait for whatever awful fate Faeterus had planned for him. Clawing at the stony ground, seeking a handhold, he hauled himself forward. His progress was pitifully slow, but it was progress. All he need do was reach the front edge of the plateau, fifty yards away, and roll over. His torment would end at last. As he dragged himself along, he tried to make peace with what he had done.

Ambition was at the root of all his trouble. He should have gone with Glanthon and the warriors when they departed the valley. Instead he'd chosen to probe secrets no mortal should ever know. Faeterus was still bellowing his invocation, but Favaronas didn't hear him. Instead, he heard Glanthon's voice calling his name. The warrior had searched a long time before assuming Favaronas was lost in the desert and riding on without him. If he could change one single moment in his life, Favaronas would never have hidden himself away from Glanthon. He would have stayed with the warriors and traveled back to Khurinost.

His path took him by Faeterus, but the sorcerer paid him no heed. Faeterus' ragged robe was stained with sweat. Blood flowed from the sole of his foot as he continued to stamp the ground. A fleeting glimpse of the sorcerer's face within the hood caused Favaronas to avert his gaze quickly. Faeterus's eyes seemed dark holes in his alien-looking face.

The pavers covering the surface of the Stairs were rough, worn by centuries of weather to a harsh, pebbled texture. The breast of Favaronas's *geb* was ripped in a dozen places. A trail of blood stretched out behind him. His fingertips were bloody, several fingernails torn away. When his accumulation of hurts grew great enough, he faltered, resting his head on the cool stone.

Faeterus's voice echoed like thunder.

Move, you useless creature, he lashed himself, and with trembling hands reached out to claim another three feet of stone.

19

The elf camp, so lately delivered from the menace of ghosts and will-o'-the-wisps, was thrown into new panic when the boiling, black cloud stained the morning sky. Most elves fled at once, seeking shelter in the outer ring of monoliths. When the cloud had swelled to match the size of the stone platform below it, the camp was blasted by wind. Air rushed toward the cloud, collapsing tents and sucking up smaller objects along the way. Cups, water jugs, and tools raced end over end on their way to the distant platform.

The spectacle confounded Gilthas and his advisors. Standing with them outside the Speaker's tent, Sa'ida was alarmed by the display. No one in the valley but Faeterus had the magical prowess to stir up such forces, she said.

Gilthas exchanged a worried look with Hamaramis. Kerian's hunting party must have failed to put an end to the sorcerer's activities. Yet Gilthas refused to give up hope. The Lioness might yet prevail.

Shouting over the wind, the old general asked Sa'ida if she could stop whatever was happening. Her reply was unequivocal. The black vortex swirling above the platform was beyond her abilities. In fact, the raw release of magical energy was making her distinctly ill. A camp chair cartwheeled past, narrowly missing her. Gilthas drew her further into the lee of the large tent, beckoning his advisors to follow.

"Can you slow it down or interfere in any fashion?" he asked. Even with the bulk of the tent behind them abating the wind somewhat, Gilthas was forced to raise his hoarse voice to its limit to be heard over the howling gale.

Little confidence showed on Sa'ida's ashen face, but she said she would try. She stepped a few feet away from the group. Lifting the Eye of Elir-Sana free of her robe, she clasped her hands around it and bowed her head. When she drew her hands apart, the amulet hung suspended in a band of bluish light connecting her hands. Her lips moved in a silent incantation, lines of concentration etching her forehead. The band of light thickened and grew brighter, and she hurled it into the sky. Caught by the wind, it flew through the debris-filled air, dwindling with distance. When it reached the cloud, there was a flare of light and the wind eased, but for a moment only. The gale resumed undiminished.

Sa'ida rejoined the group. She looked even more ill than before. "This is prodigious sorcery, Great Speaker! I don't know what Faeterus is trying to unleash, but you must take your people away. Put as much distance as possible between yourselves and this . . ." Her voice had been failing. It finally trailed away completely, and she waved a hand weakly at the huge cloud.

As a warrior supported the fainting priestess, Gilthas gave the command: "General! Everyone is to flee. Where does not matter, as long as it's away from the stone disk. Tell them to leave everything behind and run. Run, General!"

Hamaramis took the reins of his horse from an aide and offered the animal to the Speaker. Gilthas shook his head. "I stay."

The general exploded in denials. He flatly refused to leave Gilthas behind. When fear for his sovereign led him to threaten to have the Speaker carried away against his will, Gilthas's outraged expression stopped his outburst cold.

"Sire," he cried, "please forgive me! I should never have

spoken so, but you cannot expect me to—"

"I can and do, General. Take Lady Sa'ida and go. I will not say it again."

Once Hamaramis was mounted, the priestess was boosted up before him. Holding her with one hand and the reins of his nervous horse with the other, he stared down at his king. Fear and worry battled over his lean, lined face.

"It's only wind," Gilthas said, managing a smile.

Anguish unabated, Hamaramis turned his horse's head and rode away.

The palanquin was never very far from Gilthas. He seated himself in the woven chair and ordered the bearers to flee. They would not be moved. Offering no arguments or pleas, they simply sat on the ground alongside the palanquin and lowered their heads. Each grasped a handful of the Speaker's robe and held on.

It wasn't only the elves in camp who battled the wind. Kerian's company was forced to deal with it as well. The air raced down Mount Rakaris and into the valley, steady as a waterfall. the Lioness knew such a constant wind must be unnatural, and she was certain it was the work of Faeterus. When the dark cloud over the center of Inath-Wakenti became plain, she and her comrades knew at least the locus of the wind, if not the reason behind it.

The two younger elves were in the lead, with Kerian and Taranath only yards behind. The mountainside they were climbing was still washed in late-morning sunshine, but the center of the valley was as deeply shaded as though dusk had come. A column of dust and debris, like a captive tornado, slowly rose from the ground to the center of the cloud. The sight drew an anguished cry from young Hytanthas, who halted in his tracks. The others kept moving, and as Kerian came abreast of him, she gruffly told him to do the same.

"Commander, our people are there!" he protested.

"I know."

"The Speaker is there!"

DESTINY

She took his arm in a painful grip and pushed him onward. "I know!" she snapped, not even glancing at the camp. "The only way we can help them is by going on!"

They jogged to catch up with the others. Taranath was closest; Robien was a few yards ahead of him. As the Lioness and Hytanthas came abreast of Taranath, a streak of brown hurtled from the wind-whipped bushes on the right and hit Robien square in the chest. The bounty hunter went down hard. The furious wind had masked any telltale sounds. The attack had taken them all completely by surprise. Hytanthas shouted. All three drew swords and ran to Robien's aid.

He rolled over and over, clutching the neck of a furry beast. He managed to hold it away from his throat and somehow halt their tumbling with himself on top. Letting go with his left hand, he jammed a forearm against the creature's jaw. It writhed, trying to throw Robien off. He planted a knee in its ribs.

Racing to cover the distance, Taranath recognized Robien's attacker. "It's the beast the priestess banished!" he exclaimed.

"Shobbat?" Kerian was furious. She'd wanted to kill the creature when it appeared in their camp. By flinging the monster away, Sa'ida had only delayed the inevitable and put Robien's life at risk in the bargain.

"Kill him!" she shouted.

Despite the wind, Shobbat had no trouble hearing the Lioness's command. He had jumped Robien to keep the bounty hunter from leading the *laddad* to Faeterus. If the *laddad* captured the sorcerer, Shobbat might never be free of his hell of fur and fangs. The Lioness's shout caused him to fight even harder, and he had an important advantage over his foe. All the stealth and strength of his beastly form was coupled with the cleverness of a man's brain. He opened his jaws, releasing his hold on the bounty hunter's tunic, curled a long-fingered forepaw into a fist, and punched the elf hard in the face.

Robien saw three suns, as the kender say. As his head

snapped backward from the blow, he flung up an arm to ward off further strikes. Shobbat's jaws opened, ready to clamp down on the unprotected arm.

His teeth found only air. Taranath had arrived, and his sword sliced through Shobbat's short, bushy tail. Shobbat shrieked in pain. Kerian bore in, thrusting her weapon's point at his chest. Her blade found fur and slid across, but leaving a long, deep cut. While they kept Shobbat busy, Hytanthas dragged Robien out of the way. Kerian could hear the young captain frantically asking Robien where he was hurt, but she and Taranath kept their attention on the crouching beast. Blood dripped from Shobbat's chest.

"You will regret this!" he rasped.

"My only regret is not killing you sooner!"

Kerian lunged, and Taranath followed half a heartbeat later. Despite his wounds, Shobbat astonished them all. Coiling himself almost double, he sprang, not directly at his attackers, but completely over their heads. They whirled but he was faster. In two bounds he had vanished into the low brush and scrub pines.

Hytanthas was tending Robien's wound. Taranath's timely intervention had saved the Kagonesti's arm, but in his first pounce, Shobbat had scored two bloody lines on Robien's right shoulder with his fangs. Although not crippling, the injury was painful. Robien watched in stoic silence as Hytanthas bandaged the wound with a linen strip.

There was no time to rest. Robien drank from the water bottle Hytanthas pressed on him then took the lead again. In obvious pain, his face damp with sweat, he set an even more rapid pace than before his injury. The wind was destroying the trail. The fire on the mountainside had died before the gale began. Without the smoke column to guide them, they had to hurry before all signs were lost.

Eventually they spotted the tableland inset in the mountainside a few miles above. It was obviously wrought by hand and appeared a likely place for a mighty conjuration. The fast-fading traces of the trail headed directly for it.

DESTINY

Robien prided himself on his detachment. He could track the worst criminal or bring to heel the most pathetic debtor with equal efficiency and aplomb. Shobbat's attack was the latest in a line of confidence-shaking assaults and it had infuriated him. His quarry was Faeterus, but if an opportunity to slay Shobbat presented itself, Robien would seize it without hesitation.

* * * * *

Favaronas paused to catch his breath. He was nearly to his goal. The edge of the plateau was only a few feet away. In a short time, he would be free of his torment, and Faeterus would be denied whatever ugly fate he had in mind for his captive. Part of him wished he could see the sorcerer's design finished, if only to witness the unmasking of the awesome, ancient power. But Faeterus wanted him alive to test the efficacy of the spell. At least Favaronas would have the satisfaction of denying him that.

The wind was blasting relentlessly down the mountain, across the valley, and up into the writhing, black cloud. The cloud was massive, over a mile in diameter. Faeterus's bellowing chant ended abruptly. Favaronas risked a glance over one shoulder.

Palms pressed together, Faeterus thrust his hands skyward. In Old Elvish he roared, *"Now shall the Eye of Darkness seize the sun!"*

A silent concussion shook air and ground. The wind went from full gale to dead calm in an instant, as though a great door had slammed shut, and the sky darkened rapidly. The black cloud flattened out, spreading like dark oil to blot out the sky. Noon was only an hour away, yet twilight was consuming Inath-Wakenti. The air rapidly cooled.

Favaronas wrenched his attention away from the aerial spectacle and frantically dragged himself the last few feet to the lip of the plateau. He heaved his upper body over, and the drop spun before his eyes. He would fall at least forty yards before striking rocks. That ought to be more than enough to kill him.

Elves were climbing up the mountain toward him.

He gripped the plateau's edge with both hands, not daring to believe his eyes. Several figures darted among the trees. Even in the occulted light, he could see glints of metal on them. The Speaker's soldiers were coming!

As frantically as he had rushed headlong toward his own destruction, Favaronas now shoved himself back from the edge. Three, perhaps four, tiny figures moved among the sparse trees, knotted bushes, and tumbled boulders. They must be scouts, for a much larger body of warriors following behind.

Stealing a careful look at Faeterus, he saw the sorcerer had gone to consult the lengthy scroll. Relief washed through him, so strong it made his head throb. Faeterus had not noticed the approach of the scouts nor Favaronas's position at the edge of the Stair.

He looked downslope again. The scouts were no longer visible. Squeezing his eyes shut, he willed them to hurry.

* * * * *

The sudden cessation of the wind left the Speaker's loyal bearers breathless. They had held on to him as shipwrecked mariners cling to a raft, but in spite of their fears, the wind never became strong enough to endanger them. The camp was scoured clean of every small, loose object. Half the shelters—those closest to the stone platform—were a tangle of fallen canvas, broken stakes, and snarled rope.

The wind had gone, but the black cloud remained and was spreading across the open sky like a curtain falling over a vast stage. Summer day was swallowed up by summer evening. The unnatural twilight brought with it an ominous silence even more complete than usual for the Silent Vale. One of the bearers asked the Speaker what was happening. Gilthas admitted he did not know.

"We must find the holy lady. She can tell us what is going on." Although he spoke with conviction, in truth Gilthas feared Sa'ida knew no more than they.

DESTINY

Before the bearers could sort themselves out and lift the palanquin, the elf nation came streaming back to camp. Hamaramis arrived with Sa'ida mounted behind him. The old general looked sheepish.

"False alarm, sire!"

Gilthas wasn't so certain. As he'd suspected, the priestess could add little to what they already knew. A great conjuration was under way. Sa'ida had never seen its like before, but Faeterus obviously meant them harm.

"Are we sure of that?" Gilthas asked.

"No one performs a working this enormous for gentle reasons," was her grim reply.

Hamaramis dismounted and helped the priestess down. In a low voice, he asked his king whether they should evacuate.

"Where to, General?" Gilthas asked.

Gesturing broadly south, Hamaramis said, "Anywhere outside this valley."

Gilthas shook his head. It would require days for the thousands of elves to move out of Inath-Wakenti, even if they had someplace to go, which they did not. And there was no guarantee distance would offer safety from Faeterus's evil design.

The priestess left the two elves. She would retire to her tent, she said, to give serious thought to what she might do to help. If nothing else, perhaps she could tear holes in the black cloud. Sunlight might spoil Faeterus's plans.

Before departing, she examined the Speaker. His fever had risen, and he was coughing flecks of blood. He did not dispute her insistence that he must rest, but merely said he would be sure to do so when the sun shone again and his people were safe.

The elves returned to their improvised homes. Attempts were made to lift flagging spirits. Fires were kindled to ward off darkness and the chill. Flutes appeared and long-hoarded bottles of nectar and Khurish *fluq* were passed around. Songs were sung and salutes offered.

263

Hamaramis took a gloomy view of the merriment, but Gilthas did not. He called for his steward. He intended to go among his people and didn't wish to go empty-handed. Once his few potables were brought, he set his bearers in motion. With the dour general riding alongside, the Speaker made the rounds of the camp. He hailed everyone he saw, as many by name as he knew, and drank salutes with any who desired it. If his subjects were drinking fine Silvanesti nectar, then he did too. If they had nothing but raw *fluq*, then the Speaker of the Sun and Stars raised a cup brimming with Khurish liquor. Not by the smallest flicker of expression did he betray his great dislike of *fluq*.

While the brave celebrations proceeded, Sa'ida repaired alone to her tent. She had come to the forsaken valley as much to discomfort her enemies in Khuri-Khan as to aid the *laddad*. The *laddad* khan's courage and gallant manner had won her over, and she gladly applied her healing art to him. But she was well and truly frightened. Although a priestess of long and honorable service to her goddess, Sa'ida had no skill for high magic such as Faeterus commanded. Her awareness of the ancient power in the valley required no especial skill, only sensitivity. She wore a brave face for the *laddad,* but in the solitude of her tent, she let go of pretense. Her heart raced, her hands shook, and sweat soaked her white robe.

And yet she would not let fear keep her from doing what she could. Settling as comfortably as she could on the borrowed carpet, she composed her mind and set herself free of her body with a far-seeing spell. Her *naes* (the Khurish word for soul, or a person's captive spirit) rose high above the *laddad* camp. From that vantage point, the movement of the black cloud was plain. The vast mass wasn't merely thinning and expanding to cover more area, it was turning slowly on a central axis sited directly over the valley's geographical heart. The rotation was antisunwise, to Sa'ida a sign of negative power. She willed herself to move toward it, but her *naes* could not pass through the cloud. She made a second attempt and the reaction was violent. Instead of merely being halted, she was hurled back to her body. She arrived with such force, her body was thrown backward. It struck the side of the tent, knocking a support loose and collapsing half the structure. As she lay, gasping for breath, laughter sounded in the darkness.

"Woman, you cannot trifle with me!"

Sa'ida struggled to sit up. "Faeterus! What are you after here?"

"What every practitioner of our art wants: power! When I have it, the first to feel my wrath will be the spawn of those who condemned me. And after I've dealt with the elves, I shall turn to you desert-dwelling vermin."

Sa'ida lifted her hand to the Eye of Elir-Sana. It was a simple gesture, meant to shield the goddess's image from Faeterus's blasphemous presence, but contact with the jewel sent a surge of new strength through her. She concealed it, maintaining her pose of cowed weakness.

"Why do you hate the *laddad?*" she asked carefully. "You are one yourself."

"I am not!" Although the shout echoed like thunder, she knew no one else could hear it. Faeterus's voice was meant for her alone. "Chance gave me their form, but I am not of their cursed race!"

"What race are you, then?"

A figure took shape in the darkness. Faeterus allowed his *naes* to reveal his true form, without the disguise of his heavy robes. Sa'ida's hand tightened convulsively around the amulet.

"Begone," she gasped. "Go back to whatever dark place spawned you!"

Faeterus laughed. His phantom hand reached out and grasped Sa'ida's wrist. When he raised his arm, he pulled her *naes* out. Her physical body went limp.

"You will witness my triumph. It will be most instructive!"

With a speed that left Sa'ida breathless, they soared above the *laddad* camp, rising far higher than Sa'ida had done alone, then they rushed eastward. In seconds they were at a broad shelf cut into the side of Mount Rakaris, which Faeterus called the Stair of Distant Vision.

Her spirit form went sprawling as he abruptly released her. He lifted a hand, and immediately it was filled with a spear. Rather than an actual, physical weapon, the spear was the representation of a spell. He drove it through her thigh, pinning her in place, and the shock of the spiritual impalement drew an involuntary scream. But pain was a force Sa'ida understood. She conquered her agony quickly, although she could not free her *naes*. She remained firmly anchored to the stone.

None of this was visible to Favaronas. From his place at the edge of the Stair, all he saw was the sorcerer standing rigidly by the center pinnacle, head bowed. Abruptly, Faeterus lifted his face and arms to the darkened sky and broke his long silence, declaiming in a loud, clear voice. The language was Old Elvish, and Favaronas recognized the rhyme scheme and meter as an ancient bardic recitation called a *houmrya*. He had never heard it spoken before. The poetry was said to have erratic, uncontrollable magical effects, and Speaker of the Stars Sithel had banned it long, long ago.

Because Favaronas was an accomplished scholar, he detected the changes Faeterus was making in the *houmrya*. Faeterus declared himself "breaker of worlds," when the actual *houmrya* line was "maker of worlds." With such twists, he was transforming an ancient poem of creation into an evocation of destruction.

As he recited, the monoliths of Inath-Wakenti began to glow. The effect was subtle, like reflected moonlight, but in the unnatural gloom, quite noticeable. When the sorcerer entered into the second canto, the aura brightened to a steady glare.

Desperately Favaronas scanned the slope below. There was no sign of the elf scouts, and a dreadful thought came to him. Had he only imagined the figures darting among the bushes? Was his terrified mind concocting phantoms? Did he await a rescue that would never come?

DESTINY

*   *   *   *   *

The Lioness's little company was concealed behind several large boulders below the plateau. Unnerved by the glowing monuments, Kerian had sent her party into cover. When time passed and nothing else untoward occurred, she told Robien to take the lead. He studied the situation briefly then chose a narrow track winding up the southern end of the plateau. It was steep but seemed to offer more concealment than the way on the north side.

The others followed, but fired by nearness to his goal, Robien outpaced them. He glimpsed someone hiding in the rocks above and dropped on his belly to avoid being seen. A figure dressed in black was lurking behind the boulders on the slope above the plateau. Was it one of Faeterus's hirelings, guarding the sorcerer's back while he worked his conjuration? Peering at a very low angle through scattered brush, Robien saw the clear outline of a crossbow. He unslung his bow and nocked an arrow. His shoulder throbbed, but he ignored the pain, firming his right elbow. He took careful aim. After loosing the shaft, he turned downslope to warn his comrades.

"There's an archer in the rocks above the plateau!" he called, keeping his voice low.

He began to turn round again but pitched abruptly backward, his bow flying from his hand. Kerian, Taranath, and Hytanthas dropped to the ground immediately.

"Robien!" Hytanthas called hoarsely. "Robien, answer me!"

There was no reply. Hytanthas was closest to the fallen bounty hunter. He could see an arrow protruding from the Kagonesti's chest, but in the uncertain light couldn't tell whether Robien was alive or dead.

They resumed climbing and Hytanthas was amazed and relieved to find Robien still lived. The arrow had caught him high on the right side of the chest and he lay on his back, stifling gasps of pain. Hytanthas tore a strip of cloth from his own *geb* and tried to stanch the flow of blood.

Gripping his bloodstained hand, Robien gasped, "Leave me! Get Faeterus for me!"

Hytanthas gave the Lioness an anguished look. She told him to remain with the injured elf. She and Taranath resumed the slow ascent.

Above them, Favaronas had seen neither Robien's shot nor the return volley. His whole world had narrowed to Faeterus's recitation of the perverted *houmrya*. Only two cantos remained, and he was certain that if Faeterus finished it, the race of elves would be wiped from the face of Krynn. Blinking away tears, he looked out over the valley.

Columns of light had risen from the glowing monoliths. They formed a pattern on the roiling underside of the black cloud. The message that had been too agonizingly bright and fleeting when etched by the glare of the setting sun was written now in ivory light on the cloud. The knowledge feared by the ghosts of the Lost Ones teetered on the edge of Faeterus's grasp.

Perhaps he had seen warriors on the slope below, but Favaronas couldn't risk waiting. He might be the only one with even a slim hope of stopping Faeterus. He had no idea how he would do it, but it was up to him to try.

He leaned on his battered hands and pushed himself away from the edge, back toward the chanting sorcerer.

* * * * *

When the monoliths' pale glow became a dazzling glare, Gilthas ordered his people to flee to open ground west of camp, where there were no standing stones.

"Every able-bodied adult is to carry a child or help the old or infirm," he declared. "Cut all the animals loose." If there was going to be a conflagration, he wanted any living creature in its path to have a chance for escape. He also called for Sa'ida. While warriors sought the priestess, Gilthas obeyed his own orders and went to help a child wandering nearby. The boy was looking in vain for his parents.

"You're not my father!" the boy declared as the Speaker hoisted him up.

"No, I'm not. Who is your father?"

"Naratalanathas, son of Cyronaxidel."

The boy could be no more than four, yet the complicated old Qualinesti names rolled easily off his tongue. Gilthas was impressed. "Large names for so small a fellow to recall."

The child knitted pale brows. "Is your father's name hard to say?"

"Not nearly as hard as yours." That pleased the boy. He said his name was Cyronathan.

"Come along, Cyronathan. Let's get everyone to a safer place."

In going to the boy, Gilthas found himself cut off from his palanquin bearers by the rush of people. No matter; he would walk. Carrying the boy in one arm and leaning on his staff, he joined the throng streaming from camp. The frightened atmosphere infected Cyronathan, and Gilthas sought to distract the child. His first efforts failed, but mention of Eagle Eye captured the boy's imagination thoroughly. Cyronathan peppered him with questions about the griffon and asked quite seriously what exactly he must do to secure one of the majestic creatures for himself.

They passed through the outer line of standing stones and had gone some ten yards farther when a joyous voice cried out the boy's name. Cyronathan greeted his mother with relief and made plain his wish to escape.

Gilthas bent to set him on the ground and felt something give way inside. A rush of warmth flooded his chest, and a loud gasp was wrenched from his lips. The boy, not noticing his agony, dashed away to his parents, but Gilthas continued to fold, going down on his knees. Wide eyed and open mouthed, he stared at the elves rushing by on both sides. No breath would enter his lungs. He could make no sound. Slowly, he toppled to the ground. The vision in his right eye faded, submerged in a wash of red.

Screams pierced the air as fleeing elves realized who he was. In moments the Speaker's faithful bearers, still carrying the empty palanquin, rushed up beside him. Truthanar arrived on their heels.

"He's hemorrhaging!" the healer cried. He rolled Gilthas onto his back . "I need water for the Speaker!"

Pitchers, buckets, and brimming cups appeared in moments. Truthanar rinsed the still-flowing blood from his king's mouth. None of the helpful civilians or warriors gathered round could tell him where Sa'ida was. Soldiers scouring the camp for her had met with no success. Truthanar commandeered help from the multitude, and two dozen elves who'd just raced out of camp ran back in even more rapidly to seek the human priestess.

Gilthas's eyes were closed, and he no longer fought to breathe. Truthanar elevated his head and shoulders. With a slim silver lancet, the healer slashed the Speaker's *geb*, exposing Gilthas's emaciated chest. Carefully probing down the ladder of ribs, Truthanar found the spot he sought. Without explanation or warning, he plunged the lancet between two ribs. Dark blood poured from the wound. Elves clustered around screamed anew.

"Had to be done," Truthanar explained. "Accumulated blood was compressing the lung."

As the blood poured out, their Speaker's breathing eased. Everyone could see his chest rise and fall and saw the terrible waxen pallor fade from his cheeks. A few minutes longer, and the Speaker of the Sun and Stars would have drowned in his own blood. Although Truthanar's voice was calm and matter-of-fact as he said this, the hand that had just wielded the lancet so confidently shook as he worked to bind the wound he'd made.

Gilthas stirred. His eyes opened. "Keri-li," he whispered.

Tears fell from the healer's eyes. "May the gods help you, sire. May they help us all."

DESTINY

Riding up with his lieutenants, Hamaramis saw the Speaker lying on the ground surrounded by a spreading stain and feared the worst. The old general, long past leaping from the back of a still-moving horse, did just that.

"Truthanar! Does he live?" he shouted, scattering elves from his path.

"He lives, Hamaramis, but not for long." The aged Silvanesti held the hand of the ruler of the united elf nations and wept unashamedly.

* * * * *

"Cleanse, O cleanse the world, Mighty Power! Take back that which was yours!"

Faeterus spoke the last line of the fourth canto. As he drew breath to begin the fifth and final part of his great incantation, the ground began to quake. Rocks large and small tumbled down the mountainside. One struck the spire next to him, shearing it off and sending sharp shards flying.

Favaronas, edging toward the sorcerer, ducked, throwing his arms over his head. Faeterus turned away to shield his own face from flying stone.

Angrily, Faeterus intoned, *"Rabthe"*—Stillness—and the shaking stopped. He laughed. Looking at the elf cringing at his feet, he confided, "Not even the gods can stop me."

He embarked upon the final canto of his song of annihilation.

20

"M ay the Door of Heaven open wide for Him Who Bears
the Key."

Faeterus lifted his left hand. He held the long parchment,
tightly rolled, onto which had been burned the inscription
revealed by the valley's standing stones. Under the spell of
the sorcerer's oratory, the columns of light emanating from
the monoliths angled inward, converging on the bottom of the
swirling cloud at a point directly over the Tympanum.

The brilliant concentration of light, painful to behold,
must be the Door, Favaronas decided. Faeterus had reached
the climax of his conjuration. The next line of the *houmrya*
was "Let the Light shine forth so all may See." Favaronas had
no doubt the sorcerer would change the final word to "die,"
or "vanish," or some other destructive command that fit the
structure of the poem, and that would be the end. Favaronas's
exhausted brain could think of no way to stop him.

He reached up one trembling hand and clutched the hem
of the sorcerer's ragged robe.

Kerian and Taranath cautiously lifted their heads above
the edge of the plateau. The Lioness drew her sword.

Magically restrained but still a horrified witness, Sa'ida
screamed, begging her patron deity to intercede.

"Let the Light shine forth—"

DESTINY

The sorcerer's demand ended with a gurgle. Favaronas looked up.

An arrow protruded from Faeterus's neck. Blood, black in the muted light, coursed down the front of his robe. He swayed but remained upright. With his free hand he groped for the arrow. It was deeply embedded in the left side of his neck. His fingers brushed over it but failed to grasp it. A second black bolt struck him in the back, and down he went.

Unseen and unheard, Sa'ida shouted in triumph. The goddess had heeded her servant's pleas. Or had she? Would the Divine Healer send black arrows in answer to a devoted prayer?

The spell pinning Sa'ida to the rock dissolved as its maker's life ebbed, and her joy changed to frustration. She felt herself pulled back to her body, lying unconscious in the elf camp, and she fought against it. The power tapped by Faeterus must be dispersed or safely channeled. If it was not, it would run riot, endangering everyone in the valley. Whereas before, all she wanted was to escape, now she fought to keep her *naes* on the Stair of Distant Vision.

The spell that paralyzed Favaronas's legs likewise faded. His limbs came alive again, kindling into pain as if ten thousand needles pricked his flesh. He pounded on his legs with clenched fists, trying to force them to work.

Faeterus lay on his side only a few feet away, the hood fallen partly back from his face. He gurgled in helpless fury, then his lips began to move. He might yet complete his terrible design! Favaronas dug in toes and fingers and propelled himself to the sorcerer's side. He clamped a bloodied hand over Faeterus's mouth, making certain he could say nothing. Faeterus struggled weakly. Favaronas put his other hand over the sorcerer's face and leaned all his weight on them. The spasms subsided to twitches then to nothing. Faeterus's body constricted in a monumental exhalation, and the last flicker of life finally departed his grotesque body.

His death did not end the titanic conjuration he'd set in motion. The brilliant "door" at the center of the cloud remained, and the cloud itself began to seethe and twist. It spat a narrow bolt of lightning that struck the Tympanum with a loud crash. A second bolt, larger than the first, cracked the granite disk in two.

"Finish . . ."

The unknown voice caused Favaronas to whirl. A human woman knelt only a few feet away. She was translucent, like a ghost, but Favaronas recognized her at once, although he was at a loss to know how the high priestess of Elir-Sana had come to be here.

"Scroll!" she said. Her image wavered, then disappeared altogether.

Seize the key before the door opens.

The words of the ghost and the priestess's command came together. He snatched the thick scroll from the sorcerer's rigid fingers. The scroll was the Key!

A lightning bolt sizzled across the width of the valley and struck the mountainside below the Stair. Favaronas assumed the Speaker's warriors had shot Faeterus, but he didn't dare wait for them to arrive. He must finish the conjuration before the wild discharge of power tore the valley apart. He drew a deep breath and spoke the last line.

"Let the Light shine forth so all may—"

He froze. "See" was the original ending of the *houmrya,* but he had no idea what the consequences of such a command might be. He needed something less vague, but positive, and it must be similar to the verb "to see" in Old Elvish so the line would still scan. Merciful E'li, what should he say? A list of ancient verbs raced through the scholar's mind. His entire body shaking, Favaronas thrust the scroll aloft.

"Live!" he shouted. "Live! *Live!*"

Someone called his name. Before he could see who it was, the world came apart.

The monoliths went dark, extinguished in their thousands

all at once. The blazing Door they'd created in the cloud persisted for the space of four heartbeats; then it exploded. The sound was no louder than a heavy thunderclap, but the explosion blew away the glowing white corona to reveal a black core within, spinning madly. The core slowed, wobbled, then it, too, detonated.

The first explosion had sent a wave of hot wind through the valley. When the black core exploded, nothing could stand before it. Everyone in Inath-Wakenti was thrown to the ground. The monoliths burned fiercely white for an instant then dissolved into clouds of vapor. The granite Tympanum survived the blast but was cleft by a deep crack zigzagging from north to south. Trees were blown down, boulders shattered, and every source of water in the valley, from small springs to Lioness Creek shivered its contents into fine droplets and shot them into the air.

The blast occurred high above the valley, and its tremendous shock wave roared over the encircling mountains and out into the desert. Like a plow, it lifted a wall of sand and drove it across the empty wasteland. Wells were filled, oases submerged, and small towns buried in the blink of an eye. Unwary caravans caught in the open were swallowed whole, never to be found again. Enormous drifts of sand fetched up against the walls of Kortal, Delphon, and Khuri-Khan. The moving mountain of grit overtopped the low walls of Kortal, collapsing the side facing Inath-Wakenti. Upon reaching the sea, the wave dumped what remained of its sand—although ships as far out as Habbakuk's Necklace reported showers of brown dirt peppering their sails—and lifted a swelling tide of water. The mighty wave swamped the Horn of Khur and swept ships ashore all around the Bay of Balifor. In occupied Silvanesti, trees were uprooted and waves smashed the port of Kurinost, wrecking forty minotaur ships. Flagstaffs at the Towers of Eli snapped, and the new overlord's banner fluttered into the sea.

Because the Khalkist Mountains deflected the blast, Neraka, Thoradin, and Blöde suffered less. Roofs in every town and hamlet were stripped of tiles. Strange changes of pressure affected communities at high altitudes. Drains cracked and wells overflowed. Bells in the town of Neraka rang, though no hand touched their pull ropes. Towers swayed but none fell. Panes of glass shattered, and the streets filled with puzzled members of the Order, who speculated on the coming of another Cataclysm. In Thoradin the Two Hammers Bridge collapsed, dropping four thousand feet to the bottom of the gorge. Fortunately the span was empty, and no one was hurt. Landslides buried tunnel entrances and toppled mine derricks all through the dwarves' realm.

Deflected by the mountains, a weaker shock wave rolled down the western slopes. Whirlwinds drove through Sanction, blowing away awnings, shutters, and roof tiles. Ships in the harbor rolled hard. Collisions sank half a dozen. A host of smaller vessels were swamped. Alarm bells sounded and rumors ran wild in the streets. Only the strenuous efforts of the city guard returned calm to Sanction.

The blast reached a narrow beach between the New Sea and the heights of the western Khalkist Mountains. The ground shook violently, and a deep boom of thunder echoed off the peaks. The sea went white with wind-tossed waves. A column of armored warriors riding slowly south along the beach fought to control their plunging horses. Griffon riders in the air overhead had to work equally hard to calm their own beasts. Dust and dirt rained down on the soldiers.

At the head of the army, Porthios mastered his horse. Two griffons alighted on the beach nearby. Alhana and Samar dismounted and hurried to him.

"What has happened?" Alhana called.

Porthios pulled his hood farther forward to shade his eyes and looked up. The ground had ceased shaking, but a new wonder was unfolding overhead. A vast ring of clouds was racing across the sky, spreading out from some locus behind the mountains. In its wake was the clearest, cleanest blue sky they'd seen in many days.

DESTINY

"Volcano?" suggested Samar. There were no active mountains in central Ansalon, but he could think of nothing else that would cause such a powerful blast.

They searched the sky for smoke or other signs of catastrophe. Nothing was visible but the preternaturally clear vault of blue. In minutes the cloud ring had rolled over the horizon. The temperature dropped noticeably. The very air around them seemed to sparkle.

"No, something strange has happened. Strange and wonderful," Alhana murmured. Ironhead and Chisa chortled and whistled at each other as if agreeing with her.

Samar inhaled deeply. He vowed that for the first time since their departure from Khur he felt free of the desert's seared, desiccated air. It wasn't only their nearness to the sea. The purity of the air had changed completely in the aftermath of the quake.

Only Porthios seemed unaffected. "It doesn't matter," he said. "Whatever it is, it's over. We ride on."

Samar regarded him with surprise, but Alhana told her faithful second to get the column moving again. He returned to his griffon, shouting orders for the cavalry and dismounted griffon riders to resume the march.

Alhana understood her husband's indifference. He didn't trust feelings. Omens and portents were for those too weak to take destiny into their own hands. She didn't waste time mourning what he had lost in the fire that had scarred him so grievously inside and out. He was alive. They were together. Nothing in the world mattered more to her.

Yet her silence seemed to unnerve him. He'd pushed his hood back a bit, and she could see his eyes. They darted toward her, away, then back again. She suppressed a smile. He had no idea how well she could read his emotions simply by watching his eyes.

"We're not going to Sanction, you know," he said roughly. "We'd find plenty of ships there but too many laws, bureaucrats, and foreign spies. Southward the towns are smaller, but working down the coast, we ought to be able to pick up enough ships to transport the army to Qualinesti."

"I agree."

He blinked. Dispute he would have met with forceful arguments, carefully marshaled. Her acquiescence left him nothing to say.

"Samar has the column ready," she said and turned to go back to Chisa.

Porthios spoke her name. She turned back. He was holding a hand down to her and had kicked one foot free of the stirrup.

Once she was mounted behind him, the Army of Liberation set out again.

On and on the great shock wave flew. Kothas and Mithas experienced mysterious southeast winds, quite contrary to their usual patterns of weather. A dusting of brown sand fell on the islands, followed by showers of tiny yellow flowers. Traders identified the blossoms as dandelion flowers, which grew no closer than Kern. On Schallsea orchards bloomed for a second time in one season, something they had not done in recorded history.

Deep in occupied Qualinesti, Lord Liveskill was summoned from his desk in the Black Hall to witness a strange rain falling on his fortress. He emerged into the bailey amid a flurry of white flower petals. The large, waxy blossoms were from poplar trees, which were long past their blooming time. Pennants atop the battlements were whipping in a stiff northwest wind.

The rain of flowers ceased and nothing more occurred. Liveskill ordered his steward to note the anomalies in the castle's daybook then returned to his plots and his papers.

*　*　*　*　*

Hands cleared away the rocks and dirt covering Favaronas, and he beheld Lady Kerianseray and General Taranath. Both exclaimed at finding him alive. When they helped him sit up, dirt and moss rained from his head and shoulders.

"Can you hear me?" the Lioness asked loudly.

"Perfectly well, lady." Favaronas's head rang like a temple bell, but his hearing was unimpaired.

He had been thrown onto a bed of jagged rocks yet had sustained no cuts or bruises. His rescuers were in the same strange condition. Not only were they unharmed by the great explosion, they were in better shape than before it had occurred. The knife wound Kerian had received in Khuri-Khan was completely healed. The arm bore a scar but felt as strong and healthy as ever. The many injuries Favaronas had sustained during his captivity were healed as thoroughly as the Lioness's arm. Even the fingernails he'd lost dragging himself across the Stair had grown back.

"What was that blast?" Kerian asked.

"The end of a dangerous conjuration." Favaronas explained that Faeterus had solved the riddle of Inath-Wakenti then attempted to use his knowledge to tap the power held captive within the valley. The power came not from long-gone dragonstones, but from the monoliths themselves. Faeterus had intended nothing less than the utter destruction of the elf race, but his grandiose plans had been thwarted at the last moment.

"Which of you shot him?" Favaronas asked, and they answered with blank looks. "He was hit from behind, with crossbow bolts . . ." His voice trailed away as he realized neither of them carried such a weapon.

The Lioness stepped back and looked upslope. She saw no sign of anyone but sent Taranath to investigate the boulders where Robien had spotted an archer. The archer who shot Robien must also have killed Faeterus. Whoever he was, he'd had ample time to serve them the same, but no more black bolts had flown. Taranath returned and reported finding only a torn boot and bloodstained leggings. The cloth was heavyweight serge of northern origin, probably from eastern Solamnia. The boots were common Abanasinian leather. That the assassin had come from west of Khur was all Taranath could determine.

The sun was gone from the sky—not because of Faeterus's fell magic, but simply due to the natural passage of time. The blast had occurred just after midday. The elves had been unconscious half a day and dusk had come. The sky over Inath-Wakenti was cloudless as usual, but the air shimmered like cloth-of-gold, as though minute crystals had been cast into the heights to catch the failing daylight. None of them could explain the remarkable phenomenon.

A shout from below brought them to the edge of the Stair. Hytanthas was climbing up. Close on his heels was Robien.

"I thought you were wounded?" Kerian called.

"I thought he was dying!" Hytanthas retorted, grinning.

"I thought him long dead," put in Favaronas.

He and Robien were pleased to find each other again. Favaronas exclaimed over Robien's escape from Faeterus's entombment spell. The bounty hunter, uncertain how he'd survived, credited his rescue to the timely intervention of Taranath's patrol.

"And this?" Favaronas pointed at the bloody rent in the breast of Robien's tunic.

"I understand that even less. Hytanthas had managed to draw the bolt"—Robien grimaced at the memory—"but got no further. Then we awoke a few minutes ago and I was completely healed!" He fingered the rent open, showing the smooth, unbroken skin beneath.

Kerian asked Favaronas what he made of the miraculous occurrences. The scholar was silent for some time. Perhaps the healing had come about because he himself had completed the poem with the injunction "live," but the once-ambitious elf had no desire to claim credit. Besides, who could know what really had happened?

Choosing his words carefully, he answered with perfect honesty, "The healing power must have come from the valley itself."

Robien had gone to inspect the fallen Faeterus. With one

foot, he rolled the body over. As it moved, the layers of robe covering it fell away in decayed clumps. The others came in response to his shocked exclamation.

All that remained of Faeterus were bones and scraps of dry flesh. If they hadn't known better, the elves would have sworn he'd been dead for months rather than hours. He had claimed great age, Favaronas mused. Perhaps the rapid decay was due to the cessation of the preservation spells that had kept him alive for so many centuries.

Robien was disgusted. "What do I tell Sahim-Khan? He hired me to bring the sorcerer to justice."

"He's met his justice." Kerian leaned down and picked up Faeterus's skull. "Give this to Sahim. Tell him your job is done."

Disgust became curiosity as Robien studied the grisly memento. Frowning, he said, "It doesn't look much like an elf's skull."

Favaronas took it from him and quickly bound it in a square of cloth from the sorcerer's robe. "When you have the best of all possible outcomes, it isn't wise to ask too many questions!"

Dusk was fading into darkness, and a handful of stars had appeared overhead. Kerian wanted to complete the steepest part of their descent before full night set in. She told them to make ready to depart.

Favaronas had one last task he wished to perform. The blast had knocked the Key from Faeterus's hand. Scanning the Stair, he saw the parchment some yards away, unfurled and fluttering in the evening breeze. The librarian in Favaronas could not abandon so rare a text. But when he tried to pick it up, the parchment fell to pieces at his touch. Kneeling, he used the hem of his robe to cover his fingers and tried again. It crumbled further. He was staring helplessly at the remains of the Key when the Lioness came to tell him they were ready to go. He explained his predicament and the importance of the parchment.

Without a word, she walked around him and deliberately

trampled the fragile parchment beneath her boots. Favaronas was aghast.

"Now no one can try to do what Faeterus did," she said flatly.

He knew she was right. But watching the knowledge of eons ground into dust was painful. He closed his eyes against the sight.

Her calloused hand tugged gently at the neck of his *geb*. "Leave it, Favaronas. It's time to go."

They departed, descending carefully in the gathering darkness.

* * * * *

Nearly half an hour went by before Breetan emerged higher up the slope.

Blown into a crevice by the explosions, she had awakened to find her broken ankle entirely mended. Her foot wasn't even swollen. From her hiding place, she could hear the small party of elves moving about and speaking but couldn't make out what they said. They didn't seem wroth over the death of their leader, the Scarecrow. That much she could tell.

She found her sword buried in the rocky soil. It was undamaged, but her crossbow had not been so fortunate. Hurled directly into a boulder, the stock was shattered. To keep its secrets from unfriendly hands, she completed its destruction.

The Black Hall was such a long way away, she decided instead to go over the mountains and present herself in Neraka. Her mission was complete. The Scarecrow was dead. As more and more stars crowded the sky, Breetan headed for home.

* * * * *

Farther down the valley, another was awakening after the terrific blast. Wounded by the Lioness's party when he attacked the bounty hunter, Shobbat had crept under a low thread-needle bush—to rest or die, he wasn't sure which. He awoke in darkness.

DESTINY

He was human again.

Joyous relief changed quickly to alarm. The thread-needle bush was covered by sharp, inch-long spines, and he was completely naked. Little more than a nuisance to the tough, thickly furred hide of his beastly form, the spines would wreak havoc on his delicate human flesh. He inched his way very carefully out from under the bush and into the cold night air.

He couldn't possibly cross the mountains in his current state, so he went back the way he had come, through the southern pass, into the valley. He needed clothes and would have to avoid the *laddad* patrols, but he was himself again. Even shivering and exposed, Shobbat grinned in triumph.

* * * * *

Kerian's party crossed the valley in mounting excitement. Moonlight and starlight showed them the many changes wrought in the landscape. The monoliths were gone. Where the thousands of snowy quartz blocks had stood were only scorched patches of turf or shallow pits. The air was drier, with none of the clammy mists that usually clung to the ground at night.

And the valley was full of trees! Not the stubby, twisted plants they'd grown accustomed to in the benighted vale, but soaring giants such as they'd not seen since leaving their homelands. Oaks towered forty feet above their heads. Pines and cedars thrust skyward like enormous green spires. The ground was littered with palm-sized acorns and pine cones the size of melons. The air was drenched with the perfume of a riot of blossoms. The open landscape was gone. Although loathe to destroy such beauty, the elves were forced to hack a path through the newly grown foliage.

Periodically their way was blocked by water. Rivulets they'd crossed the day before in a stride or two were rushing streams. Creeks had matured into small rivers. The valley's few small springs gushed like fountains.

Passing one of the larger pits left by a departed monolith, they saw a rabbit shoot out of the hole, dart around their legs in confused fashion, and vanish into the night. On its furry heels came more creatures: a pair of squirrels, half a dozen starlings, a cloud of flies.

"The same power that cured our personal hurts has restored the animals of Inath-Wakenti," Hytanthas said.

"How so?" asked Favaronas.

Hytanthas told him about the layers of dry bones he'd found in the tunnels under the valley. Favaronas had entered the tunnels during the Lioness's original expedition and hadn't encountered any remains, but his stay had been very brief, and the captain's theory seemed logical to him. The bones of the valley's animals had been given flesh again.

Taking his theory a step further, Hytanthas exclaimed, "Commander, our comrades! All those lost to the lights will be returned to us!"

The idea was a beguiling one, but Favaronas warned against hasty assumptions. "They might be returned, but it's equally likely the 'resurrection' will affect only the original denizens of the valley."

While the men debated the point, Kerian's face acquired an odd expression. Taranath asked if something was wrong. She regarded him in wide-eyed silence for the space of two heartbeats then sprinted away, leaving them all behind. Over her shoulder floated one word.

"Gilthas!"

Comprehension quickly dawned for Taranath. Hytanthas and Robien shared his understanding. Favaronas did not, having been lost before the Speaker took ill.

"Must we run?" he complained, just before Hytanthas and Robien each took one of Favaronas's arms and hurried him along.

Mind and body in an uncharacteristic whirl, Kerian outpaced them all by fifty yards. She forced her thoughts away from the hope she dared not voice and instead tried to calm her churning belly. It was requiring all her considerable concentration to keep from being sick. The idea it might be simple hunger lasted only until she remembered the revelation Sa'ida had delivered. She was sick because she was pregnant. She tightened her grip on her sword hilt. She would not be sick. Not now. Later she could be sick but not now.

She pushed through a wall of closely growing ash saplings and found the way ahead blocked by a new lake. She waited for her companions to catch up then struck out around the lake. Ever the archivist, Favaronas insisted they name the new body of water. Robien's suggestion of "New Lake" was roundly rejected as too dull. Hytanthas offered "Lake Pathfinder," and Kerian surfaced from her distraction long enough to veto that.

"He won't thank you for it," she said. "Besides, it smacks of favor-seeking."

"Lake Planchet."

Taranath's quiet suggestion met with unanimous approval. Kerian thought it a fitting tribute to the valiant elf who had given his life in the desert to save the nation.

Lake Planchet was broad and kidney shaped, with its long axis running north-south. As they skirted its shore, a flock of geese wafted down. In moments half a hundred birds had settled, honking lustily.

Not even Qualinesti in its heyday was so rich, so bountiful. Although full night was still upon the valley, it teemed with animal life. The elves passed a cloud of bees swarming around an open fissure in the ground. Snakes glided across the path in front of them. Crickets whirred and thick clouds of fireflies glittered. Coming upon a small grove, they were overwhelmed by the sweet scent of apples. The trees were laden with fruit such as was grown in Hylo and Ergoth, apples fully ripe but green as leaves. Even Kerian could not help but follow her comrades' example and pause long enough to fill each hand with a gleaming fruit.

Favaronas bit into an apple and laughed with delight at the flavor. Juice ran down his chin. Although he hadn't tasted the fruit, Hytanthas began to laugh as well. Their shared amusement went on so long, Robien and Taranath stared at them. Hytanthas shrugged helplessly.

"I don't know," he said, his face still wearing a broad grin. "It just feels as though we've gone back to the beginning of the world!"

Taranath offered a wary warrior's smile. A surprisingly fresh, wry grin appeared on Robien's face. Suddenly all four of them were laughing, the mirth of one inciting fresh hilarity in the rest.

"Get moving!"

The Lioness's harsh voice recalled them to their senses. Embarrassed, Taranath hustled Favaronas forward, and Hytanthas and Robien sped their own lagging steps.

"It's very strange. I feel almost drunk," Robien confessed, and the others agreed.

"Perhaps it's another effect of the valley's transformation," suggested Favaronas.

By the time dawn broke, the land had become less cluttered with undergrowth. Open ground was covered by a lush carpet of knee-high grass. They were close to the valley's center, and Kerian began to run, shedding gear that slowed her down. She topped a low knoll and halted.

Below lay the circular stone platform at the valley's heart. The huge disk was bisected by a broad crack. Off to the left, the south side, lay the elves' camp. Most of the tents were down. Some had been consumed by fire, and thin spires of smoke still curled skyward.

Her four comrades arrived. Surveying the scene in dismay, Taranath said, "They must have survived!"

Kerian was already running down the hill. She covered the last mile without stopping. When she discovered the camp to be deserted, she headed for the open ground on the west side, where she and Gilthas had faced down the ghostly multitude. Her surmise proved thrillingly correct. The elf nation was there, sitting on the grass, looking quite dazed but alive and well.

DESTINY

The tall figure of Hamaramis on horseback drew Kerian. She dodged through the crowd, making straight for him. A troop of warriors was drawn up with the general. They parted ranks for her.

The palanquin sat on the ground. The bearers were seated around it, heads bowed to their knees. A dark red mantle was draped over the seat.

After all her blistering hurry, Kerian stopped so suddenly she nearly fell. She couldn't move. Her feet felt rooted to the soil. Her belly churned. He could not be gone. Not when the whole world had come alive at last!

"The chair is empty."

The familiar voice jolted through her like a bolt of lightning. She turned. Standing a short distance away was her husband. Face pale, white hair blowing in the breeze, Gilthas resembled nothing so much as one of the ghosts of Inath-Wakenti.

The Lioness covered the distance between them in three long strides and seized him by the arms. He was no ghost. He returned her bruising grip and pulled her close for a kiss so fierce, it left both of them shaken.

"You're alive," he whispered, and she laughed through tears, so perfectly had he echoed her own thoughts. She touched his face to reassure herself.

Standing straight and proud, all signs of suffering gone, for the first time in a long time, Gilthas was himself. The only lingering physical trace of his brush with death was his hair. Rather than returning to its natural blond shade, it was snowy white.

He took half a step back from her, the mantle of kingship descending on him again but his eyes remained warm and loving.

"Your mission was a success?"

"So it would seem," she said wryly.

A frown touched his face. It lasted only a moment. There would be time enough later to learn exactly what had happened. He gestured at the multitude around them. "As you see, we endured."

"You always do," she said, and it was the elf nation she meant.

He held out a hand to her. "Well, someone has to look after you—you and the next Speaker within you."

21

The camp was a shambles. But if their worldly goods had suffered, every elf felt reborn.

All had been restored to excellent health. Wounds from the war in the desert and injuries acquired from the harsh, daily battle for survival healed outright. Sicknesses endemic to the population since the fall of their homelands—afflictions such as pox, ague, and consumption—were banished. Even greater miracles were recorded. Lost faculties returned. Deafness and blindness were cured. So were madness and despair. Oddly, elves who had lost arms and legs fighting the nomads did not have these restored, but those who lost eyes to arrows or to the poisonous flies so common in the desert found those organs grown anew. The great healing followed a logic and law of its own. Many tried to fathom the Great Change (as it came to be called), but no one understood it.

Eager to explore the new-made valley, Gilthas sent scouting parties out on horseback and afoot immediately. Most were charged with finding food, and they returned quickly, their hampers overflowing. Apples, pears, grapes, and berries of every sort grew in abundance, as did wild onions, various greens, and many kinds of nuts. Sage, rosemary, basil, and other herbs grew in broad swaths like green lakes. A profusion of crops, which naturally ripened at different times during the year, had been created instantly. Mounted hunters brought back venison, rabbit, and squab and reported sighting bears, although the creatures had been extinct in central Ansalon since the First Cataclysm. One band of warriors returned driving a shaggy aurochs before them. The presence of wild oxen in the valley meant there would be not just meat, but leather too.

Water birds proved especially abundant. Flocks of geese and pintail darkened the sun as they passed over the camp. Swans and loons populated the lakeshores. Ponds and streams teemed with fish. Honeybees swarmed the fields of blossoms. Soon there would be wax, honey, and later, mead.

Other finds, seemingly less dramatic, were of equal import. Flax was discovered growing wild. The elves would be able to make linen again. The valley was filled with tall, sturdy hardwoods of the most useful species, including oak, walnut, ash, and yew. In the shade beneath the trees sprouted fantastic mushrooms, twice normal size. Every variety, from the delicate pink shell mushroom to the rare subterranean blacknut, was as common as weeds in a summer garden. The more widely the elves searched, the greater the bounty they discovered.

The valley's riches were being catalogued by Varanas and the scribes. Vixona Delambro, who had demonstrated her mapping ability in the tunnels, was commissioned by the Speaker to map the entire valley. Gilthas intended to send a warrior with her, to aid in her work and protect her from wild animals. Before he could designate an elf for the task, however, one volunteered: Hytanthas Ambrodel. In the months to come, the two would be gone for days at a time, either on horseback or mounted on Hytanthas's griffon, Kanan. It surprised no one when warrior and scribe eventually married.

To Kerian, the change wrought in Gilthas was more amazing than the entire litany of wonders they had found thus far. Every trace of the horrible disease had been cleansed from his body, leaving him thin but vigorous.

DESTINY

An equally vigorous appetite soon returned the flesh to his bones. It was almost as though, having been more ill than anyone else, he was granted the greatest healing. He positively glowed with vitality. It shone from him like some invisible aura. He seemed unaware of it, but Kerian found it nearly unbearable. When he was near, his presence intoxicated her like a draft of the most potent nectar. When he touched her, she felt almost sick with love. Even the slight contact he considered proper in public left her shaken.

They were in public at that moment, awaiting the arrival of the human prisoner Jeralund. The setting had been carefully staged. A light canopy had been erected near the northern bank of Lioness Creek, in a meadow awash in bluebells. All the newfound bounty of the valley was piled beneath the canopy. In the center of it all, the Speaker of the Sun and Stars sat in a tall wooden chair. Although hastily finished and intended as only a temporary throne, the chair was strikingly beautiful, made from a single piece of ash and embellished by carvings of intertwined oak and ash leaves. Elves skilled in wood shaping had invested each detail with loving care, relishing the chance not only to serve their king, but to practice their art for the first time in years.

Kerian watched her husband twirl an ash twig in his fingers. The shield-shaped foliage reminded her of the falls of leaves they had encountered in Khur on more than one occasion. For a long time, the presence of Faeterus had colored her view of any magic they encountered. Finally she understood the sorcerer was only one of the sources of magic that had been at work around them. The falls of ash leaves had been caused by another. Gilthas had told her of the strange rain of edible ash leaves which had saved the nation from starvation in the desert. The powerful force that had intervened to save Alhana's life at Redstone Bluffs may have been a third. Whatever their source, the different magics seemed to have counter-acted each other, allowing the elves to win through.

Gilthas let the ash twig drop from his hands as the human prisoner arrived. Jeralund gaped at the bounty arranged around the throne.

Gilthas ordered his bonds removed then asked politely, "Are you well?"

Jeralund said he was. The Great Change had healed his relatively minor injuries too.

"Have you any reason to complain of your treatment here?"

"No, Speaker."

Gilthas leaned back in his chair and gestured for Jeralund to help himself from a nearby bowl of fruit. Drink was brought. Soon the sergeant was sipping rich red berry juice.

"Although you were the consort of an assassin, I have chosen to parole you."

Jeralund choked on a mouthful of juice. Gilthas had had his suspicions about the human—plainly a soldier and not the type to enter Inath-Wakenti on his own. Kerian's description of the killing of Faeterus smacked of a Nerakan plot. The sergeant's reaction confirmed that theory. Exactly why the Order wanted Faeterus dead, Gilthas didn't know.

"I release you for one purpose: to return to your masters and tell them what you have seen here."

Jeralund wiped juice from his lips. He regarded the Speaker thoughtfully for a moment then repeated, "Tell them what I have seen?"

"In every detail. I wish it known in Neraka that we have recovered from our time in Khur. Tell them of our new strength and our new riches; then tell them to darken our doorstep no more."

With freedom in his hands, Jeralund did an odd thing. He spoke the truth.

"Why should the lords of Neraka heed your command, Speaker?" he said. "Why shouldn't they gather their armies and seize this fertile land for themselves?"

DESTINY

Gilthas glanced at Kerian. The Great Change had healed her griffon's eye, and Eagle Eye stood like a fierce statue by his mistress's right hand. Kagonesti and griffon wore similar expressions of proud disdain. It did not escape the Speaker's notice that Jeralund kept darting uncertain looks in their direction. It was impossible to know which of them unnerved him more.

"Your masters will not come here," Gilthas finally replied. "The same power that changed a sterile wasteland into a garden is still here. Consider what might happen should that power be unleashed with unfriendly intent."

"If you have such power, why not use it now to extinguish your enemies forever?"

"I am tired of war. I want to build a nation, not conquer others. Tell your lords that too. If they let us be, we will let them be. Move against us, and the consequences will be dire."

Jeralund bowed with rough grace and vowed to deliver the Speaker's message as dictated.

After he had been escorted away, Kerian asked, "How do you know he'll do what you ask? His masters don't welcome ultimatums. He may turn south and never see Neraka again."

"It might be more effective for us if he does just that. If he spreads his tale among those he meets along the way, the story will reach Neraka through a thousand channels instead of only one. The knights may be more likely to believe it."

Her eyes narrowed. "You are devious," she said. She meant it as a compliment.

The human spy dealt with, Kerian swung onto Eagle Eye's back. A question had been nagging her since the Great Change. Consultation with the high priestess Sa'ida had not supplied an answer. To quiet her concerns, a return to Mount Rakaris was in order.

Before she took off, Gilthas asked how she was feeling. It was a question he asked frequently these days. Kerian had been up at dawn, losing what remained of her dinner the night before.

"I'm fine," she said sourly. "And no, I don't want an apple." He had acquired an annoying tendency to press food upon her at every turn.

"Fruit is good for you."

"Did I say you were devious? I meant cruel," she shot back. She and Eagle Eye took wing.

Even as the breeze stirred up by the griffon's departure died away, Sa'ida arrived. Just before the Great Change, the elves had found her unconscious in her tent, a terrible gash in her thigh. The magical blast healed her wound, but she remained unconscious for hours after everyone else had awakened. When finally she did revive, she awoke screaming. Truthanar told her what had happened—the explosions, the miraculous healing, and the astounding transformation of Inath-Wakenti. She nodded, then lapsed into a natural, restful sleep.

Still looking wan and moving slowly, she bowed to the Speaker. He bade her sit.

"How are you today, Holy One? I'm told that of all the souls in Inath-Wakenti, you are the only one not strengthened by the Great Change," he said.

She admitted he was right, rubbing her forehead and grimacing. "Great Speaker, I'm not certain you realize just how much power was released here. It was"—she shivered—"overwhelming. I will live, sire, but I fear I will never practice the high art again."

Attuned to the natural world by her devotion to the goddess, Sa'ida experienced the mighty surge as a blow that struck at the very core of her being. The tremendous force had burned her soul, and she could not bear the thought of coming into contact with magic again.

"What will you do, lady?" asked Hamaramis.

"I don't know. I cannot return to the temple." In that mystic place, she would be in constant torment, and of little use besides.

"Stay with us," Gilthas offered. "You will always be welcome here."

DESTINY

Her smile was forced. "Your Majesty is generous, but the air here crackles with latent power. I cannot remain."

He did not waste time trying to persuade her. He did offer whatever she might need for her journey, including a griffon ride to the destination of her choice. Instead of aerial transport, she requested a cart and a sturdy horse to pull it. She wished to depart as soon as possible.

While the cart was stocked with food and water, Sa'ida put two sealed scrolls into the Speaker's hands. One was a letter to be delivered to her sisters in the Temple of Elir-Sana. The other, thicker roll of parchment was for Sahim-Khan. Gilthas eyed the latter as if it was a deadly serpent.

Sa'ida said, "I've told him I will not be returning to Khuri-Khan, and of my suspicions about the workings of the Nerakans in Khur and what I know of his son's condition. I'm sure he will know what to do with the information."

He promised to have both messages delivered. Robien was returning to Khur with the desiccated skull of Faeterus to collect a sizable bounty. He could carry the sealed scrolls as well as his prize.

The priestess's departure was difficult for Gilthas. If she hadn't braved the unknown and come to the valley, he would not have survived to see the Great Change. And because she had, she'd lost everything that was important to her. Truly grieving her loss, he rose and took her hand in both of his.

"If ever you need me, holy lady, you need only ask. You have the unending gratitude not only of the Speaker of the Sun and Stars, but of Gilthas Pathfinder."

Bestowing a kiss on her hand, he let her go. She limped away. Truthanar assured Gilthas the strange wound on her leg had disappeared completely, yet she still favored the limb.

The small, horse-drawn cart rolled down a natural lane of towering elms on its way out of Inath-Wakenti, eliciting little notice amid the general excitement and bustle. But General

Taranath and the warriors on duty in the pass presented arms as the former high priestess passed their way.

Outside the pass, beyond the remnants of the wall begun by the nomads, Sa'ida let the reins hang slack, giving the horse its head. It veered southwest to keep the morning sun out of its eyes.

Sa'ida was drowsing beneath her sun hat when she became aware of a presence beside her. Bolting upright, she found herself sharing the cart seat with an old man. A pair of knowing eyes looked out at her from beneath short, unkempt white hair. A circlet of green leaves rested atop his head. His priestly robe was many-times patched.

"Who are you?" she demanded. No sooner had the words left her lips than she knew the answer. A mighty name whispered in her soul. She clasped her hands reverently, exclaiming, "My great lord!"

Gesturing at the slack reins, he said, "You'd best see to your horse."

The prosaic words penetrated her awe, and she did as he bade, taking up the reins and guiding the wandering horse back onto the narrow desert track.

He settled more comfortably on the hard seat. "It's all worked out rather well, don't you think? For the elves." She nodded dumbly. "They've suffered much, but now they have a chance to make a new life for themselves."

Enlightenment dawned. "*You* saved them!"

"Well, I pointed them in the right direction. They saved themselves."

The cart rolled along the base of dunes lately sculpted by the blast from Inath-Wakenti. Sa'ida's companion took something from a fold in his robe: a brown bat.

"I don't need you anymore," he said, nose to nose with the tiny creature. It squeaked in response. He lifted his hand skyward. "Go home."

The bat took wing. As it vanished in the bright sky, Sa'ida asked why he'd been carrying it. Had he nursed the injured animal back to health?

DESTINY

"No. It was part of my costume. To veil my activities, it was necessary for me to assume the appearance of a long-dead oracle."

"The Oracle of the Tree!"

The god winked. "A useful diversion but one I no longer need." Looking to the horizon, he asked where she was going.

"Where the horse takes me."

"Ever been to Qualinesti? No? I think we'd find it a very interesting place."

He pointed a stubby finger south-southwest, and the horse immediately adjusted its course accordingly. Sa'ida opened her mouth to protest but closed it without speaking. She'd told the Speaker she didn't know what she would do. Now she did. She was bound for the elves' old homeland, and had acquired a new patron. Just what he had in mind, for her and for Qualinesti, only time would tell.

* * * * *

Like the rest of Inath-Wakenti, the broad plateau known as the Stair of Distant Vision had undergone a profound change. The once-bare rock was completely covered by wild roses and honeysuckle. Eagle Eye circled it several times as Kerian tried to recognize landmarks submerged beneath the profusion of green leaves and yellow blossoms. When she finally directed the griffon to land, he remained balanced on his rear paws for several seconds before carefully lowering his front legs into the clinging growth. Champing his beak and growling, he made his displeasure known.

"There's something I have to do," she told him. "I won't be long. Don't be so finicky."

Despite her testy words, she took time to slash a clear patch around him. He trilled softly. With a fond smile, she stroked his neck, and he settled down for a nap. Making use of her sword again, she cut a path to the broken pinnacle.

Faeterus's remains were still there. Ants were busily stripping away the last bits of dry flesh, but it was the sorcerer's bones that concerned Kerian. She'd seen for herself how the long-dead creatures of the valley had been reborn. From rabbits to aurochs, the animals of Inath-Wakenti had been remade from their ancient bones. Despite Hytanthas's hopes, none of the elves taken by the will-o'-the-wisps had been so favored. No one knew why, but the elves they remained lost.

Still Kerian could not rid herself of the nagging fear that a powerful sorcerer such as Faeterus would find some way back from death. Wise Sa'ida and well-read Favaronas had been unable to assure her that her suspicions were groundless, so she would make absolutely certain Faeterus could never again darken the world.

The joints had fallen apart, and the bones were scattered. She cut away greenery and raked through the dirt with her fingers, seeking even the tiniest bones. As she found each one, she laid it atop the sorcerer's rotted robe. When she was satisfied she'd left none behind, she soaked the pile and the dirty fabric with lamp oil and set it alight.

The pyre blazed up, sending a stream of dirty yellow smoke skyward. She fed the fire with vine cuttings and windfall limbs, turning it into a genuine bonfire.

The morning passed. Kerian sat on the edge of the Stair and ate wild blueberries. The view was spectacular, and she allowed herself to be captured by it. Fluffy clouds floated high over Inath-Wakenti, dappling mighty trees and lush foliage with patterns of light and shade. Flocks of starlings wheeled overhead. Nearby, squirrels leaped from treetop to treetop, and birds trilled and sang.

She kept the bonfire hot, adding kindling and splashes of oil. Only when the sun hovered above the western peaks did she allow the flames to die out. Raking through the ashes with a tree branch, she crushed any remaining bits of bone to dust. The hot ashes and bone dust went into a clay pot that she carried back to Eagle Eye.

The last scraps of the creature that called itself Faeterus

would not remain in Inath-Wakenti. Kerian and Eagle Eye winged down the valley toward the pass. They flew far out into the desert before the Lioness upended the clay pot. The cloud of ashes was taken by the wind and scattered across many miles of Khurish sand.

* * * * *

A line of nomads riding on the shady side of a dune spied a very odd thing: a lone figure walking toward them. No one but foolish *laddad* went about in the desert on foot. The nomads—they were Weya-Lu, as it happened—halted their horses and watched in cautious curiosity, hands resting on sword hilts. The stranger wore only a ragged breechcloth. His skin was burned by the sun to the color of cinnabar. He was either mad, possessed by a desert spirit, or a monster in disguise. He hailed them.

"Stand where you are!" the eldest nomad commanded. He drew his sword and pointed its curved blade at the sun-baked apparition. "Name yourself!"

"I am Shobbat, son of Sahim, Khan of All the Khurs!"

That decided the issue. He was a madman.

Advancing slowly, hands held high, he cried, "Look upon me and know the truth!"

"What truth?"

"I have come from the land of the dead—from the Valley of the Blue Sands. I, who was cursed and given the form of a beast by a vile foreign sorcerer, have been cured by the gods! Now I return to cleanse the land of Khur!"

His words fell upon fertile ground. The Weya-Lu, still grieving the loss of so many of their kin as well as their Weyadan, listened. They let the stranger come into their midst. Under the deep-desert burn, the features of the khan's eldest son were apparent. Still, their allegiance was not so easily won.

"How long have you been in the desert?" one man asked.

Shobbat shrugged. "I don't know. I awoke in the valley,

naked as the day I was born. I set out each morning with the rising sun on my right shoulder, three mornings so far."

The Weya-Lu exclaimed. He carried nothing with him; had he once had provisions? None at all, he said. Immediately, they pressed a waterskin on him. He drank, not with the desperate thirst that should have afflicted him, but slowly, his actions those of a true child of the desert, who is always careful not to waste a drop of precious water. The nomads were awed. Surely Those on High were watching over the prince. How else to explain his not simply surviving in the desert for three days, but being in such good health?

"May we escort you back to Khuri-Khan, Highness?" asked the eldest.

"In time." Shobbat took another drink. "When I return to the city of the khan, I will wipe clean the stain of corruption there. My father treats with all manner of foreigners. He takes their coin, fawns over them, and protects them, all the while oppressing the righteous believers of his own nation, those who follow the Condor."

The nomads nodded their approval of the epithet. Not even Torghan's own children used his true name lightly.

Shobbat added, "I will not allow this to continue. Those on High have spared me to lead the righteous against a corrupt and unworthy ruler!"

The fire of righteousness blazed from Shobbat's eyes. Each man felt it, breath-stealing as a dash of icy water in the face. One by one, swords were drawn and lifted high. The nomads likewise lifted their voices, shouting, "Hail the Desert-Blessed Prince! Hail the Son of the Avenger!"

The shouts continued for a long time. Shobbat stood in the center of the ring of men, soaking up the acclaim as a tree soaks up spring water. These dozen Weya-Lu were his first converts. More would follow, many more, and the walls of Khuri-Khan would tremble.

epilogue

Emissaries arrived before summer ended. They came from Solamnia and Ergoth, Sanction and Schallsea, and numerous other cities across the land. The soldiers among the delegations noted with practiced eyes the great wall being erected across the mouth of the valley. The design was typically elven: elegant and clean with soaring buttresses and high towers whose slender shapes belied their great underlying strength. Behind the outer wall, a second had been started, and beyond it lay the foundations of a third. The mountains ringing Inath-Wakenti were rich in granite. No effort was being spared to make the walls high and thick. It would be some time before the defenses were complete, but when they were, no army could hope to force the passage.

The visitors were conducted along a road of finely crushed blue granite to the budding city in the center of the valley. There they were received by the Speaker of the Sun and Stars in a palace complex being built atop the largest single slab of stone any of the visitors had ever seen. None knew the significance of the Tympanum, but all wondered at the broad crack bisecting it.

Before winter claimed the outer world, a special emissary arrived from Khuri-Khan. General Hakkam led a party of forty high lords from the court of Sahim-Khan. All were attired in the panoply of Khur, a splendid display, if barbarous to elf eyes. Clan totems were rendered in gold atop broad-brimmed helmets. Every shoulder, every elbow bristled with a shining steel spike, and each man's hooded sun mantle was spotlessly white—the color of wealth in dusty Khur.

Although city-dwellers rather than superstitious nomads, the Khurish delegation still preferred not to enter the Valley of the Blue Sands. As a conciliatory gesture to his reluctant ally, Gilthas broke protocol by meeting them just inside the uncompleted valley wall. He arrived on foot, shaded from the late-autumn sun by a long canopy of flowers supported by a dozen young elves. Although large, the canopy weighed very little and rippled in the slight breeze. The canny Speaker also wore white. Even his aurochs-leather sandals were pale as mountain snow. The only touches of color were the square-cut amethysts decorating the ends of the cord tied around the waist of his robe.

Hamaramis, Taranath, and a retinue of warriors followed their sovereign. They, too, were clad in white and bedecked with flowers. The display had been carefully orchestrated, and it had just the impact Gilthas intended. As desert-dwellers, the Khurs regarded flowers and green plants with deep reverence. Presenting his people awash in blossoms—so near winter, no less—proclaimed Gilthas's power far better than gilded raiment would have. The elves presented a pageant of wealth and success, the kind that fills bellies and swells coffers with income from trade.

The Khurish delegation halted their horses and watched with barely concealed amazement as the *laddad* khan approached. In lieu of a silver or gold crown, Gilthas wore a circlet of green ivy. When he stopped, the youths also halted, sending a slow undulation along the length of the floral canopy.

"Hail, Great Speaker! May you reign a thousand years!" Hakkam cried.

"Oh, not *quite* that long," Gilthas replied genially, turning the Khur's hyperbole into a subtle reminder of the long life spans of elves. Hamaramis and Taranath both bit back smiles.

Somewhat taken aback, Hakkam blinked but forged ahead.

"You are well, Great Speaker?"

"I am. How fares my friend, the mighty Sahim-Khan?"

"The Khan of All the Khurs feasts on the fear of his enemies!"

"No doubt. What news do you bring, General?"

"The mighty Sahim-Khan bade me tell you that when the autumn stars were high in the sky, he drove out the ambassador from Neraka and all his hirelings."

"Good!" Hamaramis said. Gilthas waited a long moment to reply, silently rebuking the general for speaking out of turn, then inquired of Hakkam what had precipitated the expulsion.

The human frowned. "It is well known the over-the-mountain men have long stirred up treason against our august khan. Your Majesty sent proof of that to my master months ago."

Gilthas had had no word from Robien on the success or failure of his embassy to the khan. He was glad to know the bounty hunter had gotten the priestess's message through.

"Yes," he said benignly. "*Many* months ago."

Hakkam leaned on his saddle pommel, scowling at the implied criticism. "The roots of bribery and treachery were deep. It took the khan's loyal vassals time to bring all to light."

Gilthas offered congratulations to Sahim-Khan and his steadfast defenders. "Is that all?" he asked.

The forty Khurish lords stirred on their horses. Plainly, that was not all Hakkam had come to say, but he seemed to have difficulty choosing his words. Finally, he said, "A rebellion has broken out in the south of our country. The tribesmen have rallied around a treacherous leader."

Many of the elves present immediately thought of Porthios. But he'd gone to Qualinesti. He should be nowhere near Khur.

"Who is this leader?" Gilthas asked.

"He who was Shobbat."

Despite his surprise, Gilthas made careful note of that phrasing: not "Crown Prince Shobbat" nor "His Highness," but only "Shobbat." He expressed his regret at the turn of events, saying "Family wounds are always the deepest."

Hakkam drew a short, rolled scroll from inside his gauntlet. Taranath rode forward to convey it to Gilthas.

"My master, the mighty Sahim-Khan, proposes an alliance. In that document are his terms. If the Great Speaker would care to read—"

"I shall." Gilthas tucked the scroll into his belt. "When I have done so, I will give you my answer."

He turned away. The canopy bearers about-faced. Hamaramis and the warriors turned their horses, and the entire entourage departed the way it had come. The Khurs were left fuming. All Hakkam could do was lead his own delegation back beyond the unfinished walls where they would make camp and await the Speaker's answer.

Gilthas returned alone to his tent—not the large, open structure in which he conducted the daily affairs of state, but a smaller habitation that would serve as his private quarters until the new palace eventually was completed. The focus of construction in Inath-Wakenti was on humbler structures than the palace, by Gilthas's own decree. More important to him was that his people have strong roofs over their heads. When those were done, then work would resume on the Speaker's royal residence.

Within, he found Kerian reclining in a sling chair. Her face had taken on a rosy flush, and her hair had grown long enough to brush her shoulders. Her pregnancy was well advanced, and she did not bother trying to rise when he entered.

The gestation had gone much more quickly than usual. Truthanar believed the Great Change had somehow sped up the process. All the elf women in Inath-Wakenti who were pregnant were much further along than normal. An odd but popular belief was that the souls of those warriors lost to the will-o'-the-wisps were returning in the bodies of newborn babes. Kerian openly scoffed at the notion, but Gilthas could not. His own losses were severe enough that he would never deny solace to others. He knew he would grieve the deaths of his mother and Planchet for the rest of his days.

"How was old Hakkam?" she asked, shifting uncomfortably in the chair.

"Piratical as ever."

He went to a small sideboard and poured them both some fruit juice. As he handed her a cup, he pulled the scroll from his belt. "He gave me this. Sahim wants an alliance. Shobbat's rebellion is gaining ground."

"What are you going to do?"

He sat down facing her and placed a hand on her belly. "Talk to my son."

"We don't know it will be a boy."

"Truthanar says so." Gilthas closed his eyes. *Hello, son. How are you today? If you are well, give us a sign.*

Whether Gilthas was communing with their child or not, the baby did kick his mother quite vigorously. Opening his eyes, Gilthas smiled broadly. Kerian shoved his hand away, but a grudging smile lightened her expression.

"Stop teaching *her* bad habits." Growing serious again, she said, "You remember our bargain?"

He sighed. "You still intend to hold me to it?"

"Yes!"

"And what of our child? Can you leave him alone so easily?"

"Alone? Gil, there'll be scores of elves vying for the chance to tend him!"

"A child needs his mother."

"And his father. And a homeland."

It was an old argument, given new urgency by a stream of news from the west. Word had come from Alhana that the revolt in Qualinesti was stalled. The Army of Liberation had landed on the east coast in midsummer and driven inland, swiftly cutting the country in two. Samuval's army was pushed back over the border into Abanasinia. It seemed the end of the bandits' reign, but local Nerakan forces south of the Ahlanlas River counterattacked, breaking the siege and freeing Samuval's army. A vicious back-and-forth war raged: one side would take a town only to lose it the very next week. Central Qualinesti had become uninhabitable, full of abandoned villages and despoiled farms. The cruel impasse served no one, as thousands of Samuval's troops battled hunger as well as the elves. Kerian was determined to join the fight, and she'd struck a bargain with Gilthas. Once the baby was born, she would fly to Qualinesti. He had agreed, believing that when the time actually came, she wouldn't be able to leave their baby. He'd been berating himself for a fool ever since. When had the Lioness ever shown herself unwilling to join a fight, whatever the cost to herself?

Argument was pointless, but he still had to try. He took her hand. "Can you really leave us?"

"Only with your blessing." She gripped his hand hard. "Do I have it?"

Misery filled his eyes, and she pulled him close. What use was there in wishing her to be other than what she was? Would he change her if he could? Of course not. But a part of him couldn't help wishing she would give up placing herself in danger.

Burying his face in her neck, he whispered, "Whatever you choose to do, you have my blessing."

He was proud of her courage and, ultimately, shared her desire to regain the lands they'd lost. But he didn't have the luxury of following that dream. At moments such as this, he hated being Speaker, unable to deny the higher cause of his country in favor of his own family. Such was the price of kingship.

*　*　*　*　*

DESTINY

Their child was born on the first day of the new year. Naming a son was a father's privilege, and Gilthas chose the name Balifaris, meaning "Young Balif."

Hamaramis, standing in as the mother's father, held Kerian's hand through the delivery. Afterward, he swore it was more painful for him than it had been for her. His hand did indeed sport a bandage, but Truthanar assured him the breaks would heal cleanly.

Soaked in sweat, Kerian held her son close. Mother and child had drifted off to sleep. In a whisper, the old general asked the Speaker the significance of the name he had chosen.

"Balif, although cursed and cast out, forged a new nation. I hope my son can do the same." His strange hallucination while at the brink of death had left Gilthas with a feeling of kinship to the long-dead Silvanesti.

Kerian was a loving if plainspoken mother. She was also true to her word. Three months to the day after Balifaris was born, she bade son and husband an emotional farewell, mounted Eagle Eye, and flew off into the late-afternoon sky.

When she and her griffon were lost from sight, Gilthas felt a hand on his shoulder. It was his old archivist, Favaronas.

Since the Great Change, the Speaker's favorite librarian had been little seen, spending all his days writing down his strange experiences in the Silent Vale. His close association with the sorcerer Faeterus had left him with startling conclusions about the origin of Inath-Wakenti and its power. Dragonstones and godly magic were not behind the valley's weird nature, he believed. For centuries before and after the founding of the first elf realm, Speaker Silvanos, supplemented by a corps of powerful mages, had worked to suppress all clerical opposition to the throne. Mage by mage, enemies of the Speaker had their powers stripped away and sealed into the standing stones of Inath-Wakenti. The Brown Hood Society of wild sorcerers were wiped out to the last elf, for example. Later, the mage Vedvedsica tried to create his own race, using arcane magic to transform animals into the semblance of elves. The transformations did not last. Exposed as abominations, his creations were confined in Inath-Wakenti for all time, together with their maker. Vedvedsica was "the Father Who Made Not His Children" mentioned in the scrolls.

Floating lights were set to guard the valley, keeping the beast-elves in and all other animals out. But one creature escaped, perhaps with Vedvedsica's help, and with illicit longevity spells kept himself alive so he might one day avenge the treatment of the exiles. That sole escapee was Faeterus, who loathed the elf race and plotted its obliteration.

With his chronicle complete, Favaronas had accepted a new role, that of tutor to the Speaker's son.

"Come, sire," he said softly. "It's time for the child's lessons to begin."

Pulling his attention from the clouds that had swallowed his wife, Gilthas regarded him with surprise.

"But he's only an infant."

The scholar shouldered a large bag of scrolls. "Yes, sire. And he has so much to learn."

* * * * *

At the empty volcanic shell that once had housed the Oracle of the Tree, an old man sat on the sand, his back against the black stone spire. He'd found the guise an excellent one. Being old—visibly old, like a human—conferred many advantages. Listeners were respectful. They didn't fall on their faces and cower, nor did they expect him to perform impossible feats with a snap of his fingers. He came and went mysteriously, gave suitably obscure advice, and gently guided the affairs of mortals rather than directing them. It was a most satisfactory arrangement.

Was.

DESTINY

For his interference in the elves' fate, he had earned a severe punishment. As autumn painted the forests of old Qualinesti in every shade of gold, russet, and red, he found himself plucked up and judged. The sentence was five hundred years' banishment, the loss of his divine powers, and (a twist he considered particularly ironic) confinement in the feeble body he once had used only as a disguise. As of today, he had four hundred ninety-nine years and ten months to go.

He put back his head and laughed. The sound rang off the stone spire at his back and carried across the empty sands until distance consumed it. He was banished, confined to a weak and pain-riddled form, but the elf race would survive.

It was worth it.

RICHARD A. KNAAK

THE OGRE TITANS

The Grand Lord Golgren has been savagely crushing
all opposition to his control of the harsh ogre lands of
Kern and Blöde, first sweeping away rival chieftains, then
rebuilding the capital in his image. For this he has had to
deal with the ogre titans, dark, sorcerous giants who have
contempt for his leadership.

VOLUME ONE
THE BLACK TALON

Among the ogres, where every ritual demands blood and every ally can
become a deadly foe, Golgren seeks whatever advantage he can obtain,
even if it means a possible alliance with the Knights of Solamnia, a
questionable pact with a mysterious wizard, and trusting an elven slave
who might wish him dead.

December 2007

VOLUME TWO
THE FIRE ROSE

With his other enemies beginning to converge on him from all sides,
Golgren, now Grand Khan of all his kind, must battle with the
Ogre Titans for mastery of a mysterious artifact capable of ultimate
transformation and power.

December 2008

VOLUME THREE
THE GARGOYLE KING

Forced from the throne he has so long coveted, Golgren makes a final
stand for control of the ogre lands against the Titans . . . against an
enemy as ancient and powerful as a god.

December 2009

A World of Adventure Awaits

The FORGOTTEN REALMS® world is the biggest, most detailed, most vibrant, and most beloved of the DUNGEONS & DRAGONS® campaign settings. Created by best-selling fantasy author Ed Greenwood the FORGOTTEN REALMS setting has grown in almost unimaginable ways since the first line was drawn on the now infamous "Ed's Original Maps."

Still the home of many a group of DUNGEONS & DRAGONS players, the FORGOTTEN REALMS world is brought to life in dozens of novels, including hugely popular best sellers by some of the fantasy genre's most exciting authors. FORGOTTEN REALMS novels are fast, furious, action-packed adventure stories in the grand tradition of sword and sorcery fantasy, but that doesn't mean they're all flash and no substance. There's always something to learn and explore in this richly textured world.

To find out more about the Realms go to www.wizards.com and follow the links from Books to FORGOTTEN REALMS. There you'll find a detailed reader's guide that will tell you where to start if you've never read a FORGOTTEN REALMS novel before, or where to go next if you're a long-time fan!

R.A. SALVATORE

The *New York Times* best-selling author and one of
fantasy's most powerful voices.

DRIZZT DO'URDEN

The renegade dark elf who's captured the imagination of a generation.

THE LEGEND OF DRIZZT

Updated editions of the FORGOTTEN REALMS® classics finally in their
proper chronological order.

WELCOME TO THE

WORLD

Created by Keith Baker and developed by Bill Slavicsek and James Wyatt, EBERRON® is the latest setting designed for the DUNGEONS & DRAGONS® Roleplaying game, novels, comic books, and electronic games.

ANCIENT, WIDESPREAD MAGIC

Magic pervades the EBERRON world. Artificers create wonders of engineering and architecture. Wizards and sorcerers use their spells in war and peace. Magic also leaves its mark—the coveted dragonmark—on members of a gifted aristocracy. Some use their gifts to rule wisely and well, but too many rule with ruthless greed, seeking only to expand their own dominance.

INTRIGUE AND MYSTERY

A land ravaged by generations of war. Enemy nations that fought each other to a standstill over countless, bloody battlefields now turn to subtler methods of conflict. While nations scheme and merchants bicker, priceless secrets from the past lie buried and lost in the devastation, waiting to be tracked down by intrepid scholars and rediscovered by audacious adventurers.

SWASHBUCKLING ADVENTURE

The EBERRON setting is no place for the timid. Courage, strength, and quick thinking are needed to survive and prosper in this land of peril and high adventure.

During the Last War, Gaven was an
adventurer, searching the darkest reaches
of the underworld. But an encounter with
a powerful artifact forever changed him,
breaking his mind and landing him in the
deepest cell of the darkest prison in
all the world.

THE DRACONIC PROPHECIES

BOOK I

When war looms on the horizon, some see it as more
than renewed hostilities between nations. Some see the
fulfillment of an ancient prophecy—one that promises
both the doom and salvation of the world. And Gaven may
be the key to it all.

THE STORM DRAGON

The first EBERRON® hardcover by veteran game designer
and the author of *In the Claws of the Tiger*:

James Wyatt

SEPTEMBER 2007